VENDETTA
Lucky's Revenge

Jackie Collins

VENDETTA
Lucky's Revenge

WHEELER
PUBLISHING, INC.
ROCKLAND, MA

★ AN AMERICAN COMPANY ★

Published in Large Print by arrangement with
HarperCollins Publishers, Inc.
in the United States and Canada.

Wheeler Large Print Book Series.

Set in 16 pt Plantin.

Library of Congress Cataloging-in-Publication Data

Collins, Jackie
   Vendetta: Lucky's revenge/Jackie Collins.
       p. (large print) cm.(Wheeler large print book series)
   ISBN 1-56895-435-2 (hardcover)
   1. Large type books. 2. Motion picture industry—California—Los
Angeles—Fiction. 3. Businesswomen—Fiction. 4. Los Angeles (Calif.)—
Fiction. I. Title. II. Series
[PR6053.O425V4 1997b]
823'.914—dc21   97-2922
                                                                                   CIP

For my Italian hero,
Ti amo,
Jake

VENDETTA
Lucky's Revenge

Los
Angeles

1987

Prologue

Donna Landsman's icy slate eyes darted around the expensive mahogany conference table, fixing on her three high-powered lawyers and her mild-mannered husband, George. "How much more time before we acquire enough shares to take control of Panther Studios?" she demanded impatiently. "It's taking too long."

One of her lawyers spoke up, a florid-faced man with close-together bushy eyebrows and a bulbous nose. "Donna, it's true, it is taking longer than we anticipated. However, as you know, I've never been in favor of this—"

Donna crushed him with a contemptuous glare. "Do you hear me, Finley?" she interrupted. "Because if you don't, get out of my sight. Negativity fails to interest me. If I want something, *nobody* tells me no. And... I...want...Panther."

Finley nodded, sorry he'd spoken. Donna Landsman never listened to anybody's advice. She was queen of the hostile takeover, every company she went for made her another fortune. This was one of the reasons Finley couldn't understand why she was so anxious to wrest control of Panther. It was a studio in trouble, with massive debts and a rocky cash flow—hardly a money-making proposition.

"Yes, Donna," he said. "We all know what you want, and believe me, we're working on it."

"I should hope so," Donna said, making a mental note to tell George that soon it might be time to replace at least two of their lawyers. Finley would be the first to go.

She stood up, indicating the meeting was over. No point in wasting more time.

George stood up, too. He was an undistinguished-looking man in his fifties with plain features, heavy spectacles, and flat brown hair cut too short. Everyone knew he was the financial brains behind Donna's empire. She was the flash and he was the cash. They were a formidable combination.

"I'll see you later," Donna said to her husband, dismissing him with a wave of her hand.

"Yes, dear," he replied, unfazed by her abrupt attitude.

Donna strode from the conference room to her office—a palatial suite of interconnecting rooms with a breathtaking view of Century City. For a moment she paused in the doorway, taking it all in.

Lawyers—what did they know? Exactly nothing. The only thing they were truly competent at was sending enormous bills. Fortunately she had someone in place who was able to do exactly what she required. Her team of lawyers had no idea how smartly she'd worked this one—even George had no clue.

Donna smiled to herself.

Everyone has a weakness.
Seek and ye shall find.
She'd found.

She entered her private bathroom, pausing before the ornate antique mirror above the sink, peering intently at her reflection.

She saw a woman of forty-three with streaked blond hair pulled back into an elegant chignon. A woman with sculpted features—the pride of her plastic surgeon. A slim woman who wore her Chanel suit and Winston diamonds with flair.

She was attractive in a hard, manufactured, "I am very rich" way. She was attractive because she'd forced herself to become so.

Donna Landsman.

Donatella Bonnatti.

Ah, yes...she'd come a long way from her humble beginnings in a dusty little village nestled on the southeastern corner of Sicily. A long, long way...

And when she brought Lucky Santangelo to her knees, she'd make sure the bitch knew exactly who she was dealing with.

Book One

1

Lucky Santangelo Golden steered her red Ferrari through the ornate metal gates of Panther Studios, waved a friendly greeting to the guard, then drove across the lot to her personal parking space located directly outside her well-appointed suite of offices. Lucky was a wildly beautiful woman in her late thirties with a mass of tangled jet curls, deep-olive skin, a full, sensual mouth, black-opal eyes, and a slender, well-toned body.

She'd bought Panther in 1985, and since then she'd been running the studio. After two action-packed years, it was still exciting, for there was nothing she enjoyed more than a challenge, and running a Hollywood studio was the biggest challenge of all. It was more absorbing than building a casino/hotel in Vegas—something she'd done twice, or managing her late second husband's shipping empire—a task she'd relinquished, handing everything over to a board of trustees.

Lucky *loved* making movies—reaching out to America—putting images on the screen that would eventually influence people all over the world in a thousand different ways.

It wasn't easy. The opposition to a woman taking control of a major studio had been formidable. *Especially* a woman who looked like

Lucky. *Especially* a woman who seemed to have it all together—including three children and a movie-star husband. Everyone knew Hollywood was just one big boys' club—female members not exactly welcome.

The legendary movie mogul, Abe Panther, had sold her Panther only after she'd proved she was capable of taking over. Abe had challenged her to go in undercover as a secretary and work for Mickey Stolli—his devious grandson-in-law who was running the studio at the time. Abe's deal was, if she could find out everything Mickey was into, he'd sell her Panther.

She'd found out more than enough to close the deal. It turned out Mickey was skimming big bucks every way he could; his head of production was snorting coke and supplying two-thousand-dollar-a-night call girls to movie stars and VIPs; the head of distribution was smuggling porno flicks overseas along with Panther's legitimate productions, scoring an under-the-counter bundle; the movies Panther was making were soft-core exploitation crap full of sleazy sex and outrageous violence; producers were getting massive kickbacks; and women around the lot were treated as second-class citizens—it didn't matter whether they were star actresses or mere secretaries, chauvinism ran rampant.

Lucky offered Abe a great deal of money and salvation for a studio whose reputation was being slowly ruined.

Abe Panther liked her style.

He sold.

Lucky took over in a big way.

Abe had warned her that bringing Panther back to its glory days was going to be a struggle.

How right he was.

First of all, she'd refused to continue making the kind of cheapo garbage Panther had been churning out. Then she'd fired most of Mickey's key executives, putting a new, first-rate team in place. After that, it had been a question of developing new projects—a slow process that took time and patience.

The studio had been running at a loss for years, with astronomical bank loans. Lucky and her business advisor, Morton Sharkey, had been forced to arrange another massive loan just to keep the studio operating. Then, after the first year's disappointing net loss of nearly seventy million dollars, Lucky took stock and decided it was time to recoup some of her initial investment and diversify. Morton suggested selling blocks of shares to several corporations and a few private investors. It seemed like an excellent idea.

Morton had taken care of everything—finding the right investors who would basically leave her alone to run the studio; setting up a board of directors who wouldn't interfere; and making sure she still owned 40 percent of the stock.

The good news was that currently Panther had two big movies on release, both of them

11

performing extremely well. *Finder*, a showy vehicle for the controversial superstar Venus Maria—who also happened to be one of Lucky's best friends. And *River Storm*, a sharp-edged detective thriller starring Charlie Dollar—the middle-aged hero of stoned America. Lucky was especially delighted, as both movies had been put together under her regime. She hoped this was the start of the turnaround she'd been working toward. "Give them good, interesting movies and they will come," that was her motto.

She hurried into her office, where Kyoko, her loyal Japanese assistant, greeted her with a lengthy typed phone list and a morose shake of his head. Kyoko was a slight man in his thirties dressed in a Joseph Abboud jacket and sharply creased gray pants. He had glossy black hair pulled back in a neat ponytail, and an intelligent expression. Kyoko knew every aspect of the movie business, having worked as personal assistant to several top executives since graduating from college.

"What's the matter, Ky?" Lucky asked, throwing off her Armani jacket and settling in a comfortable leather chair behind her oversized Art Deco desk.

Kyoko recited the day's business: "You have fifteen phone calls to return; a ten-thirty with the Japanese bankers, followed by a production meeting regarding *Gangsters;* then a noon appointment with Alex Woods and Freddie Leon; lunch with Venus Maria; another production meeting at three; your interview with a reporter from *Newstime;* a six o'clock with Morton Sharkey; and—"

"Dinner at home, I hope," she interrupted, wishing there were more hours in the day.

Kyoko shook his head. "Your plane departs for Europe at eight P.M. Your limo will pick you up at your house no later than seven."

She smiled wryly. "Hmm...a twenty-minute dinner break—you're slipping."

"Your schedule would kill a lesser person," Kyoko remarked.

Lucky shrugged. "We're a long time dead, Ky. I don't believe in wasting time."

Kyoko was not surprised by her answer. He'd worked as Lucky's personal assistant since she'd taken over the studio. She was a dedicated workaholic who never ran out of energy. She was also the smartest woman he'd ever met. Smart and beautiful—a devastating combination. Kyoko loved working for her as opposed to his last boss—an edgy mogul with a relentless coke problem and a small dick.

"See if you can get Lennie on his portable," Lucky said. "He tried reaching me in the car this morning, the connection was deadly, couldn't make out a word."

Lennie Golden, the love of her life. They'd been married for four years and every day it seemed to get better.

Lennie was her third husband. Right now he was on location in Corsica shooting an action/adventure film. Three weeks apart was a killer; she couldn't wait to join him for a long weekend of lounging around doing nothing except making slow, leisurely love.

Kyoko connected with the production office in Corsica. "Lennie's out on a beach location," he informed her, covering the mouthpiece. "Shall I leave a message?"

"Yes. Tell them to have him call his wife pronto. Mrs. Golden can be interrupted wherever she is." She grinned when she said Mrs. Golden—being Lennie's wife was the most fun of all.

Lennie's movie was, regrettably, not a Panther production. Early on they'd both decided it wasn't a wise move for it to be perceived that he was working for his wife. He was a big enough star in his own right, and making a movie for Panther would only induce false rumors of nepotism.

"Get me Abe Panther," she instructed Kyoko.

Occasionally she called Abe for advice. At ninety he was a true Hollywood legend. The old man had seen it all—done most of it—and was still as canny and quick-witted as a man half his age. Whenever she spoke to him, he was always full of encouragement and wisdom, and since the banks were coming down on her big time, she needed his assurance that with two blockbuster movies their attitude would soon change.

Once in a while she drove up to Abe's grand old mansion overlooking the city. They would sit out on the terrace watching the sunset, while

Abe regaled her with outrageous stories about Hollywood in the far-off, golden days. Abe had known everyone—from Chaplin to Monroe— and he wasn't shy about telling fascinating tales.

She felt like visiting him today, but there simply wasn't time. As it was, she was hardly going to see her children—two-year-old Maria and baby Gino, who was six months. Bobby, her nine-year-old son from her marriage to deceased Greek shipping billionaire Dimitri Stanislopolous, was spending the summer with relatives in Greece.

"Mr. Panther is unavailable," Kyoko said.

"Okay, we'll try him later."

She glanced at her children's photographs, proudly displayed in silver frames on her desk. Bobby—so cute and handsome; baby Gino, named for his grandfather; and Maria, with her huge green eyes and the most adorable smile in the world. She'd named Maria after her mother.

For a moment she let her mind wander, thinking about her beautiful mother. Could she ever forget the day she'd found her floating in the family swimming pool, murdered by her father's lifelong enemy, Enzio Bonnatti? She'd been five years old, and it had seemed like her world was ending.

Twenty years later she'd taken revenge— killing the slime who'd ordered her mother's murder, getting retribution for the Santangelo family—for it was Bonnatti who'd also masterminded a hit on her brother, Dario, and the first great love of her life, Marco.

15

She'd shot Enzio Bonnatti with his own gun, claiming self-defense. "He was trying to rape me," she'd told the police, stony-faced. And she was believed because her father was Gino Santangelo and he had money and pull in all the right places. The case had never even gone to court.

Yes, she'd taken revenge for all of them and never regretted it.

"Shall we start with the phone calls?" Kyoko asked, interrupting her reverie.

She glanced at her watch. It was already past ten; the morning had flown by even though she'd been up since six. She picked up her phone list; Kyoko had arranged the names in order of importance, an order she didn't agree with. "You know I'd sooner talk to an actor than an agent," she chided. "Get me Charlie Dollar."

"He wants a meeting."

"About what?"

"He doesn't like the poster art for *River Storm* in Europe."

"Why?"

"Says they've made him look overweight."

Lucky sighed. Actors and their egos. It was never ending. "Is it too late to change it?"

"I spoke to the art department. It can be done. It'll be costly."

"Worth keeping a superstar happy?" she asked, sounding only mildly sarcastic.

"If you say so."

"You know my philosophy, Ky. Keep 'em smiling and they'll work all the harder to promote the movie."

Kyoko nodded. He knew better than to argue with Lucky.

Lennie Golden hated bullshit, and the worst thing about being a movie star was that half the time he was knee deep. People reacted to fame in such a weird fashion. They either fell all over him or insulted the hell out of him. Women were the worst. Getting laid was on their mind the moment they met him. And it didn't have to be him—any movie star would do. Costner, Redford, Willis—women had no preference as long as the man was a celebrity.

Lennie had learned to ignore the come-ons, he didn't need the ego boost of constantly scoring, he had Lucky, and she was the most special woman in the world.

At thirty-nine Lennie was a charismatically attractive man with an edgy style all his own. Tall, tanned, and fit, he was not conventionally handsome. He had longish dirty-blond hair and very direct ocean-green eyes, plus he worked out every day, keeping his body in excellent shape.

He'd been a movie star for several years—which surprised him more than anyone. Six years ago he'd been just another comedian looking to score a gig, a few bucks, anything going. Now he had everything he'd ever dreamed of.

Lennie Golden. Son of crusty old Jack

Golden, a stand-up Vegas hack, and the unstoppable Alice. Or "Alice the Swizzle" as his mother was known in her heyday as a now-you-see-'em, now-you-don't Vegas stripper.

He'd split for New York when he was seventeen and made it all the way without any help from his folks. His father was long dead, but Alice still caused trouble wherever she went. Sixty-seven years old and as frisky as an overbleached starlet, she'd never come to terms with getting older, and the only reason she acknowledged Lennie as her son was because of his fame. "I was a child bride," she'd simper to anyone who'd listen, batting her fake lashes and curling her overpainted lips in a lascivious leer. "I gave birth to Lennie when I was twelve!"

He'd bought her a small house in Sherman Oaks, where she ruled the neighborhood—having decided that since she was never going to be a star, she'd become a psychic. A wise move, for now—much to Lennie's embarrassment—she appeared on cable TV on a regular basis and sounded off about anything and everything. Quietly he'd christened her "my mother the mouth."

Sometimes it all seemed like a fantasy—his marriage to Lucky, his successful career, everything.

Leaning back in his director's chair he narrowed his eyes and surveyed the beach location. A blond in a bikini was busy strutting her considerable assets. She'd paraded in front of him several times with a definite yen to get noticed.

He'd noticed, all right—he was married, not dead, and spectacular blonds with bodies to die for had once been his weakness. Earlier in the day she'd asked to have her picture taken with him. He'd politely declined—photos with fans, especially attractive ones, had a nasty habit of ending up in the tabloids.

She'd gotten the message and returned a few minutes later with a strapping bodybuilder type who spoke no English. "My fiancé," she'd explained with a dazzling smile. "*Please!*"

He'd obliged and had a photo taken with the two of them.

Now the blond did another turn. Long legs. Rounded butt in an almost nonexistent thong. Firm tits with erect nipples straining the flimsy material.

Looking was okay.

Taking it any further was not.

Marriage was a commitment that worked both ways. If Lucky was ever unfaithful to him, he'd never forgive her. He was confident she felt the same way.

The blond finally zoomed in for a landing. "Mr. Golden," she purred in a Marilyn rip-off voice with a slight French accent, "I *loove* your movies. It is such an honor to be appearing in this one with you." Deep breath. Nipples threatening to break through.

"Thanks," he mumbled, wondering where the fiancé was now.

Adoring giggle. "*I* should be the one thanking *you*." Small pink tongue darting out to lick pouty pink lips. Invitation to fuck shining in her overeager eyes.

Rescue swooped over—Jennifer, the pretty American second assistant. She wore shorts, a tight T-shirt, and a Lakers baseball cap. Temptation was everywhere.

"Mac's ready to rehearse, Lennie," Jennifer said, ever protective.

He shifted his lanky frame out of the director's chair and stretched.

Jennifer raked the blond in the bikini with a condescending look. "Try and stay with the other extras, dear," she said crisply. "You never know when you'll be needed."

The blond backed off, not happy.

"Talk about silicone city!" Jennifer muttered.

"How do you know?" Lennie asked, wondering why women were so much more knowledgeable at spotting fake tits than men.

"It's obvious," Jennifer replied disdainfully. "You men fall for anything."

"Who's falling?" he said, amused.

"Not you," Jennifer said, flashing him a friendly smile. "It's a pleasure to work with a star who doesn't expect a blow job along with his morning coffee."

Jennifer, Lennie decided, was Lucky's kind of woman.

He couldn't help smiling when he thought of his wife. Tough exterior. Soft interior. Drop-dead gorgeous. Strong, stubborn, sensual, street smart, vulnerable, and crazy. The package that was Lucky was really something.

Lennie had been married once before. A quickie marriage in Las Vegas to Olympia Stanislopolous, the willful daughter of Dimitri Stanislopolous, who—at the same time—was married to Lucky.

Olympia had died tragically, overdosing in a hotel room with Flash, a drugged-out rock star.

Dimitri had suffered a fatal stroke.

Soon Lucky and Lennie were together, where they belonged.

Olympia left behind a daughter from a previous marriage, Brigette, now nineteen and one of the richest girls in the world. Lennie was very fond of her although he didn't get to see her as often as he would like.

"I want you to meet Lucky when she's here," he said to Jennifer. "You'll like her, she'll like you. It's a done deal."

"She won't be interested in meeting *me*," Jennifer said modestly. "She runs a studio, Lennie. I'm just a second assistant."

"Lucky doesn't care. She likes people for who they are, not what they do."

"If you say so."

"And hey," he said, boosting her confidence, "there's nothing wrong with being a second assistant—you're working your way up. One day you'll be directing. Is that the plan?"

Jennifer nodded. "I've arranged for a car to meet your wife at Poretta Airport tomorrow," she said, all business.

"I'll be in it," Lennie said.

"You might be shooting."

21

"Have them shoot around me."

"You're in every shot."

"Fake it."

"I *never* fake it."

Yes. Lucky would definitely like this one.

2

Alex Woods had a smile like a crocodile—wide, captivating, and ultimately deadly. His smile held him in good stead with the movie executives he was forced to deal with on a daily basis. It caught them off guard, unbalancing the delicate power structure between writer/producer/director and studio honcho who could usually make or break any filmmaker—however famous and talented. Alex was a powerful presence, capable of making a lot of people nervous.

Alex Woods and his lethal smile had written, directed, and produced six big-budget major movies over a ten-year period. Six controversial, sex and violence–drenched masterpieces. Alex called them masterpieces, not everyone agreed—although each of his movies *had* been nominated for an Academy Award and had never won once. It pissed him off. Alex liked recognition—a lousy nomination didn't do it for him. He wanted the fucking gold statue on his Richard Meier–designed beach house mantelpiece so he could fucking shove it up everyone's ass—metaphorically speaking, of course.

Alex was not married—even though he was

forty-seven years old, tall, and good-looking in a darkly dangerous way, with compelling eyes, heavy eyebrows, and a strong jawline. No woman had ever managed to nail him. He didn't go for American women, he preferred his female companions to be Asian and petite, so that when he made love to them he felt like the big, conquering hero.

The truth was that Alex had a submerged fear of women whom he might in any way consider his equal. This fear originated from his mother, Dominique, a fierce Frenchwoman who'd dispatched his father—Gordon Woods, a moderately successful film actor who'd specialized in playing best-friend roles—to an early grave when Alex was only eleven years old. They'd said it was a heart attack, but Alex knew—because he'd been a silent witness to many of their violent fights—that she'd tongue-lashed his poor father to death. His mother was a vicious, calculating woman who'd driven her husband to find solace in a bottle of booze whenever he could. Death was his cunning escape.

Shortly after his father's funeral, Madame Woods had sent her only child off to a strict military academy. "You're stupid—exactly like your father," she'd said, her tone allowing no argument. "Maybe it'll make you smart."

The military academy had been a living nightmare. He'd hated every minute of the rigid discipline and unfair rules. It didn't matter, because whenever he'd complained to

Dominique about the beatings and solitary confinements, she'd told him to stop whining and be a man. He'd been forced to stay there for five years, spending vacation time with his grandparents in Pacific Palisades while his mother dated a variety of unsuitable men, virtually ignoring his existence. Once he'd caught her in bed with a man she'd made him call Uncle Willy. Uncle Willy was lying back with a giant hard-on while Mommy was on her knees next to the bed, completely naked. It was a scenario that stayed with him forever.

By the time he'd left the academy and tasted freedom, his anger was insurmountable. While his contemporaries had rocked and rolled their way through high school, screwing cheerleaders, getting drunk and high, he'd been shut in a windowless room on detention for some petty misdemeanor, or getting paddled on his bare ass because they didn't like his attitude. Sometimes detention lasted ten hours with nothing to do except sit on a hard wooden bench staring blankly into space. Torture for rich kids whose parents didn't want them around.

Alex often thought about the lost years of his youth and it filled him with rage. He hadn't even gotten laid until college, and that had been no memorable experience—a fat, greasy whore in Tijuana who'd smelled of stale tacos and worse. In fact, he'd hated it so much he hadn't tried sex again for a year.

The second time was better—he was a film student at USC, and a serious blond who'd admired his budding talent had given him head twice daily for six months. Very nice, but not enough to keep him satisfied. Eventually, he'd gotten restless and one drunken night he'd enlisted in the army. They'd sent him to Vietnam, where he'd spent a shattering two years—experiencing things that would haunt him forever.

When he'd returned to L.A. he was a different man, unsettled and edgy, ready to explode. He'd left town after two weeks—hitching his way to New York, leaving a short note for his mother that he'd be in touch.

Ah...revenge...He didn't call her for five years, and as far as he knew she'd never sent anyone looking for him. When he finally called, she acted as if she'd spoken to him the week before. No sentimental bullshit for Madame Woods.

"I hope you're working," she'd said, her voice as cold as cracked ice. "Because you'll get no handouts from me."

Big surprise.

Yeah, Mom, I've been working. Hustled my ass for a couple of months so I could eat. Guarded the door at a low-class strip joint. Ran interference for a busy hooker. Cut up carcasses in a meat factory. Drove a cab. Chauffeured a car for a degenerate theater director. Bodyguarded a criminal. Lived with a rich older woman who reminded me of you. Procured drugs for her friends. Managed an after-hours gambling club. Worked as an assistant editor on a series of cheapo slash/horror stories. And finally, the big break—wrote and directed a porno movie for a lecherous old Mafia capo. Tight pussies. Big cocks. Erotic porno. The kind that really turns people on. And a story. Next thing, Hollywood beckons. They know good pornography when they see it.

"I'm on my way to the Coast," he'd said. "Universal has signed me to write and direct a movie for them."

She was unimpressed. Naturally. A long pause. "Call me when you're here." And that was it.

Some broad, his mother. No wonder he didn't trust women.

That had been eighteen years ago. Things were different now. Madame Woods was older and wiser. So was he. They maintained a love/hate relationship. He loved her because she was his mother. Hated her because she was still a mean bitch. Occasionally he dined with her. Severe punishment.

In those eighteen years his career had soared. From one low-budget no-brainer he'd risen to the top, gradually gaining a reputation as an innovative, risk-taking, original moviemaker. It hadn't been easy, but he'd done it, and he was proud of his success.

It would be nice if his mother was, too. She never praised him, although criticism still fell easily from her thin scarlet lips. Alex knew if his father had lived he would have been happy and supportive of everything he'd achieved.

Now he had a meeting with Lucky Santangelo, the current head of Panther Studios, and it did not please him that he had to go to a female to try and keep his latest project—a movie called *Gangsters*—in a go position. He was Alex Woods, for crissakes—he didn't have to kiss anyone's ass, especially some broad who had a reputation for doing things her way.

Nobody did things their way on an Alex Woods movie.

All he needed was for her studio to put up the money on account of the fact that Paramount had dropped out at the final hour. Their excuse was that *Gangsters* was too graphically violent. He was making a movie about Vegas in the fifties, for crissakes. Hoodlums, hookers, and gambling. Violence was a way of life back then.

The trouble with the studios was that they were running scared because of criticism from all those do-good politicians who were busy screwing whores on the side while their wives stood beside them with fixed smiles and dry pussies. Some freaking double standard!

Alex hated hypocrisy. "Tell the real truth and nothing but" was his motto, and that's exactly what he did in each of his movies. He was a controversial filmmaker—garnering either bitter criticism or brilliant reviews. His movies made people think, and that could sometimes be dangerous.

When Paramount folded, his agent, Freddie Leon, had suggested taking *Gangsters* to Panther. "Lucky Santangelo will do it," Freddie had assured him. "I know Lucky, it's her kind of story. Plus, she needs a hit."

He hoped Freddie was right, because if there was one thing Alex hated, it was the waiting game. He was only happy when he was immersed in making one of his movies. Fulfillment was being in action.

Freddie had suggested they get together before their meeting with Lucky; he'd asked Alex to meet him for a late breakfast at the Four Seasons.

Alex dressed all in black—from his sneakers to his T-shirt—and drove to the hotel in his black Porsche Carrera. When he arrived, Freddie was already at the table skimming a copy of *The Wall Street Journal,* looking more like a banker than an agent.

Freddie Leon was a poker-faced man in his early forties with a quick, bland smile and cordial features. He was not just another agent, he was *the* agent. Mr. Super Power. He made careers, and he could break them just as easily. He'd worked hard for the privilege. His nickname around town was "the Snake" on account of the fact that he could slither in and out of any deal. Nobody dared call him "the Snake" to his face.

Alex slid into the booth. A waitress appeared and poured him a cup of strong black coffee. He took a quick gulp, burning his tongue. "Shit!" he exclaimed.

"'Morning," Freddie said, lowering his newspaper.

"What makes you think Panther will do *Gangsters?*" Alex asked impatiently.

"I told you—Panther needs hit movies," Freddie replied evenly. "And it's Lucky's kind of script."

"How come?"

"'Cause of her background," Freddie explained, pausing for a moment to take a sip of herbal tea. "Her father built a hotel in Vegas back in the early days. Gino Santangelo— apparently he was quite a character."

Alex leaned forward in surprise. "Her father's Gino Santangelo?"

"Right. One of the boys. Made himself a fortune and moved on. Lucky built her own hotels in Vegas—the Magiriano and the Santangelo. She'll understand your script."

Alex had heard of Gino Santangelo—he was not as notorious as Bugsy Siegel or any of the other high-profile gangsters—but in his day he'd certainly made his mark.

"The story is that Gino named his daughter after Lucky Luciano," Freddie added. "From all accounts she's had quite a life."

In spite of himself, Alex couldn't help being intrigued. So Lucky Santangelo was not just some ballsy broad out of nowhere. She had a history—she was a Santangelo. Why hadn't he put it together before?

He downed the strong black coffee in three big gulps and decided this deal could turn out to be more interesting than he'd thought.

Three Japanese bankers, very correct, very conventional. The meeting went well, although Lucky sensed they were not thrilled to be dealing with a woman.

Ah...the story of her life. When would men learn to relax and realize it wasn't all one big pissing contest?

She needed the Japanese bankers to put up the money for a chain of Panther stores around the world. Merchandising was hot, and Lucky knew the smart move was to get in at the beginning.

The bankers deferred to her head of marketing—a man—and seemed to be on the verge of saying yes when they left, promising a decision within a few days. As soon as they departed, she called her father at his Palm Springs estate. Gino sounded fine, and so he should. At eighty-one, he—like Abe Panther—was married to a woman a little over half his age—Paige Wheeler, a sexy, redheaded interior designer who took excellent care of him. Not that Gino needed looking after, he was as active as a much younger man, full of drive and vigor, channeling his considerable energy into playing options on the stock market, a hobby that got him up at six in the morning and kept him alert.

Lucky concluded her conversation with a promise to visit soon.

"Make sure you do," Gino said gruffly.

"An' bring the bambinos—I gotta start teachin' 'em things."

"Like what?" she asked curiously.

"Like never you mind."

Lucky smiled. Her father was something else. Through the bad times, when they weren't even talking, she'd hated him with a burning passion. Now, she loved him with an equal passion. They'd survived so much together. Fortunately, it had made them both stronger.

She remembered the time he'd exiled her to boarding school in Switzerland when she was sixteen—then punished her after she'd run away from the strict private school by forcing her into an arranged marriage with Craven Richmond, Senator Peter Richmond's boring son. What a nightmare! But she'd had no intention of staying trapped. When Gino fled America to avoid jail for tax evasion, she'd seized her opportunity and moved in to run the family business. Gino had expected her brother, Dario, to take over. Dario was no businessman, so Lucky had completed the building of Gino's new hotel in Vegas—proving herself capable in every way.

When Gino finally returned, there'd been a major battle for control. Neither had won. Eventually they'd reached a truce.

That was all in the past. They were too alike to be enemies.

Lucky hurried into the boardroom for a brief production meeting before seeing Freddie Leon and Alex Woods. She'd already made up her mind to green-light *Gangsters*. She'd read the script and considered it brilliant. Alex Woods was a fine writer.

After speaking to her team individually, she was pleased that they'd each agreed with her decision to go ahead. Collectively she needed assurance they were all in sync that the movie could make a lot of money for the studio. Alex Woods was a controversial and dangerous filmmaker, but when he delivered, everyone knew he was worth the trouble.

The heads of production, domestic distribution, foreign, and marketing were duly assembled. They were a top-rate group of people, and after a short meeting Lucky felt assured of success.

She returned to her office, and was just about to call her half-brother, Steven, in England, where he and his family had recently moved, when Kyoko put his head around the door. "Alex Woods and Freddie Leon are here," he announced. "Should I keep them waiting?"

She glanced at the Cartier clock on her desk—a present from Lennie. It was exactly noon. She replaced the receiver, reminding herself to call Steven later. "Show them in," she said, well aware that the most important and secure people never kept anyone waiting.

Freddie led the way with his bland smile and expressionless slate-gray eyes.

Lucky rose to greet him. The thing she liked about Freddie was his businesslike attitude. No phony deal with him, he had a purpose and he got right to it.

Alex Woods followed Freddie into her office. She'd never met Alex, but had read many interviews about him and had often seen his photograph in newspapers and magazines.

The photos did not prepare her for the man's actual presence. He was tall and well built, with darkly powerful good looks and a killer smile—a smile he immediately flashed in her direction.

For a moment she was quite taken aback. It was a rare occurrence for Lucky to feel vulnerable—almost girlish—it was like she was seventeen, checking out a hot number, and in her single days she'd had enough hot numbers to last several lifetimes.

Freddie introduced them. She shook Alex's hand. His grasp was firm and strong—a secure man.

She withdrew her hand and started speaking a shade too quickly, pushing back her long dark hair. "Uh…Mr. Woods, it's a pleasure to finally meet you. I'm a big admirer of your work."

Hmm…Spoken like a true dumb fan. What was *wrong* with her? Why was she reacting like this?

Alex flashed the smile again, giving himself time to digest this woman's extraordinary beauty. She was dazzling in an offbeat way. Everything about her was incredibly sensual, from her tangle of jet curls to her watchful black eyes and full, soft mouth. Her very fuckable mouth.

He found his eyes dropping to her rounded breasts, concealed beneath a white silk shirt.

She was not wearing a bra and he could make out the faint shadow of her nipples. He wondered if she was wearing any underwear at all.

Jesus! What was going on here? He was halfway to a hard-on. Why hadn't Freddie warned him?

Lucky was well aware of his scrutiny. "Please sit down," she said, willing herself to keep her mind on business.

Freddie was oblivious to the sexual tension heating up the room. He had an agenda and he stuck to it. Smooth agent talk slipped from his lips like nectar. "Panther needs a film-maker like Alex Woods," he said. "I don't have to tell you how many times his movies have been nominated."

"I'm well aware of Mr. Woods's illustrious record," Lucky said. "And we'd love to be in business with him. However, I understand the projected budget on *Gangsters* is almost twenty-two million. That's an enormous commitment."

Freddie was right there with an answer. "Not for an Alex Woods film," he said evenly. "His movies always make money."

"With the right casting," Lucky pointed out.

"Alex's casting is impeccable. He doesn't need stars—the public comes for him."

Alex leaned forward. "Did you read the script?" he asked, watching her closely.

Her eyes met his with a level gaze. She knew he was waiting for compliments—she also knew it was better to keep him off balance—

for now. "Yes, I did," she said without blinking. "It's violent, but truthful." A pause. "My father, Gino, was in Vegas at that time. He built the original Mirage Hotel. You might enjoy meeting him."

His eyes remained fixed on hers. "I'd like that very much."

She refused to be the one to break the look. "I'll arrange it," she said coolly, pretending they weren't locked into some subliminal eye-contact power struggle. "He lives in Palm Springs."

"I can drive down there any time you say."

"So," Freddie said, sensing closure. "Do we have a deal?"

"More or less," Lucky replied, switching her attention to Freddie and then getting mad at herself for being the first to look away.

Freddie ignored the fact that her reply was somewhat ambiguous. "This is a winning combination," he predicted enthusiastically. "'Panther Studios presents Alex Woods's *Gangsters*.' I can smell the Oscar now!"

"Just one small thing," Lucky said, picking up her favorite silver pen—another present from Lennie—and tapping it impatiently on her desk. "I'm aware that Paramount passed on this project because of the graphic violence, and I'm not asking you to tone it down. However...about the sex..."

"What about it?" Alex demanded, challenging her to object.

"The script makes it clear several of the

actresses are naked in certain scenes—yet it seems our hero and his friends remain modestly covered."

"What's the problem?" Alex asked, genuinely not getting it.

"Well..." Lucky said slowly. "This is an equal opportunity studio. If the females get to take it off—so do the guys."

"Huh?" Alex said blankly.

Suddenly Lucky was back in control. "Let me put it this way, Mr. Woods. If we get to see tits an' ass, we get to see dick, too. And I'm not talking Dick Clark." A small smile as Freddie and Alex reeled at the thought. "And if we can work that out, then, gentlemen—we've got a deal."

3

"How old are you, sweetie?" the fifty-five-year-old lech in the Brioni suit asked the exceptionally pretty, fresh-faced honey blond sitting across from his desk.

"Nineteen," she replied truthfully, although she'd already lied about her name, substituting Brown as her surname instead of Stanislopoulos. Brigette Stanislopoulos was a mouthful, whereas Brigette Brown had a certain ring to it. Plus, Brown was anonymous, and Brigette had no intention of anyone finding out who she was.

"Well," Mr. Fifty-Five-Year-Old said and cleared his throat, wondering if anyone had nailed this delectable piece of female flesh.

"You've certainly got all the attributes to have a very successful career as a model." His eyes lingered on her breasts. "You're tall enough, pretty enough, and if you lost ten pounds, you'd be thin enough." A pause. "Get rid of the baby fat and I'll arrange for you to have test shots taken." Another pause. "In the meantime, I'll take you to dinner tonight and we'll discuss your future."

"Sorry," Brigette said, rising to her feet, "I'm busy tonight." She paused at the door. "But, uh...I, like, certainly appreciate your advice."

Mr. Lech jumped up. He was surprised she hadn't accepted his invitation—they usually did. Girls who wanted to be models were always hungry on account of the fact that they usually had no money and a free meal was a free meal; dinner with him was considered a coup.

"How about tomorrow night?" he suggested with an encouraging leer.

Brigette smiled sweetly. She had a lovely smile, as innocent as spring flowers. "Do you want to fuck me or get me started as a model?" she asked, shocking the socks off Mr. Lech, who was not used to being spoken to in such a fashion by a junior piece of ass.

"You have a dirty mouth, little girl," he said angrily.

"All the better to say good-bye with," she said, slipping through the door, calling out a final "See you on the cover of *Glamour*!"

She hit the street, steaming at his conde-scending attitude. Men! What pigs! Lose ten pounds indeed, she was not fat—in fact, she was as thin as she'd ever been. And did he honestly think she would go to dinner with an old cretin like him? *No way.* "Read my lips, old man," she said aloud as she bounced along Madison Avenue. "You are *not* a contender!"

Nobody took any notice. This was New York, and here you could get away with anything.

Brigette was five feet eight inches tall and weighed a hundred and ten pounds. She had sun-kissed honey-blond hair, which she wore shoulder length and straight. Her lips were full and pouting, her eyes blue and knowing, and her skin had a glistening, luminous quality. She radiated health and energy. Most men found her fresh-faced sex appeal irresistible.

Brigette loved the city. She was crazy about the hot, dirty sidewalks and the way a person could get lost in the rushing crowds. In New York she was not Brigette Stanislopoulos—one of the richest girls in the world. In New York she was just another pretty face desperately trying to carve out a career.

Thank God Lucky and Lennie had understood when she'd informed them she wanted to skip college and take a shot at making it as a model in New York. They had not objected; in fact, they'd convinced her maternal grandmother, Charlotte, she should go for it, but only on the condition that if it didn't work out, in six months she'd go to college and continue her education.

No chance. Because it *was* going to work out.

Brigette was a true believer, something good *had* to happen for her.

So far her luck had not been the best. Okay, so she was wealthy, but what did that mean? It wasn't like she'd earned the money herself, her fortune was just sitting there—inherited from her billionaire grandfather, Dimitri, and her mother, Olympia. Both of them dead and buried. A lot of good the money had done them.

Her real father, Claudio Cadducci, was also dead. Not such a sad thing, for she'd never known him; her mother had divorced him as soon as she'd given birth to Brigette because of his constant indiscretions. They'd been married when Olympia was nineteen and Claudio forty-five. According to all reports, Claudio had been a handsome Italian businessman with immense charm and an expensive wardrobe. Part of his divorce settlement had included two Ferraris and three million dollars. Unfortunately, Claudio never had time to enjoy the cars or the money because a few months later he'd stepped out of a limo in Paris and been accidentally blown to pieces by a terrorist's bomb.

Olympia immediately married again, this time to a Polish count who lasted exactly sixteen weeks. Brigette didn't remember the count at all, the only stepfather she'd known was Lennie, whom she adored.

Sometimes she missed her mother with a deep feeling of emptiness that nothing could fill. She'd been twelve when Olympia had died and there'd been nobody to take her place—except Grandmother Charlotte, a New York socialite who had an extremely active social life; and Lucky and Lennie, who were both so involved with their work and their kids that even though they made time whenever they could, it wasn't enough.

Brigette knew she had to find something to fill the void.

It certainly wasn't going to be a man. Men were not to be trusted. Men were after only one thing. Sex.

She'd had sex and she didn't want it again. Not until she was the most famous supermodel in the world.

Last year she'd gotten engaged for about ten minutes to the grandson of one of her grandfather's business rivals. They'd had a great time together until she'd discovered he was a total coke freak. Brigette wasn't into drugs. She'd ended the engagement quickly, and taken off for Greece, where she'd spent time with her grandfather's relatives.

Stopping off at Bloomingdale's, she perused the makeup counters, buying a pale-bronze lipstick and some shiny lip gloss. She loved makeup as long as it was natural-looking. It was fun experimenting—trying new looks. When she was a star, she planned on launching a personal makeup line. Oh yes, she was going to amass her own fortune—it was merely a matter of time.

She'd been in New York for seven weeks and Mr. Fifty-Five- Year-Old Lech was the third modeling agent she'd seen. It wasn't easy getting appointments, and since she had no intention of using her connections, she'd simply have to keep slogging away. An annoying thought, for Brigette was impatient, she expected it to happen yesterday.

She took a cab back to the apartment she shared with another girl in SoHo. Both Charlotte and Lucky had insisted she have a roommate although Brigette was sure she would've been perfectly fine on her own.

Lucky had personally found Anna, the girl she shared with. Anna was in her late twenties, a thin girl with long brown hair and dreamy eyes. She wrote poetry, stayed home most of the time, and was always available to do anything Brigette wanted. Brigette suspected Anna was a paid spy planted to keep an eye on her. She wasn't bothered; after all, she had no secrets.

Anna was cooking eggs when Brigette got in. "How'd it go today?" she inquired, adding too much pepper to the runny eggs.

"Okay," Brigette said, thinking that it had not gone well at all. It never did. Oh, God! Maybe she was doomed to failure.

Anna brushed a lock of fine hair out of her eyes. "Do they want you?"

"Ha!" Brigette replied, not pleased. "They want me to lose ten pounds."

"You're not fat."

Brigette pulled a face. "Don't I know it," she said, smoothing down her extra-short skirt. "He said I had baby fat."

"Baby fat!"

"Yes. What a retard!"

Anna continued to stir the eggs. "So what next?"

Brigette shrugged. "I'll keep trying."

Later she ordered pizza and sat out on the fire escape eating it because the apartment was so uncomfortably hot. She could have been living in luxury in an air-conditioned penthouse on Park Avenue. That was not for her—she preferred the struggle.

Munching a slice of pizza, she thought about her life and the twisted turns it had taken.

Sometimes it was difficult to believe.

Sometimes she burst out crying for no reason.

Sometimes the memory of Tim Wealth came back to haunt her and she couldn't get him out of her mind.

Tim Wealth. Hot young movie star.

He'd taken her virginity at fifteen. And gotten himself murdered for his trouble.

How well she remembered him. How many nights she shuddered at the memories.

Poor Tim had gotten in the way of Santino Bonnatti—a lifelong enemy of the Santangelos—just when Santino was in the middle of a kidnapping attempt on Brigette and her younger half-brother, Bobby.

Santino's men had brutally murdered Tim and left him dead in his apartment, while she and Bobby were forcibly taken to Santino's house and sexually abused. She could still recall in sickening detail cowering naked and terrified in the center of Santino's bed while the perverted freak, clad only in his underwear, stripped off her little brother's clothes and prepared to commit an obscene act.

It was then she'd spotted the gun placed casually on a bedside table, and as Bobby's anguished screams filled the room, she'd known she had to do something.

Silently sobbing, she'd crawled across the bed and reached for the weapon.

Santino was too busy with Bobby to notice.

With shaking hands, she'd picked up the gun, pointed it straight at the monster, and squeezed the trigger.

Once.

Twice.

Three times.

Good-bye, Santino.

She shook her head vigorously—trying desperately not to remember.

Shut out the memories, Brigette.

Forget the past.

Concentrate on now...

"She's a crazy bitch," Alex said irritably.

"She's putting up the money for your movie," Freddie replied mildly.

"What's her fucking problem?" Alex steamed.

"Didn't know she had one."

"Christ! You heard her."

Freddie sighed patiently. "What?"

"She wants to see actors with their cocks

hanging out. What kind of shit is that? Doesn't she realize there's a double standard?"

"Don't let it bother you."

"It *does* fucking bother me," Alex said angrily as they reached their cars.

"Why?" Freddie asked, one hand on the door of his gleaming Bentley Continental. "Whatever you shoot'll have to be cut. She can't afford an X rating, it'll kill the grosses, plus the theater chains won't book an X. She'll realize that."

"She must be some sick broad," Alex muttered.

Freddie laughed. "Well, she sure got to you, I've never seen you like this."

"Because she's stupid."

"No," Freddie said quickly. "That's one thing Lucky's not. She took over Panther two years ago and she's doing an excellent job. She had no previous experience in the film industry, yet she's definitely turning things around."

"Okay, okay, she's a fucking genius—but I'm not asking any of my actors to march around stark naked."

"Nicely put, Alex. I'll call you later."

Freddie got in his Bentley and took off.

Alex stood beside his black Porsche, still fuming at Lucky's request. Didn't she realize women were not turned on by male nudity? It was a well-known fact.

He got in his car and drove to his production offices, located on Pico. He'd called his production company Woodsan Productions—because it sounded peaceful and still incorporated his name. He owned the building—one of his better business investments.

He had two assistants, Lili, a softly pretty Chinese woman in her forties without whom he claimed he could not function. And France, an exquisite Vietnamese twenty-five-year-old who'd once been a bar girl in Saigon before he'd chivalrously rescued her and brought her to America. He'd slept with both of them, but that was in the past and now they were nothing more than loyal assistants.

"How was your meeting?" Lili asked anxiously.

He slumped in a worn leather chair behind his enormous littered desk. "Good," he said. "*Gangsters* has a new home."

Lili clapped her hands together. "I knew it!"

France brought him a mug of hot black tea, stood behind him, and began massaging his shoulders with relaxing, kneading movements. "Very tense," she scolded. "Not good."

He could feel the pressure of her small, firm breasts against the back of his neck while her surprisingly strong hands dug deep. It was comforting. Asian women were the best.

"Let me ask you a question," he said, still uptight about Lucky's request.

"Yes?" both women chorused.

"Do you get off looking at naked guys?"

Lili's expression was impassive as she tried to figure out the answer Alex wanted. France burst out in giggles.

"Well?" Alex demanded, none too pleased by their hesitation.

"*What* naked men?" Lili asked, stalling for time.

"On the screen," Alex said shortly. "Actors."

"Mel Gibson? Johnny Romano?" France said hopefully.

"Jesus!" Alex exclaimed, fast losing patience. "It doesn't matter *who* they are."

"Oh, yes it does!" France retorted, abruptly stopping his massage. "Anthony Hopkins—*no!* Richard Gere, *yes!*"

"Or Liam Neeson," Lili added, a faraway look in her eyes.

"I'm not talking about just their upper torso," Alex said ominously. "I'm talking about everything—the whole caboodle."

Lili figured out the answer he required, and even though she didn't mean it, she knew how to keep her boss happy. "Oh, no," she said quickly. "We don't want to see that."

"Exactly," Alex exclaimed triumphantly. "Women don't *want* to see it."

"I do," France murmured, low enough for him not to hear.

"Why are you asking?" Lili inquired.

"'Cause Lucky Santangelo is a crazy bitch who's under the false impression women want to act like men."

"Crazy bitch," parroted France, thinking to herself that Lucky Santangelo must be a really interesting woman whom she couldn't wait to meet.

"I don't get it," Alex muttered, deciding that the next time he saw Lucky Santangelo he'd definitely set her straight. She had to learn a thing or two—and who better to teach her than the master himself.

4

Venus Maria was in spectacular shape. She worked at it diligently, rising at six every morning to run up and down the Hollywood Hills with Sven, her personal trainer, before returning to her house for a punishing hour of aerobics and light weights.

Jesus! Staying in spectacular shape took some doing. Her routine was a major pain in the ass, but she never slacked off, because slacking off meant she would no longer have the best body in Hollywood. And fuck 'em—one thing they couldn't bitch about was her glorious bod.

Virginia Venus Maria Sierra had first come to Hollywood in her early twenties with her best friend, Ron Machio—a gay would-be choreographer. They'd hitchhiked their way from New York and had survived in L.A. by taking any gig they could get. Venus had worked in a supermarket bagging groceries, as a nude model for an art class, as a movie extra, and various one-nighters singing and dancing.

Ron had attempted waiting tables, running errands for a messenger service, and chauffeuring limousines. Together they'd managed to survive, until one night Venus was discovered by a small-time record producer who'd hung out at the same all-night clubs she and Ron frequented. With some heavy persuasion she'd gotten him to cut a record using her, then she and Ron had put together a sexy on-the-edge video to go with it. Venus had planned the look and the style, while Ron had come up with all the right moves.

Overnight they'd scored, for within six weeks their record was number one and Venus Maria was launched.

Now, five years later, at the age of twenty-seven, she was a major superstar with an enormous cult following. And Ron was a hot director with two hit movies behind him. It helped that Ron's current boyfriend was Harris Von Stepp, an extraordinarily rich show business mogul who'd financed Ron's first film. As Venus often pointed out, if Ron hadn't possessed the talent, it would never have happened for him. She didn't like Harris, he was twenty-five years older than Ron and icily controlling.

As an actress Venus was creamed by the critics, even though every one of her movies did mega box office. Her latest, *Finder*, had already made over eight million its first weekend out. She was one of the few female stars able to open a movie.

It obviously pissed off the mostly male critics that a woman could be as daring and outspoken as Venus, and *still* manage to have a fantastic career. Journalists were always writing about her in derogatory terms—saying she was finished, tapped out, gone with the wind.

Finished! Ha! Her last greatest hits CD had leaped into the charts at number one and stayed there for seven weeks.

Finished, indeed! Who were they kidding? She had legions of loyal fans, and if the critics didn't like her, too bad; she was around for the long haul and they'd better get used to it or bail out.

Two years ago she'd gotten married to Cooper Turner—a classically handsome movie star with a major stud reputation. Even though he was hitting forty-seven—twenty years older than she—she'd recently found out that her dear husband was unable to keep his dick in his pants. He adored women, and although she was sure he loved her, there was nothing she could do about his wandering cock. Cooper was a player who couldn't help it. Too bad, because they made a dynamite couple.

When they'd first met, she'd been involved in an affair with one of his best friends, the New York property tycoon Martin Swanson. At the time Martin was very hot for her and *very* married. Their affair had culminated in the suicide of Martin's wife in front of them.

Cooper had been there for her all the way. Tragedy had brought them together and they'd fallen in love and gotten married.

At one time Cooper had mentioned wanting to start a family. She'd told him she wasn't ready because she knew exactly what would happen— *she* would have the babies while *he* cruised the club scene; *she* would lose her figure while he stocked up on Armani suits; *she* would sit home with them while *he* would be out showing off the famous Cooper cock.

No. Starting a family with Cooper was not for her.

Marriage, she realized, had probably been a mistake, and lately she'd been considering getting a fast divorce.

That would send the tabloids into a frenzy. She was their darling, their favorite. Ever since her dear brother Emilio the slob had sold them the story of her life, there'd been no getting rid of them. Every week they ran a sensational new story about her. According to the tabloids, she'd slept with everyone from John F. Kennedy Jr. to Madonna!

If they only knew the truth. She'd been the faithful wife, while Cooper put it about like a drunken hooker on a Friday night. Well, damn him, the time had come for a showdown.

After working out, Venus took a shower, then sauntered downstairs to greet her masseur, Rodriguez, a sizzling Latino of twenty-two with the experienced hands of a man twice his age. Rodriguez was all sinewy muscle, with dark wavy hair and smoldering eyes—just the way Venus liked 'em. She had a weakness for extremely handsome men—especially men with tight, curved butts, and arms and legs to cream over.

Lately she'd been considering having an affair with him, but wouldn't that be baby snatching?

50

No way, she decided. Twenty-two was hardly a baby, and Rodriguez seemed *very* worldly. He was from Argentina, and delighted in regaling her with tales of his love trysts with older married women whose rich husbands failed to satisfy them.

That was one problem she *didn't* have. Cooper was an extraordinarily accomplished lover. He had a slow hand—the best kind. He truly loved women, and got off by making sure he gave them the ultimate pleasure trip.

Too bad the trip was soon coming to an end.

Venus was late for lunch. This didn't bother Lucky, who'd taken advantage of the time by using her cellular to return a few calls.

When Venus entered the commissary, all conversation stopped as the platinum blond casually sashayed across the crowded room to the private executive dining area in the back. There was something about Venus that screamed "SEX!" There were actresses in Hollywood taller, thinner, younger, more beautiful—but Venus had it over all of them; she managed to look vulnerable, smart, and incredibly slutty all at the same time. It was an irresistible combination. Women admired her strength and men couldn't wait to fuck her.

Sliding into her seat, she immediately ordered a white wine spritzer.

"Fifteen minutes; I'd like an excuse," Lucky said, tapping her watch.

"I was considering screwing my masseur," Venus murmured provocatively.

Lucky nodded; nothing Venus said surprised her. "Seems like a good excuse to me."

"*I* thought so."

"And what *did* you decide?"

Venus rolled her eyes and licked her lips. "Mmmm...I'm sure he's *very* talented."

"And you're *very* married."

"So is Cooper," Venus said sharply, her mood quickly changing. "I don't see it stopping *him*."

Lucky had been waiting for this moment. Everyone knew about Cooper and his out-of-control libido. Venus had chosen never to discuss it, and even though they were close friends, Lucky hadn't wanted to rock the friendship. She'd simply assumed Venus chose to ignore her famous husband's indiscretions.

"I've about had it," Venus said with a defiant shake of her platinum curls. "At first I thought flirting was his thing—which was okay with me 'cause I'm not exactly a slouch in that department myself. Now I realize he's jumping everything that breathes." She paused, shaking her head again. "I don't get it," she continued with a perverse twist of a smile. "He's got *me*— every man's wet-dream fantasy. What more can he possibly want?"

"Have you confronted him?" Lucky asked, knowing Venus was hardly the kind of woman to lie back.

"Fuck, no!" Venus steamed. "According to my hairdresser—who knows everything—

my dear, philandering husband is now in bed with Leslie Kane." A defiant pause. "As far as I'm concerned, he can stay there. I'm not mad at him, I merely want a divorce."

"Well..." Lucky paused for a moment. "If there's anything I can do..."

"Yeah," Venus said fiercely. "Don't believe a word you're gonna read, 'cause the rags'll come down on me big time." She frowned, before adding indignantly, "*He's* the one fucking his way through this town, and *I'm* the one who'll get the whore/slut headlines."

Lucky agreed. It was a well-known fact that men were always the protected ones, while women got the blame for everything. If Meryl Streep starred in a movie that flopped, she was instantly denigrated. If Jack Nicholson made three duds in a row, they lined up to pay him millions of bucks for the next one. Not at Panther. Lucky made sure women were treated equally in every way—including star salaries.

"Why couldn't I have gotten to Lennie before *you* picked him off?" Venus complained. "Lennie's so great. You won't find *him* screwing his costar."

And if I did, I'd probably kill him, Lucky thought calmly. She had a vengeful streak that was not to be messed with.

"Leslie Kane!" Venus snorted. "Is Cooper the only guy in town who doesn't know she used to be one of Madame Loretta's hookers?"

"Have you told him it's over?"

"Leslie's having a dinner at her house tonight.

I'm considering announcing it over dessert, that way everyone gets to share in the good news. May as well dump him with a bang."

Lucky shook her head. "You're really bad— you know that?"

Venus raised an eyebrow. "*I'm* bad? Try blaming the motherfucker who's screwing around on me."

The rest of the lunch they discussed business, including the grosses on *Finder,* a couple of scripts Venus was interested in developing, and the future plans of her personal production company. Then Venus wanted advice on whether she should switch agents. Freddie Leon had been pursuing her and she felt like a change.

"Freddie's the best," Lucky said, sipping Perrier. "In fact, I had a meeting with him and Alex Woods this morning." A casual pause. "Do you know Alex?"

Venus didn't miss a beat. "Big talent. Big dick. Only fucks Orientals. Doesn't give head, but *loves* getting it."

"How come you know everything?"

"Spent a stoned evening at a party with one of his ex's—a spicy Chinese piece. She gave great detail."

"We're doing his next project. A movie called *Gangsters.*"

Venus couldn't conceal her amazement. "*You're* making an Alex Woods movie? *You?* Surely you know he's supposed to be a total chauvinist prick?"

"With a dynamite script."

"Boy—lots of luck on this one."

Lucky smiled. "Thanks, but I don't think I'll need it."

The second production meeting of the day went smoothly; possible casting on *Gangsters* was discussed, and although some good names came up, Lucky knew Alex Woods would have his own ideas. She was aware that he didn't usually work with stars, but Freddie had called her after lunch to tell her he was pushing the Latino movie idol, Johnny Romano, for one of the leads. Lucky liked the idea—Johnny, with his huge following, could guarantee a big-bucks opening weekend.

"You've got *my* vote," she said.

"Good. I'll tell Johnny."

After the production meeting was over, the last thing she felt like doing was an interview for a magazine. However, she was well aware of the power of good PR, and bringing Panther back to where it belonged was important. With *Finder* and *River Storm* doing so well, it was time to put out a positive PR spin—even though she was extremely wary of the press and usually did everything possible to stay out of print.

Mickey Stolli, the former head of Panther—now running Orpheus—was constantly making negative statements to the press, saying Panther was finished, that none of its movies made money. Even though everything he said was a blatant lie, it wasn't good PR. The time had come to retaliate.

Lucky settled in with an earnest black man in his thirties and spoke eloquently about her plans for the future of the studio. "Panther's making the type of movies *I* like to see," she said firmly, pushing a hand through her unruly black curls. "In my kind of movies, women are smart. They are not relegated to the kitchen, bedroom, or whorehouse. They're strong, well-rounded women with careers and lives of their own who do not live their life through a man. *That's* what intelligent women want to see. I'm putting into development and production the movies Hollywood *should* be making."

Alex Woods called in the middle of the interview. "Can I take you up on that visit to your father?" he asked, speaking in a low, fast voice. "How about this weekend?"

"Uh, I don't know," she said hesitantly. "I'll have to arrange it with Gino."

Alex sounded like a man on a mission. "You'll come with me. It's important."

She had not planned on accompanying him. "I'm away this weekend," she said, wondering why she felt the need to explain.

"Where?" he demanded like he had a right to know.

None of your fucking business. "Uh...I'm spending a couple of days with my husband."

"Didn't know you were married."

Oh, really? Where have you been? "To Lennie Golden."

"The actor?"

"Very good."

He ignored her sarcasm. "When *can* we go?" he asked impatiently.

"If you're that anxious, I'll set it up for next week."

Very insistently, "And you *will* come?"

"If I can."

Alex Woods was the kind of man she could get into trouble with. Before Lennie...before her life had become so structured with kids and a studio to run and all the other things she was involved with.

She tried to return her attention to the interviewer, but two thoughts kept buzzing around in her head, vying for attention.

Alex Woods was a dangerous temptation

Lucky refused to be tempted.

5

Donna Landsman, formerly Donatella Bonnatti, resided in a fake Spanish castle perched atop a knoll above Benedict Canyon. She lived with her husband, George—who was her late husband Santino's former accountant—and her son, Santino Junior, a truculent, overweight sixteen-year-old. Her other three children had all left home—willing to face anything rather than life with their domineering and controlling mother.

Santino Junior—or Santo, as he was known—had elected to stay because he was the only one who could successfully manipulate her. Plus, he was sharp enough to realize that *someone* had to inherit the family fortune, and that someone was going to be him.

Santo was Donna's youngest child and only son. She worshiped him. In her mind he could do no wrong.

For his sixteenth birthday—against George's advice—she'd bought Santo a green Corvette and a solid-gold Rolex. Then, in case this was not enough, she'd handed him an American Express card with unlimited credit, five thousand dollars in cash, and thrown him an enormous party at the Beverly Hills Hotel.

She wanted her son to own the world.

Santo was in complete agreement.

George, however, did not agree. "You're ruining him," he'd warned Donna on many occasions. "If you give him everything at such an early age, what does he have to look forward to?"

"Nonsense," Donna replied. "He lost his real father, he's entitled to whatever I can provide."

George had given up arguing. It wasn't worth the battle. Donna was a difficult and complex woman; sometimes he felt he didn't understand her at all.

Donatella Lioni was born in a small village in Sicily to a poor, hard-working family. She'd spent the first sixteen years of her life taking care of her many younger brothers and sisters, until one day, an older cousin who lived in America visited her village and picked her out as a bride for the very important American businessman, Santino Bonnatti. Her father agreed it was an excellent match, and even though he'd never met Santino, he'd accepted a thousand dollars in cash and sent her on her way to the United States without any thought for her feelings.

The truth was, he'd sold her to a stranger in a faraway country, forcing her to leave the love of her life—Furio—a boy from her village. Donatella was heartbroken.

Arriving in America she was taken straight to Santino Bonnatti's house in Los Angeles. He'd looked her over with his beady eyes and given her cousin the nod. "Okay, okay, she ain't no beauty, but she'll do. Buy her some clothes, have her taught English, an' make sure she knows who I am, 'cause I ain't puttin' up with no crap."

Her cousin had taken her to his girlfriend's house—a parrot-faced blond imported from the Bronx. She'd stayed there several weeks while the blond attempted to teach her English. It was a disaster. The little English Donatella mastered came with a heavy Sicilian accent.

The second time she saw Santino was at their wedding. She wore a long white dress and a frightened expression. After the ceremony, Santino strutted around smoking a fat Cuban cigar, swapping dirty jokes with the boys while practically ignoring her.

Her cousin told her not to worry, everything would work out fine. Later she discovered Santino had paid him ten thousand dollars in cash for her delivery.

After the reception they'd gone back to Santino's house. Santino was not like the love she'd left behind in Sicily—he was older, short, in his late twenties, with thin lips, a rapidly receding hairline, and an exceptionally hairy body. She found this out when he stripped his clothes off, dropping them on the floor with an impatient shrug. "Get naked, honey," he leered. "Lemme get'a load of t'goods."

She ran to the bathroom, shivering in her satin wedding dress, tears staining her cheeks, until Santino marched in, and with no ceremony, unzipped her dress, ripped off her bra, pulled down her panties, and bent her over the sink, entering her from behind, grunting like a hog.

The pain was so staggering that she screamed aloud. Santino didn't care; covering her mouth with a hairy hand, he continued pumping away until he was satisfied. Then he walked out without a word, leaving her in the bathroom with blood dripping down between her legs.

That was the start of their marriage.

In quick succession she bore him two daughters, hoping this would make him happy. It didn't. His fury that she hadn't given birth to a son mounted daily—he desired an heir to carry on the great Bonnatti name.

When she didn't get pregnant again, he sent her to doctors, who poked and prodded and found nothing wrong. Santino belittled her, telling her she was a failure as a wife.

One day she suggested he have his semen tested. She'd been reading American magazines, such as Cosmopolitan, and it had dawned on her that failure to conceive wasn't always the woman's fault.

Santino was livid. He whacked her across the face so violently she lost two teeth. It was the first time he hit her. It certainly wasn't the last.

As time passed, she discovered he kept many mistresses. She didn't care, the less he came near her the better.

She found solace in fixing big bowls of pasta, which she consumed for breakfast, lunch, and dinner. She baked soft, doughy rolls and ate those, too. In the supermarket she stocked up on cookies, chocolate, and ice cream. Soon she was huge.

Santino was disgusted. He spent more and more time with his svelte mistresses, although occasionally he fell on top of Donatella in the middle of the night when he was drunk enough, forcing himself inside her.

He never gave her sexual pleasure, she was merely a receptacle for his maleness. All Santino required was a son.

She finally got pregnant again and he was ecstatic, but when their third child turned out to be another girl, he was so angry he moved out for six months.

Donatella considered those six months the happiest of her marriage.

When Santino came home, she hardened her heart against him. She was older and wiser and refused to take any more of his garbage.

Santino accepted her new attitude. From a stupid peasant girl she'd turned into a nagging balls breaker. Finally he had a wife he could respect.

He made love to her once a month to keep her quiet, until eventually she got pregnant again, and this time she gave birth to a boy. At last Santino was a happy man.

Donatella threw all the love she didn't get from her husband into her relationship with her son. Santino loved the boy, too. They vied with each other to see who could give little Santo—the name they called him—the most attention. As soon as the boy reached an age where he could understand, he *played them against each other, although he always favored his father.*

Donatella accepted that her life wasn't so bad. She lived in a three-million-dollar mansion in Bel Air, once the residence of a silent screen star. She was the wife of an important businessman. She had four healthy children, and she was able to regularly send money to her relatives in Sicily.

Occasionally Santino suggested she learn proper English, claiming her strong accent embarrassed him. He also nagged her to lose weight.

She ignored both his requests, laughing in his face.

One day, in the summer of 1983, Steven Berkely, a black lawyer, turned up at her door and informed her that Santino was the lowest form of human life. Ha! As if she didn't know.

She invited him in, curious to find out what he had to say.

He threw a copy of a pornographic magazine on her coffee table and angrily told her the naked woman on the cover was his fiancée. "Her face on somebody else's body," he said harshly, thrusting the magazine at her. "These are fake pictures."

"I no look'a this dirt," Donatella said, sorry she'd invited him in.

"My fiancée tried to kill herself because of these pictures," Steven said roughly. "All because your sick, sadistic husband publishes this filth."

She knew Santino owned a publishing company. He'd always told her they published technical books, not disgusting magazines. Now she had pornography in her own house, and an angry lawyer claiming Santino was responsible.

The phone rang. Glad of the diversion, she rushed

to answer it. "There's a house on Bluejay Way where your husband keeps his favorite mistress," a husky female voice whispered. "Come see for yourself. His car's outside."

Donatella hustled the lawyer out. If she could catch Santino with one of his mistresses, she'd make the lying swine pay. Muttering to herself, she hurried to her car and set off to bust her cheating husband.

Donatella had no trouble finding Bluejay Way. She parked behind Santino's car and marched up the driveway of the house, then rang the doorbell.

Within moments the door opened an inch, and Zeko, one of her husband's bodyguards, peeked through the crack.

Donatella gave the door a hefty kick, hurting her foot in the process. "Where you putta my husband?" she demanded.

"Mrs. Bonnatti," said a stunned Zeko, opening the door wider, failing to notice two men coming up the driveway behind her.

"FBI," one of the men said, holding up identification.

Ignoring the two men, Donatella barged into the house, coming face-to-face with a willowy blond. "Mrs. Bonnatti," the blond said, as if she were expecting her.

Donatella glared at her. "You gotta my Santino?"

"He's here," the blond replied calmly. "Before you see him, you and I should talk."

"He sleepa with you?" Donatella shouted.

The two FBI men shoved past Zeko and burst into the house waving guns. Zeko lumbered after them.

"Who's these people?" yelled Donatella.

"Get against the wall and shut up," one of the men commanded.

Then an almighty crash came from the back of the house, followed by several gunshots.

Donatella crossed herself. Ignoring the FBI men, she rushed down the corridor toward the noise.

A man was hustling a child and a young teenage girl into the hallway. Donatella pushed past him and entered the room they'd come from.

Santino's body was sprawled on the floor next to the bed. He was covered in blood and very dead.

"My God! My God! My God!" shrieked Donatella.

A dark-haired woman was still in the room. Donatella recognized her as Lucky Santangelo, the Bonnatti family's longtime enemy.

"Whore!" Donatella screamed hysterically. "You shota my husband. You killed him. I saw you!"

The rest was confusion. The police arrived and arrested Lucky Santangelo for Santino's murder. Months later, when the case came to court, it turned out that the real culprit was not Lucky, it was Brigette Stanislopoulos, a teenage heiress whom Santino had held captive, and while he'd been molesting the girl's six-year-old stepbrother, Bobby—Lucky's son—she'd shot him. Everything had been captured on videotape, evidence that was produced in court.

Brigette walked and so did Lucky.

Donatella was left a widow with four children to raise. She was filled with an unforgiving rage. Santino might have been an unfaithful pig, but he was her unfaithful pig and the father of her children. Something had to be done to avenge his murder; after *all, she was Sicilian, and in Sicily, if a family member is brutally murdered, their death has to be avenged. It was a matter of honor. It made no difference how long the vendetta took.*

Carlos, Santino's older brother, came to see her, offering to take over all of Santino's businesses, cutting her in for a paltry 5 percent. Donatella told him she'd think about it, although she had no intention of doing so. Instead she met with Santino's accountant, George, and got herself an education. Santino's main business was import/export, which she soon discovered brought in millions of dollars a year, most of it in cash. He also owned real estate, interests in two New Jersey casinos, and a very lucrative publishing company—which did indeed publish technology books, along with a selection of soft- and hard-core pornography.

Donatella found out from George that she was Santino's legal partner. He'd often dumped documents in front of her, making her sign. She'd never dared question him. The payoff was that everything was now hers.

George Landsman was an unassuming man who faded into the scenery with his mild manners and low voice. He'd been Santino's trusted lieutenant—there wasn't anything he didn't know about the various businesses. Quiet he might be, but George was a financial wizard with numbers. After watching him for a while, Donatella realized he was more than capable of keeping things running smoothly. With George's help and encouragement, she began familiarizing herself with everything—soon realizing that if she planned to take over, she'd have to rid herself of her cartoon accent, lose weight, and get her long hair styled.

Once she started on her quest to improve herself, she couldn't stop. First the accent went, then the weight; plastic surgery gave her a smaller nose, firmer chin, and higher cheekbones; she had breast reduction surgery, and got her hair cut and dyed; she purchased a closetful of designer clothes and several pieces of important jewelry.

Somewhere along the road to improvement she married George, who, it turned out, had always lusted after her—even when she was fat and could barely speak English. The word "orgasm" entered her vocabulary for the first time. She was considerably happier than she'd ever been before, especially when she discovered she possessed great skills as a capable businesswoman.

With George's tutoring she soaked up a lifetime of knowledge in a very short period of time. And when she finally felt she was ready, she began making her own deals with George's sound advice to back her. First she sold the publishing firm, using the money she raised to take over an ailing cosmetics company. Months later she got rid of the cosmetics company, and with that profit, took over a chain of small hotels. Six months later she sold the hotel chain at more than double the price she'd paid.

From that moment on, she was hooked. Takeovers became her game of choice.

Carlos, Santino's brother, was impressed. He came to see her again, this time suggesting a partnership. She turned him down, which didn't sit well with Carlos, who thought she should have kissed his ass.

"What're you doing about Lucky Santangelo?" she demanded of Carlos. "We know the Santangelo

family is responsible for Santino's murder, and you're letting them get away with it. If you don't do something, I will."

Carlos glared at his dead brother's wife. This broad was something else. From a dumpy, stupid hausfrau she'd turned herself into some kind of business dynamo, even learning to speak the language without that crazy accent. But did she really think she was capable of taking care of Lucky Santangelo?

No freaking way.

"Yeah. What'll you do?" Carlos asked, barely concealing a contemptuous sneer.

"Where I come from we honor our traditions," Donatella replied ominously, thinking he was more of a deadbeat than his brother.

"Don't sweat it," Carlos replied, angry that a woman would dare talk to him in such a way. What she needed was a proper man to slap the tongue right out of her plastic face. "I got plans for that Santangelo cunt."

Donatella arched her eyebrows. "Really?" she said.

"Yeah, really," he countered.

Carlos's plans did not pan out. In December of 1985 he suffered an unfortunate fall from the nineteenth floor of his Century City penthouse. Nobody knew how it happened.

Donatella knew.

Lucky Santangelo was responsible.

Donatella made the decision that it was up to her to ruin Lucky permanently. And with that end in mind, she'd come up with a devastating plan to destroy her.

Every day at four o'clock, Santo arrived home from school. He made the most of the few hours of peace before his stupid mother descended and began fussing the crap out of him. Fortunately, she and his nerdy stepfather were never home before seven, so that gave him plenty of time to do whatever he liked without either of them sticking their interfering noses in.

He hated his mother. Every day he thought about how much he hated her, and how unfair it was that she was still alive while his father was dead.

Why hadn't *she* been killed?

Why wasn't *her* dumb ass buried ten feet beneath the ground?

The only good thing about her was that she was easy. He could usually get anything he wanted—especially since all his siblings had taken off, leaving him in position numero uno.

As for George, he hated him, too. The man was an ineffectual jerk—whom Donna kicked around good. He was no stepfather. He was nothing.

Santo considered the hours between four and seven his special time. First he smoked a couple of joints; next he stuffed himself with ice cream and candy; after that he flicked through his extensive pile of porno magazines hidden in a locked closet. If the girls turned him on, he jerked off—although mostly he saved that activity for HER.

SHE was the special one created for his pleasure.

SHE was everything a man could ever want.

Not that he was a man. He was sixteen, and being sixteen sucked.

Every morning when he got up and saw himself in the bathroom mirror, Santo wished he was older and thinner. If he was older, he might have a better chance of scoring with HER. If he was thinner, he might be able to make out with some of the more popular girls at school—the pretty ones with the Beverly Hills attitudes, nose jobs, silky skin, and long fair hair. These little tramps didn't care that he had plenty of money and a fancy car. They were too stupid to notice. Instead, they ran after the dumb jerks who played football and worked out. Big, sweaty assholes. He hated all of them. He didn't want them anyway. Not when he had HER.

SHE was a startlingly sexy blond with everything in the right place. And SHE didn't mind showing it. He'd seen her tits, her ass, and her hairy pussy. He'd read her thoughts and knew what she wanted from a man.

Today he decided to concentrate on HER and forget about the other whores. After locking his bedroom door he went to his closet, reached in the back, and pulled out a suitcase filled with his collection—a collection that included early nude photos where she sat around with her legs open, exhibiting a big, black bush of pubic hair; magazine layouts reflecting her rise to fame; CDs; posters; videos of her singles; taped TV appearances and interviews.

Reading her interviews was a major head trip. She was a maniac—talked about sex like she was one of the guys.

Santo devoured every word, memorizing her preferences. She liked men who went down on her—that was in *Playboy;* she'd made love with a woman—*Vanity Fair;* she wanted sex constantly and fantasized about black men—*Rolling Stone.*

Yeah! She was some hot ticket. And he was rich enough to buy a ride straight up her wet pussy.

One day he knew he'd get the opportunity to do it with her.

One day Venus Maria would see him coming in more ways than one.

He leered at the thought. It made every day worth living.

6

"I can't believe I have an hour free before my next meeting," Lucky said, collapsing into the leather chair behind her desk.

"Not exactly," Kyoko said apologetically. "Charlie Dollar's on the lot. I told him it was okay to stop by at five, and if you'd finished your interview, you'd see him."

"Oh, *great,*" she groaned. "Why'd you do that?"

"He *is* one of Panther's biggest stars," Kyoko reminded her. "And I happen to know

Mickey Stolli sent him a script he's interested in. So..."

"I know, I know...you're right, Ky. I should see him—keep him happy."

"It would be prudent."

She loved the way Kyoko spoke, he was always so proper.

"Okay, order two margaritas and a dish of guacamole from the Mexican place across the street. Then put on my Billie Holiday CD. I need a mind break and I suppose Charlie's the perfect person to have it with."

Kyoko nodded, pleased she agreed with him.

The fiftyish Charlie strolled into her office five minutes later with a shit-eating grin and a bouquet of purple roses—her favorite.

Charlie—like most actors—could be a total pain in the ass. Lucky didn't care. She was fond of Charlie because he didn't take himself too seriously and he had a sardonic sense of humor that made him stimulating company. In fact, if there hadn't been Lennie, there might have been Charlie—he was certainly attractive enough in a Jack Nicholson off center kind of way.

Charlie settled down on her couch and proceeded to light up a joint. "Didja get my message?" he asked, dragging deeply.

"Couldn't miss it," she replied, taking in his uncombed hair, scuffed Reeboks, rumpled T-shirt, and ill-fitting pants. Somehow or other it all worked, the tramp look suited Charlie.

He patted his stomach. "We're gonna dump the gut. Right?"

"Wouldn't want your fans to think you've lost it," she said caustically.

"Smart lady."

"You're so full of shit, Charlie," she said, smiling affectionately.

He raised an indignant eyebrow. "Why? 'Cause I wanna present the movie star image everyone knows an' loves?"

"Nope. You're just full of shit, period. Maybe *that's* why I love you."

Charlie took another deep drag before offering the joint to her. She declined. Maybe with Lennie, but not now, not with another meeting coming up.

Charlie mock sighed. "Lucky, Lucky, Lucky—what'm I gonna do with you?"

She helped herself to some guacamole, savoring the tangy flavor. "Certainly not the same as you do with every other woman," she said tartly.

"Hey," Charlie objected, extravagant eyebrows shooting up again. "Can I help it if they all wanna jump my decrepit old bones? Lady, I do not encourage it. Truth is, I'm gettin' too old to choo choo all night."

"Oh, yeah, sure," she said sarcastically.

He ignored her sarcasm. "And I've *definitely* had it with baby chicks," he continued. "Went out the other night with one who'd never heard of Bruce Springsteen. Get *that* deal."

Lucky shook her head. "Life's tough, Charlie, when you won't date anyone over eighteen."

They both laughed, enjoying their irreverent friendship.

"Word is, you're off for a dirty weekend," Charlie remarked, leaning back on the couch, examining his unmanicured nails.

She observed his comfortable gut—barely hidden beneath his baggy T-shirt, and wondered if he'd ever considered working out. "Does it count as a dirty weekend if I'm spending it with my husband?" she asked.

A lopsided leer. "I sure hope so."

She grinned, aching to see Lennie. "I'll only be gone three days. Do me a big one, Charlie, try to save any other complaints until I get back."

He nodded. "Gonna do my best, Mafia Princess."

"Don't call me that!" she protested.

He shook a knowing finger at her. "C'mon, babe, y'know you love it."

"I do not," she said indignantly. "My father was never into the whole mob scene. Gino was a very savvy businessman who just happened to have connected friends."

"Sure, an' I drive a limo in my spare time." A crooked grin. "So, how's Gino doin'? The old guy's still got it goin' for him—I admire that in a senior citizen."

"Balls of steel," Lucky said dryly. "Runs in the family."

Charlie blew a lazy smoke ring. "Never got a chance to see for myself," he drawled.

"Is that a come-on?"

"Hey—balls of steel—my big turn-on."

"Gee, I never knew you cared."

"Sure I care." A perfectly timed pause.

"Change my poster and I'll care even more."

Actors! They always had an agenda. And somehow or other it always managed to put them in first position. "Okay, Charlie," she said with a small sigh, "it's done. Now can we relax for five minutes?"

A very big Charlie Dollar grin. "Whatever you say, babe."

"Brigette?"

"Nona? Wow—Nona! How *are* you? When did you get back? And how did you *find* me?"

"Called your grandmother. After a brief interrogation she gave me your number. *Radical* security, babe. I could've been anyone."

Nona Webster, ex–best friend whom she hadn't seen in two years on account of the fact they'd drifted apart when Nona's rich, bohemian parents, Effie and Yul, had sent their only daughter off on a world tour. They'd attended boarding school together, and shared many an escapade.

"It's so great to hear from you!" Brigette exclaimed animatedly. "Where are you staying?"

"Big downer, I'm stuck at home 'cause I haven't had a chance to scope out my own place. At least I've got a job—researcher at *MONDO*."

Brigette was impressed. "Wow! Cool magazine."

"Yeah—Effie scored me the job. So…what

are you doing in New York? Didn't you tell me L.A. was the only place?"

"It was, for a while. Then I, like, changed my mind."

"I get it—you met someone."

"I wish," Brigette said wistfully.

"Listen—we've *gotta* get together. I've *sooo* much stuff to fill you in on."

"How about lunch?" Brigette suggested, anxious to fill Nona in on a few things herself.

"Perfect," Nona replied. "Can't wait to see you!"

They met at Serendipity, devouring foot-long hot dogs while catching up on each other's news. Nona was more interesting-looking than pretty. She had startlingly natural red hair, slanted eyes, and a freckle-covered face. She dressed in a funky-stylish way, and her personality was disarmingly direct. As soon as they sat down, she confessed to three current boyfriends—each living in a different country.

"I can't decide which one's the best for me, so I made a daring escape," she said with a wicked grin. "They all wanna do the marriage thing. I feel like such a slut!"

"You *are* a slut," Brigette retorted crisply. "What else is new?"

"Thanks!" Nona exclaimed.

"You always *were* the biggest flirt around," Brigette pointed out. "Made *me* look like an amateur."

"That's true," Nona agreed. "But enough about me. What's going on with *you*?"

"Trying to be a model," Brigette confessed.

"A model! Get outta here!"

"What's so funny about that?"

"I dunno…it's such a shitty profession. All looks, no brains."

"I can do it, Nona. All I need is a chance to get started."

"Okay, so you're goin' for it, that's cool. I mean, you *look* amazing—still got those fantastic tits, and I must say you lost weight in all the right places."

"So did you."

"Ugh!" Nona said, pulling a face. "The food in some of the countries I visited—pigs' ears, snake bile, buffalos' balls. Who could eat!"

"Tell me about your three would-be husbands," Brigette said, dying to hear every detail.

Nona rubbed her freckled nose. "All *very* cute. One of 'em's black—my parents will freak—or maybe not, you know how liberal *they* are. Oh—by the way, they're throwing one of their parties tonight, you're invited."

"How's Paul?" Brigette asked casually.

Paul Webster, Nona's handsome artist brother. Brigette had harbored a big crush on him—unreturned for a long time, until she'd gotten engaged. Only then had Paul stepped forward and declared his love for her. Too late. By that time she was over him.

"Married, with a *baby*!" Nona exclaimed. "Amazing what happens to people."

"Is he still painting?" Brigette asked, recalling Paul's ferocious talent.

"*Nooo*. He's a stockbroker on Wall Street.

Very straight. Isn't that the funniest thing you ever heard?"

"I can't imagine Paul with a proper job and a family. He must've really changed."

"Yeah—but I got a sneaky feeling he's still a bad boy underneath."

"Do me a favor," Brigette said earnestly. "Impress upon your parents that I don't want *anyone* knowing who I am. Right now I'm Brigette Brown. After all the past scandal, it's better this way."

"Fine with me," Nona said, looking at her watch and letting out a shriek. "I gotta get back to work," she said, grabbing the check. "I'll see you tonight. Nine o'clock. Wear something outrageous!"

Brigette nodded. "I'll be there."

Cooper Turner was a connoisseur of women, and Leslie Kane was irresistibly gorgeous. It was no surprise that in a short period of time, America had fallen in love with this vision of clean-cut American beauty with her flowing red hair, full, luscious lips, and gorgeous body. She'd appeared in two movies, becoming an instant star. Currently she was shooting a film with Cooper, and even though he was forty-seven and Leslie only twenty-three, they were an on-screen love match. Hollywood liked its leading ladies young; it didn't matter how old the guys were.

Leslie was in bed with Cooper on-screen and

off. He'd only had to look at her with his knowing ice-blue eyes and she'd turned to mush.

When she was fourteen, she'd had his picture taped to the wall above her bed. Cooper Turner. Hunk. How she'd hated all the women she'd read about him dating in the fan magazines she'd so avidly collected. Didn't he *know* he was supposed to wait for her?

Whenever her stepfather had staggered into her bedroom late at night with beer on his breath and a swollen gut, she'd always clung to Cooper's image hovering above her rickety bed, watching over her, while her obese stepfather grunted and groaned on top of her. She'd yearned to kick him in his rancid balls and run. But she couldn't go, not while her mother lay sick in bed with a terrible cancer eating away at her.

The day her mother died she'd taken off with a thousand bucks stolen from her stepfather in her pocket and plenty of ambition to fuel her journey.

Good-bye, Florida.

Hello, L.A.

She was eighteen and quite stunning, so it hadn't taken long for her to be discovered by Madame Loretta, a woman who recognized a moneymaker when she saw one. For many years Madame Loretta had been supplying exquisite young girls to all Hollywood. She required them fresh and unused, so as soon as she'd spotted Leslie, she'd lured her from the Rodeo Drive boutique she was working at, and set her up in a luxurious apartment.

Leslie was a natural. With her glowing looks, and small-town charm, she soon beguiled all her clients, who, much to Madame Loretta's delight, became instant regulars.

Leslie had harbored no intention of remaining a call girl forever. Servicing rich, jaded men was not her life's ambition. She'd wanted more. She'd wanted true love, and one day—while waiting for her car at the Santa Palm car wash—she'd found it with Eddie Kane, a former child star who was then the head of distribution at Panther Studios.

Eddie Kane was a true Hollywood character and no slouch when it came to women. One look at Leslie and he'd mentally burned his fat black book. At first he'd had no idea she'd once been one of Madame Loretta's high earners, and although she'd gone to great lengths to make sure he never found out, eventually he'd discovered the truth, causing an immediate split between them.

It was an unhappy time for Leslie, but she'd been determined not to return to her old life. Instead, she'd taken a job as a receptionist at a fashionable beauty salon, where several weeks later she'd been discovered by Mickey Stolli's wife, Abigaile. Abigaile had insisted Mickey screen-test this incandescent beauty. In the meantime, a coked-out Eddie had smashed his precious Maserati into a concrete wall, leaving Leslie a very young widow.

The very young widow's screen test was a big success.

A year later she was a star.

Leslie often reflected that it was true—in Hollywood—if you wished hard enough, anything could happen.

Now she was in bed with Cooper Turner, and he was everything she'd ever imagined and more. He was her fantasy come to life.

She leaned over, softly trailing her manicured nails up and down his smooth, bare back. It was lunch break and they were in a motel near the studio. Cooper's idea of lunch was eating her pussy for a solid half hour. She'd come so many times she'd lost count. This man was an unbelievable lover.

Cooper lay beside her, asleep, a satisfied smile spread across his still boyishly handsome face.

The motel had been his idea. They'd sneaked off without telling anyone—highly unprofessional. Leslie knew the hair and makeup people would kill her when she returned to the set, because it would take at least an hour to put her back together before she could step in front of the camera looking picture-perfect again.

"Sweetie pie, wake up," she purred, satisfaction coloring her breathy voice. "C'mon, we have to get going."

Cooper opened one eye, lazily reaching for her breasts. Gorgeous, like the rest of her. He pushed them together, gently caressing both nipples with his fingertips.

She sighed with pleasure, her nipples hardening to his touch.

He rolled over on his back, positioning her

on top of him, her long legs spread wide across his thighs. Very slowly he inserted two fingers, savoring her anticipation. "Lower yourself on me, baby," he commanded, loving the fact that he could get her so hot and creamy. "Do it slowly."

"But Cooper..." she protested, knowing it was useless to say no. She would do exactly as he asked and he knew it.

"*C'mon*, baby," he urged. "What're you waiting for?"

She caught her breath as she felt him slip inside her. Flexing her muscles tight, she held him a willing captive.

"That's it, baby, that's it," he moaned, grasping her ass and squeezing. "You're sensational!"

7

"What's your mother like?" Tin Lee asked.

Insane, Alex wanted to reply. *Selfish. Mean. Self-obsessed. A tyrant. A nag. She drove my father to drink and an early death. And even now—with all my success and fame—she's constantly putting me down.*

"You'll like her," Alex said shortly. "She's a fine woman."

"I'm sure," Tin Lee said. "After all, she raised you, Alex, and you are a wonderful man."

Oh, Jesus. One good fuck and they think they know it all.

"I'm excited to meet her," Tin Lee continued, clutching her tiny hands together. "It is quite an honor that you wish me to accompany you and your mother on her birthday."

Baby, baby, if you only knew. I can't be alone with dear old Mom. I can't stand her company. When we're alone together, we rip the flesh from each other's throats. We're a fucking horror show.

They were standing in the front hall of Alex's Wilshire condo. He never took his girlfriends to his main residence—the modern house at the beach. That was private property not to be invaded by transient girlfriends.

Tin Lee was six weeks old in Alex Woods's life. From Thailand, she was petite and pretty, an actress in her early twenties. She'd come in for an audition and he'd invited her out. He'd only made love to her once and had no real desire to do so again. She didn't make him feel young, she made him feel old and decrepit. But tonight he desperately needed her as a buffer between him and his mother.

"I hope she likes me," Tin Lee said anxiously.

"She'll love you," Alex assured her.

Right. And if you believe that, you're dumber than I thought.

"Thank you," Tin Lee said gratefully.

Oh, Jesus, Dominique would pick this poor girl to shreds. "Another gook, dear?" she'd ask when Tin Lee visited the ladies' room. "Another Asian bar hooker? Why can't you settle down with a decent American girl? You're not getting any younger, Alex. You're forty-seven, and look your age. Soon you'll be losing your hair, and then who'll have you?"

Sure, he knew exactly what his mother would say before the words left her brightly smeared crimson lips. She was going to be seventy-one years old and time had not mellowed her.

But what could he do? She was his mother and he was supposed to love her.

Morton Sharkey was a tall, slim, hawk-nosed man in his late fifties. He was also a brilliant lawyer and well-respected business advisor. He was the man who'd helped Lucky buy Panther, and even though he was a pessimist, his instincts were usually impeccable.

They had their fights. Ever since she'd bought Panther, he'd been carrying on about it being a losing proposition.

"Don't sweat it, Morton," she'd told him on numerous occasions. "I've built hotels in Vegas, run Dimitri's shipping empire—I sure as hell know how to make a movie studio work."

"The movie business is different," Morton had warned, a stern note in his voice. "It's the most creatively dishonest business there is."

If he knew so much about the movie business, then surely he realized it took time to turn things around. Besides, when she'd sold off

60 percent at his insistence, she'd practically recouped her original investment. So what was he so worried about? Everything was under control.

Morton listened as she filled him in on her meeting with the Japanese bankers. "If this merchandising deal goes through," she said, "it'll raise plenty. And that's exactly what we need to keep the banks happy. That, and our two hit movies."

"Good," Morton said.

"I thought you were going to be at the meeting," Lucky added, noticing that Morton seemed to be somewhat preoccupied.

"I got held up."

"Shouldn't wear a Rolex," she joked.

He didn't get it.

"I'm visiting Lennie this weekend. When I'm back we'll discuss everything. If the Japanese deal is a go, and our two movies keep performing, I think we're finally in excellent shape, don't you?"

He cleared his throat. "Yes, Lucky."

There was something wrong with Morton today. She hoped he wasn't going through some bizarre midlife crisis. He acted as if he couldn't wait to get out of her office.

"Are you all right?" she asked.

"Why wouldn't I be?" he countered in a defensive way.

"I'm only asking."

Morton jumped to his feet. "Got a feeling I'm coming down with the flu."

"Bed rest and liquids," Lucky said sympathetically. "Oh, yeah, and Nate 'n Al's chicken soup."

"Have a nice weekend, Lucky."

"I plan to!"

★ ★ ★

Morton Sharkey left Panther in his pale beige XJS Jaguar convertible—his personal salute to middle age. He drove two blocks before pulling over to the side of the street and speaking furtively into his car phone. "Donna?" he questioned hoarsely when a woman answered.

"Yes."

"We're nearly there. You'll have what you want shortly."

"Make sure it happens as soon as possible."

Click. She hung up without another word.

He'd met some ice queens in his time, but this one took the prize. She acted like she was ruler of the whole goddamn planet. He hated her attitude. Most of all he hated that she had something on him.

How could he have been so foolish?

How could he, Morton Sharkey, have gotten himself caught in the oldest trap of all?

Morton Sharkey, married, with two grown children, a well-respected member of the business community, a *family* man with excellent values and a place on the board of several prestigious charity committees. All his life he'd worked hard and given back, helping others less fortunate than himself. His wife,

Candice, was still a very attractive woman. More than that, she was a caring, faithful wife, and in twenty-six years of marriage he'd only strayed twice.

Until Sara.

Seventeen-year-old Sara with the long red hair and skinny white thighs and bitten nails and smart mouth and expressive lips and tiny breasts and tangerine pubic hair and...

Oh God—he could go on and on about Sara. She was the bittersweet dessert of his life, and even now, in spite of what had taken place, he still lusted for her.

Sara was younger than his daughter.

Sara was a free spirit.

Sara was a would-be actress.

Sara had accepted twelve thousand dollars to set him up.

And still he loved her.

Or obsessed about her.

It didn't matter which, because there was no way he was prepared to give her up.

What was that expression he'd heard so many times?

Ah, yes...There's no fool like an old fool.

How very true.

And yet...when he was with Sara, enveloped by her soft young flesh and wraparound legs, enjoying their fantasies together, nothing else mattered. Not even blackmail.

He hadn't wanted to betray Lucky. He'd been given no choice.

Donna Landsman had promised to destroy him if he didn't.

★ ★ ★

Lucky's house in Malibu was set back from the ocean, with a clear view of the coastline. It was a comfortable Mediterranean-style house, filled with simple rattan furniture and plenty of books, paintings, and objects she and Lennie had collected together. They'd both decided this was the perfect spot to raise children.

She arrived home just in time to catch little Maria toddling around the living room, looking adorable in a cute orange jumpsuit. Sweeping her daughter up in her arms, she swung her high in the air. Maria giggled uncontrollably—exactly like her mother, she craved action.

"She wouldn't go to bed until she saw you," explained Cee Cee, Maria's pretty black nanny.

"Wouldn't go to bed, huh?" Lucky teased, tickling her daughter until Maria screamed with even more excitement. When she quieted down, Lucky kissed her on the forehead and said, "Mommy's going away for a few days, so you've got to be a very good girl and let Cee Cee look after you nicely."

"Mommy go," Maria said, wriggling out of Lucky's arms and proceeding to race unsteadily around the room. "Mommy, GO GO GO GO!"

"Mommy go, but I'll be back soon," Lucky assured her.

"Good Mommy," Maria crooned, running

over and stroking Lucky's face with her soft baby hands. "Nice Mommy. Mommy *good* girl."

The joy of having such wonderful children was overpowering. After tucking Maria safely into bed, she crept in to check on baby Gino, asleep in his cot with his tiny thumb stuffed firmly in his mouth.

Watching her son sleep, she realized that moments like this made everything worthwhile.

She went into her bedroom, checked her weekend bag, then grabbed a quick snack in the kitchen before calling her father and telling him about Alex Woods. "He's written a fantastic script," she said enthusiastically. "Very realistic. Can't wait for you to read it."

"Yeah, yeah," Gino said gruffly. "I'll look at it, meet the guy, maybe give him an education, huh?"

"How about we come down to Palm Springs at the end of next week?" Lucky suggested, nibbling on a chocolate cookie.

"You're comin' with him?"

"Well, yeah. I'm not leaving Alex alone with you, you'll frighten the crap out of him, then he won't make his movie at my studio."

Gino chuckled, "Are you sayin' he's a chickenshit?"

"I don't know him that well."

"Tell ya what, kid, I'll fill you in if he's got balls."

"Gee, thanks!"

As soon as she put the phone down, it rang again.

"Sweetheart!" said Lennie, calling long-distance.

Four years of marriage and her heart still jumped when she heard his voice. "Lennie!" she said, smiling broadly. "I've been trying to reach you all day."

He chuckled. "Here I am, babe. Bored and horny."

She laughed softly. "Don't try and sweet-talk me with your romantic come-ons."

"Why not? You're so easy."

"Yeah?"

"Yeah."

"How's everything going?"

"Usual problems, nothing I can't deal with." He paused. "I need you, Lucky. Right here next to me."

"I'm leaving for the airport any moment," she assured him.

"I miss you so much, sweetheart. It's not the same when you aren't around."

"I miss you too, Lennie," she said softly. "So do the kids. Maria runs back and forth all day chanting 'Daddy! Daddy!' It's her new mantra."

"How's her walking?"

"Impressive."

"Takes after her mommy, huh?" He paused for another moment. "Sweetheart, you're *sure* you want to do this? Fly all those hours just to spend two days with me?"

"Ha!" she exclaimed. "Try stopping me."

"No escape, huh?" he joked.

"My husband—the comedian."

"Yeah, and don't you love it."

"I love *you*," she murmured.

"Love you, too. Kiss the kids, tell 'em Daddy's thinking about them."

"How about *my* kiss?"

"You'll get yours in person."

She gave a low laugh, anticipating their time together. "Ohh...baby, baby, *that'll* make the trip worthwhile."

"I'll be at the airport to meet you. Fly safely."

"If you say so, I will." She hung up with a big smile on her face.

Her limousine was on time, driven by Boogie, her longtime bodyguard, private investigator, and driver. An ex–Vietnam vet, Boogie was protective and smart; Lucky trusted him implicitly.

They rode in companionable silence to the airport—Boogie never spoke unless it was absolutely necessary.

The limo dropped her next to the Panther Lear jet. She didn't feel like talking, but the pilot insisted on giving her a full weather report. And the steward, a mop-top gay guy, regaled her with some outrageous gossip he'd recently heard about Leslie Kane and Cooper Turner. Like she hadn't had an earful at lunch with Venus. Why were people so fascinated with boring, mindless gossip?

As the plane took off, she leaned back, closing her eyes.

A weekend with Lennie...she couldn't wait.

8

"Hi, gorgeous," Cooper Turner said, entering Venus Maria's all-white, luxurious bathroom.

She was sitting at the vanity, brushing her hair. He sauntered up behind her, slid his hands onto her breasts, tweaked her nipples, and kissed the back of her platinum-blond head.

She didn't move a muscle. This was her show, and she'd run it her way. "How'd work go today?" she asked casually.

"Pretty good," Cooper replied, walking over and peering at himself in another mirror. "Do I look tired?" he asked, turning back for her approval.

"Hmm...a little bit," she replied, knowing this would drive him crazy. Cooper thrived on compliments.

"You really think so?" he said, frowning.

"It can't be helped, baby," she said, falsely sympathetic. "You're working hard. I mean, my *God*—you're at the studio morning, noon, and night. I bet you hardly have time for lunch. What *did* you eat today?"

Pussy, he was tempted to reply. But he controlled himself. It wouldn't do for Venus to find out he was in bed with Leslie Kane. His wife had a fierce temper, and Leslie was merely a temporary distraction.

"Uh...just a salad," he said vaguely. "What about you?"

"Lunch with Lucky."

"How's she doing?"

"Great. Panther's financing the next Alex Woods movie."

"Jesus!" Cooper exclaimed. "Alex answering to Lucky. They'll kill each other."

Venus continued brushing her hair. "Do you know him?"

"We've spent a few out-of-control nights together. Alex is a wild man."

"Mmm…" Venus said, smiling slyly, going for the dig. "With one of the biggest dicks in Hollywood."

She had Cooper's attention. "How do *you* know?" he asked quizzically.

"'Cause *I* know everything."

Cooper was fully confident of her answer. "Bigger than mine?"

"You're so conceited."

He grinned. "No, just realistic, honey, just realistic."

Yeah, Venus thought, *let's see how realistic you'll feel after we have our little confrontation at Leslie's dinner tonight. Let's see how you'll handle that.*

Brigette strolled into the Websters' party as if she were already the most famous supermodel in the world. She'd watched the elite squad of girls strut the runways enough times to know the walk, to master the look. The look said *I own the world and you're all dogs.* The walk confirmed it. Brigette had them both down.

She'd taken her time dressing for the party, discarding several outfits before settling on a drop-dead Hervé Leger black wrap dress and very high Manolo Blahnik pumps. She knew she looked hot with no bra and her honey-blond hair casually caressing her shoulders.

It was her intention that tonight somebody was going to discover her, because she was determined that any moment would be the start of her modeling career.

Nona's parents greeted her at the door, startled at her transformation. They remembered Brigette as a cute, cuddly blond. Now this statuesque beauty marched into their party full of sass and attitude. She paused at the entrance to the living room.

"My dear, you look wonderful," Nona's eccentric mother said admiringly.

"So do you, Effie," Brigette replied, her bright blue eyes scanning the party, searching for the right people to impress.

"Nona tells me you're modeling now," said Nona's father, Yul, a tall, imposing man.

"Uh...yes."

"That must be very exciting."

"It is," she lied.

"Well," Yul said, leading her through the enormous room crammed with an eclectic group of guests. "I'm sure you'll see dozens of people you know."

"Thanks, I'm sure I will," she said, looking around. The truth was, she didn't know anyone. She couldn't even see Nona. *Great*. She'd made this fabulous entrance and now she was standing there like the town idiot.

For a moment she panicked, then she thought about how Lucky would handle a situation like this—Lucky, who was always in control. *Think Lucky! Think Lucky!* Head tilted high, she headed for the bar.

"Brigette?"

The first person she bumped into *would* have to be Paul, Nona's brother and *her* ex-crush. She hadn't seen him for at least a couple of years. He looked different. Gone was the long hair, unshaven chin, and single gold earring. Now he wore a respectable blue blazer, gray pants, white shirt, and a conservative tie. As if this weren't enough, his hair was cut extremely short. He was a preppy nightmare!

"Paul!" she exclaimed.

"*You* look fantastic," he said, standing back with an appreciative smile.

"Hmmm… *you* look different," she responded, hating the way he looked.

"Uh, this is my wife, Fenella," he said, placing a proprietary arm around an anorexic brunette and pulling her into the conversation. "Honey," he said, "meet Brigette Stanislopoulos. Remember, I told you about her? Nona's best friend."

He obviously hadn't told wifey dear that they'd once almost been an item.

"Nice to meet you," Fenella said in an uptight Bostonian accent. "So you're Nona's friend?"

"Right," Brigette said, turning her attention back to Paul. "By the way, it's Brigette Brown now. Please don't mention that other name."

"Sorry."

"That's okay." An awkward silence. She broke it with, "I hear you've got a baby."

"A boy," Paul said proudly.

Fenella clung to his arm possessively. "Yes, little Military's the image of his daddy."

Brigette stopped herself from laughing out loud. "Military?" she said, shooting Paul a surely-you-can't-be-serious look.

"We wanted an unusual name," Fenella said.

This is so weird, Brigette thought, *once I would have done anything for this man, now I'm standing here talking to a total stranger. A stranger who named his kid Military! What kind of a nerd has Paul turned into!*

"Well, lovely seeing you," she said, trying for a fast getaway. "Guess we'll bump into each other later."

She moved across the room, feeling Paul's eyes on her back. Several men tried to start conversations. She ignored them and kept moving.

At last she spotted Nona holding court by the window. She made her way over, still trying to maintain the walk and the look. From the attention she was getting, it seemed to be working.

Nona leaped up and embraced her. "I'm *so* glad you're here," she said, smiling mysteriously. "Big things have happened since lunch."

"Like what?" Brigette asked curiously.

Nona pulled a handsome black man dressed in a flowing African robe to his feet. "Meet my fiancé, Zandino!" she announced triumphantly.

Zandino bowed from the waist and beamed. His teeth were dazzling.

"Zandino," Brigette repeated, slightly dazed.

"Yup. Zan flew in today and surprised me," Nona said happily. "We met when I was visiting Africa. Zan's father's a chieftain, but Zan went to college here, so it's not like he's a stranger to America."

"Wow!" Brigette said, shaking her head. "This is some surprise."

"I know," Nona said, grinning sheepishly.

Brigette turned to Zandino. "Will you be living here?"

Zandino's wide, toothy smile was irresistible. "I shall be doing so," he said in very precise English. "I hope to study law."

Nona winked at her. "Isn't he the *best*?" she whispered, leaning close to Brigette's ear. "*And*—he's got the biggest dick I've ever seen!"

"Nona! This is your future husband you're talking about!"

"It's true," Nona said, laughing happily. "'Course, that's not the only reason I picked him. Zan is simply the kindest, sweetest guy I ever met."

"That's great," Brigette said, gazing around the room. "You know, Nona, I have to make connections tonight. Who do you think I should meet?"

"Well…I suppose I *could* introduce you to my boss from *MONDO*. And there's a couple of hot photographers here. And…let me see, hmm…Michel Guy—he's that aging French stud who runs the Starbright Modeling Agency."

"I want to meet everyone," Brigette said, a determined light shining in her eyes.

"Okay, okay, don't get anal about it. I'll take you on a tour, and we'll hit on anybody who can deliver."

Brigette nodded. "What are we waiting for?"

Leslie Kane lived in a small but charming house on Stone Canyon Road in Bel Air. She'd bought the place as soon as she'd started making money, hired an interior designer, and was more than pleased with the results. For the first time in her life, she had a home, a place that was truly hers. Now all she needed was a man to fill it, and Cooper Turner was the perfect candidate.

Minor detail: He was married.

Very minor detail: Leslie had supreme confidence when it came to men. After all, she'd been taught by the great Madame Loretta, and Madame Loretta had handled some of the most successful girls in the business—girls who had gone on to marry movie stars and major moguls.

Leslie knew she was on the right track with

Cooper. He was certainly enthusiastic enough, every break they got he was hot to tango. Mister permanent hard-on. Quite impressive for a man his age.

As she dressed for her dinner party, Leslie thought about Madame Loretta's three cardinal rules for keeping a man happy.

Rule One: Find something about him that you consider the most wonderful thing in the world and praise him constantly.

Rule Two: Make sure you tell him he's the most exciting lover you've ever had.

Rule Three: Whatever he says, be amazed at his knowledge. Gaze adoringly at him and insist he says the most intelligent and clever things you've ever heard.

Leslie had put these three rules into practice and found it worked every time. Of course, now that she was a famous movie star she didn't need to impress anyone, men came running merely for the chance to say they'd stood next to her. Not that they got to do anything more than that, because she was extremely choosy. Sleeping around did not appeal to her.

What appealed to her was a settled relationship.

What appealed to her was a wedding ring.

What appealed to her was Cooper Turner.

She put on a clinging lace dress made especially for her by Nolan Miller. The neckline was demure, but the lace revealed her body down each side, clinging to her curves provocatively.

Admiring herself in the mirror, she wondered

what Venus Maria would wear. Probably something trampy.

Leslie simply couldn't understand why Cooper had married Venus. The woman had no class, with her dyed blond hair and slutty looks. Leslie might once have been a whore, but she'd always managed to look like a lady.

Well...he wouldn't have to put up with Venus much longer, because when Leslie wanted something, she usually got it. And she wanted Cooper.

Tonight she'd invited Jeff Stoner, a young, good-looking actor who had a small part in the movie. In the past Cooper had often teased her about Jeff, saying he had a big crush on her, so she knew having Jeff at her house would irritate Cooper and hopefully make him jealous.

Whenever Cooper had mentioned Jeff, she'd laughed and dismissed him as just another boring actor. But tonight, when Cooper was sitting next to his trampy wife, and she was playing hand on the thigh with Jeff, it would force Cooper into making some kind of decision about their future together. A serious commitment was exactly what she had in mind.

Satisfied with her appearance, she strolled into the living room, ready to greet her guests.

9

"Let's stop for a drink," Alex suggested, his nerves already on edge.

"Won't that make us late for your mother?" Tin Lee countered.

"She'll wait," Alex said. His throat was so parched he had to have something. Before leaving his apartment he'd popped a Valium and smoked half a joint, not enough to get him through the evening.

Tin Lee nodded. "Whatever you say." She liked Alex and hoped he liked her. Meeting his mother was an encouraging sign.

Alex considered her to be most agreeable. They'd been out on several occasions and she'd never nagged him about anything. He liked that in a woman. A calm acceptance that the man is always right. None of that feminist shit.

In bed she'd ministered to him, unconcerned about her own fulfillment. There was nothing worse than a woman who expected equal everything, especially in the bedroom.

He gave his four-door Mercedes to a parking attendant at the Beverly Regent, and entered the bar, Tin Lee close behind him. He'd left the Porsche at home tonight so they could accommodate his mother.

They sat against the wall on the plush leather banquette seating. Tin Lee ordered cranberry juice, explaining that she didn't care for alcohol. Alex ordered a double Scotch on the rocks and lit a cigarette. He had all the vices and knew it. He smoked too much, drank too much, popped pills, and smoked grass. The good news was, he'd given up blow and crack. Even Alex knew the danger line. His shrink had explained that if he kept doing the hard stuff, he couldn't expect to see fifty. Point taken.

Tin Lee coughed delicately. He continued smoking.

"Alex," Tin Lee said, placing her hand on his thigh. "Is something bothering you?"

Nothing that my mother dropping dead won't cure.

"Bothering me? What would be bothering me?" he asked, a feeling of irritation crawling over his skin.

"I don't know. That's why I ask." A wistful pause. "Is it something about me?"

Aw, shit, he was in no mood for a talk about "their relationship," such as it was. And he knew it was coming. Women always took everything personally.

"Nothing's wrong with you," he assured her, hoping he sounded sincere enough to stop her carrying on.

"Then why," Tin Lee asked plaintively, not quite smart enough to leave a good thing alone, "haven't we made love since the first time?"

No different than any of the others. Talk, talk, talk. Sex, sex, sex. Was that all women ever thought about?

"Don't I please you, Alex?" she asked, twirling a thin gold bracelet on her tiny left wrist.

He picked up his glass and gulped a couple of mouthfuls of Scotch as he contemplated his reply. Had to be careful, he needed her around this evening.

"No, honey, it's not you," he said at last. "It's me. I'm always tense when I'm preparing to shoot a new movie. I've a lot on my mind."

"Sex is good for taking things off your mind," Tin Lee said boldly. "Perhaps, later tonight, I can relax you with a massage. A very...personal massage."

She wanted to be in his movie, that was for sure. And why not? Everybody wanted something.

A dark-haired woman entered the bar. He noticed her passing, and for one unsure moment he thought it was Lucky Santangelo. Something about the way she moved across the room reminded him.

No. Lucky was much more beautiful—in a wild and intriguing way.

"One more drink and we're on our way," Alex said, gesturing for the waiter.

"What's *he* doing here?"

Cooper's furious whisper was enough to satisfy Leslie. "Why *shouldn't* he be here?" she said guilelessly.

"You know he wants to fuck you," Cooper said, steamed.

"So do a lot of men," Leslie responded calmly. "That doesn't mean I have any desire to return the compliment."

He frowned. "Are you sure?"

"Positive," she said, waving a greeting at a

well-known country singer and his plain wife as they entered her house. "Excuse me, Cooper," she said, secretly thrilled she'd gotten to him. "I must go greet my guests."

He watched her walk away in her tantalizing gown with half her body on show, and he couldn't help but feel a small frisson of jealousy—even though he knew she was doing it purposely, trying to piss him off because he was with his wife.

Meanwhile, Venus was settled at the bar downing shooters while charming Felix Zimmer, an aging producer known for his quirky habit of telling every woman he met that his specialty was eating pussy. Felix was oversized and no Mel Gibson—but his conversational gambit sure helped him score with a lot of women, that and the fact that he was a very successful producer.

"Hey, babe," she called, beckoning Cooper over. "Do you know Felix?"

"Know him," Cooper said with a thin smile, "I taught him everything he boasts about!"

Venus laughed. Cooper thought she looked exceptionally pretty tonight in gold lounging pajamas with her hair piled casually atop her head. He decided he really should consider spending more time at home.

Leslie had put together an eclectic group: Felix and Muriel, his "rumored to be a lesbian" wife; the country singer and *his* wife; Cooper and Venus; a hot director with his extremely young model girlfriend; a sulky-faced woman who designed clothes for an Emmy-nominated TV show; and Jeff Stoner.

Cooper suspected Leslie had arranged the party solely for his benefit. For some perverse reason, she wanted Venus in her house.

For a moment, he felt guilty. How would *he* feel if Venus did the same thing to him?

She wouldn't. Venus might appear sexually over the top and outrageous in her videos and movies, but in real life she was the perfect, faithful, supportive wife. He could trust her, and he did.

"My son," Dominique Woods announced, fluttering diamond-beringed fingers. "Used to be the most handsome man in the world—just like his father. Now look at him, he's dissipated, old—time has not been kind to my Alex."

"Excuse me?" Tin Lee said politely, shocked by the older woman's harsh words.

"It's true, dear," Dominique continued matter-of-factly. "He had enough talent to have been a famous actor like his father. The tragedy is that he threw it all away."

"I never wanted to be an actor," Alex said grimly. "Always wanted to direct."

"It's a damn shame," Dominique said, her voice rising. "As an actor you could have amounted to something—received *real* recognition."

Jesus Christ. Six Oscar nominations were not enough for her. This woman wanted blood.

"Anyway, it's too late now," Dominique continued, a cruel twist to her mouth. "You lost your looks years ago; soon you'll be losing your hair."

Every time, the same thing. What was her fucking problem? Anyone could see that his hair was thick, dark, and wavy—no way was he anywhere near losing it.

His mother was insane—she seemed to take a perverse pleasure in putting him down. His shrink had advised him that fighting with her was pointless. All he could do was ignore her dumb comments.

"Alex has lovely hair," Tin Lee said, rallying to his support.

"For now," Dominique said ominously. "However"—a meaningful pause—"baldness runs in the family. His grandfather was as bald as an ape's ass."

"When he was eighty-five," Alex muttered, ordering another drink.

"You can't avoid the march of time," his mother said. "*I* fight it every day." Now she turned coy. "And I'm winning," she added, focusing her attention on Tin Lee. "Can't you see I'm winning, dear?"

Tin Lee nodded, too startled to say anything else. Alex took a long, hard look at his mother. She was thin and very chic. Fashionably dressed, she wore a short-cropped black wig over thinning hair. Her problem was too much heavy makeup for a woman her age. Her skin was as white as alabaster. Her lips as red as blood. And her eyes were surrounded with black charcoal—giving her an overly dramatic Norma Desmond look. From a distance she could pass for a woman in her late fifties, but close up, the game was over. To his knowledge she'd had her face lifted at least twice. Even at seventy-one, appearance meant everything to Dominique.

Alex had often tried to figure out what she was so bitter about and why she took it out on him. Was it because his father had died, leaving her with a child to raise by herself? Was it because she'd never married again? According to her, no man had been prepared to take on the responsibility of a woman with a son. Over the years she'd constantly reminded him. "Who would have me when I had a boy your age to raise? It's *your* fault I'm alone now. Remember that, Alex."

How could he ever forget when she was constantly reminding him.

Fortunately, she'd always had a certain amount of money. Not that she'd ever put any in his direction. Not that he'd ever wanted any.

Tin Lee rose to her feet. "I'm going to the ladies' room," she said.

His mother had the grace to wait until Tin Lee was out of earshot before she launched into her usual stream of criticism. "Don't you know any American girls, Alex? Surely some of the actresses in your films would be suitable for you to take out? Why are you always with these Asian women? They arrive here searching for the good life however, I'm sure you're aware that in their own country most of them

106

were no better than cheap street prostitutes."

"You have no idea what you're talking about," he said, trying not to get too pissed off at her stupidity.

"I certainly do," Dominique replied, tapping a talonlike finger on the table. "I'm the disgrace of my ladies' bridge club because of you."

"Me?"

"Yes, Alex, you. They read about you in those tabloid papers. They tell me appalling things."

"What things?"

"Why can't you settle down with a decent American girl?"

How many times had they had this conversation?

How many times had he blown up and screamed at her?

He'd learned, after years of therapy, that it simply wasn't worth it anymore. What she said was completely meaningless, and he refused to take any notice of her cruel barbs.

By the end of dinner, he was drunk. When they left the restaurant, Tin Lee automatically slid behind the wheel of the Mercedes.

"I can drive," he objected, teetering on the sidewalk.

"No you can't," she said, firm but nice. "Get in the back, Alex."

"Smart little cookie, this one," his mother murmured, climbing in the front passenger seat.

Like *she* would know. Dominique knew nothing. Nada. Shit. She was a mean, bigoted, hateful woman. And yet she was his mother, so therefore he had to love her, didn't he?

He slumped across the backseat of the car, moodily silent until they dropped Dominique off at her condo on Doheny.

"It was such a pleasure meeting you, Mrs. Woods," Tin Lee said, still rallying. This girl had impeccable manners.

Dominique nodded imperiously, "You, too, dear." A pause. "However, take a word of advice from an older and wiser woman. Alex is not for you, he's too old. Be a clever girl and find a boy your own age."

Gee, thanks, Mom. Fuck you, too.

Dominique swept into her building without looking back.

"She's uh...very nice," Tin Lee said, groping for words.

Alex laughed uproariously. "Very nice, my ass. She's a raving bitch, and you know it."

"Alex, please don't talk about your mother like that. It's bad karma."

"I don't give a shit about karma," he said, drunkenly fondling her small breasts from behind. "Drive me home, baby, I'm gonna show you how a bald, ugly has-been gets it on. I'm gonna light up your fuckin' world!"

Jeff Stoner circled the room, summing up the action.

Cooper watched him, understanding every move. He'd been like that once—ambitious, hungry for the big time. Jeff had the look that Cooper knew so well, and he didn't like it because he was well aware that if he didn't act to prevent it, tonight Jeff Stoner was definitely going to score with Leslie. She looked too delectable to be left alone after everyone had gone home.

Cooper knew exactly how Jeff would operate. He'd stay for a nightcap, bombard her with compliments, get her talking about herself, and then POW—he'd zero in for his big chance. After all, apart from being gorgeous, Leslie was the star of the film, she had the director's ear; therefore—with a small amount of effort—she could convince the director to enlarge Jeff's minor role.

"Something wrong?" Venus interrupted his thought process with a beringed hand on his arm. She'd finished talking to Felix, whose sexual boasting had finally bored her.

"Nothing," Cooper replied vaguely.

Bastard, Venus thought. *Lousy, lying, cheating bastard.*

"Where's the john?" she asked.

Trick question. He knew enough not to fall into *that* trap. "How would I know?" he said casually. "I've never been here before."

Big lie. He'd spent several steamy afternoons at Leslie's house when filming had quit early.

"Come find it with me," she said, pulling him into the hall. Together they discovered a powder room near the front door. "Come in with me, baby," she said persuasively.

He followed her into the mirrored room.

She turned around, locking the door behind them.

Cooper peered in the mirror. Yes, he *did* look tired. When he finished the movie, it was definitely health-spa time.

Venus didn't hesitate; throwing her arms around his neck, she pressed his back up against the marble sink and began provocatively tonguing his lips.

He made a mild attempt to push her away.

"I'm *veree* horny," she whispered, persevering. "Humor me, baby. Got a little something I've been imagining doing to you all night."

Instant reaction as her hand snaked down, unzipped his pants and rapidly began freeing him from the confines of his Calvin Kleins.

"Nice..." she murmured with a throaty laugh, firmly caressing his positive response. "*Veree* nice."

Venus could elicit a hard-on from a stone statue!

All of a sudden he forgot about Leslie and Jeff as she slid to her knees. His wife was a very accomplished woman. Very—

"God!" he groaned, arching his back as her tongue began flicking lightly back and forth across the tip of his penis.

"Shhh..." She silenced him by reaching up and placing a finger on his lips. "We wouldn't want anyone to hear."

Then, after a few moments of teasing, her full mouth enclosed his hardness and nothing else mattered as he gave himself up to the sensation of riding the wave as she sucked him dry of all desire, leaving him spent and extraordinarily satisfied.

The entire event took less than three minutes. Fast sex, like fast food, could sometimes do more than all the gourmet meals in the world.

"Jesus!" he exclaimed, totally content. "That was really something!"

Venus rose from her knees, plucked a Kleenex from a box on the vanity, and daintily dabbed her lips. "Figured you seemed a touch tense, Coop. Thought I'd relax you."

"You're unbelievable!" he said and laughed.

"I try to please," she said, gazing at her reflection in the mirror.

"Well, you do," he replied, stretching his arms high above his head.

"You'd miss me if we weren't married, wouldn't you, Coop?" she teased, staring at him through the glass.

He turned her around, cuddling her close. "I miss you every minute we're not together," he said seductively, the full Cooper Turner charm machine on alert.

Lying,
cheating
sonofabitch.

Gently, she pushed him away. "We'd better get back. I'm sure Felix has plenty more to tell me about his talented tongue."

"Talking of talented tongues..." Cooper said. "When we get home tonight..."

"Yes?"

"You'll see," he said confidently.

"I will?"

"Oh, yes, you will. I owe you one." He zipped up, took one last glance in the mirror, and unlocked the door. "Let's leave early tonight, honey, I can't wait to be alone with you."

"Whatever you like," Venus replied, obliging to the end. "Whatever turns you on."

10

"How come you haven't been in to see me?"

"Just your bad luck, I guess," Brigette replied with exactly the right amount of sass.

Michel Guy's heavy-lidded eyes swept over her, lingering on her breasts, provocatively on show in her sexy Hervé Leger dress. "Come to my office tomorrow," he said. "Bring your book."

"I would," Brigette replied agreeably, "only I'm kind of on an assignment."

"Doing what?"

"A foreign catalogue."

"Which one?"

"Uh...it's a favor for a friend," she said vaguely.

"Who's the photographer?"

"Uh...the photographer..."

Michel started to chuckle. "You're a very pretty girl," he said. "*Very* pretty. However, *ma chérie,* there are a lot of pretty girls in New York trying to be models. A word of advice—don't fake it—be truthful."

"I'm always truthful," she said, "when it works."

112

He scratched his chin. "Have you done the rounds?"

"I've only been in New York a short time."

"So you haven't seen any other agents?"

To hell with truthful. "Not yet," she lied.

"Here's my card," he said. "Be at my office, ten A.M. tomorrow. There might be something you're right for."

Brigette couldn't wait to find Nona and thank her for the introduction. "This is, like, *soo* great," she enthused, her eyes gleaming excitedly. "I've been trying to get an appointment with Michel Guy for ages."

"Michel's got a reputation as an ass grabber," Nona warned. "He's living with that English model—Robertson—you know, the one who's so skinny you could slide her through a crack in a French window. Everyone knows he's taken. It doesn't stop him—he still hits on all the girls."

Brigette was determined. "If he's with Robertson, he's hardly likely to come on to me, she's incredible."

"When has that stopped any man?" Nona said, tossing back her bright-red hair. "So, tell me...what do you think of Zandino?"

"Major cute. Only I thought you wanted somebody who was already...y'know, established."

"Nobody *old*," Nona said, wrinkling her nose. "They have to be under thirty. I can't deal with anybody, like, you know, older than that. Can you?"

Brigette hadn't really thought about it. So

far, all her relationships had been with younger men.

She took another look across the room at Michel Guy. He had crinkly grayish-blond hair, a weathered tan, and faded blue eyes.

"How old do you think Michel is?" she asked.

"Forty-something. Pretty ancient."

"Forty-something isn't ancient."

"Keep it business," Nona said sternly, wagging a warning finger.

"I'm not about to *sleep* with him." Brigette laughed. "Although he *is* attractive."

"There's my boss," Nona said, on to the next subject. "Charm her. Maybe she'll put you on the cover of *MONDO*."

"You think?"

"Just kidding, but you may as well meet her." They headed across the room for another opportunity.

★ ★ ★

"Get on top," Alex demanded.

"It's enough, Alex, I've had enough," Tin Lee cried, her compact, naked body slick with sweat.

Alex had been pumping away inside her for twenty minutes and to her dismay he remained ramrod hard. He'd popped two amyl nitrate capsules and was still drunk.

Tin Lee was not enjoying herself. This man was big and rough and not a gentleman in bed. She wanted out.

114

Alex grabbed her around the waist, hauling her on top of him. She felt herself impaled, like a thing, an object. He wasn't treating her nicely. No foreplay. No touching. Nothing except a relentless pounding.

And yet...the truth was...she *did* want a role in his upcoming movie. And he *was* Alex Woods—a very important and famous director. And maybe...if he'd let her...she could teach him things in bed—like how to pleasure a woman—because right now, what she was going through was uncomfortable and humiliating. Wasn't he *ever* going to come?

Alex shut his eyes and attempted to concentrate. The problem was that when his eyes were closed, the world took off, leaving him dizzy and confused. God, he hated drinking. Hated the effect. Hated getting up the next morning and suffering from his excesses.

His mother drove him to it every time. His fucking mother and her fucking put-downs. Why couldn't she leave him alone?

Tin Lee moaned on top of him. Or was it more an anguished cry of exhaustion?

He didn't know. He didn't care. Dominique was right. Tin Lee should go out and find a nice boy her own age. What the fuck was she doing with *him*?

Abruptly he rolled away from her. Still hard, he finished himself off.

This did not make Tin Lee happy. She jumped off the bed and ran into the bathroom. When she emerged a few minutes later, she was fully dressed.

"I'm going home, Alex," she said in a small, flat voice.

He nodded, too tired and disgusted to say anything.

She left his apartment and he heard silence— an eerie, earth-shattering silence that was enough to drive a man crazy.

Burying his head under a pillow, he fell into a troubled sleep.

Leslie Kane was nervous. Something had happened and she didn't know what. Cooper had definitely cooled toward her and she couldn't figure out why. He sat on her right at the round dining table, Jeff on her left. She'd imagined this would drive Cooper crazy with jealousy. It didn't. He seemed disinterested— almost cool as he chatted amiably to Felix's dyke wife. Leslie knew Muriel Zimmer was a dyke because in her past life as a highly paid call girl, she'd been summoned to the Zimmers' mansion one night with two other girls; the three of them had been given diaphanous robes and elaborate Venetian masks and then been led into an all-black bedroom with a huge circular waterbed, where Mrs. Zimmer had awaited them wearing nothing but thigh-high rubber wading boots and a big, toothy leer.

Leslie remembered the evening well. Mrs. Zimmer obviously didn't. Thank God she was into masks!

Leslie could not stop herself from saying

something to Cooper, although she knew it was hardly an appropriate time. "Have I done anything to upset you?" she whispered, groping for his thigh under the cover of the long damask tablecloth.

"Huh?" He looked at her vaguely, like they were nothing more than casual acquaintances.

"Cooper..." she murmured, thinking of how he'd been earlier in the day—his head buried between her legs, his expert touch burning into her skin.

"Not now, Leslie," he muttered, removing her hand as he turned once again to Muriel Zimmer.

Leslie felt a horrible lump in her throat. She...was...losing...him.

How had it happened so quickly? When he'd walked into her house two hours ago, he'd been all over her.

Jeff Stoner leaned toward her, speaking in a low, intimate voice. He resembled a young Harrison Ford. She didn't care, he did not captivate her interest one iota.

"Leslie," he said earnestly. "Inviting me here tonight was so damn sweet. In the Hollywood scheme of things, I'm nothing, a nobody. Only you don't care, 'cause you see me as a guy you like, a friend. No bullshit. You're somethin' else."

Oh, God, Jeff thought she was so sweet, yet all she'd been doing was using him. Now her clever scheme to make Cooper jealous was backfiring.

Venus Maria, who'd been holding court at

the table with the country singer and the clothes designer, suddenly stood up, tapping the side of her champagne glass with a fork. "Can I say something here?" she said, silencing the table. "I think *somebody's* gotta say something, 'cause this is such a special night." She smiled at Leslie—a warm, loving smile. "Leslie, dear, you've put on such a *very* impressive show. Company interesting, food delicious—I mean, what more can any of us want? In fact, I feel so comfortable here tonight that I'm about to share a big secret with all of you."

Cooper wondered what his unpredictable wife was going to share now.

"Everyone, raise your champagne glasses," Venus continued. "First we're toasting our lovely hostess, Leslie Kane. Oh, and I know this might surprise some of you, or maybe not— but this toast is also for Cooper—my fantastic husband. You see, the truth is..." A long, provocative pause. "Leslie and Cooper are having an affair."

Jaws dropped around the table, and a heavy silence descended.

"And although I'm a *very* understanding wife," Venus continued brightly, "and *extremely* open-minded, there comes a point in every relationship when one has to say enough is enough. So...dear Cooper," she tilted her glass at him, "I'm taking this opportunity to tell you and Leslie," she lifted her glass toward Leslie, who sat in stunned silence, "that you can continue your affair as long as you care to. Because, my dear Cooper, I'm divorcing you."

Muriel Zimmer said, "Ohmigod!"

The rest of them were silent.

Venus carried on. "Even as we sit here, Coop, your clothes are being moved out of our house and into the Beverly Hills Hotel, where I'm sure you'll be very happy. That's, of course, if you don't move in with Leslie. I have no idea how accommodating she is. Maybe she's getting it on with young Jeff here, who knows? Anyway, Coop, I don't want you to be surprised when you try to get into our house and find your key doesn't work."

Cooper stood up, his face flushed with anger. "Is this some kind of joke?" he asked tightly.

"That's *exactly* what I thought in the beginning," Venus said pleasantly. "You screwing Leslie *had* to be a joke—'cause little Leslie here, *sweet*, innocent Leslie, the darling of America, used to be a hooker."

Leslie's stomach dropped.

Another "Ohmigod!" from Muriel.

"Really, Coop," Venus admonished. "You must be the only guy in town who doesn't know Leslie was one of Madame Loretta's girls."

A nerve twitched in Cooper's left cheek as he listened to his wife. No point in trying to stop her, she was on a roll.

Venus turned to Leslie again. "Not that I hold it against you, dear, everybody has to do whatever they can to survive; *I* certainly did. But, you know what? You've also got to learn who you can fuck and who you can't. And if you jump into bed with *my* husband, you'd bet-

119

ter be sure I approve, 'cause if I don't, I can be *very* mean, and you wouldn't want that, would you?"

Leslie sat absolutely still as her world crashed around her. She loathed Venus with a hatred she'd only felt for one other human being, and that was her stepfather—the man who'd molested her night after night with sickening regularity.

"Anyway," Venus continued cheerfully, "allow me to finish my toast. This evening was great, but right now I gotta go. I have a hot date waiting at my house, and I hate to keep 'em waiting when they're *really* hot. Oh, yes, and Felix," she added, winking boldly at the lecherous producer, "thought you'd like to know...Cooper gives great head." She returned her attention to her errant husband. "So... Coop, guess I'll see you around, babe."

And with that she blew him a kiss and made a very effective exit. So effective that nobody noticed the tears in her eyes.

11

Nona's boss, Aurora Mondo Carpenter, was a tiny, brittle woman with watery eyes and cut-glass cheekbones. She was of an indeterminate age, but Nona confided to Brigette that she had to be in her seventies.

Brigette was amazed. "Wow!" she said. "She doesn't look like any grandmother *I've* ever seen."

Aurora's personal stamp was all over *MONDO*. She'd created the magazine and been at the helm for over twenty-five years. She was married to one of New York's top architects, and often wrote coy little articles about him in her magazine, claiming they had the best sex life in New York. Aurora was quite a character.

Nona was not in awe of her, she'd known her since she was a small child, and Aurora was a close friend of her mother's, so she felt quite comfortable taking Brigette over to meet her.

"This is my friend," she announced. "Brigette's the hottest model in L.A."

"Really?" Aurora said, raising a thinly penciled eyebrow. "How many covers have you appeared on, dear?"

"Actually," Brigette said, thinking fast, "I recently returned from Europe."

"How many *European* covers were you on?"

"Oh, God!" Nona said, quickly butting in. "You can't even count them, there were so many!"

"Why haven't you mentioned Brigette before?" Aurora inquired.

"She wasn't in the country. Thing is— Aurora, I had this brilliant idea that *MONDO* should be the first to use her. I mean, she's going to be *huge*. Michel Guy wants to sign her."

Aurora nodded agreeably at Brigette. "Come along to my office tomorrow, dear, we'll take tea together."

"I'd love that," Brigette said, bright blue eyes shining with enthusiasm.

121

"Bring your portfolio," Aurora said. "So I can peruse your covers. And don't forget your test sheets."

"I'll be there," Brigette assured her.

As soon as they were out of earshot, Nona said, "Have you *got* photographs?"

"I didn't think I'd need them until I landed a job."

"You're impossible," Nona said, shaking her head in disbelief. "Surely you *knew* you had to be prepared? No wonder nothing's happened for you."

"It's not as if I've been doing this all my life," Brigette said huffily.

"Okay, okay, everything's under control, 'cause I've come up with a cool idea."

"Like what?"

"Like *I'm* going to be your manager."

"*You?*" Brigette exclaimed, choking back a derisive laugh. "What do *you* know about being a manager?"

"Who got you an intro to Aurora Bora Alice?" Nona said. "Who fixed you up with Michel Guy? Who's gonna get you test shots?"

"Well, since you put it like that..."

"Ten percent," Nona said firmly, "which right now is ten percent of nothing. A deal?"

"I guess we could give it a try," Brigette said hesitantly; after all, she had nothing to lose and everything to gain. The truth was, there was nobody pushier than Nona.

Nona nodded, satisfied with her reply. "There's Luke Kasway. *I'll* do the talking. The good news is, he's gay. The bad news is, he can be a bit testy. If he insults you, take no notice."

"Why would he insult me?"

"It's his way. He calls it 'constructive criticism.' Luke is such an awesome photographer that he gets away with it."

Luke Kasway was short and compact with a spiky crew cut. He wore a multicolored Versace shirt, baggy blue jeans, white sneakers, and owl-like rimless glasses. Two gold earrings adorned one ear, while the other featured a small diamond stud.

Nona did her usual introduction, praising Brigette big time.

Luke didn't fall for it. "Get real, Nona, your friend's never modeled in her life."

"She's big in Europe and L.A.," Nona insisted.

Luke laughed disbelievingly. "I'm in L.A. all the time, *I've* never seen her." He gave Brigette a penetrating stare. "Be honest, have you done anything at all?"

Brigette brushed a nervous hand through her hair, wondering which way to play it. "Actually," she confessed, "I haven't."

"I like a girl who tells the truth," Luke said, pushing up his glasses, which had a habit of slipping off his nose. "When I've got time, we'll take some test shots, 'cause I gotta admit—you do have a certain quality."

"Told you!" Nona said triumphantly.

"Whether that quality will shine through the lens is another thing," Luke continued. "Some girls can be insanely sexy in real life, trouble is—if they can't make out with the camera, they're dead meat."

"When can we do this?" Nona asked, grabbing the opportunity. "She's got an interview with Michel Guy tomorrow, and Aurora's considering her for a cover."

"I'm booked for the next three weeks," Luke said. "Then I'm off to the Caribbean, where I'm doing nothing but lying on the beach checking out hot young cabana boys."

"Oh, *c'mon,* Luke," Nona wheedled. "You can do this favor for me."

"Can't, sweetheart," he replied, regretfully shaking his head. "I'm booked solid."

"What about *now*?" Nona pleaded. "Let's go to your studio and take a few shots tonight. *Pleeese,* Luke, it means so much to me."

"You're pushy, exactly like your mother," Luke said peevishly.

"*Nobody's* pushy like her," Nona retorted.

He laughed. "Okay, okay," he said, turning to Brigette. "Are you up for it?"

She nodded. *This* was the opportunity she'd been waiting for.

"Then let's go."

"Can I bring my fiancé?" Nona asked.

"Didn't know you were engaged."

"He's horny and major cute, you'll fall in love. Hands off!"

"Bring him, as long as he doesn't talk."

Nona pouted. "You're so mean, Luke."

"Excuse me?"

"Nothing."

Luke Kasway's studio was in SoHo—near the Tribeca area. Brigette, Nona, and Zandino arrived by cab, following Luke, who'd gone ahead in his own car. They piled out of the cab outside his building.

"This is so cool!" Nona said excitedly. "Luke's the greatest!"

Zandino rang the bell downstairs. After a few moments, Luke buzzed them in. The three of them climbed into an open freight elevator and rode to the top of the large industrial building.

"Welcome kids," Luke said, greeting them at the heavy stainless steel door.

"We're here!" Nona exclaimed. "Ready for action!"

"I can see that," Luke said, ushering them into his enormous studio.

"Incredible space!" Brigette said, taking in the blowup photographs of all the top models adorning the whitewashed walls.

"Who wants a drink?" Luke asked.

"I don't drink," Brigette replied, still staring at the photographs, wondering if she'd ever be as famous as the girls in them.

"I'll have a bourbon and water," Nona said.

"That's a very grown-up drink for a kid I've known since she was twelve," Luke remarked, walking over to a functional all-white and glass-block bar.

"I'm a *very* grown-up girl," Nona retorted, following him.

"So I can see."

"Oh, Luke, this is Zandino, my fiancé," she said, beckoning Zandino over.

Luke gave Zandino an appreciative once-over. "Drink?" he said.

Zandino beamed his toothy grin. "Coca-Cola, please."

Luke squinted at him. "Nice robe," he said.

"Traditional," Zandino replied, still beaming.

Nona giggled. "We thought we'd blow my parents' minds if he wore it to their party tonight."

"*Nothing* would blow Effie's and Yul's minds," Luke said. "They're the most liberal couple in New York, *and* the most interesting." He handed them their drinks. Then he stepped back, taking a long, critical look at Brigette. "Okay," he said. "What are we doing here?"

"*You're* the photographer," Nona pointed out.

Luke ignored her. "Okay, babe," he said to Brigette. "Kick off your shoes and go stand in front of the camera over there."

She stepped out of her Blahnik pumps, placing herself in front of a plain blue backdrop.

Luke threw a switch on the stereo and Annie Lennox's throaty voice flooded the studio.

"Major point—relax," he said, loading film into two cameras. "I'll shoot a couple of rolls of black-and-white, some color, and we'll see what happens. No big deal. Don't get nervous on me."

Now that she was finally in front of a camera, Brigette felt her confidence level sink. She was suddenly awkward and unsure about what to do. She'd imagined herself on a Paris runway, strolling snootily along, clad in a top designer's outfit, giving everybody that disgusted look like they should drop dead because she was so hot. But standing in front of an actual camera was totally intimidating.

"Imagine the camera's your lover," Luke said, positioning himself behind it. "You've had a lover, haven't you?"

"Of course," she replied indignantly.

"Good. So make out with the camera, get those pretty eyes working. Let your hair fall over your face...that's it...now bring your head down, we're gonna see if we can create magic here."

She began to pose, gradually getting into it as the music swept over her.

As soon as she did anything Luke considered obvious, he started yelling. "Be natural," he shouted. "Natural! Natural! Get it?"

He clicked off several rolls of film, then produced his Polaroid and ran off more photos.

Nona and Zandino stood on the sidelines, cheering her on.

After an hour of nonstop activity, Luke was finally ready to quit. He yawned and stretched. "I think we got it," he said. "Whatever *it* might be."

"When can we see the photos?" Nona asked.

"Call my assistant in the morning."

Brigette was on an adrenaline high. She began wandering around the studio again, still fascinated by all the photos on the walls. Among the models there was a scattering of celebrities: Sylvester Stallone in a cowboy hat, Winona Ryder wearing a red bustier, Jon Bon Jovi bare-chested. "Do you know all these people?" she asked Luke.

"Of course he does," Nona replied, picking up a giant blow-up photograph of Robertson and Nature—another famous model, wearing nothing but skintight blue jeans and alluring smiles, their hands covering their breasts.

"*Some* picture," Nona exclaimed.

"Yeah," Luke agreed. "That's the ad campaign I'm doing for Rock 'n' Roll Jeans—you heard of them?"

"Nope."

"You will. They're gonna be bigger than Guess and Calvin Klein combined."

"Really," Nona said, her interest perking up. "The only thing is," she added, studying the photo, "there's nothing unusual about this ad. Two girls...every guy's fantasy, only it's been done a million times. Robertson and Nature have been on every cover, from *Vogue* to *Allure*. It's not cutting edge, Luke. Using them for a hot new ad campaign is, like—you know—kinda old news." She paused, gazing at him innocently. "You don't mind me saying that, do you?"

"Yeah, I mind," Luke replied, not pleased with her criticism.

"I'm just being truthful."

He pushed his glasses onto his nose. "Do me a big one, Nona—go be truthful somewhere else."

"Don't get uptight. *I'm* the girl who's going to buy the product."

He looked at her, perplexed. "Are you telling me you wouldn't buy these jeans simply because the models have appeared in ads for other things?"

She shrugged. "It's nothing I haven't seen before."

He snorted with aggravation. "You're a pain in the ass, Nona—you always were."

"I'm an *honest* pain in the ass," she said, taking a long pause before adding, "Now, if *Brigette* was wearing the jeans."

"I suppose you want me to photograph her in them, is that your game?"

"What's to lose?" Nona said, wide-eyed.

Luke sighed. "Okay, Brigette, go in the dressing room. You'll see a rack of jeans, pick out your size and put 'em on, then come back out here. No top."

"I'm not doing nudity," Brigette objected. Luke Kasway might be a big-deal photographer, but she wasn't taking off her clothes for anyone.

"Cover your boobs with your hands," Luke said. "Copy what those girls are doing in the photo."

Nona nodded her approval. "Go ahead."

Oh, yeah, fine for Nona to say go ahead, it wasn't *her* stripping down.

She went into the dressing room, found jeans in her size, and wriggled into them.

She felt like an idiot covering her breasts with her hands, then she assured herself that all models did a certain amount of nudity; after all, it wasn't as if she were posing for *Playboy*.

She emerged, waiting for Luke's instructions.

"Okay, over there," he said, gesturing to a different setup—this time a brick-wall backdrop. "Face the wall, legs apart, swing around when I tell you."

She did as he asked.

Luke peered through his lens, making grunting noises. "Nice one, Brigette. Lower your head, bring your eyes up, lick your lips. That's it."

Zandino, standing on the sidelines, said, "It looks good."

Luke glanced at him. "You ever had any pictures taken?"

Zandino beamed. "Snapshots when I graduated."

"Another idea," Luke said, snapping away. "Does he have a body, Nona?"

She rolled her eyes. "Does he have a body!"

Luke grinned. "I should've known. We always shared the same taste, even when you were twelve!" He turned back to Zandino. "Go in the dressing room, find jeans in your size."

Nona saw the possibilities. "Yes, Zan, do it," she encouraged, giving him a little push. "It's just for laughs."

"Really?" Zandino asked unsurely.

"Really," Nona assured him.

A few minutes later Zandino emerged. His body was toned, taut, and a delicious deep-chocolate hue. The jeans fit him as if they were sprayed on.

"Wow!" Nona said, pointing gleefully at his crotch. "Terrific view of your assets!"

Zandino frowned.

"Lighten up," she said and giggled. "At least they're major!"

"Okay, we're getting there," Luke said, running his hands through his spiky hair. "Over there with Brigette. Let's see how the two of you interact. Do stuff in front of the camera."

"Like *what* stuff?" Brigette asked, nervous of Zandino invading her space.

"I dunno...back to back, face to face. Zan, put your hands over her boobs, whatever. We need to go for something different."

"*Wait* a minute," Nona objected. "*His* hands on *her* boobs? Forget it!"

"Listen, didn't you tell me you were her manager? This could fly."

Nona nodded. "I'm getting the idea," she said. "'Black and white—Rock 'n' Roll Jeans.'"

"Right!" Luke said enthusiastically. "What's rock 'n' roll all about? *Black* music. *White* music. It's a fit!"

At first they were tentative, stiff.

"Get into it," Luke screamed. "Relax, for crissakes!"

Fine for him to say, Brigette thought, *he wasn't standing there with some strange man holding his boobs. Oh, God, she was so embarrassed!*

Sting blasted from the speakers as gradually they started to relax and began working together.

Luke moved fast, using several cameras as he shot roll after roll of film.

As soon as she relaxed, Brigette found herself enjoying it—posing was hard work, but fun.

By the end of the session, everyone was exhausted.

"Whew!" Brigette exclaimed, grabbing a towel. "I'm dead, but what an experience. Awesome!"

"Don't go getting excited," Luke warned. "This *could* turn out to be a waste of everyone's time."

"No," Nona said, very secure. "This'll be your new campaign. You'll see, Luke. I'm never wrong."

12

Lucky slept most of the long flight to Europe, not even waking when they stopped to refuel. She'd planned on reading a couple of scripts, viewing the dailies on two of her movies currently in production, in fact, generally getting a lot done.

It was not to be. Instead she had a light meal, settled back with a glass of Cointreau, and fell into a deep sleep.

Her last thoughts before drifting off were that she was going to forget about business this weekend and concentrate on having a wonderful time with Lennie. They both deserved it.

After being out on the beach location all day, Lennie wasn't tired, so instead of going straight to his room, he joined some of the cast and crew in the hotel bar and had a few beers.

He couldn't stop thinking about Lucky arriving. God, how he loved her. There was nobody else in the world for him, and this from a man who'd once been a major womanizer. Things had certainly changed. Now he was Mr. Married and loving every minute.

"Gotta go," he told Al, the first AD. "Wanna get a good night's sleep."

"Grab an eyeful of *that* little beauty!" Al replied, nudging him as a blond with a body that didn't quit approached.

Lennie took a look. It was the same blond who'd been parading in front of him on the set earlier. Instead of a bikini she now wore a crotch-high skirt and midriff-baring tank top. Every guy in the bar was immediately transfixed.

She came right over to him. "Hi, Lennie," she murmured in her softly accented voice. "Mind if I join you?"

What was with the "Hi, Lennie" crap? He couldn't believe she was acting as if they were old friends.

"No, luv, he don't mind at all," said the focus

puller—a randy Englishman with a Rod Stewart haircut and a lascivious leer. "'S matter of fact, y'can park it right here—next ta me."

"Excuse me?" she said coolly, hardly glancing in his direction.

"I'm outta here," Lennie said, quickly getting up. "You guys can do what you like."

"Thanks, mate," Al said with a ribald chuckle. "Didn't know we needed your permission!"

Lennie made a swift exit before the blond had a chance to hit on him again. Instinct told him she was big trouble.

Up in his room he threw off his clothes, lay on top of his bed, and began studying the pages for the next day's shooting.

The phone rang. He grabbed it, hoping it was Lucky calling from the plane.

A provocative purr. "Lennie? Are you lonely?"

"Who's this?" he said, although he was immediately aware it was the blond.

"How about buying me a drink?" A short pause, then, "Say...in your room."

"My mother told me never to drink with strangers," he said, trying to make light of what could turn out to be an awkward situation.

"I wouldn't be a stranger for long," she replied, her sexy voice full of promise.

"Hey—you know what," he said shortly, "maybe tomorrow, when my wife's here, we'll *both* have a drink with you."

The blond chuckled softly. "Ooohh...you like threesomes. *Très* cozy!"

"Honey, go hit on somebody else," he said,

realizing this was not an easy one to get rid of. "I'm not interested."

"You would be if you saw what I had to offer."

"I've seen it," he said sharply. "So has everyone else."

She still wouldn't go away. "So...you are Mr. Straight and Faithful."

"Get lost," he said, slamming the phone down. A few minutes later, it rang again. He almost didn't answer, thinking it was Miss Persistent. "Yeah?" he snapped.

"Ha! *You* sound in a good mood."

"Oh, Jennifer. What's going on?"

"I got your call changed. You're free to go to the airport tomorrow. I have a car picking you up at noon. Your new call's two P.M. Don't forget."

"You're the best."

"Thanks, she said, sounding pleased."

"By the way—d'you remember the blond? The one who was trailing me on the set today?"

"What about her?"

"Can you believe she just called my room?"

"Yes, Lennie." Jennifer sighed. "I can believe anything about the army of silicone blonds who follow you day and night."

"Let's not get carried away."

"What did you tell her?"

"Let me see—" he said sarcastically. "Oh, yeah—I told her to come up to my room with a bottle of vodka and a supply of condoms. What do you *think* I told her?"

Jennifer was unamused. "Would you like me to accompany you to the airport?"

"No," he said dryly. "I'm sure I can manage a reunion with my wife by myself."

"Don't forget, Lennie, your new call is now two P.M."

"Okay, okay."

"I know what you're like—write it down."

"Got it." He replaced the receiver, reached for his script, and started reading.

A few minutes later, there was a knock on the door. He knew it was Jennifer. She didn't trust him and was personally delivering his new call sheet to make sure he had it right.

He grinned, got off the bed, and opened the door. Standing there was Miss Silicone City herself, wearing nothing but high heels, a loosely belted terry cloth robe, and a seductive smile.

"I'm sure you *are* lonely," she purred. "Big American movie star all by himself—it's not right."

This woman never gave up. "Listen," he said patiently, "I don't know how to tell you this, but I am perfectly happy, so go home—wherever that might be."

"Are you sure, Lennie?" she said, staring directly into his eyes as she untied her robe, allowing it to fall open. Naturally, she was wearing nothing beneath it.

"Oh, shit!" he muttered, taking in every inch of her incredible curves.

"Am I changing your mind, Lennie?" she said, sexy voice at full throttle.

"Listen," he said sternly, "do everyone a favor and get out of here."

She had no intention of going anywhere. "You don't mean that," she said confidently, a woman used to getting results.

"Yes, I mean it. I don't want to see it. I don't want to touch it. So make a fast exit, okay?"

She licked her index finger, bringing it down to caress an erect nipple. "Don't you like what you see?"

"I'm calling hotel security if you don't leave right now."

She shrugged off her robe. It fell in a heap at her feet, leaving her totally naked. "Go ahead, Lennie. I'll tell them you lured me to your room and attacked me."

Now he was angry. "Get the fuck away from me," he said, attempting to slam the door on her.

Before he could do so, she flung her arms around his neck, clinging to him tightly.

From the end of the corridor a photographer appeared, camera flashing.

Lennie struggled to shove her away, realizing too late that this was a setup.

Managing to disentangle himself from the naked blond, he made a run for the photographer.

The man with the camera immediately took off.

Lennie started to give chase before realizing that all he had on were his undershorts. What a picture *that* would make. Better to deal with the blond and find out what her game was.

He turned around, sprinting back to his room.

She was gone. They'd gotten their pictures and now they'd both vanished.

Grabbing the phone, he demanded security.

A few minutes later, the manager of the hotel was at his door. "Yes, Mr. Golden?" the manager said, trying to appear formal, although it was obvious he'd been roused from a deep sleep.

What was he going to say? That there was a naked woman in his room with a photographer? Somehow it didn't sound like anyone would believe him.

The smart move was to forget it and hope the photographs wouldn't surface, although he had a nasty feeling they would.

"Uh...thought I heard someone trying to break in," he said lamely.

"I will take a look around personally, Mr. Golden," the manager said with an imperceptible bow.

"You do that."

Lesson to be learned. The paparazzi would go to any length to get the pictures they needed to sell to the tabloid rags back in America. Tomorrow he'd call his lawyers, tell them exactly what had taken place so they'd be prepared to stop publication if the pictures surfaced.

He picked up the phone and tried Jennifer's room.

"Yes, Lennie?" she said patiently.

"What was that blond's name?"

"Lennie!" Jennifer scolded. "Your wife's coming in tomorrow. I thought you were one of the nice guys."

"Get me her name and phone number."

"Oh, yeah, right," Jennifer said sarcastically. "How about her measurements and diaphragm size?"

"It's not what you think."

Jennifer gave an "all men are pigs" long-suffering sigh. "Whatever you say, Lennie. You're the star around here."

He knew she didn't believe him, but Lucky would, and that's all that mattered.

In the morning, he was up long before it was time to leave for the airport.

This weekend he was going to make his wife a very happy woman indeed.

Lucky was dreaming. In the dream she was lying on a raft in the sea while the water gently rocked the raft back and forth. Then Lennie was beside her, massaging her shoulders, telling her he loved her.

"Miz Santangelo...Miz Santangelo. We'll be landing in an hour. Thought you might want to freshen up."

She opened her eyes with a start. Tommy, the plane's steward, was standing over her. Lennie had merely been a dream.

"Coffee and orange juice, Miz Santangelo?" Tommy inquired solicitously.

She yawned, still half asleep. "Great, Tommy. I'll take a quick shower and be right out."

The Panther jet was equipped like a luxurious hotel suite. In the bathroom, she stood under a cold shower, jolting herself awake. When she emerged, she felt refreshed and full of energy. She applied fresh makeup, fixed her hair, and dressed in a loose silk top and wide pants.

It was crazy, really, she and Lennie had been married four years, yet she was as excited about seeing him as if they were going on their first date.

Who ever said passion didn't last?

"Is my car here?" Lennie asked the doorman.

The doorman snapped his fingers, and a chauffeur-driven old Mercedes pulled up. Different car, different driver.

"Where's Paulo today?" Lennie asked, getting in the backseat.

"Sick."

"We're going to the airport."

"I know," the driver said as the Mercedes took off fast.

The Panther jet zoomed in for a smooth landing at Corsica's Poretta Airport. Lucky couldn't wait to disembark, to feel Lennie's arms around her, see his face, just to hug him.

She hurried off the plane and was disappointed to discover he wasn't at the airport. An airport official asked if she'd like to wait in a private room. She agreed, although she was wild with impatience.

The first thing she did was call Lennie's hotel. They put her through to his room. A breathy female voice said, "Hello."

"Lennie?" Lucky questioned, frowning.

"Oh…Lennie…he left early this morning," the voice said.

Lucky detected a faint French accent. Could it be the maid? "Who's this?" she asked suspiciously.

"A friend of his. Who's *this*?"

"His wife."

Whoever it was hurriedly hung up.

Lucky began to steam. Was it possible Lennie was screwing around?

No way. He wasn't the kind of man who would let her down. They had something special between them, they trusted each other. They had a special bond.

THEN WHO THE FUCK WAS IN HIS ROOM?

She marched from the little office and found the airport official. "Get me a car and driver," she said. "I've decided not to wait."

13

Venus didn't have a hot date waiting at her house, she'd made that up to infuriate Cooper. When she arrived home, she wished that she *had* arranged for Rodriguez to be there. She needed a warm, sensual body. She needed to know somebody loved her.

Was it too late to call him?

Yes. It wouldn't do to look desperate.

God! Cooper's face. She'd certainly rattled his ego. All his life he'd screwed around on every woman he'd been with, never suffering the consequences. The day they'd gotten married he'd promised that things would be different.

Well, guess what? He hadn't changed, and she wasn't waiting around for it to happen again.

So now she was alone in her mansion, Cooper's clothes and personal possessions packed up and gone, his presence removed as if he'd never lived there.

Kicking off her shoes, she wandered around the house barefoot, staring at the numerous photos of them together.

It was too soon to remove his image from the silver frames, but she was sure she'd never take him back.

In the morning she was up at six to jog

with Sven. Jogging prepared her for the day, made her feel alert and focused.

They toiled up and down the Hollywood Hills, puffing and sweating. Back at the house they headed straight to the gym, where Sven put her through a vigorous workout that included an hour on the treadmill and three quarters of an hour working her upper and lower body with free weights. Ha! And people thought it was easy getting this body.

At nine o'clock, she asked Sven to put on the TV so she could watch Kathie Lee and Regis—their early-morning banter was always an entertaining exchange—especially when Kathie Lee was in one of her feisty moods.

The talk-show hosts were just getting into it when they were interrupted by a special news break.

Venus watched and listened to the news-caster's words in shock.

"Movie star Lennie Golden was reported killed early today in a fiery car wreck on the isle of Corsica, where he was currently on location shooting his latest movie. A spokesperson for Wolfe Productions issued a statement…"

Lennie Golden killed.
Lennie, Lucky's husband.
Lennie, her good friend.
"I've got to get to Lucky," she mumbled, frantically running from the room.

143

Cooper had not bothered going back to his house. If Venus said she'd moved his clothes and changed the locks, he sure as hell knew she'd done it.

After leaving Leslie's, he'd driven directly to the Beverly Hills Hotel, where he'd found himself already prechecked into a bungalow. Venus had thought of everything.

Leslie had begged him to stay, something he'd had no intention of doing.

"How did Venus find out?" he'd asked. "Who did you tell?"

"No one. People aren't stupid. They saw us together."

He'd paced around the room trying to figure out how he'd gotten screwed. "You *wanted* her to find out, didn't you?" he'd demanded.

"No," she'd said stubbornly. "It's the last thing I wanted."

"Well, anyway, Leslie, it's not smart for me to stay."

Her eyes had filled with tears. "But, Cooper, I need you."

"You should've thought about that before."

He'd left her house, cursing himself for being so indiscreet. All he could think about was how he could make things right with Venus, because the truth was, he truly loved her.

After sleeping fitfully, he awoke late, immediately groping for the phone. He called room service requesting bacon, eggs, orange juice,

144

muffins, and coffee—the kind of breakfast Venus never allowed because she was always on a health kick.

When the waiter entered his bungalow, Cooper greeted him curtly. The man looked like a talker, and he wasn't in the mood.

"Terrible news about Lennie Golden," the waiter remarked, removing the eggs and bacon from the hot plate under the room service cart. "He often used to lunch here. Everyone'll miss him."

"What news?" Cooper asked, pulling up a chair.

"He was in a bad car accident."

"He's all right, isn't he?"

"His car went over a cliff."

"IS HE ALL RIGHT?"

"No, Mr. Turner. He's...he's...dead."

Cooper shook his head in disbelief. Not Lennie. Not his friend Lennie. This couldn't be possible.

"Where did you hear this?" he asked.

"It's all over the news. I'm sorry, Mr. Turner, I thought you knew."

"No," Cooper said blankly. "No, I didn't know."

Alex rolled into his offices hungover and late. It was past noon, and he was in a foul mood. All he could remember of the previous evening were his mother's insults. She did it to him every time, got him so crazy he couldn't think straight. Now she'd ruined his day because he'd blown a very important meeting with his line producer and location manager and they were both pissed at him.

He felt like a drink. So far he'd resisted the temptation, last night was punishment enough.

"Good morning, Alex." Lili greeted him with a faintly disapproving lilt to her voice. "Or should I say 'good afternoon'?"

"I know, I know, I shoulda been here at nine," he grumbled. "Something came up."

"I called your house," she said pointedly.

"Had the phone shut off."

"Hmmm..."

France brought him a mug of steaming-hot black tea. "Drink it," she ordered sternly. "Later you'll thank me."

He held back an urge to throw up all over his desk. "Send Tin Lee flowers," he muttered.

"How much do you wish to spend?" France inquired.

"A lot," he said ominously. God knew what he'd put Tin Lee through. She probably wasn't talking to him anymore.

"Alex," Lili said. "Have you heard about Lennie Golden, Lucky Santangelo's husband?"

"What about him?"

"He was on location. There was a car wreck."

"Where?"

"In Corsica. The car he was traveling in went over a mountain."

"Jesus! When did this happen?"

"It was on the radio this morning."

Alex remembered Lucky had told him she was on her way to visit Lennie. "Was Lucky with him?" he asked urgently.

"Don't know," Lili replied, making a vague hand gesture. "They didn't say..."

Alex jumped up. "Get me Freddie."

Lili hurried to the phone. "Yes, Alex."

Brigette and Nona headed down Madison, laughing and talking nonstop about the previous night's party and the incredible photo session with Luke.

Brigette realized how much she'd missed her best friend, and how great it would be having Nona as her manager. Together they *could* make it happen, they'd always brought each other luck.

As they passed a newsstand on Sixty-fifth Street, her eye caught the headline on the *New York Post*.

LENNIE GOLDEN KILLED
CAR CRASH IN CORSICA
MOVIE STAR MEETS FIERY DEATH

"Ohmigod!" she gasped, clinging to Nona. "Ohmigod! *No! No! NOOO!*"

★ ★ ★

Donna Landsman was not surprised. She read the newspapers and smiled to herself. Everything was working out just fine.

Lucky Santangelo. How does it feel, bitch? How does it feel to lose your husband, just as I lost mine?

How does it feel to be left alone with three young children to raise all by yourself?

Well, bitch, now you'll find out exactly how it feels.

And, I can assure you, this is just the beginning.

14

Lucky sat very still, gazing straight ahead. She knew she should be crying, screaming, anything other than this icy calm that seemed to have crept over her, seeping into every pore, deadening her feelings.

Lennie was dead.

Her Lennie was *gone.*

And yet...she remained lucid and in control, as if her life moved around her in a kind of blurred slow motion.

She was numb with grief. Devastated. And yet...the tears didn't flow.

She sat on Lennie's bed in a hotel room in a foreign country and her husband was dead and she did not weep.

Little Lucky Santangelo. She was five years old when she'd discovered the mutilated body of her mother floating in the family swimming pool; twenty-five when they'd gunned down her first real love, Marco; even younger when her brother, Dario, was shot and thrown from a car.

Death was no stranger to the Santangelos. Lucky knew what it meant only too well.

And now Lennie was gone...her Lennie, the love of her life.

Or was he?

She considered the circumstances.

THE FUCKING CIRCUMSTANCES.

Riding from the airport to the hotel. Grabbing the key to his room from a surprised desk clerk. Noting a DO NOT DISTURB sign on his door.

She'd entered Lennie's world away from her and was disappointed to find he wasn't there.

The bed was unmade, the room an untidy mess. Well...Lennie had never been known for his housekeeping skills.

Details...details...She'd absorbed them one by one. The overflowing ashtrays on both bedside tables. A nearly empty bottle of champagne...two glasses, one rimmed with lipstick. A silk chemise crumpled on the floor, half hidden beneath the bed.

THIS MUST BE THE WRONG ROOM.

No. It wasn't. There was her picture with the children turned facedown on a table. Lennie's clothes were everywhere, his script, phone book, his special silver pen—the one she'd bought him at Tiffany's, matching the one he'd bought her.

She'd called the production office, trying to locate him. By that time, news was trickling through of a horrible accident on the treacherous mountain roads.

They came and got her, the line producer and a production executive. They took her with them in a car up the twisting narrow road, where they all stood in horror, watching as rescue teams went to work, trying to recover the wrecked car hundreds of feet below where it had smashed onto rocks and burned before ending up in the angry sea swirling beneath them.

Lucky had known with an overwhelming feeling of dread that she would never see Lennie again.

Now, she sat alone in his hotel room. Cleaned by maids, the champagne gone, the ashtrays washed and pristine, her picture with the children back in position.

FUCK YOU, LENNIE. HOW COULD YOU LEAVE US?

The phone kept on ringing. She ignored it, having no desire to speak to anyone. Her plane was on standby, awaiting instructions. Right now she was incapable of making a decision about anything.

They'd recovered the body of the driver, fished from the sea and identified through medical records. Lennie was still missing.

"They didn't have a chance," one of the police detectives had explained through a sympathetic interpreter.

After a while, Lucky got up and mechanically began packing Lennie's things. His T-shirts, socks, sweaters. His workout clothes. A favorite jacket. His collection of denim work shirts that he liked to wear every day. She did it slowly, methodically, almost as if she were in a trance.

When she was finished with his clothes, she gathered together his script, and several yellow legal pads—the first draft of a script he was writing. Then she pulled open the drawer of the bedside table, where she discovered several Polaroids of a naked blond. She stared at them for a long, silent moment. The blond was exceptionally pretty, her legs spread wide, a seductive smile on her dumb-ass face.

FUCK YOU, LENNIE. FUCK YOU. YOU WERE SUPPOSED TO BE DIFFERENT.

No tears. Disappointment. Hurt. Anger. A tremendous feeling of letdown and betrayal.

She remembered when she'd walked in on her second husband, Dimitri, in bed with the opera singer, Francesca Fern. She hadn't cried then. There was no reason for her to do so now.

"Be strong," that was her motto. Over the years, it was the only way she'd managed to survive.

There were more photos to be found. Lennie standing with the blond, her naked body wrapped intimately around him. Another shot of the two of them, apparently taken on the set. Lennie with his arm across her shoulders. Very cozy.

AND NOW YOU'RE DEAD, YOU SONO-

FABITCH. AND YOU CAN NEVER EXPLAIN.

Not that she wanted explanations.

Who cared?

Who gave a damn?

Lennie Golden was just another guy with a hard-on. Another horny actor on location.

WELL, FUCK YOU, LENNIE GOLDEN. FUCK YOU.

And the pain of loss was unbearable.

She finished packing his stuff into two suitcases and jammed them shut. The photographs she slipped into a zippered compartment in her purse.

After a while she picked up the phone and called her father in Palm Springs. They'd spoken earlier when she'd asked Gino to take the children. He had them safely with him.

"Come home," Gino urged.

"I will," she replied listlessly. "I'm waiting for them to recover Lennie's body...I want to bring him back with me."

"Uh...Lucky—it could take awhile. You should be with your kids."

"I'll give it another twenty-four hours."

"There's nothin' you can do there. When they find him, the production office will make arrangements. You gotta come home now."

"I...I need some time."

"No!" Gino said harshly. "You should be with your family."

She didn't care to be lectured to. She didn't care about anything. "I'll call you, Daddy," she said, her voice quiet and low.

Before he could argue further, she replaced the receiver and began roaming aimlessly around the room. Lennie. So tall. So sexy. That great grin. Those penetrating green eyes. That lanky body.

Lennie. *Her* Lennie.

She couldn't put him out of her mind. She could feel his skin, smell his smell, and she wanted him more than she'd ever wanted anything in her life.

Lennie.

Cheater.

FUCK YOU, LENNIE.

YOU BETRAYED ME AND I CAN NEVER FORGIVE YOU FOR THAT.

Book Two

Two Months Later

"Hi," Lucky said. She was seated behind her massive desk twirling Lennie's silver pen as Alex Woods entered her office for their six o'clock meeting.

"Hello," Alex responded, pausing at the door. He hadn't seen her since the tragedy, although it wasn't for want of trying. She'd been difficult to get hold of—elusive, always on the run. Even Freddie had been unable to arrange a meeting.

"People handle grief in different ways," Freddie had explained. "There's always problems at the studio. Lucky's thrown herself into work."

"*I'm* work," Alex had pointed out. "And I've got to have a meeting."

Actually, there was no necessity for them to meet. Everything was being taken care of. Budget approval, casting, location choices—Lucky's head of production was on top of it, Alex had no complaints. If all continued to proceed at such a timely pace, they'd be able to commence principal photography within weeks.

"Come in, sit down," Lucky said.

He walked in, observing she looked tired; there were smudgy dark circles under her eyes and an edginess he hadn't noticed before.

She was still the most beautiful woman he'd ever seen.

"Look," he said, "before we get into anything, I want you to know how sorry I was to hear about Lennie—"

"Forget it," she interrupted briskly. "It's the past." She knew she was probably coming across as hard and uncaring, but she couldn't worry about how Alex Woods perceived her. It didn't matter. Nothing really mattered.

She leaned back, automatically reaching for a cigarette. Her bad habits had come back to haunt her with a vengeance.

Earlier in the day she'd had a strangely disturbing meeting with Morton Sharkey. Her gut reaction told her Morton was up to something, only she couldn't figure out what. For once, things were running smoothly at the studio, the banks were quiet, and the Japanese had said yes to the merchandising deal. The truth was that businesswise, things couldn't be better.

After Morton left she'd downed a couple of Scotches, wondering what it was about him that was making her uneasy. Their meeting had gone well except for one thing—Morton had been unable to look her in the eyes, and from past experience she knew this was a bad sign.

But she had other things to worry about. She was well aware that personally she was in big trouble. Something inside her was ready to explode. Something that had been deeply buried for the last two months.

Lennie was dead, and she was carrying on

as if nothing had happened. Business as usual.

Well, fuck business. Fuck everything. She was tired and despondent and very, very angry.

Alex Woods was staring at her, she could feel the heat of his eyes. "Everything going well?" she asked, returning to the present. "Or are you here to complain?"

"As a matter of fact, I have no complaints," he said, noting that she was in a defensive mood.

"*That* makes a pleasant change," she said coolly. "Everyone else is driving me nuts." She paused; he hadn't shaved, and the faint stubble on his chin added to his attractiveness. "Congratulations on signing Johnny Romano," she said. "He's an excellent choice."

"Glad you approve."

"I wouldn't have okayed him if I didn't." She picked up her list of phone messages, stared blankly at it for a moment, then put it down. "How about a drink?" she suggested, anxious to have another one herself.

Alex consulted his watch; it was past six, definitely martini time. "You look like you've had a heavy day," he said. "How about we go to the bar at the Bel Air Hotel?"

"A fine idea," she said, buzzing Kyoko. "I'm outta here. Cancel my other appointments."

"But Lucky—" Kyoko began.

"Don't give me a song an' dance, Ky," she said sharply. "I'll see you tomorrow." She got up from behind her desk, grabbed her jacket, and joined Alex at the door. "Christ!

If I can't do what I want occasionally, then what's it all about, huh?"

"You won't get a fight from me," he agreed, smelling the faint aroma of Scotch on her breath.

She smiled, a dazzling smile. "Good. Because I am so bored playing the poor little widow."

He was too surprised to say anything as they walked outside.

"My car or yours?" she said, standing still for a moment.

"Where's yours?" he asked, trying to keep his eyes off her long legs. After all, this was business.

"Parked over there, the red Ferrari."

Naturally. "I'm the black Porsche," he said.

"Then, my dear Alex, the black Porsche it is—'cause I've a feeling I will not be in a driving mood later."

All he'd expected was a meeting; this was turning out to be more than that. But he was into it, even though he had an eight o'clock date with Tin Lee, a date he knew it was highly unlikely he'd keep.

Lucky got in his car, leaned back, and closed her eyes. Oh, how sweet it was making a daring escape. She'd had it with meetings and budgets and business decisions and SHIT SHIT SHIT. She'd had it with the goddamn studio. She'd had it with the responsibility of being a mother and a respectable pillar of society and the proper widow. It was too fucking much. She was going insane. She

160

had no outlet for the fierce anger that was beginning to consume her.

Lennie had left. Checked out. Gone.

Lennie was an unfaithful sonofabitch and she couldn't forgive him for that.

They drove in silence for a few minutes.

"You're looking well," Alex said.

She didn't bother with pleasantries. "Do you have any family?" she asked.

"A mother," he replied carefully, wondering what this was leading to.

"Are you close?"

"Like a snake and a rat."

"Snakes eat rats."

"You got it."

Lucky laughed dryly. It occurred to her she'd picked the perfect drinking companion, and that's exactly what she required tonight, someone who could keep up with her and not fall by the wayside.

"I need a joint," she said restlessly.

"No problem," he said, reaching in his pocket and handing her a half-smoked roach that he just happened to have with him.

She pushed in the dashboard lighter, waited for the glow, then lit up, taking a long, satisfying pull. "You're very obliging, Alex."

"Not always."

She gave him a quizzical look. "Making an exception for me 'cause my studio's putting up the money for your movie?"

He went along with her mood. "Yeah, sure, that's it."

She gazed at him steadily. "Or maybe you feel sorry for me 'cause I lost my husband?"

He kept his eyes on the road. "You can take care of yourself."

She sighed. "That's what everybody thinks."

He shot a quick glance at her. "Are they right or wrong?"

"Hey," she said restlessly. "How about we drive to the Springs and visit Gino? You said you wanted to meet him. Catch me while I'm in the mood."

"Sure."

"Oh, boy, you're an agreeable one."

If she only knew! Alex Woods had never been called agreeable. Difficult—yes. Sexist—yes. Moody, demanding, a perfectionist—all of those things. But agreeable? No way.

"You might be getting a false impression of me," he said, speaking slowly. "Y'know, nice guy helping out beautiful woman who seems to be troubled. I've got that chivalry thing buried somewhere inside me."

"Glad to hear it," she said, staring blankly out the window. "Let's get a drink before we hit the freeway."

They stopped at a Mexican restaurant on Melrose. Lucky downed straight tequila while Alex opted for a margarita. Then he ordered a pitcher to go while Lucky visited the ladies' room, called home, told Cee Cee she wouldn't be back tonight and that she could be reached at Gino's house in Palm Springs.

Lucky was well aware she had nothing to complain about, everyone around her had been incredibly supportive, from Gino to Brigette, who'd flown in from New York and stayed at the house for several weeks. Even her half-brother, Steven, and his wife had come in from London to attend Lennie's memorial service. The service had been special. She'd gotten through it with strength and grace. Little Maria had clung to her while baby Gino stayed in Cee Cee's loving arms. Later, she'd thrown a party at Morton's with all of Lennie's friends and colleagues because that's what he would have wanted. His eccentric mother had insisted on making an embarrassing speech.

Dry-eyed, Lucky had gotten through it all.

Now, two months later, she was ready to crack.

Alex didn't bother calling Tin Lee. For a start, he couldn't remember her number. And second, who cared? It didn't matter anyway, Miss Compliant was on a fast train out of his life.

"Hey—Alex." Lucky touched his sleeve as they left the restaurant. "Whatever I say tonight—promise not to hold it against me. I'm in a weird place."

He looked at her, somewhat intrigued. "What might you say, Lucky?"

"Anything I feel like," she answered boldly.

Alex had a strong suspicion this was going to be an interesting journey.

16

Venus had a lot on her mind. Since throwing Cooper out, it was almost like starting over. She'd given Rodriguez a chance to show his stuff, but to her disappointment, he wasn't in Cooper's class sexually. Too young and sure of himself. Every move planned to give pleasure, but with no real feeling behind it. Unfortunately, Rodriguez simply didn't do it for her.

The truth was, she missed Cooper—not enough to take him back, even though he'd made several attempts. They'd seen each other at Lennie's memorial service where he'd cornered her and told her what a mistake she was making.

"It's *you* who made the mistake," she'd said, trying not to get upset. "You took me for granted, Coop, not a good move."

"But, honey," he'd said, attempting to embrace her. "I love you, and only you."

"You should've thought about that before," she'd replied, and quickly escaped.

After that he'd sent her flowers on a daily basis, and phoned continually. She'd changed her private number and had the flowers forwarded to a children's hospital. Eventually he'd stopped.

She'd wanted to talk to Lucky about it. Impossible, because since returning from Corsica, Lucky had gone back to work as if nothing had happened.

It puzzled Venus. She considered herself one of Lucky's best friends, but even *she* couldn't get her to talk about her loss, there was no getting close to her.

The good news was that she'd signed with Freddie Leon. He was the kind of agent she'd always dreamed of—a man with ideas bigger than hers. Recently he'd been trying to talk her into considering a pivotal cameo role in Alex Woods's *Gangsters*. "It's not the lead," he'd warned her. "However, it's an Oscar-nomination role, and you should do it."

She'd read the script and was excited. Set in the fifties, *Gangsters* was a steamy, brutally honest film about Las Vegas and two powerful men. One a sadistic mobster. The other a famous Latin singer owned by the mob. Johnny Romano was playing the singer. They had yet to cast the mobster. The role Freddie had in mind for her was Lola, the original good-time girl who becomes involved with both men. It was not a huge role, but very showy.

"Alex has agreed to meet you," Freddie said.

"How very generous of him," Venus drawled sarcastically, wondering if Freddie really understood who she was and what she'd achieved.

Freddie chose to ignore her sarcasm. "You'll read for him."

Venus gave a brittle laugh. "Not me, Freddie, I don't read. I'm *way* beyond that."

"Listen," Freddie said, his bland features unperturbed. "Marlon Brando read for *The Godfather* and look what it did for *his* career. Frank Sinatra auditioned for *From Here to Eternity*. When big actors realize a role is special, they'll do anything to get the part. If you want to play Lola, you'll have to convince Alex. It's the only way."

The meeting was set up for noon the next day at Alex's office.

Just as she'd expected, the tabloids had gone headline crazy with the news of her separation from Cooper. The two of them were spread all over the front pages of the supermarket press. So was Leslie Kane—who somehow or other had managed to get herself portrayed as the sweet, innocent girl next door, while Venus was painted as the sexually voracious superstar who'd driven her husband into another woman's arms.

God! These papers were so full of crap. If they only knew the truth about Leslie, it would blow their minds.

The other bad news was that she'd heard her bum brother Emilio had returned from Europe, where he'd been hanging out with an aging Eurotrash contessa. Emilio made a living out of being her brother; he was even now probably trying to sell more stories of her early days to the tabloids.

One of her spies told her Cooper had left the Beverly Hills Hotel and returned to his former high-rise penthouse on Wilshire. It made her sad to think of him going back to his old ways, but then, she wasn't responsible for him. If he chose to be an almost fifty-year-old playboy screwing a different woman every night, that was *his* problem.

More news flashes from the set informed her he'd broken up with Leslie. It wasn't important, their real problem was never Leslie.

Rodriguez was on his way over again. She'd decided to give him another chance to exhibit his sexual skills.

The truth was, she was not fond of being alone in the house; at least Rodriguez was company.

Ah…the life of a superstar. Not as glamorous as everybody seemed to think.

Leslie Kane had taken up with Jeff Stoner— the small-time actor from her current movie. Not because she'd wanted to—he meant nothing to her—but because she'd had to do something. Cooper's behavior toward her was too humiliating. After Venus's cruel and nasty speech at her dinner party, she'd hoped that Cooper would finally be hers.

No. It was not to be. He'd turned against her as if she had some unspeakable sexual disease, the bastard was barely polite to her. And what made it worse was the way he treated her on the set. When they were shooting their love scenes he was fine, then as soon as the director yelled "Cut!", he was cold and unapproachable.

What had *she* done to merit this kind of treatment?

Nothing. Except make love to him whenever he was in the mood. And before her dinner party he'd been in the mood all the time.

Was it because he'd found out she was once one of Madame Loretta's highly paid call girls?

Probably.

Men were so two-faced.

Jeff, on the other hand, didn't seem to mind at all. Well, he was much younger than Cooper—by about twenty years. And younger men, she'd discovered, were far less judgmental.

Jeff *loved* being her boyfriend. He blossomed in the limelight. She was his career booster, giving him the high profile he'd always yearned for.

Cooper hadn't liked it when she'd spoken to their director and gotten him to enlarge Jeff's part. It wasn't much—an extra scene at the end of the movie and a few close-ups—but it sure pissed Cooper off. And he couldn't do a thing about it, because *she* was the real star of the movie on account of the fact that her career was sizzling hot while Cooper's flame was turned kind of low and steady.

Sexually, Jeff came nowhere near Cooper's stellar performances. He was a beginner—all stamina, with no finesse. The trouble with a lot of men was that they had no idea how to make love, all they knew how to do was fuck. Jeff was no exception.

She missed Cooper's slow sensuality, the

way he knew exactly where to touch her and when, his long, steamy kisses, his probing tongue and sensitive hands. Oh yes, there was no substitute for real experience. Cooper's moves were still the best.

Jeff came bounding out of the bathroom all hyped up because they'd been at a party where she'd introduced him to his hero, Harrison Ford.

"What a guy!" Jeff enthused. "So *nice*. Kinda like you, Les."

"I'm not so nice," she said, casually brushing her long hair.

"Yes, you are," Jeff said. "Even if you won't admit it." He took the hairbrush out of her hands, put his arms around her, and kissed her on the mouth.

His kisses were too hard, she could barely breathe. And he had this thing he did that she hated. He rolled his tongue and shoved it in her mouth. Not a winner.

If only he knew how to kiss...

Two minutes of kissing and his hands were on her breasts. One minute of fingering her nipples, a quick suck on each one, and he was inside her, pumping away, probably under the false impression that he was the world's greatest lover.

She wasn't in the mood to teach him otherwise.

Later, while Jeff snored beside her, she lay in bed thinking about Cooper and how to win him back. There had to be a way.

If there was, she'd find it.

★ ★ ★

Back in New York, Brigette was more determined than ever to make things happen. She'd truly loved Lennie, and now he was gone. His death had brought her up with a resounding jolt, forcing her to realize how fast a life could be snuffed out.

In L.A. she'd spent as much time as possible with his kids. Lucky was always at the studio, and seemed so completely swamped with work that Brigette hardly got to see her even though she was staying at the house.

A few weeks after the memorial service for Lennie she'd told Lucky she was returning to New York. Lucky hadn't seemed to mind, she'd wished her luck and assured her good things were about to happen for her.

Now she was back, and there'd be no more sitting around. She was going to be somebody. And she was going to be somebody *soon*.

Anna was pleased to see her. "Nona phoned three times today," she said as Brigette dumped her suitcases. "She said for you to call her immediately."

She'd only spoken to Nona a few times while she was in L.A. Nona had promised she'd still get her in to see Aurora Mondo Carpenter and Michel Guy, and that Luke would have photos ready when she returned. At least she had *something* to look forward to.

She went in the kitchen, opened a Seven-Up, sifted through her accumulated mail, then called Nona.

"About time!" Nona exclaimed. "Where *were* you?"

"On a plane. It was late leaving L.A. I only just walked in."

"Well, get ready to walk out again. Luke Kasway wants to see us at his studio. And he wants to see us now!"

Rodriguez arrived on time, his smoldering eyes gazing eagerly into Venus's. "My beautiful one!" he exclaimed, lifting her hand to his lips.

Venus, clad only in a short Japanese kimono, smiled. There was something delightfully decadent about the fact that she was paying Rodriguez. She got off on it, and even though he was not the lover she'd expected, who was?

"I'm tired," she complained in a little-girl voice. "My bones are weary."

"Ahhh!" he said soothingly. "Rodriguez will make your bones sing, your muscles come alive. Your whole body will tingle from my special touch."

He'd certainly mastered the art of corny English. They went to her massage room in her classic-modern, all-white house. She clicked on the CD player and K. D. Lang proceeded to serenade them.

Rodriguez removed his jacket. He wore a sleeveless black T-shirt and thigh-hugging black jeans. The muscles in his arms rippled invitingly. He had a deep tan and minty breath. All in all, he was some studly package.

171

He smiled at her, his dark eyes full of sexual promise. "On the table, my beautiful one," he commanded.

She slipped off her kimono, revealing a black lace thong and nothing else.

Rodriguez's eyes swept over her appreciatively, fixing on her full breasts. "Perfect!" he exclaimed. "You are perfection, my Venus."

I am not your Venus, she wanted to say. *I'm your client. You're giving me a massage and we're both getting our rocks off, but that doesn't mean I belong to you.*

Without a word she climbed onto the table and lay facedown, her arms stretched out above her head.

Rodriguez produced a bottle of exotic perfumed oil, poured a small amount in the palm of his hands, and began to lovingly massage her shoulders and back.

Slowly, surely, she felt the tension leaving her body. Oh, God, he did have extremely talented fingers.

"How long have you been in L.A.?" she questioned, her skin tingling.

"Since I was sixteen," Rodriguez replied. "I came here with a married woman running from her husband. She promised to buy me my own beauty salon."

"What happened?"

"Her husband arrived to claim her. The man was a billionaire." Rodriguez shrugged. "She loved me, but she was forced to go with him. I was too young to fight it."

"What did you do then?"

"Another woman. They have always been my weakness."

"No, Rodriguez," Venus corrected. "You've been *their* weakness."

His hands moved down to the small of her back, very slowly peeling off her lace thong. Tossing it aside, he began kneading her bare buttocks with his masterful hands.

"Wow..." she sighed luxuriously, feeling the heat. "That's *sooo* damn good."

"I learn from the best," Rodriguez boasted. "My father—he was the most famous masseur in Argentina. The women of Buenos Aires would do anything for my father."

"I was thinking," Venus Maria murmured as his fingers hit the crack, "how would you like to be in my new video?"

"Doing what?"

"Playing yourself. It's for the song I've written called *Sin*. I see the video as being very surreal and sensual."

"I would be honored."

"My casting agent will call you."

His hands were inside her thighs now, spreading her legs, delving down, exploring her most private places.

She did nothing to stop him, she needed the release.

So what if she had to pay him? That was part of the perverse thrill.

And best of all, she was in total control.

Brigette took a cab over to Luke Kasway's studio. Nona had sounded excited on the phone, although she hadn't revealed anything other than "Get your ass over here fast."

She knew she wasn't looking her best in baggy jeans and a shapeless plaid shirt, her honey-blond hair braided down her back. Fortunately, she'd just purchased a pair of cool Guess shades, so she covered her eyes with those even though it was dark out. She didn't want Luke to be disappointed when he saw her. After all, the last time they'd met, she'd been all dressed up.

Nona was pacing the sidewalk, waiting for her.

"What's going on?" Brigette asked, paying off the cab.

"Dunno. Luke was totally psyched when he called. Insisted on seeing us immediately."

"Do you think he's got a modeling job for me?"

"I bloody well hope so," Nona said. "And even if he hasn't, we'll get to see the pictures. Tomorrow we'll take 'em up to show Aurora. Now you're back, I'll call Michel, we'll go see him, too."

"Sounds good to me."

"Don't worry, girl," Nona said encouragingly. "We'll get it going."

Luke was in the middle of a session when they entered the studio. His assistant, a skinny girl in khaki overalls and scuffed combat boots, led them over to the bar and told them to wait.

Luke was busy shooting Cybil Wilde, the gorgeous blond model. Cybil wore lingerie of the see-through kind and a toothpaste-ad smile. It didn't seem to faze her at all that the studio was packed with people.

"Who *are* all these bodies?" Brigette whispered.

"Ad executives, hair, makeup, stylists," Nona replied. "When they shot my mom for *Vanity Fair*, there were more people than this."

Loud rock music blasted from several speakers. A side table was set up with a full salad bar and plenty of snacks. The atmosphere was tense even though Cybil seemed to laugh a lot.

Every time Luke took a break, people sprang at Cybil, fussing with her hair, touching up her makeup, adjusting the tiny red lace bra and bikini panties that barely covered her luscious curves.

Brigette tried to imagine herself in Cybil's place. Would it be fun? Would she like it?

When Cybil finally went off to change, Luke came over to the bar. "Hello, ladies," he said, running a hand through his spiky hair.

"What's the panic?" Nona asked. "You told me to get Brigette up here immediately."

"Let me finish this gig," Luke said. "Then I'll take you two girls out for dinner."

"I'm supposed to be seeing Zan later," Nona objected. "And Brigette's exhausted. She only just got off a plane."

"Have Zan meet us. In fact, I want him there, too."

"Can we at least go home and change?" Nona grumbled.

"Yeah, yeah, whatever. I didn't realize this session was going to run over. Tell you what— let's meet at Mario's, eight o'clock. We'll get into everything then."

Nona frowned. "Exactly *what* are we getting into?"

"Oh, didn't I tell you?" Luke replied ingeniously, like it was no big thing. "Rock 'n' Roll Jeans want Brigette and Zandino to carry the ad. You were right, Nona—they're gonna be superstars!"

17

Lucky finished off most of the pitcher of margaritas before falling asleep. When she awoke she experienced a fleeting moment of confusion—where the hell was she?

Then she remembered. She was in a car with Alex Woods and they were on their way to visit Gino in Palm Springs.

She glanced over at Alex. He had the demeanor of a man who'd always gotten his own way—strong profile, rugged jawline, probably a selfish sonofabitch with women.

She couldn't help wondering if he was a good lover.

No...too into himself.

"Hey—" she said, languidly stretching. "Where are we?"

"On the road. You drank everything in sight and fell asleep."

She laughed softly. "It's a habit I have."

"That's okay."

"Gee…thanks," she murmured, reaching for the pitcher of margaritas wedged precariously against the back of her seat. She took a couple of healthy swigs. "Guess I should call Gino, warn him we're heading in his direction."

"You didn't call him from the restaurant?"

"Don't sweat it, he'll be thrilled to see us."

"He's *your* father."

"Yeah, and he's the greatest, although…I have to admit…we didn't always get along."

He had a feeling she wanted to talk. "How come?" he asked, making it easy for her.

"Gino wanted a boy. Got me instead. I turned out to be more than he could handle." She grinned at the memories. "I was a wild child. Uncontrollable."

"And now?"

"A mere shadow of my former self."

"What was so wild about you, Lucky?" he asked, genuinely interested.

"Oh, the usual," she said casually. "Ran away from school, fucked a lot of guys, tried to take over my father's business, threatened to cut off one of his investor's dicks if he didn't put up the money he owed."

"A nice, simple girl," Alex said sarcastically.

"Trust me, it worked. When you mess with a guy's dick, it *always* works."

"And now you're running a studio. Perfect."

"Y'know," she said thoughtfully, "Gino always warned me to check on everyone around me—and to double-check everyone around *them*. In other words—" she put on a tough guy voice—"don't trust no one. *Capishe?*"

"He sounds like a smart guy."

"Yeah," she said ruefully. "He sure is."

"Want to tell me about it?"

"There's nothing to tell. I've simply got this gut feeling that something bad is about to happen. Don't ask me why."

They drove in silence for a few minutes, then Alex said, "I didn't think nice Italian girls fucked around."

She laughed good-naturedly, "Oh, baby, baby...what a sheltered life *you've* led."

"*Me?*" he said incredulously. Hadn't she read his press clippings?

She paused and lit a cigarette. "How come out of everything I said, the only thing you commented on was that nice Italian girls aren't supposed to screw around? Hmmm...Could it be that the bad boy of movies, Mr. Sexually Anything Goes is—deep down—dare I say it—a prude?"

"Are you out of your fucking mind?"

She smiled slyly. "Girls do talk, y'know. Wanna hear what the word is on you?"

He couldn't resist falling into the trap. "What?"

Dragging on her cigarette, she blew a steady stream of smoke into his face. "Big boy on campus. Doesn't give head."

"*Jesus!*"

"Oh, sorry," she said innocently. "Am I shocking you?"

He was completely perplexed. Lucky Santangelo was certifiably crazy.

"You say things to get a reaction, don't you?" he asked.

"Isn't that the whole point?"

He drove on in silence, trying to figure her out.

"Why'n't we pull off at the next exit?" she suggested. "We're all out of margaritas."

Alex had to admit, he was intrigued. He had not expected Lucky to be so unpredictable. She had an aura of strength about her, as if she could handle any situation and come out on top. It was unnerving. He was not used to women who projected such confidence.

So far she hadn't mentioned Lennie, and it didn't seem appropriate for him to bring it up; if she wanted to talk about it, she'd no doubt do so.

He changed lanes and pulled off the freeway. The territory was desolate—there was not much going on except a gas station, a hamburger joint, and a seedy roadhouse with a neon sign flashing LIVE NAKED GIRLS.

Alex slowed the car. "We're in the wastelands," he said. "This appears to be it."

"Define *live* naked girls," Lucky said, frowning. "Is that as opposed to *dead* naked girls?"

"Not your kind of place, huh?"

"Seems our choice is limited."

He shrugged. "Don't blame me."

"Alex, when you know me better you'll realize I *always* accept responsibility."

"Former wild child straightens out. I like it."

"Fuck you," she said casually.

He looked her straight in the eye. "Is that a threat or a promise?"

"You'd better leave me alone tonight, Alex. I wouldn't want to see you get hurt."

And as she said it, it came to her. That's *exactly* what she needed to do. Hurt someone the way Lennie had hurt her. It was bad enough that he'd gotten himself killed—but when he'd gone, he'd left enough evidence of infidelity to make her hate him forever. There was only one way to even the score.

They parked the car and entered the crowded bar. Big surprise—it was filled with men, most of them swigging bottled beer.

A harassed underage waitress in boots, a cowboy hat, and micro skirt darted about carrying a tray. She was topless, with small, droopy breasts and a lackluster smile. At one end of the bar was a circular platform where a large blond stripper undulated her out-of-shape body up and down a shiny pole wearing only a frayed pink G-string and fake silver cuff bracelets. Dolly Parton blared from the jukebox. Every time the stripper squatted down, rolls of excess flesh doubled over her stomach and hips.

"Lovely," Lucky muttered, taking a seat at the bar while every guy in the place checked her out.

Alex slid on the stool beside her. He carried an unlicensed gun in his car; after taking a look around, he was sorry he hadn't brought it in with him.

"Tequila," Lucky said to the bartender, a gnarled old man with sunken cheeks and a permanent scowl. He ignored her, waiting for Alex to give him the order.

"Tequila for the lady," Alex said, getting the picture. "And I'll have a bourbon and water."

"Make mine a double," Lucky said, impatiently tapping her fingernails on the bar. The bartender shuffled off.

The big blond stripper reached the end of her act, snatched off her G-string, turned her back to the crowd, bent over, and shook her huge blob of an ass at the paying customers. There was a scattering of groans and catcalls.

"What a bunch of pathetic losers," Lucky said, checking out the place. "I mean, take a look at these jerks—why aren't they at home with their wives?"

"I didn't promise you the Ritz in Paris," Alex said. "And keep your voice down."

"You didn't promise me shit," Lucky replied, the booze finally getting to her. "But, hey— we're here, let's make the most of it."

The bartender returned with their drinks. Lucky downed her tequila in one shot. A John Travolta clone, perched on a stool on the other side of her, let loose an admiring whistle.

"Another one," Lucky said.

"Are we ever gonna make it to your father's?" Alex sighed, signaling the bartender.

"Tell me the truth," Lucky said, swaying slightly on the rickety bar stool. "Is that the only reason you're with me tonight? To meet Gino?"

"What do *you* think?"

"I think we're together 'cause we both have a need for something different." She fixed him with a long, knowing look. "Am I right?"

"Perceptive."

"Oh, yeah, that I am. So fucking perceptive that I truly believed Lennie was faithful."

"And he wasn't?"

"Don't wanna get into it," she snapped, sorry she'd mentioned something so private.

A short man clad in a too tight leisure suit jumped up on stage. "Okay, folks," he bellowed, his cheeks red from the effort. "Here's the moment we've all been waiting for—the star of our show! Give her a great big hand—and we all know where!" Snicker, snicker. "Here she is—our special queen of the night—Driving Miss Daisy!"

An extremely ugly black woman with an incredible body hit the stage with a burst of unbridled energy. She was clad in a white fringed bra, bikini panties, and a peaked chauffeur's cap. The Rolling Stones were on the jukebox and Driving Miss Daisy immediately began taking it off to the strains of "Honky Tonk Woman." The audience went wild.

Alex considered her almost naked ebony flesh. "I should find a walk-on for her in *Gangsters*," he mused. "She's got quite a look."

"Why not?" Lucky replied coolly. "What would your movie be without the obligatory strip scene?"

She had a smart answer for everything. "Hey,

it's what's happening, Lucky," he said, knowing she'd give him an argument.

"Maybe it is, but how come you moviemakers are so predictable? It's always two actors sitting in a strip joint while the camera spends the entire scene zooming in for close-ups of the stripper's tits and ass. When are you guys gonna realize those scenes have been done to death?"

"What *is* it with you? The first time we met all you could talk about was actors taking it off."

"Did that offend you?"

"Women don't want to see that. It's a man's world."

"You'd *like* it to be a man's world," she said forcefully. "You'd like it to *stay* a man's world. But women do what they want today, and women don't mind taking a peek at naked guys. Why do you think Richard Gere is a star today? 'Cause he flashed his nuts in *Looking for Mr. Goodbar*, and women loved him for being so honest."

Driving Miss Daisy did something obscene with the pole, causing quite a commotion among her audience. Several guys threw dollar bills onstage.

"A friend of mine was in the hospital and I took her *Playgirl* to read," Lucky continued, getting into it. "Now, you'd think the nurses would've seen *plenty* of male equipment. But let me tell you—they went apeshit when they got a load of the guys in this magazine. They grabbed it, showed it to every other nurse on the floor. They were *thrilled*."

He shook his head. "You don't get it."

She smiled, unperturbed. "No, Alex, *you* don't get it."

Driving Miss Daisy was divesting her clothes at a rapid pace. Flinging her bra into the audience, she twirled the two fringed pasties barely covering each erect nipple. Her bikini bottom was long gone, replaced by a hardly there G-string. Coated with a fine film of sweat, she moved like a sinewy gazelle.

"I wonder how she got here," Lucky mused. "This seedy two-bit bar in the middle of nowhere."

"That's *my* deal," Alex said. "Finding out people's stories."

"Then writing about them and turning them into a movie."

"Beats packing meat."

Driving Miss Daisy squatted down, cleverly picking up dollar bills between her thighs. The John Travolta clone on Lucky's left yelled his appreciation.

"Asshole," Lucky muttered.

"From what I hear, yours is a pretty interesting story," Alex ventured, curious to hear what she had to say.

"I told you—I was a wild child," she said lightly. "I didn't tell you about the guy I shot. Self-defense, of course."

Jesus! She *was* a wild one. "No, you didn't tell me that," he said quietly.

"Enzio Bonnatti, he was the man responsible for killing my mother and brother, and, uh...there were a few other minor incidents along the way that made me who I am today."

She was actually sitting there calmly telling him that she'd killed somebody. Perhaps they had more in common than he'd thought. He'd killed in Vietnam, only he'd had an excuse, it was called war.

He wondered if she suffered from the same nightmares that often crept up on him without warning. Middle of the night panic attacks.

"You're a very unusual woman, Lucky," he said, clearing his throat.

She watched him carefully for a moment. He didn't know the half of it. Maybe she was talking too much; it might be prudent to change the subject before he got too intrigued. "And you, Alex? Ever been married?"

"No," he said guardedly.

"Never?" She shook her head disbelievingly. "How old are you?"

"Forty-seven."

"Hmm...that means you're either very smart, or you have a fatal flaw."

He picked up his drink. "What are you—a shrink?"

She regarded him steadily. "Guys who aren't married by your age usually suffer from major hang-ups—otherwise some woman would've picked you off long ago."

"There's a simple answer. I've never met anybody I'd be prepared to spend the rest of my life with."

"I've done it three times," she said lightly. "It's not so nerve-racking after the first time."

"And the first time was... ?"

"Craven Richmond. Senator Peter Richmond's little boy. God, was he a moron! And I was stuck with him." She laughed at the memory. "Gino married me off because he could. Peter owed him a favor."

"Must've been some favor."

"It was."

"Do I get to hear about it?"

"Not until I know you better."

"And after Craven?"

"Dimitri Stanislopoulos, a man old enough to be my father." She paused for a moment. "Actually, he *was* the father of my best friend, Olympia." She giggled, recalling her juvenile delinquent past. "We were two little bad girls who ran away from school together."

"You must've really been something."

"Oh, yeah! I gave jailbait a whole new meaning."

"I bet you did."

"Anyway, while I was married to Dimitri, I caught him in bed with Francesca Fern—the opera singer. She was a rival of Maria Callas's, and *very* demanding. He didn't want to leave me, but, boy, he sure wanted to fuck the life out of *her*."

"The man was obviously insane."

"After Dimitri, there was Lennie." She stopped speaking, her eyes clouding over. "Lennie was my soul mate," she said at last. "We were everything to each other. I loved him so much." She gazed deeply into Alex's eyes. "Have you ever felt that kind of connection with another person?"

"No," he said, wishing he could say he had.

"It's the greatest feeling," she said wistfully. "There's this incredible chemistry...."

"It must have been hard for you, Lucky," he interrupted. "The accident...losing Lennie..."

"Some things are meant to be," she said, abruptly reaching for her drink. "I haven't told anyone this, Alex, but I found out Lennie was screwing around. There were photos in his hotel room with a blond draped all over him. Nude pictures of her stashed in the bed-side drawer. He was obviously with her the night before I arrived. I don't know why he didn't cover his tracks—he must've thought the maid would clear everything up while he was at the airport." She took a long, deep breath. "Anyway, it's been hard, because, uh...I believe in fidelity. You know, screw around all you want when you're single, but when you marry somebody—well...for me that's the ultimate commitment."

"Ah..." Alex sighed. "She has-old fash-ioned values."

"What's wrong with that?" she responded vehemently, sorry she'd revealed so much of herself. "I find it crazy that we live in a country where everybody says it's okay if a guy goes out and gets laid because he's a guy. It's *not* okay with me. I loved Lennie, and he let me down. That's not playing fair." She stopped talking and lit another cigarette, angry with herself for becoming so emotional. "I'm getting maudlin," she said, making a rapid recovery. "Let's have one more drink."

"You're almost blasted, Lucky."

She looked at him coolly. "Sometimes you just gotta blow it out, Alex." She clicked her fingers—summoning the bartender. The old man shuffled over. She waved a twenty-dollar bill under his nose. "Give this to Driving Miss Daisy. Tell her we'd like her to join us, and bring me another double."

"What are you *doing*?" Alex said, creasing his forehead.

"I'm curious to know how this ugly woman with this amazing body ended up here, stripping for a living. Aren't you?"

"I'm more interested in meeting Gino."

"We'll get there. Don't worry."

The John Travolta clone leaned into their conversation. He wore a yellow shirt and mud-brown pants. His hair was long and greasy. "You-all from L.A.?" he asked, rubbing the tip of his nose with a dirty fingernail.

"Now what makes you think that?" Lucky said, tilting her head.

He placed his bottle of beer on the bar, suggestively fingering the wet rim. "'Cause you sure don't look like you're from these parts."

"Aw, shucks," Lucky drawled, almost flirting. "And I was hoping I'd fit right in."

The young guy guffawed. "Name's Jed. This here's the hottest place around," he boasted. "You picked good."

"Really?" Lucky said, her dark eyes drawing him in.

Jed leaned closer, leering at her. "You one of them Hollywood actresses?"

Alex could smell the dumb jerk's hard-on. "She's with me," he interrupted. "And we're not looking to have a third party join us." *So keep it in your pants, shithead, and get the fuck away.*

"No offense," Jed said, backing off. "Just bein' friendly."

"Lucky," Alex said in a low voice, "I'm not interested in getting into a fight, so do me a favor and stop encouraging the local talent."

She regarded him mockingly. "Thought you might get off taking a walk on the wild side, Alex. Isn't the wild side your territory?"

"In case you haven't noticed, I'm considerably outnumbered."

"Oh... *sooo* sorry." She held her empty glass toward the bartender. "Set me up again."

"Jesus Christ!" Alex muttered. "Whaddya have—a hollow leg?"

"Something like that."

"I'm going to the john," he said curtly. "Try to stay out of trouble. When I get back, we're taking off."

She mock-saluted. "Yes, *sir*!"

The moment Alex was out of sight, the local stud returned to the business of picking her up.

"Didn't mean no offense," he said, sliding nearer.

"None taken," Lucky responded, noticing he had no side teeth. It did not add to his sex appeal.

"Would that be your husband?" Jed said, gesturing to Alex's seat.

"No. That would *not* be my husband," she said, amused.

"Then mebbe I kin buy you a beer."

"I'm drinking tequila."

"I kin go for that." He signaled the bartender. "Put the lady's drink on my tab."

The bartender was a man who sensed trouble long before it happened. "Not a good idea, Jed," he said warningly.

"The guy she's with ain't her husband," Jed explained, like that took care of everything.

"Still not a good idea."

Jed stood up, red in the face. "I'm fuckin' buyin' her a drink," he said, angrily slamming the bar with his fist.

"Christ!" grunted the bartender, disgusted.

"Let's not make this a major incident," Lucky said, staring at the crusty old man.

"You people should stay where you belong," the bartender growled, glaring at her. "Comin' in here as if y'own t'place. Drinkin' tequila like you're some kinda *man*."

"Screw you," Lucky said, starting to lose her temper.

Jed grabbed her arm. "Better not insult t'old bastard. C'mon, I'll take you somewhere else."

She shook her arm loose. The booze was clouding her judgment. Alex was right, encouraging the local talent was not a good idea.

Jed went for her arm again. She slapped his bony hand away.

"What's your freakin' problem, lady?" Jed exploded.

"Don't touch me, asshole," she warned fiercely, her black eyes suddenly deadly.

His face reddened even more. "Whaddaya call me, *bitch*?"

Alex chose that exact moment to return from the men's room.

18

"Your fans, they must drive you crazy," Rodriguez remarked, lazily stroking Venus's platinum hair as they sat, naked, in her outside Jacuzzi, the city lights spread out beneath them like a shimmering blanket of rare jewels.

"Sometimes," she said thoughtfully. "When I'm out in public, and they try to touch me. You never know if they've got a knife or a gun. You can never tell if *they're* the maniac who's going to get you."

"Is that why you have a guard at your house?"

"Protection is necessary. Think about it—everything we do today needs some kind of protection."

"Like sex."

"Exactly. You told me you hate wearing a condom. Well, *I* hate having to live my life with guards. Sadly, these are things we're forced to do."

"Rodriguez does not have any disease."

"I'm sure you don't."

"Then we throw away the condoms?"

"No. We do not."

"Why, my beauty?"

"Get an AIDS test and we'll see."

He touched her breasts with his fingertips, rubbing insistently.

She shivered as her nipples became erect. Tonight he'd been better than the two previous times. Tonight he'd made her moan with pleasure. As a reward, she was allowing him to stay awhile.

He reached for the bottle of champagne perched on the side of the Jacuzzi and held it to her lips. She allowed the golden liquid to trickle down her throat.

"Aren't you having any?" she asked, slowly licking her lips.

"I'll show you how Rodriguez drinks champagne," he said, boldly picking her up and placing her on the edge of the Jacuzzi.

"What are you *doing*?" she objected, but not too strenuously.

"Silence, my lovely," he murmured, spreading her legs and caressing the soft inner part of her thighs. Then he took the champagne bottle and tipped the bubbly liquid over her pubic area. "*This* is how Rodriguez drinks champagne," he said, lapping the liquid from between her legs, continuing to work his smooth Latin tongue until once more she sighed with pleasure and decided that maybe Rodriguez was a keeper after all.

Mario's was a noisy and colorful Italian restaurant packed with models, agents, art dealers, and writers. "It's *the* happening place," Nona informed Brigette as they pushed their way past the jammed bar to Luke's booth, Zandino trailing behind them.

They'd both rushed home and changed. Nona wore a bright-green satin Dolce Gabbana shirt and tight black pants, while Brigette had settled on a skimpy white Calvin Klein shift dress and strappy sandals.

Luke was not alone. Cybil Wilde and her hair stylist were sitting in his booth. Cybil had a Christie Brinkley glow about her that automatically made her the center of attention. She was so glossily pretty that Brigette was immediately intimidated—even though they were about the same age.

"Squeeze in, everyone," Luke said, greeting them warmly. "I'm sure you all know Cybil, and this is the great Harvey, who makes even *my* hair look halfway passable."

Harvey reached up and touched a lock of Brigette's honey-blond hair. "Nice, luv," he said in a heavy Cockney accent. "No coloring—none of them stupid streaks all the girls are into. Keep it this way."

"Thanks," Brigette said, sliding in next to him.

"And as for *you*, madame," Harvey added, checking out Nona's blazing red hair. "Veree *au courant*. An' natural too, I bet."

Brigette took a moment to study Harvey. A man of about thirty, he had a white-blond buzz cut with a side streak of green, black-leather wrist cinchers, and a small diamond embedded in the side of his nose.

"What would you do to my hair?" she asked, curious to get his opinion.

"Nuffin'," he said. "You're a little darlin' just the way you are."

Talk about an ego booster! Brigette was pleased.

Nona was more interested in getting down to business. "Can we talk here?" she asked Luke.

"Absolutely," he replied, waving at several friends.

"Well?" Nona demanded impatiently. "*What?*"

Luke grinned, behaving like an asshole.

"*What?*" she repeated, pulling on his arm.

"I showed the ad agency the pictures of Brigette and Zan. They took 'em to the client, and wham, bam—we got ourselves a gig!"

"Ohmigod!" Nona exclaimed, nudging Brigette. "Did you hear that?"

"Great."

"Great," Nona shrieked. "GREAT. It's absolutely AMAZING!"

"I got *my* start modeling for a May Company catalogue," Cybil interjected, smiling prettily. "I was sixteen." Her smile widened, causing dimples in her cheeks. "A very well-developed sixteen!"

"When will the photos appear?" Brigette asked Luke. "And where?"

"We haven't taken 'em yet," Luke said, laughing at her naivete. "First you get your agent to make a deal. *Then* we shoot a proper session. After that, my sweet girl, you'll be in every magazine from here to the moon! Rock 'n' Roll Jeans spends *money*."

"How come *I* wasn't up for this job?" Cybil asked, pouting.

"'Cause you're—as Nona so tastefully puts it—like dog shit. Oh, don't worry," Luke added quickly. "You're in excellent company—Robertson, Nature—they all got Nona's seal of disapproval."

"Guess we need an agent," Nona said thoughtfully. "Like yesterday."

Brigette thought of all the agencies who'd refused to see her. The only one who'd shown any interest was Michel Guy.

"Elite," Cybil said, trying to be helpful. "They're the best."

"No. The Ford Agency," Luke argued. "They'll protect her. She's a virgin in this biz, she'll need armored guards to keep the aging playboys from jumping her innocent little bones."

"Those men are so gross," Cybil squealed, turning up her snub nose. "Total *perverts*! Prince this and Count that, and all they want to do is snort coke, get head, and show you off to their equally disgusting decrepit old friends."

"Tell us how you *really* feel, dear," said Harvey, sipping a margarita through a straw.

"Be warned!" Cybil said to Brigette. "I'll give you a list of the worst offenders."

"Thanks," Brigette responded. Cybil was so open and friendly it was impossible not to warm to her.

"What's your take on rock stars?" Luke asked Cybil with a sly smile.

Cybil giggled; she'd just started dating English rock star Kris Phoenix. "I'm in love!" she cooed. "Kris is *sensational!*"

Brigette remembered another English rock star, the infamous Flash. Her mother had overdosed and died while in his company— both of them drugged out of their minds in a cheap hotel room in Times Square.

Oh, God! Nobody must find out her real identity. It was imperative she protect her anonymity. Maybe she should change her first name just to be sure.

"I can get you in to see any agent in town," Luke boasted. "Tell me who."

"Michel Guy," Brigette said quietly, hardly believing that this was finally happening.

"No problem," Luke said. "He's sitting two tables away with Robertson—only when she finds out she's not doing the Rock 'n' Roll Jeans campaign, you may not be a welcome addition to Michel's family."

"We'll see," Brigette said with a small confident smile.

After Rodriguez left, Venus found she could not sleep, so instead she did her usual night-time prowl around the house. It was not late enough for her to settle down. Rodriguez had satisfied her sexually, but mentally he was a blank. She must be getting old, because now she needed more than just a great body and a horny disposition. She craved a companion, someone she could talk to when the sex was over. Cooper excelled at both.

She tried to decide who she could wake up at this time of night. Maybe Lucky, who never wanted to talk anymore unless it concerned business. Well, too bad, this might be the perfect time to reach her.

"Miss Santangelo is in Palm Springs visiting her father," Cee Cee informed her over the phone.

"How's she's doing?" Venus asked.

"She works too hard," Cee Cee replied, sounding concerned.

"Tell me about it! I never see her anymore, she's always too busy."

After putting the phone down, she attempted to read a magazine and found she couldn't concentrate. She was so restless it was crazy.

Hmm...she thought, who else would be up?

Ron, of course. Her best friend, Ron, who, since he'd been with major mogul Harris Von

Stepp, was also on the missing list. She'd nicknamed Harris "Major Mogul" to get back at Ron, who'd called Martin Swanson the same thing when she and Martin had been an item.

Ron was not amused. "Don't *ever* let him hear you call him that," he'd warned. "Harris has no sense of humor, he'll throw a complete fit."

"Harris is too tight-assed," she'd replied. "Couldn't you have latched on to a *fun* faggot?"

"Control your language, girl," Ron had scolded. "Faggot is *not* a politically correct word."

She missed Ron. Not seeing him as much as she used to was like breaking off with a favorite lover.

The hell with it, she decided to call him.

"You'll never guess who this is," she announced when he answered the phone.

"Oh, like *quelle surprise*!" Ron said, totally unsurprised. "Are we experiencing a *crisis*?"

"As a matter of fact, we are. I was kind of wondering if you could come over, sit around and talk, y'know…get cozy like we used to…"

"Certainly, popsicle," he said crisply. "That will go down *very* well with Harris. I'm sure he's simply *dying* for me to run into the bedroom and say, 'Just shooting out to visit Venus.' The man is a jealous wreck as it is. *Especially* of you."

"Why *me*? I'm a girl."

"*Ohh*... you've just answered your own question. *Clever* little minx!"

"When *can* I see you?"

"Seriously, poppet, if it's urgent, I'll risk Harris's wrath and come over now."

"No, no, it can wait, but I *do* miss you."

"Miss you, too. How about lunch tomorrow?"

"Excellent."

"I'm in the editing room all morning. Let's see, we could meet, say, one-thirty?"

"I can tell you all about Rodriguez."

"Ahh...you finally did it with your masseur."

"But of course!"

"Then I'll surely be there. Details are my life!"

When she hung up, she had this insane desire to call Cooper. *Come back, all is forgiven,* she'd say. No, she'd learned at an early age that it was suicidal to repeat past mistakes.

Cooper would never change. And unless she was prepared to accept his infidelities, she was better off without him.

19

"Aw, Jesus!" Alex groaned as he approached the bar and caught the action.

"It's okay, I promise you, it's okay," Lucky said quickly, jumping to her feet.

Jed was flexing his power. "What's *with* you, bitch?" he demanded belligerently, facing her right on. "Too freakin' good for us?"

"Back off," Alex said with a granitelike expression as he stared Jed down.

Jed swayed on his feet. "Don't freakin' tell *me* what to do, Grandpa!"

"Fuck!" Alex muttered, wondering how he'd ever gotten caught up in this scene. And what was with the Grandpa shit? He should knock this snot-nosed pisshead out of the ring.

Instead, he reached into his pocket, produced a wad of bills, threw them at the barman, and grabbed Lucky's arm. "We're outta here," he said, pulling her to the door without looking back. It was a trick he'd learned in Vietnam. If you want to fight, stay eyeball to eyeball with the enemy. If you don't, get the hell out. And do it fast.

"Hey," Lucky objected as they reached the door. "What about the twenty bucks I gave the bartender?"

Alex tightened his grip. "What about getting in the car and shutting the fuck up."

"You're a lot of laughs," she complained.

"If it's laughs you want, you picked the wrong guy," he said tersely.

"Let me jog your memory, Alex, *you're* the one who came running into my office asking me out for a drink."

"I came for a business meeting," he reminded her. "Did I know you were going to be sitting there half ripped?"

"Half ripped?" she said, outraged. "I'm perfectly sober." Although even as she said it she knew she was teetering on the edge.

"Yeah, yeah," he muttered, hustling her

over to the Porsche. Out of the corner of his eye he observed Jed emerging from the bar with a couple of his rowdy friends. He shoved Lucky in the passenger seat, bent down, and reached for his gun in the glove compartment.

"What are you *doing?*" Lucky said.

"Protecting us. Do you mind?"

"Are you *crazy?* You can't shoot the jerk just 'cause he came on to me."

"I'm not planning on shooting anybody. I'm buying us time to split."

"Gino taught me never to pull a gun unless you're prepared to use it."

"He taught you well, 'cause if those punks come at me, I'm shooting 'em straight in their scrawny balls."

"I can see the headline now," Lucky said, not taking him seriously in spite of the fact that his gun appeared to be the real thing. "'Studio head an' bad boy filmmaker. *Busted*!'" She broke up at her own humor.

Jed and his friends hesitated at the entrance. Maybe they'd seen the glint of the metal, or maybe they'd changed their minds. Whatever, to Alex's great relief, they didn't venture farther. Which was fortunate, because he'd meant what he'd said.

Lucky doesn't know me, he thought grimly, *she has no idea that in Vietnam I was forced to kill people more than once.*

It wasn't something he cared to remember, only in his nightmares.

He got behind the wheel of his Porsche, revved the engine, and took off at high speed.

"Shame," Lucky sighed, snuggling down in her seat, feeling no pain. "I was *sooo* interested in talking to Driving Miss Daisy."

This woman is crazy, Alex thought as he got back on the freeway. What am I doing with her? She's crazier than me.

They'd been driving for five minutes when Lucky realized she'd left her purse at the bar. She sat up abruptly to announce the fact.

"We are *not* going back," Alex said tersely. "No fucking way."

"Oh, yes we *are*," Lucky retorted. "My credit cards are in it, my Filofax, driver's license—everything. We *have* to go back."

"You're a difficult woman," he said sourly.

"So I've been told."

He couldn't believe he was doing it as he took the next exit off the freeway, making a sharp turn. "Listen to me," he said sternly, his eyes fixed on the road ahead. "You stay in the car with the engine running while I go in and collect your purse. Understand?"

"You're not taking your gun in."

"Don't tell me what to do."

"No, don't tell *me* what to do."

"Oh, I can see we're going to have a fascinating time making this movie."

"You'd better believe it."

Did she *always* have to have the last word?

He pulled his Porsche up outside the roadhouse and got out. In spite of Lucky's warning, he shoved his gun down his belt, at the back of his pants. Better prepared than not, small-town hotheads were the worst kind.

When he walked in, another stripper was busily working the stage, grabbing everyone's attention. Chinese this time. They certainly went in for variety.

Alex hurried over to the bar. "My companion left her purse," he said.

The grizzled old barman fished under the bar, silently handing over Lucky's purse. "We don't want no trouble in these parts," the man said sourly. "You L.A. people with your money and flashy cars. Stay away."

"Listen, buddy, it's a free country," Alex pointed out, putting Lucky's purse under his arm and walking out.

His Porsche was exactly where he'd left it. There was only one problem. Lucky was not in it.

He stood by his car, totally pissed off. He'd *told* her to stay in the goddamn car—was that so difficult? Too independent. That was the problem with Lucky Santangelo. One thing was sure. He'd never met a woman like her.

He considered teaching her a lesson, driving away and leaving her stranded. Then he decided he couldn't do that, nobody deserved to be left in this pisshole; besides, her studio was financing his movie. He went back inside, looking for her.

The bartender was busy shifting heavy crates of beer; he shook his finger when he saw Alex—as if to say, Not you again.

"Did you see the lady I was with?" Alex asked.

"I told you," the bartender repeated, "your kind ain't welcome here."

Alex was fast running out of patience. "Where's the ladies' room?" he asked.

"Out in the parking lot," the bartender said. "An' don't come back."

Like he would ever want to.

The outdoor ladies' room doubled as a dressing room for the strippers. They scurried in with their plastic makeup cases and see-through carryalls, changing clothes in the cramped space. When Lucky entered, Driving Miss Daisy had just finished getting dressed in an alarmingly tight, scarlet catsuit.

"Hi," Lucky said. "My friend and I wanted to buy you a drink, only it didn't seem like we were welcome here."

The stripper peered at her reflection in the cracked mirror over the once white basin. "Girl, this place is two-tone shit," she remarked, busily rubbing lipstick off her teeth. "Why're you here?"

"I'm with Alex Woods, the film director," Lucky explained. "And we're both kind of curious to know why you're wasting the best body we've ever seen in *this* dump?"

Driving Miss Daisy adjusted what appeared to be a long red wig. "Listen, girl, there's times a person don't have no choice. I work plenny a places—private parties, ole boys' reunions, crap clubs, an' dives like this. Thing is, girl—*that's* what pays the rent."

"We'd pay you—"

"Oh, *no, no no*," Driving Miss Daisy said, shaking her finger at Lucky. "I ain't into any of them *kinky* scenes, so don' go gettin' no fancy ideas jest 'cause I take my clothes off."

"Absolutely no kinky scenes," Lucky assured her. "All we want is to hear your story. Alex is interested in putting you in his new movie."

"His movie, huh?"

"Would a hundred bucks give us twenty minutes of your time?"

"This is too weird," the stripper said, shaking her long red wig.

"What's weird about it? It's an opportunity. Seize it."

The woman pursed her lips. "Never *had* no *opportunities*," she said thoughtfully.

"So take it," Lucky urged.

"I got another gig t'go to."

"We'll come with you."

"I dunno..."

"Where is it?"

"A pool hall... 'bout twenny minutes from here."

"A deal," Lucky said quickly, before the stripper changed her mind.

They walked outside, running straight into an irate Alex.

"I told you to stay in the car," he said, glaring.

"I don't take instructions well."

"That's obvious."

"Alex, this is Driving Miss Daisy…or, uh…" She turned to the stripper. "I guess you've got a name, right?"

"Why y' wanna know my name?" the woman asked suspiciously.

"'Cause I feel a little foolish when I have to keep saying Driving Miss Daisy. It's not like I'm turning you in to Social Security or anything."

The stripper narrowed her eyes. "Jest 'cause I'm black, y' think I'm on welfare? That's *shit*!"

"Did I say that?"

"Lucky," Alex interrupted impatiently. "Can we go?"

"We're going to see…what's your real name?"

"Daisy," the woman muttered.

"Fine. We'll catch uh…Daisy dancing at another place, and then she'll have a drink with us."

"I'm *not* stopping at another one of these shit-holes," Alex said, still glaring.

"I promise," Lucky said sweetly, "no more trouble."

Alex didn't believe a word. "Yeah, like *you* can control it," he said.

"I can," she assured him.

He shook his head. "You're something else, Lucky."

"So are you, Alex," she said. "But we'll get into that another time." She turned to the stripper. "Daisy, we'll follow you, where's your car?"

"Y'all are *real* strange," Daisy said, rolling her eyes.

"You can say that again," Alex muttered.

"I'm the yellow Chevrolet over there," Daisy said, pointing to a wreck of a car.

"We'll be right behind you," Lucky said.

"Are you insane?" Alex asked when they were settled in his Porsche. "Why are we doing this?"

"If you're not into it, drop me at the next bar and I'll call a limo," she said, fed up with Alex's nagging.

"I can't leave you here," he said flatly, adding a surly, "Much as I'd like to."

She desperately wanted another drink, it seemed that every drop of alcohol she'd consumed had no effect. "C'mon, lighten up," she said, turning on the charm. "It'll be a blast. Another tequila. A game of pool. What's so bad?" She nudged him, trying to lure him into the spirit of things. "Twenty bucks says I can beat you."

He studied her for a moment. "You think you can beat me at anything, don't you?"

"Maybe I can," she said, thinking that maybe she could.

"Your ego has a life of its own."

"I suppose yours is just a shadowy little thing?" she countered, groping for a cigarette.

He couldn't help laughing. "I bet you're always used to getting your own way."

"Like *you're* not?" she said, wondering why she felt this continuing urge to needle him.

He regarded her steadily. "I worked my ass into the ground to be able to get my own way."

"What do you think *I* did?" she replied, meeting his gaze.

"Then I guess we're more alike than we realize."

The yellow Chevrolet exited the parking lot.

"Let's go," Lucky said. "We're following an adventure about to happen!"

20

Morton Sharkey met with Donna Landsman in the privacy of her fake Spanish castle. As he drove up the long winding driveway, he tried not to think about how he was betraying Lucky. He knew that what he was doing was wrong, but the downward spiral he was caught up in was too strong to stop. Besides, he was being blackmailed, so he was also a victim.

And yet...in spite of everything, he was still obsessed with Sara. When he was with her, nothing else mattered.

An Asian butler opened the front door and led him through a baronial hallway into a grand, high-ceilinged living room. Morton noticed a lot of portraits of other people's ancestors hanging on the walls.

Donna stood in the middle of the room dressed in Escada, her face impeccably made up, a martini glass in her hand. "Morton," she said, formal and cold, not offering him a drink.

"Donna," he responded.

She did not ask him to sit down. "I understand you have good news for me," she said.

"It's the news you've been waiting for," he replied evenly. "All the investors are in place. As of tomorrow, you will be in control of Panther Studios."

She smiled a thin, almost evil smile. "I'm delighted you decided to cooperate with me."

As if he'd had a choice. He tried not to stare at her; a nerve began twitching under his left eye. "When do I get the tapes, Donna?"

"The moment I'm sitting behind the desk in Lucky Santangelo's office."

"Exactly what day *are* you taking over?"

"Tomorrow," Donna said, her face an unemotional mask. "I hope you'll be there to congratulate me."

"I wasn't planning on it."

"That's not very friendly of you, Morton," she chided. "Surely you wish to witness my moment of triumph?"

"Not really."

"Too bad." Her voice hardened. "Because you *will* be there. I'm sure at this late stage you would not want the videotape of you and that *inventive* young lady becoming public property."

Witch! Scheming witch! Why was she doing this? What made Panther Studios so important to her? That was something he hadn't figured out.

"Very well, Donna, I'll be there."

Another evil smile. "Good."

She waited until Morton had left, then she went to the bar and fixed herself another congratulatory martini.

She sipped it slowly, relishing the thought of what joy tomorrow would bring.

Revenge was sweet. So very, very sweet.

As soon as he was out of there, Morton drove directly to Sara's apartment, an apartment he paid for. When he'd met Sara, she'd lived in a place too dreadful to contemplate; he'd always imagined getting mugged on his way in. Now he'd installed her in a respectable high-rise, and he felt secure traveling up in the elevator from the private underground garage.

He let himself in with his key. At first she'd objected to his having a key, but as he'd pointed out, if he was paying the rent, why shouldn't he?

Sara was not alone, which infuriated him. He'd told her repeatedly that when he visited he did not want her friends around.

Even though he'd informed her he was on his way over, her friend Ruby was there—a sulky-looking girl with stringy black hair and a bad attitude. The two of them were sitting on the living-room floor surrounded by trashy magazines, candies, and an army of colored nail polish bottles. Both of them were barefoot, giggling as they painted each other's toenails.

"We're experimenting," Sara said, waving.

"Hi'ya, *Morton*," Ruby said, mocking his name.

He nodded, standing awkwardly over the two girls, expecting them to get up. Neither of them did.

"Sara," he said at last, "I'd like to speak with you."

"Go ahead," she said, busily painting black polish onto Ruby's big toe.

"Privately," he said, annoyed that she didn't treat him with more respect.

She pulled a face. "Say what you want—Ruby don't care."

He wondered how much Ruby knew. Was she aware that Sara had put him in the most compromising position of his life? Did she know that Sara had banked twelve thousand dollars to do so? And she wasn't even embarrassed or sorry when he'd found out. "It's a lotta money, Morty," she'd said, completely without guilt. "Couldn't turn it down." Then she'd made love to him in a way that he'd never been made love to before. And he'd continued seeing her.

He was sick. He knew that.

Lovesick. Only now he made sure there were no hidden cameras concealed in the apartment.

Ruby took the hint. She stood up and yawned. "I'm goin' by Tower Records," she said. "Want anything?"

"Wouldn't mind comin' with you," Sara said, wistfully entertaining the idea until she noticed Morton's furious expression. She grimaced. "Guess not."

Ruby slipped on a pair of ugly sandals and left.

"I can't imagine why you're friendly with her," Morton said, standing stiffly in place.

"That's 'cause you got no imagination," Sara said, popping a Gummi Bear in her mouth. She jumped up, throwing her arms around his waist. "That's okay, Daddy, 'cause I got 'nuff for us both, don't I, honey buns?"

"Yes, Sara, you do," he said, feeling an overpowering rush of excitement, the kind of sexual anticipation he hadn't experienced in twenty-five years.

Sara pulled her skimpy tank top over her head and dropped her shorts. She wore no underwear. She was as skinny as a ten-year-old boy, but her lack of curves only heightened Morton's ferocious excitement. His eyes fastened on her almost pubescent nakedness, drifting down to her thick tangle of tangerine pubic hair.

"What's it gonna be?" Sara asked with a sly smile. "Waitress? Lawyer? Schoolgirl? Or maybe you're in the mood for the little *boy* thing..." She smiled knowingly, twisting her pubic hair. "C'*mon*, bunny rabbit, it's your call."

"Little boy," he said, his voice constricted.

"Ohhh...you *are* naughty today. If I was playing nanny, I'd be forced to spank a bad boy like you."

And so the games began.

And Morton Sharkey gave no more thought to his betrayal of Lucky Santangelo.

★　　★　　★

Santo had noticed that his mother was in an extremely good mood. This meant he could ask her for anything he wanted and more than likely get it.

He wandered into the kitchen where she was busily preparing pasta sauce.

"Hi, Mom," he said, slouching over to stand beside her.

Donna beamed. "Santo. Come. Taste," she said, shoving a spoonful of steaming, rich meat sauce into his mouth.

It burnt his tongue. *Dumb cunt!* he wanted to yell. Instead he said, "S'good," hating the garlicky flavor almost as much as he hated her.

Donna knew that when she cooked—which wasn't often—she was the best. "Only good?" she questioned, confident of his answer.

"Awesome!" Santo responded. He knew what was expected of him.

"I'm freezing a batch of it," Donna said. "You can invite friends over and enjoy it together."

She was so stupid she didn't even know he had no friends. The kids at school shouted names at him like "Rich Jerk" and "Fat, Greasy Wop." They hated him, and he hated them back.

He didn't care. One day he'd burn the whole friggin' school down with everyone in it, then she could meet his so-called friends all laid out in the morgue—burnt to a crisp.

"I was thinkin', Mom," he said, perching his

considerable bulk on a stool. "Wouldn't it be bitchin' if I got a new car?"

"What are you *talking* about?" Donna exclaimed, expertly chopping zucchini. "I bought you a Corvette for your birthday."

"Since I had that dumb accident, it's not the same," he complained, hunching his shoulders.

"We had it repaired."

"I know—but, Mom," he waited until he had her full attention, "I *really* want a Ferrari."

"A *Ferrari*?" she said, shocked.

"Why not?" he whined. "Mohammed's dad bought him one, and Mohammed's the geek of the decade."

"It's not a practical car for school," Donna said sternly, adding the chopped zucchini to her pasta sauce.

"I'd drive it weekends, and take the Corvette to school," he explained, making it sound like an extremely sensible idea.

"Well..." She hesitated. It was so damn difficult saying no to her son.

"C'mon, Mom," he said persuasively. "It's not like I do drugs, or go out an' get wasted like most of the kids in my school. I could, like, *really* do things that'd bum you out."

Donna shook her head. Was this a veiled threat? No, not from her sweet boy. Santo was too good. "Two cars," she mused, thinking it over. "George will never agree..."

"Who cares what George says," Santo said bitterly, his puffy features hardening. "He's not my father. My father was killed, and you can't replace him with George, so don't try."

"I would never do that," Donna objected.

Santo went for a new angle. "Putting George's feelings first sucks," he said, scowling.

"I put *you* first, Santo," Donna replied, crushed that he would think otherwise.

He glared at her accusingly, as if he didn't believe her.

"When I was your age we had nothing," Donna said, shaking her head at the memories. "We were so poor—"

"'S'not the same," Santo interrupted. "You lived in some little village."

"A village I shall take you to one of these days," Donna promised, remembering her humble roots with a certain amount of nostalgia. "My relatives will be so proud of you. *I'm* so proud of you."

"If my dad was alive, *he'd* buy me a Ferrari," Santo said, going for the full guilt trip. If this didn't get her, nothing would.

Donna stared at her son, finally capitulating because it was too difficult saying no. "If it's what you really want," she said and sighed.

He beamed. She was so damned easy.

"Go to the showroom, pick out the model you like."

He jumped up and hugged her. "You're the best mom in L.A."

The title alone was worth the expenditure. "George is staying in Chicago overnight," she said. "If you like, we can catch a movie, then have dinner at Spago."

Much as he wouldn't mind pigging out on the delicious pizza at Spago, he couldn't face an evening alone with his mother. "No, Ma, I can't," he mumbled. "Too much homework."

"Oh," she said, her face sagging with disappointment. "Can't it wait?"

"You'd be bummed if I fell behind on my grades, wouldnja, Ma?"

"I suppose so." She paused; the two martinis she'd had earlier were giving her a nice, steady buzz. "It's just that this afternoon I concluded a very exciting deal. I thought we could celebrate."

Like her closing some big deal was anything new. "What deal?" he said, not interested but smart enough to know that since she'd agreed to the Ferrari he should jolly her along.

"I'm taking control of a Hollywood studio," she announced proudly. "Panther Studios."

This was more like it. Thoughts of stardom raced through his head. "Can I be an actor?" he asked, imagining the possibilities.

Donna's thin mouth curved into an indulgent smile. "You can be anything you want."

Shit! This was good news. A Hollywood studio. Venus Maria was an actress, and all actresses were prepared to do anything to get into movies, everyone knew that. If his mother owned a studio, the power would reflect on him. In fact, he'd be able to make sure Venus Maria starred in every film the studio made.

This was a sign. First the Ferrari, now a big movie studio. The time had come to contact Venus.

Of course, he wouldn't reveal his identity

yet, instead he'd write her an anonymous letter informing her he was on her side, and that soon, when the time was right, they'd be married, joined together in every way.

"Gotta go, Mom," he said, sliding toward the kitchen door. "See ya later."

Once up in his room he hunched over his computer and began composing his first letter to HER.

Recently he'd purchased a stars' map and looked up Venus's address. Then he'd taken an investigative drive up to her house in the Hollywood Hills, gotten out of his car, and peered through the large wrought-iron gates. A guard had emerged and waved him away.

Freaking moron. Didn't he know that one day he, Santo, would live there with Venus, it was only a matter of time.

He'd thought about telling the asshole that's what was going to happen. The jerk probably wouldn't believe him.

No. He could wait. One day, everyone would know.

He did his best to concentrate on the letter, but somehow or other it was impossible to stop his mind from wandering.

He imagined Venus without her clothes, naked and available, licking her jammy lips, prancing around the stage just for him...

And when she saw what he had to offer...Oh boy! Venus Maria would be some happy babe.

Jeez! He was getting the biggest boner just writing to her. Why hadn't he done it before?

He unzipped his pants, fumbled for his

dick, and thought about her some more. She was some horny piece of ass, and one day she would be all his.

He decided he had more exciting things to do with his hands than play with a computer. Her letter would have to wait.

21

It was past ten when Lucky and Alex drove up to Armando's Strip Palace and Pool Bar—a gaudy, sprawling place that once again appeared to be in the middle of nowhere.

"Another classy joint," Lucky remarked, taking in the signs, which proclaimed the usual LIVE NUDE GIRLS, and the unusual—NAKED WICKED WILD WILD WIMMIN!

"Sure you wanna go in?" Alex asked, pulling into the jammed parking lot right behind Daisy's yellow Chevrolet.

"Yes," Lucky said, feeling light-headed and ready for anything. "This looks like a happenin' place."

Alex realized there was no way she was backing out. Not Lucky Santangelo. Not this woman. "Okay, let's go," he said, resignedly parking his Porsche.

Daisy met them as they got out of the car. "I gotta go in the back way," she mumbled. "Armando's shitty rules. Where's my hundred bucks?"

"Don't you trust me?" Lucky asked, thinking this woman was the least likely candidate to have a name like Daisy.

"I ain't in this business t'trust no one," Daisy retorted, hands on hips.

Lucky fumbled in her purse, pulled a hundred-dollar bill from her wallet, and handed it over.

"Tell the guy at the door you're friends a mine," Daisy cackled. "*That'll* get you a bad seat." She teetered off on stiletto heels, still laughing.

"Lucky," Alex said with a deep sigh of resignation. "What the *fuck* are we doing here?"

"Getting a drink," she said, pushing back her long dark hair.

"How about food?" he said, adding sotto voce, "To put in your hollow leg."

"Ha ha!"

They entered Armando's. It was four times as big as the last place and just as overcrowded. Three pool tables were lined up on one side of the room. A live band blasted their version of a well-known Loretta Lynn song, and a long, curved bar on which a red-haired stripper cavorted was jammed with beer-swigging cowboys and a scattering of women all dressed up in their cowgirl best.

"Hmm..." said Lucky, surveying the room with a jaundiced eye. "It seems to be one of those country and western deals with a twist. Wanna do a little quick-stepping, pardner?"

"There's something seriously wrong with you," Alex said sternly.

"Why?" she replied, feeling pretty good.

"You're not normal."

"What's normal?" she asked flippantly, deciding that in spite of himself Alex was quite a sport.

"Well..." He thought for a moment. "You're not exactly quiet."

She burst out laughing. "Oh, I see. You're into quiet, subservient women, is that it?"

"You know what I mean," he said, aggravated.

No. She didn't know what he meant, and quite frankly, she didn't care. He was here for a purpose, and that purpose was to entertain her.

God! Her world was starting to spin. Better get a grip. Better get it together.

There were no free tables, so once again they found two seats at the bar, crowding in between a couple of surly cowboys. Alex slipped the hostess a twenty, informing her he expected the next available table.

"Jesus!" he muttered as they sat down. "If I don't get into a fight tonight, I'm the luckiest guy around."

Once again Lucky brushed back her long hair and laughed. She knew she was drunk, but it didn't matter. Tonight she wasn't Lucky Santangelo—businesswoman, head of a movie studio, mother. Tonight she was single and free, and she could do whatever she felt like. And right now she felt like having another drink. Only problem—Alex wasn't keeping up with her.

"One tequila," she said, concealing a hiccup. "We'll watch Daisy do her thing, play a game of pool, then we're on our way. That's a Santangelo promise."

"You and your promises," he said grimly, glad that he'd stayed comparatively sober. *Somebody* had to know what they were doing.

"No, really," Lucky insisted. "You *will* meet Gino later. You're gonna love his stories."

Alex knew there was no way he was getting anywhere near Gino tonight. "Yeah, yeah," he said.

"Y'know, Alex," Lucky said, placing an understanding hand on his shoulder. "I've been doing all the talking. Isn't it about time we got into you?"

"Why?" he said, stone-faced.

"I still can't get over the fact you never married."

"Hey, listen, just because *you* were married three times..."

"My take is you must have an overpowering mother whom you secretly hate."

"That's not funny," he said, frowning.

"Did I hit it right on?"

He didn't reply.

The waitress came over and told them she had a ringside table ready for them. They moved over just as Daisy bounced onto the stage like a dynamo.

Instead of a pole, Armando's had a fake silver palm tree stuck in the middle portion of the long bar. Daisy worked the palm tree like it was her most intimate lover, doing things to it most people only dreamed about.

The audience began throwing money, stamping, and whistling their approval. Daisy got off on the applause. She squatted down, thighs spread, and began collecting dollar bills.

"Amazing muscle control," Lucky murmured. "I hope they bring a guy on next."

"Are you *crazy*?"

"C'mon, Alex, surely you're into equality between the sexes?"

"Bullshit."

"Scratch a movie director and find a chauvinist," she taunted.

"What is it with you?" he asked, exasperated.

"Nothing you'd understand."

By the time Daisy took it all off, the audience was out of control. Daisy sure knew how to play a crowd. When she was finished, she joined them at their table, out of breath and triumphant, her jet skin glistening with perspiration.

"What you wanna know?" she asked, flopping into a chair.

"Alex, *you* do the talking," Lucky said.

He shot her a look. *She* was the one who'd dragged him to this joint, and now she expected *him* to ask the questions. Surely she knew he couldn't give a damn about this black stripper, even if the woman did have an unbelievable body.

Still...visually...in his movie, Daisy would definitely score. Especially the picking up the money with her thighs bit.

"What's your story, Daisy?" he asked wearily. "Fucked by your father? Beaten by your stepfather? Raped by an uncle? Then you ran away from home…Am I getting there?"

Daisy twirled her fingers through her long red wig and ordered a beer. "My ole man was a Baptist minister," she said primly. "Wouldn't allow no sex talk in our house. My daddy was one *strict* motherfucker. Me? I'm a workin' girl with two kids an' a lover. I make enough t'see my kids are done right by."

"Not exactly the story you were expecting, huh, Alex?" Lucky said, needling him.

"Where's your lover tonight?" Alex asked, ignoring Lucky and concentrating on Daisy.

"Babysitting. She's into stayin' home."

"*She?*" Alex questioned.

Daisy winked at Lucky. "Honey, *y'*know what I mean. Once you-all had pussy, y'don' wanna bother with some big, dirty ole *man*. Cock ain't all it's cracked up to be—right, baby?"

"Thanks for sharing that," said Alex, not fond of the direction this conversation was taking.

"So," Lucky said, amused at Alex's discomfort. "Where can we reach you?"

Daisy swigged beer from the bottle. "Why you wanna reach me?"

"In case Alex puts you in his movie."

Daisy held out both her hands, admiring her long, curved nails painted a deep, sparkly purple. "I ain't no actress," she said modestly.

"No acting involved," Alex said.

"Absolutely not," Lucky added. "You'll be in the strip scene. Y'know—that's the one where two guys are talking…"

Daisy got it. "Yeah, *that* ole scene," she said.

223

"Two guys with some babe behind them shovin' her big titties in their faces."

"Right!" Lucky said. Daisy was smarter than she'd thought.

They both laughed.

"Write down a phone number where my casting people can reach you," Alex said, handing her a book of matches and a pen.

Daisy scrawled her name and number.

Alex wanted out. "Can we go now?" he said to Lucky.

"One game of pool. You promised."

He looked over at the pool tables and was relieved to see they were all occupied. "No free table," he said, trying not to sound too pleased.

"*I'll* get us one," Lucky said, jumping up.

"No," he said forcefully. "We're outta here while we're still walking."

Her eyes were dark and challenging; she liked a man who fought back. "Don't wanna get beat, huh?"

He was too sober and she was too drunk. It wasn't worth an argument.

They said good night to Daisy and headed for the parking lot.

The cold night air hit Lucky like a block of cement. She stumbled, almost falling.

Alex caught her in his arms. "Whatever happened to your hollow leg?" he asked, breathing in her sensual, musky scent.

"Don't feel so good," she mumbled, leaning heavily against him.

He couldn't help enjoying her sudden vulnerability. This was a new, dependent Lucky. This was how women were meant to be.

Without thinking, he brought his lips down on hers, kissing her roughly, passionately.

It was an electric kiss, surprising both of them.

Lucky knew she was drunk, knew she shouldn't be doing this, knew it was a big mistake. But all she could see were the pictures of Lennie with the naked blond flashing before her eyes. And all she could feel was hurt and disappointment that he'd let her down.

Lennie had deserted her so cruelly. There was only one way to get even.

And Alex was it.

Two lovers in a cheap motel. Thrashing around on the bed, their clothes leaving an untidy trail across the threadbare carpet. They both felt the urgency of instant sex. No foreplay required. He was harder than he'd ever been, and she was ready.

He touched her breasts, so very beautiful...

She touched his cock, thrilling to the urgent throbbing of his desire...

She moaned when he entered her. An anguished moan of passion and carnal abandon.

They were both into the ride. It was pure, lustful pleasure tempered by no inhibitions— nothing more than a great, uncomplicated fuck.

It was exactly what Lucky needed. And when she came, it released the pent-up anger and hurt and pain and all the other frustrations she'd been holding on to.

Alex shuddered to a climax simultaneously. "Jesus *Christ*!" he exclaimed.

She didn't respond. She rolled away from him, curling into a tight ball, hugging her knees to her chest.

He didn't pursue her.

Within minutes they were both asleep.

Book Three

22

Lying near the southeastern corner of Sicily—high above the dusty road from Noto to Ragusa—was a tiny village that was Donna's birthplace. She was born in a small house still occupied by her eighty-seven-year-old father, two of her younger sisters and their husbands, her brother Bruno and his wife, and various nieces and nephews. Donna supported everyone, sending them regular food packages, clothes, and luxuries unheard of in such a primitive place.

Since her father had sold her off as a young girl, she'd only visited once; however, she was a legend in the small village and spoken of in revered terms.

Donna's village was mostly rugged terrain, but a forty-five- minute walk down through the steep hills led to a cliff, below which was the seashore and a catacomb of mysterious caves. Folklore said they were haunted; very few people ever went near them.

As children, Donna, Bruno, and her young love, Furio, had spent much of their spare time exploring the caves. They were not frightened of ancient rumors, although the village elders spoke of ghosts and even worse. Legend had it that after the disastrous earthquake of 1668 that destroyed many towns, the caves became a place where thieves and murderers made their home. When one of them raped and killed a local girl, the village men—filled with wrath—raided the caves and butchered them all, burying them beneath the ground in a mass grave.

Donna, Furio, and Bruno did not believe the stories; the caves were their playground and nothing could spoil it.

When Donna was taken off to America to become a bride, Bruno and Furio stopped going there.

It wasn't until Donna sent for Bruno and told him of her plan that he even thought of going back. When she explained what had to be done to avenge the murder of her husband, Bruno was in complete agreement that the caves presented the perfect solution. Located at the bottom of the cliff—dank, deserted, difficult to get in or out of—they were a natural prison.

Lennie Golden knew this to be true. For Lennie had been held captive for eight long weeks, his left ankle shackled to an unmovable rock, allowing him only enough room to hobble around the musty cave.

Every morning he awoke to the same demoralizing sight: a shaft of light filtering in from somewhere high above; the walls of his cave mossy and damp; and he could hear and smell the sea somewhere close.

How close? The dampness made him think that it was dangerously close. What if there was a storm? Would his cave be flooded?

Would he die a grim and watery death because there was no way he could escape?

His home.

His cell.

His place of incarceration.

And the worst thing of all was that he had no idea why he was there. He could only assume he'd been kidnapped for ransom. But if that was the case, why hadn't Lucky or the studio paid the money?

He'd been imprisoned for eight interminable weeks of misery. He knew exactly how long it was because he'd been gouging marks into the walls of the cave as each day passed. During that time, the only people he'd seen were the two men who brought him his daily meal of bread and cheese. Once a week they replaced the cheese with a hunk of indigestible meat, and twice they'd given him fruit. Right now he was so hungry he would have eaten anything.

Neither of his captors—both surly-looking men in their late thirties—spoke English. They avoided having anything to do with him, shunning eye contact and all conversation.

One or the other of them appeared every day at the same time, placing the food on an upturned crate and leaving immediately. Every few days they emptied the bucket that was his makeshift toilet, at the same time replacing another bucket—filled with murky water—that was his only washing facility.

There was no mirror, or anything to groom

himself with. He suspected he resembled a wild man, with long matted hair and an eight-week growth of beard. His clothes were filthy. Once he'd tried to wash them, discovering it wasn't worth freezing to death while waiting for them to dry.

He could accept the food and toilet situation. He could even accept the bone-chilling cold and damp, and the rats that scurried around the cave all night long—sometimes running over his legs as he lay on the stiff wooden planks that did duty as his bed.

What he could not accept was the hopeless despair and never-ending boredom of having nothing to occupy his mind. Day after day, sitting there, unable to read or write, listen to music or watch TV.

Nothing.

HE...WAS...SLOWLY...GOING...CRAZY.

Lately he'd begun talking aloud. Listening to himself was a small comfort, for at least it was the sound of a human voice. He'd started going over old routines from his stand-up comedy days, and scenes from his movies. Sometimes he spoke to Lucky as if she were there with him.

In his mind, he often retraced the events of that fateful morning. He remembered being so happy because Lucky was flying in. He'd created a vivid mind picture of her running off the plane into his arms. They fit so well together, they always had.

He recalled leaving the hotel, the doorman pointing to his car. A new driver, not his regular one. Shortly after they'd set off for the airport, the driver had offered him coffee. He'd accepted, gulping down the hot liquid—enjoying the strong, almost bitter flavor.

After that—nothing—no more memories until he'd awakened on the floor of the cave, chained like a rabid dog, with nobody there to explain what was happening.

When the first of the men had appeared, he'd thought he was saved. But no, it was merely the beginning of his nightmare.

Now there was nothing he could do except wait, desperately trying to keep himself sane. And to hope that Lucky was searching for him.

Sometimes he wondered...

Was he dead?

Was this hell?

HE DIDN'T KNOW.

23

It was five-thirty in the morning when Lucky awoke. Her mouth felt like a rat had died in it. Her head was pounding relentlessly. She was aching all over and craved a cigarette.

She turned her head and sneaked a look at Alex. Naked and snoring, he was sprawled across the rumpled bed, completely relaxed.

Oh, God! What had she done?

Moving quietly, she got off the bed and set about stealthily gathering her clothes from the floor. Then she crept into the cramped bathroom and hurriedly dressed, not bothering to shower because she had only one thought in mind—a fast, silent exit.

Outside the motel room, in the middle of Nowheresville, it was murky and still dark. Bypassing Alex's Porsche, she walked briskly to the deserted renting office where she punched a bell on the desk, waiting impatiently for someone to respond. A mangy dog sniffed her ankles and wandered off. She shivered, pulling up the collar of her jacket.

Finally a tousle-haired teenager appeared, tucking a grubby Star Trek T-shirt into his pants. "Kinda early, ma'am," he said, with sleep in his eyes. "What kin I do for you?"

"I need a limo," Lucky said, drumming her fingers on the counter, fervently hoping she could be on her way before Alex discovered she was missing.

"A what?" the teenager asked blankly.

"Limousine. Hired car. Anything to get me out of here."

"I dunno..." the boy said vaguely. "The gas station won't open 'til six, an' I don't reckon they got no limousines. My grand-dad'll know. Only thing is, he's sleepin', an' it ain't worth my butt t'wake him."

"Do *you* have a car?"

He rubbed his chin. "Me?"

"Yes. You."

"I got me a sixty-eight Mustang," he said proudly. "Souped it up good."

"Will it get me from here to L.A.?"

"Lady—"

"*Will* it?"

Wrinkling his brow he mumbled, "'Scuse me, ma'am, but ain't you in that foreign car parked outside cabin four?"

She sighed impatiently. "Let's make this a short story. I have to get out of here now. How much will it cost me to borrow your Mustang?"

Five hundred dollars later she was on her way, putting as much distance as possible between herself and Alex. She didn't regret what had happened. She'd wanted it, in fact, she'd been moving toward it ever since Alex had stepped into her office.

In retrospect, though, maybe she would have been better off sleeping with the Travolta clone from the bar. Less complicated.

Oh God! She hoped Alex wasn't going to turn out to be a problem.

No way. He used women, she was sure of that. It shouldn't bother him that the situation had been reversed.

Alex Woods.

In future she'd make sure it was all business.

The teenager in the Star Trek T-shirt had told the truth, his old Mustang sped along the freeway like a revved-up sports car. She tuned the radio to a soul station, listening to Otis Redding sing the classic "Dock of the Bay" as she cruised along the freeway.

Instead of heading for L.A., she drove toward Palm Springs. She'd promised Alex he would meet Gino, but it was not to be. She wanted to be alone with her father—if Alex insisted on meeting him, he could do so on his own time.

When she arrived at Gino's estate she found him up and dressed, busily screaming at his stockbroker on the phone, red in the face and as happy as a teenager who'd just gotten laid.

"Kiddo!" he exclaimed, covering the mouthpiece. "What in hell *you* doin' here? Doncha know it's earlier than shit?"

Dear old daddy. He certainly had a way with words.

She hugged him, marveling that he never seemed to age. Gino was eighty-one years old, and looked about sixty-five with his thick, slightly graying hair and youthful grin. He was fit and feisty, with all his own teeth, and from the smile on Paige's face, an active sex life. In his Brooklyn youth he'd been nicknamed "Gino the Ram." Oh yes, her father certainly had a colorful past; he'd traveled a long way from his humble beginnings.

He finished with his stockbroker and banged the phone down. "The guy's a putz," he complained. "Always tellin' me the wrong thing t'do. Dunno why I listen to him, the dumb bastard costs me money every goddamn day."

"Why *do* you listen?" Lucky asked, collapsing into a chair, rummaging in her purse for a cigarette.

Gino peered at her. "What's up, kiddo? I got a strong suspicion it ain't a social call at this time of mornin'."

"I got blasted," she said ruefully. "Thought I'd share my hangover with you."

"Still livin' your life like a guy, huh?" Gino

said, shaking his head disapprovingly. "Doncha know, ladies don' get shit-faced."

She found a cigarette and lit up. "I told you once, Gino, a long time ago"—she assumed a tough guy voice—"I ain't no lady, I'm a Santangelo—just like you."

He grinned. "Yeah, yeah, could I ever forget it. You were some problem kid."

She fixed him with a winning smile. "The problem kid turned out good, huh?"

"I got no complaints." He paused a moment. "How're you *really* doin'?"

She shrugged, edgy, tired, and confused. "I'm getting there," she said, not sure *how* she was feeling.

He looked at her knowingly. "It takes time, kid."

"Yes, Gino," she nodded, wishing for a split second that she was a little girl again and could run into the protective custody of his arms. "I know that."

"We've been through a lot together, kiddo," he said, studying her with his black eyes that matched hers.

"I know that, too," she said quietly.

"Okay, so you're a Santangelo, don't ever forget it."

She smiled softly. "As if I could."

He stood up—even at his age, always on the move. "You want some tea? Coffee?"

"Nothing, thanks," she said, stifling a yawn. "Is it okay if I take a shower?"

"Use the guest room. I'll tell Paige you're here."

"Don't wake her."

"Ha! The friggin' Russian army wouldn't wake *my* wife if she wasn't ready!"

The guest room was decorated in English country pastels. It wasn't Lucky's taste, although she had to admit that Paige had done a good job.

She wandered over to the large picture window, gazing out over a manicured green lawn, a profusion of lush, purple bougainvillea bushes and an azure, kidney-shaped pool. Swimming pools gave her a bad feeling—ever since that fateful day she'd discovered her mother's body...

No! She was not taking that soul-destroying trip down memory lane. Not today.

Throwing off her clothes, she entered the bathroom, pausing for a moment in front of the full-length mirror, studying her reflection. Youthfulness ran in the family; her body—even after three children—was olive-skinned, lithe, and slender, with firm breasts and long legs.

Alex Woods hadn't seen it. After that one passionate kiss in the parking lot, things had moved at a rapid pace. A roadside motel. No conversation. Such was their lust they'd fallen on top of each other with none of the sexual niceties. Dark, fast fucking. The driven kind.

It reminded her of her wild years, when she'd bedded as many men as she'd felt like with absolutely no guilt. "Don't call me, I'll call you"—that had been her motto.

God! It seemed like a million years ago. Long before AIDS.

And then she'd met Lennie. Her true love. Her soul mate. And for the first time, her life was complete.

Thinking of Lennie, the tears finally came. She slumped down on the bathroom floor, silently sobbing out her anger and hurt and frustration until she was totally spent.

It was a cleansing, a renewal. She'd exorcised Lennie's unfaithfulness; now, finally, she could mourn him properly.

She jumped up off the floor, took an icy-cold shower, and quickly dressed. She had a sudden great yearning to see her children, hold them close and love them more than anything in the world. Gino would understand if she left immediately, so she decided to drive straight back to L.A. and spend some time with them before going to the studio.

Family first.

Business second.

And she'd still make Panther the biggest success story in town.

Lennie would want her to go on.

Lennie would want her to achieve nothing but the best.

Alex surfaced slowly. Light was creeping into the room, playing tag on his eyelids. He tried throwing his arm across his face to block the rays of early-morning sun. It didn't work.

He stretched and groaned, slowly opening his eyes. It was definitely time to get up.

For a moment he lay there, completely dis-
oriented, until gradually it all started to come
back.

Lucky Santangelo. The girl with the hollow
leg.

Lucky Santangelo. A beautiful, exciting
woman.

They'd made love in this godawful motel
room, urgent, passionate love. Now it was
morning and...where was she?

He got off the bed, tripping over his shoes
on the way to the bathroom.

She wasn't in there.

He went to the window, pulled back the
shade, and peered outside. His Porsche was
parked where he'd left it last night. Good
sign, it meant she couldn't have ventured far.

He hoped she'd gone to get them coffee. Boy,
he could sure use a cup of strong black coffee.

Picking his clothes off the floor, he returned
to the bathroom. The shower was broken,
spewing a thin stream of rust-colored water.
Forget that.

Glancing at his watch he was shocked to see
it was almost nine. He was always up by six-
thirty. Must have really needed the sleep.

Jesus, he felt good—didn't even have a
hangover. *She* was the one with the hangover.

Lucky Santangelo. Thinking of her brought
a smile to his face. In a strange way she was
a mirror image of him—a rebel—completely
unpredictable. And so wildly beautiful...

The smart move would be to take a shower back in L.A. He threw on his clothes and left the small, depressing motel room, walking the few yards to the renting office, where he encountered a weather-beaten old man sitting outside shelling peanuts while chewing tobacco.

"'Morning," Alex said cordially.

"'Morning to you, too," the old man replied, barely raising his head as he continued to shell his peanuts.

"Where's the nearest place for coffee around here?"

"There's a cafe across the street, kitty kat to t'gas station," the old man said. "Try some a Mabel's blackberry pie, s'damn good."

"Thanks," Alex said. "I'll remember that." He began to walk away, stopped, and came back. "Did you see the lady from cabin four go across there?" he asked.

"That woman took off over three hours ago," the old man said, his lined and weathered face impassive. "Borrowed my grandson's car. Gave him five hundred bucks." The old man chuckled. "He reckoned you people was drug dealers with that kinda money t'throw around."

"She gave your grandson five hundred bucks to borrow his car and then *left*?" Alex said incredulously.

The old man spat a wad of tobacco onto the ground. "That's what I said."

"I can't believe she did that."

"Wimmin," the old man said, wearily shaking his head. "Once they got you, it's damn trouble all the way. Tol' my grandson that. He don't take no heed a me, the boy's out chasin' skirt like a trackin' dawg after a bitch in heat."

"How's he getting his car back?"

"Said she's sending a driver with it. Gave him her fancy card an' everything. When he read she was with a big Hollywood studio, he said okay. If he don't get his car back, it's his own sorry fault."

Alex was in shock. How could she take off and leave him? Something about Lucky should have warned him she was not to be trusted.

On the other hand, maybe she'd observed how soundly he was sleeping and hadn't wanted to disturb him.

Whatever. The least she could have done was to leave a note.

Coffee would have to wait. He had to get back to L.A. immediately.

24

Mornings were always a busy time at Venus's house. Anthony, her handsome blond assistant, arrived early, Sven was there to take her jogging and work her out, several maids cleaned the house, and the phone never stopped ringing.

She began studying the *Gangsters* script as soon as she awoke. Lola was such a complex character—sexy and yet sad. Venus was sure she could get inside her and capture the despair and heartbreak of the woman.

She couldn't decide what to wear for her meeting with Alex Woods. Should she dress as herself? Or should she take a chance and go as Lola?

In a quandary, she called Freddie. "What do *you* think?" she asked. "I could be me, provocative, sensual, all of that." She paused. "Although he's probably seen *that* me in my videos....I mean, he *does* know who I am, doesn't he?"

"Why do you think I had such a hard time getting you in?" Freddie said, making a point.

Sometimes Freddie pissed her off. "Oh, that's nice. You sure know how to make a person feel secure."

"It wasn't easy, Venus. I had to break the image barrier, shatter his preformed opinion of you."

"Keep going, Freddie, you're really pumping my ego!"

"Go as Lola. If I know Alex, it will impress him."

Next decision. *What* was she going to wear?

She scoured her wardrobe, rejecting everything in sight, mad at herself for not thinking of it yesterday. She should have gone to one of those vintage shops on Melrose and gotten something really sensational.

What would a good-time girl in the fifties wear? Hmm...think Marilyn, or even Jayne Mansfield.

Digging deep in her closet she finally found the perfect dress, a silk number, cut on the bias, ending just above her knees. It revealed plenty of cleavage, and was form-fitting, with cute little cap sleeves that hugged the top of her perfectly shaped arms. With it she wore very high heels, gold hoop earrings, and arranged her hair on top of her head in a kind of bird's nest.

As soon as she was dressed, she ran around her house eliciting opinions. "You like this look?" she asked Sven, who was still in the gym arranging for new torture equipment to be delivered.

"Very nice," he replied, hardly noticing.

She showed her English assistant, twirling in front of him. "What do *you* think, Anthony?"

Anthony had shoulder-length white-blond hair, a muscled body, and a beauteous smile. "Divine!" he exclaimed.

Why were all the best-looking men gay? It was such a waste. Mental note—introduce him to Ron. Perhaps Anthony with his precise English accent and extra-long eyelashes could lure Ron away from Major Mogul and they could all live happily ever after.

"This was on the doorstep this morning," Anthony said, handing her an envelope marked "Personal."

She tore open the letter; it was short and to the point.

Hi, Venus,

You're hot stuff, sexy and horny. I know everything about you. Your big tits and your hairy pussy turn me on. Don't worry—I'll never

*let anyone harm you, because you're mine. I'll
always love you, even after we're married.
You'd better wait for me—it won't be long.*

X X X
An Admirer

*P.S. I jerk off thinking of you every day—I
don't have sex with anyone except you. I hope
you feel the same way.*

"Oh, Jesus!" she said, throwing the letter down
in disgust. "Another obsessed sex maniac.
How do these morons get my home address?"

Anthony shrugged. "It was here when I arrived
this morning."

"What did he do, climb over the gates?
Where was my guard?"

Anthony shrugged again. "I have no idea."

"I hate this!" she said, feeling vulnerable.
"It makes me nervous. The last time this
happened some freak got into my *bedroom*—
fortunately, I was in New York at the time."

"What did he *do*?" Anthony asked, eyes
bugging.

"I dunno, 'cause I didn't press charges.
Couldn't face going to court."

"Maybe it's *him*," Anthony said dramatically.
"Is he *dangerous*?"

"Quit making a big deal out of this," she said
sternly, not liking his tone. "Call my security people—have them check out the letter. And
always be careful who you let in."

"Yes, Venus," he said obediently.

Rodriguez appeared at the door just as she

was leaving for her meeting. He carried a bunch of white roses and had dressed for the occasion in a dark brown silk shirt, impeccably cut beige pants, a thin alligator belt that showed off his slender waistline, and snappy two-tone leather shoes.

"My princess!" he exclaimed.

She wasn't pleased that he felt free to show up unannounced.

"What do you want?" she asked none too politely.

He handed her the roses. "I am here because my heart would not stop beating, and as each beat took place I thought of you."

"Rodriguez, you really have to get some new dialogue," she said, frowning.

"What do you mean, my sweet?"

She tossed the roses at Anthony. "I don't appreciate you turning up here without calling first. I'm on my way to an important meeting."

"I thought we could have lunch."

"Not today. I'm very busy."

"Did you call your casting person? I so look forward to being in your video."

Hmm...so *that* was the reason for his enthusiasm. Everybody wanted to be a star.

"I'll have Anthony do it," she said abruptly. "Go home and wait for the phone call."

His face drooped with disappointment.

Too bad. If he thought he was going to move in on her, he could think again.

Brigette was alive with energy. It was so great waking up in the morning with something to look forward to. She couldn't wait to phone Lucky in L.A., although right now it was too early. Instead she raced into the kitchen where Anna was sitting at the table, writing.

"Guess what?" she said excitedly.

"What?" Anna asked, putting down her pen.

"Everything's starting to happen for me. I told you it would! I'm *so* buzzed!"

"I gather last night was a success?"

"Brilliant! Michel Guy asked me to come to his office today, and the photo session with Luke is set for next week. Isn't that *fantastic*!"

"You deserve it," Anna said.

"I do, don't I?" Brigette replied, laughing because she couldn't quite believe it.

Later she met with Nona, who'd devised a plan of action. First they were going to see Michel Guy, then visit Aurora to tell her about Rock 'n' Roll Jeans, and ask her if she wanted to be the first to put Brigette on *MONDO's* cover.

"Sounds good to me," Brigette said.

"Listen," Nona said. "Zan and I are going to move in together, his father has a shitload of money so rent's no problem, and I can't wait to get out of my parents's house. We wondered if you'd be interested in sharing an apartment with us?"

Brigette giggled. "*That'll* be a laugh riot,"

she said. "Zan, you—and then *me* tagging along. I don't think so."

"It's a terrific idea," Nona said persuasively. "After all, we'll be working together, and what better than to be living in the same place?"

"Well..." It *was* kind of an interesting thought. "Maybe I'll mention it to Charlotte."

"You're nineteen, Brigette, you don't need anybody's permission."

"Okay, so I'll *tell* Charlotte."

"Good. 'Cause I see wild times ahead!"

"I'm all for that," Brigette said, thinking that it was about time she started enjoying herself again. "When am I moving?"

Alex drove back to town in a state of confusion. He couldn't believe Lucky had walked out on him. Women *never* left him, it was always the reverse. How many times had he instructed his answering service to call at a certain hour to inform him of an emergency. "Sorry, gotta go," he'd say regretfully. And his female companion would obediently get up and drive herself home. Damn! This just didn't happen to him.

There had to be an excuse, a good excuse.

He tried calling the studio from his car. Kyoko informed him that Ms. Santangelo was not in yet. He felt like a fool because he didn't have her home phone number, and he wasn't about to ask her assistant. Of course, he could probably get it from Freddie. *Oh, hey—Freddie, it's me, Alex. I fucked Lucky Santangelo last night, only I never got her private number, and now she's walked out on me. Can you give it to me?*

No way.

He got through to his office.

"Where are you, Alex?" asked Lili with her usual disapproving sniff. "Everyone is worried. Your mother called three times."

"My mother's worried about *me*?" he asked, not believing it for a moment.

"Apparently Tin Lee panicked when you didn't show up for your date last night. She waited at your apartment three hours, then called Dominique. Now they've bonded. They imagined you'd been kidnapped, murdered—something like that."

"I got sidetracked."

"By a bottle of Scotch?"

"Not your business, Lili."

There was a twist of venom in her voice. "Well, Alex, if you expect me to run your production company *and* make excuses for you, I'd appreciate it if you'd let me in on your secrets."

He hated it when Lili got pissy. "I had to go to Palm Springs to see Gino Santangelo about the script," he explained.

"You could have told me."

"You're beginning to sound like a wife, Lili, and I don't even get to fuck you!"

She was unamused. "May I remind you, Alex, that you've missed two meetings this morning? And Venus Maria will be here at noon. Also, you're due to go on a location scout to Vegas this afternoon. Your plane leaves at three."

"What's Venus coming in for?"

"She's reading for Lola. You promised Freddie you'd see her."

"Does she have to?" He groaned, not looking forward to it.

"You made an appointment. It's unprofessional to cancel at this late hour."

"Fine, Lili, stop worrying, I'll be there."

"What shall I tell your mother?"

"Exactly nothing."

2 5

Lucky did a lot of thinking on the drive back from Palm Springs. In a way, she felt as if she were emerging from a dense fog—Lennie was gone, and hard as it was, she had to learn to accept it.

She drove directly to her house, where she spent time with her children. She picked up baby Gino, holding him close, allowing herself to be enveloped by his soothing warmth and helplessness. The realization that her children needed her swept over her. One thing she knew for sure—she would always be there for them.

Maria was racing around the house as usual. She had more energy than her mother—which was really saying something. She jumped up and down with delight when Lucky told her they'd spend the morning together. "Mommy, Mommy, read me story...I wanna story... *Pleeease!*" she begged.

"Okay," Lucky said, and sat down and read to Maria from a colorful book about Larry the Lamb and Petey the Petunia.

Maria collapsed with mirth as she listened to her mother assume the various voices. "Now we go swimming, Mommy. Now! Now!" she shrieked when Lucky finished reading.

Instead of swimming, Lucky took her daughter for a long walk along the beach, then promised that over the weekend they'd go out and choose her a puppy. Maria was ecstatic.

Cee Cee informed her that Venus had called. Lucky was well aware she'd been neglecting her friends, and she resolved to do something about it.

Arriving at Panther after twelve, she drove across the lot, parking in her usual spot.

Kyoko was at his desk in the outer office.

"I'm sorry about yesterday, Ky," she said on her way into her private domain. "I had to get out of here or go totally insane. Did you reschedule the appointments I missed?"

"Everything's taken care of," he replied, following her in. "I thought you might be late, so I canceled all your morning meetings, too."

"Why?" she said wryly. "Was I that out of control yesterday?"

"It seemed like you were about to be."

"Very astute, Ky. I had an interesting trip, and now I'm back."

"You probably needed the break," Kyoko said sympathetically.

"I did. Only today I'm being punished big time. I have a *major* hangover—any aspirin around here?"

He fetched her aspirin, a mug of strong black coffee, and a large glass of fresh orange juice. Then he placed her phone list in front of her.

She scanned the names, noting that Alex Woods had called twice. She had no intention of calling him—it was probably better to give him time to cool off, then, when they met again, it would be merely business.

For a moment she allowed her mind to wander, remembering Alex in bed...hot, fast sex...

No! Alex was a one-night revenge fuck. It would *never* happen again.

"Uh, Ky..." she said, trying to sound as casual as possible. "If Alex Woods phones back, find out what it's in reference to. I don't want to speak to him unless it has something to do with *Gangsters*. Take care of it, okay?"

"Yes, Lucky," Kyoko said. It was not for him to ask questions that were obviously none of his business.

"And get Venus for me," Lucky added, gulping down two aspirin with the orange juice.

Kyoko connected with Venus's house and spoke to Anthony. "She's not home," he said. "Shall I try her on her car phone?"

"Please."

A few seconds later Venus was on the line, sounding delighted. "This is like thought telepathy," she said. "Did Cee Cee tell you I tried to reach you at home last night?"

"I'd *really* like to see you," Lucky said. "It's been too long since we got together. You don't happen to be free for lunch?"

"Unfortunately, no," Venus said, sounding disappointed. "How about dinner tonight?"

"Works for me. I'll have Kyoko make a reservation at Morton's."

"Great! We can trash every guy in town, I love doing that!" Venus paused for a moment before continuing. "Uh...I wasn't going to mention this, 'cause I know it's your movie, but I'm on my way to see Alex Woods. I'm reading for Lola in *Gangsters.*"

"Lola?" Lucky said, surprised that Venus would consider such a small part. "That's not a starring role."

"I know, but *your* friend and *my* agent, Freddie, assures me I should do it, 'cause it'll showcase me in a different light."

"Trust Freddie to come up with a good idea."

"I've been studying the script, which I *love. Now* I know why you wanted to make this movie."

"Are you seeing Alex today?"

"In about ten minutes. So...if he should ask you about me..."

"Alex has the final say on who he casts. If it were my decision, you'd be Lola—although you'd bust the budget. Last week Alex signed Johnny Romano."

"According to Freddie, he had to fight to get me in to see the great Mr. Woods, which—as you can imagine—does not thrill me."

"I'm sure it doesn't."

"*You've* been working with him, what's he like?"

Lucky reached for a cigarette, her addiction worsening every day. "I thought *you* were the one who knew all about him," she said in a non-committal tone.

"Only the stuff one of his ex-girlfriends couldn't wait to tell me."

"What was it she said again?"

"Hmm…let me see…oh, yeah—only screws Asians and doesn't give head."

"Sounds like a great guy," Lucky said dryly.

"You should know."

"What do you mean by *that*?"

"C'mon, Lucky," Venus pleaded. "Give me the goods. Is he the pain in the ass everyone says he is?"

"Alex seems to be an okay guy," Lucky said, choosing her words carefully. "He's gotten a bad rap in the press. I'm sure you'll get along with him."

"If you happen to speak to him later, find out what he thought of me."

"Sure," Lucky said casually. "Maybe I will."

And then again, maybe I won't.

★ ★ ★

By the time Venus finished talking to Lucky, she was pulling up to Alex's production offices.

A guard waved her into the parking lot with a welcoming beam and an enthusiastic, "Can I have your autograph for my sister? She's your biggest fan."

How many times had she heard *that* line.

She got out of her car, smoothing down the skirt of her clinging silk dress. The guard's eyes were all over her, inspecting every available inch as she scrawled her signature on the grubby slip of paper he thrust her way. Her security advisors had warned her never to drive around L.A. by herself. Too bad—she enjoyed being alone in her car, listening to the latest CDs, thinking about things, generally relaxing. If she used a driver, it was a whole different trip. Although since she and Cooper had broken up, she never went anywhere unaccompanied at night.

Marriage to Cooper had been fun while it lasted; she'd been comfortable being faithful to one man.

A pity he hadn't felt the same way.

An exquisite Asian girl met her at the entrance to Alex's building. "Hi, I'm France," the girl said, extending a small, well-manicured hand. "Welcome to Woodsan Productions. We are honored to have you here. Please follow me."

Hmm…nice greeting. Perhaps Alex Woods was anxious to see her after all.

France led her into a large reception area with framed posters of all of Alex's movies on the walls. An impressive collection.

"Alex is running a few minutes late," France said apologetically. "May I get you something? Tea? Coffee? Spring water?"

Venus settled for an Evian and the latest issue of *Rolling Stone*. This was a new experience—she hadn't been kept waiting in years. Was he testing her? Seeing if she was a prima donna?

After a twenty-minute wait, by which time she was getting more than a little impatient, another Asian woman appeared. This one was older and strikingly attractive.

"I'm Lili, Alex Woods's executive assistant," the woman said, introducing herself with a warm smile. "Alex had to go out of town unexpectedly last night. He extends his heartfelt apologies for being late, he should be here momentarily."

"How momentarily?" Venus asked. She was not inclined to wait much longer, it wasn't good for her image.

"Very soon," Lili assured her, adding a convincing, "He's so looking forward to meeting you."

I bet, Venus thought, her confidence level sinking fast. *Freddie forced me on him. He's never heard of me, and if he has, he hates everything about me.*

Why was she putting herself in this vulnerable position when she didn't have to? She was a star, for crissakes, it wasn't necessary to wait around for anyone—especially Alex Woods with his chauvinist reputation.

"Another Evian?" Lili inquired.

Venus stood up. "You know what," she said pleasantly. "I can't wait any longer. Please tell *Mr.* Woods, it was uh...a pleasure *almost* meeting him."

What she really wanted to say was *I'm pissed off, I'm out of here, and tell your rude, fucking boss to shove it.*

Lili looked visibly distressed as she tried to think of a way to stop Venus from leaving. "He'll be right here," she said soothingly. "I spoke to him on his car phone minutes ago and he was almost downstairs."

"That's all right," Venus said graciously. "We'll reschedule."

Freddie Leon's image flashed before her eyes. "No Oscar," he said sternly. "Forget about your pride and stay."

Sorry, Freddie, not even for you.

She was at the door, with Lili trailing her, when Alex made his entrance. Unshaven and harassed, he brushed past Venus, not even noticing her. "Shit!" he said to Lili. "The goddamn traffic. Don't blame me."

"Alex," Lili said evenly, but with an underlying edge of steel, "this is Venus Maria. She was just about to leave; however, I am sure *you* can persuade her to stay."

He took a look at the platinum blond superstar. Not bad. She'd dressed as her interpretation of Lola and it almost worked.

"Sorry, honey," he said, flashing the little-boy killer smile that had gotten him out of a million predicaments. "Why'n't you come back in, an' we'll talk."

The "honey" didn't please her. Too patronizing.

The smile was cute. Calculated though; he probably used it on women purely to get his own way.

He was not perfectly handsome like Cooper. He was bigger, rougher, more masculine. In fact, he was quite attractive in an overpowering, macho way.

Bet you love getting blow jobs, she thought. *Wonder why you don't return the compliment.*

"Five minutes," she said boldly. "I'm sure that's long enough to convince you I'm your Lola."

26

A Chanel suit seemed appropriate. Navy blue with white braid trim and neat gold buttons. Daytime diamonds. Her hair styled to reflect the life of an extremely successful business-woman.

Donna Landsman, née Donatella Bonnatti, stood back from the full-length mirror, admiring her reflection.

Yes, she looked the part—no vestige of Donatella visible. There was no way Lucky Santangelo would ever know. And Donna was not about to tell her. Not yet.

Donna often wondered what her late husband's reaction would be if he could see her now. So cool and sophisticated. So worldly. In her new role, she wouldn't look twice at an uncouth lout like Santino, with his disgusting bathroom habits and foul mouth. In spite of his faults, she'd willed herself to never forget that Santino was her children's father, and as such he deserved the respect of having his death properly avenged.

So far, she was doing an excellent job. First Lennie Golden—and today Lucky's precious Panther Studios. She'd even discovered where Brigette Stanislopoulos was, and she had a plan in mind to deal with her, too.

Yesterday she'd spoken to her brother, Bruno, in Sicily. He'd assured her everything was under control. Lennie was their prisoner, and nobody except he and Furio knew. Just as she'd thought, the caves were the perfect hiding place.

It gave her a great sense of exhilaration to know that she had Lucky Santangelo's husband captive in a place where nobody could find him. In fact, even better, everyone thought he was dead. What a masterful piece of planning *that* was.

Of course, eventually, Lucky would find out, Donna would make sure of that. But not until Lucky was involved with another man— maybe even planning marriage. *That's* the time Donna would arrange to have Lennie set free and returned to his wife. *That* would be Lucky's real punishment.

In the meantime, after taking over Panther she would give the order to deal with Lucky's father, the infamous Gino. He was an old man now, he'd be easy to take care of.

It made her proud that she was going to be responsible for the downfall of the Santangelo family. Bad blood had existed for so many years, and the Santangelos had always come out on top.

Well, she, Donna Landsman, was finally changing all that.

With that thought foremost in her mind, she set off for Panther Studios and retribution.

"See if Charlie Dollar's on the lot, and ask him if he'd like to lunch with me," Lucky said, thinking that she wouldn't mind a dose of Charlie's light relief.

Kyoko did as Lucky asked, and informed her that Charlie *was* on the lot and would be delighted to see her.

They met in the private dining area in the commissary—Charlie as dapper and as mismatched as ever in baggy corduroy pants, a flapping Hawaiian shirt, and blacker than black shades. Lucky, cool in a white Armani suit.

Charlie grinned his maniacal grin. "Hi'ya, gorgeous," he said. "It's about time you came up for food an' conversation."

"It's great to see you, Charlie. How was Europe?"

He gestured expansively. "The old movie

star slayed 'em. My film's doin' boffo biz— a direct quote from *Variety*."

Lucky nodded. "I know, I'm excited with the figures."

Charlie pressed his stubby, nicotine-stained fingers together. "I'll tell you what it is. Give the great unwashed something they wanna see, and they'll fight their way into the theater."

"You underestimate yourself, Charlie. It's you and your special magic that pulls them in."

"No, babe," he quipped. "It's that scene in the shower where they get an eyeful of my bare butt. *Nobody's* seen an ass like that in years!"

"Same old Charlie," she said, reaching over and squeezing his hand affectionately.

"S'good t'see you, too, Lady Boss."

"Hey," she objected, "how come you've always got some crazy title for me?"

He raised his extravagant eyebrows. "Maybe you prefer Mafia Princess?"

"Let's not start with that again," she said sternly.

He threw up his hands in mock dismay. "Okay, okay, don't shoot!"

"Very amusing."

"I always like t'go for the laugh."

"Don't you just."

He raised his black shades, peering over them. "So what's happenin'?"

"I saw Gino this morning."

"Is the big man in town?"

"No, I drove down to Palm Springs last night."

"How come you didn't call? I'm the best on

a car ride. I sing, give directions, eat crack-
ers, make twenty-five pit stops."

"You're always good company, Charlie."

He chuckled. "That's what my proctologist
says!"

She smiled. "Was the European trip fun? Did
you finally meet *the* girl?"

"My love life sucks," he drawled. "They only
wanna fuck me 'cause I'm a movie star. An'
they wanna do it *fast*, so they can run off an'
boast about it to their friends. That's their whole
deal."

"I'm sure there's a nice girl out there for you
somewhere."

He laughed sardonically. "A nice girl? In
Hollywood? Baby, what planet are *you* from?
They're all hookers or actresses. Take your
pick—there ain't much difference."

"Mr. Cynicism."

"Hey," he said, waving at a couple of producers. "Here's your task. *Find* me a nice
girl, and you can be best man at my wedding."

"How about Venus?"

"How about checking your sanity?"

"She and Cooper are split."

"Big freakin' surprise."

They were in the middle of lunch when
Kyoko rushed over to their table in an extremely agitated state. "Lucky, you'd better come
to your office right away," he said.

"Is it the children? Has something happened?" she asked, imagining the worst.

"No, no...they're fine. It's business," Kyoko

said, his usual calmness ruffled. "Please, Lucky, come with me right now."

"Anything you need my help with?" Charlie offered. "'Cause you know I'm your resident movie icon in shining armor."

Lucky stood up. "Stay here. I'll be right back."

She followed Kyoko from the restaurant, waiting until they were outside before she turned on him. "What the *hell* is going on?"

"There's a woman in your office. She refuses to go."

"*What* woman?"

"I don't know. Morton Sharkey's with her. They walked right past me into your private office. They wouldn't stop."

Lucky felt a shiver of apprehension. She'd suspected Morton was up to something, she'd sensed it the other day. But what?

They walked across the lot without speaking. She entered Kyoko's office and strode through it into hers. Sitting behind her desk was a woman in a Chanel suit. Hovering nearby was an uncomfortable-looking Morton Sharkey.

"You'd better have a good explanation for this," Lucky said, her voice full of steel. "A *very* good explanation."

Donna swung around in Lucky's chair, locking eyes with the enemy. "I'm Donna Landsman, the new owner of Panther Studios," she said, her voice even colder than Lucky's. "And you, my dear, are fired."

"What?" Lucky gasped.

"I'm taking over as of now," Donna said, satisfied to note that not a flicker of recognition had crossed Lucky's face. "You have thirty minutes to clear out your personal possessions and get off the lot."

"What the *fuck* is going on?" Lucky said, angrily turning to Morton.

He cleared his throat. "It's true, Lucky," he said in a strained voice. "Mrs. Landsman has gained control of fifty-five percent of Panther stock. This gives her a controlling interest."

"It's not possible," Lucky said, in shock.

"Oh, yes." Donna gloated, savoring the moment. "It's *very* possible. And, I can assure you, it's done."

An icy calm came over Lucky. She was under attack, had to get a grip, find out exactly how this had happened. "Did you know about this, Morton?" she asked, her voice a tight coil of anger about to erupt.

He couldn't look at her. "I...heard something was going on."

Lucky's black eyes were suddenly deadly. "Don't give me that bullshit, Morton. You knew. You *had* to know, there's no way this could have happened without you."

"Lucky, I—"

Her heart was beating so fast she thought it might explode. "I bet you even helped her. Didn't you? DIDN'T YOU, MORTON?"

He shrugged helplessly. "Lucky...I had no choice."

"No choice? NO FUCKING CHOICE?" She was well aware she was screaming, but it was impossible to stop herself. "How can you stand here and say that to me? Have you no shame, you double-dealing hypocrite?"

"This is no time for name-calling," Morton muttered, truly ashamed but caught in a trap from which there was no escape.

"Oh, isn't it?" she said furiously. "Whatever happened here, Morton, *you're* responsible. *You* were the one who put together the stock deal for me. *You* brought in all the investors and told me I never had to worry. Now this woman marches in and informs me she has control of my studio." She turned on Donna. "Who the fuck are you, anyway?"

"Unbecoming language for a supposedly smart businesswoman," Donna said cuttingly, relishing every second of her triumph.

Lucky was enraged. "I need to see proof of this."

"I have all the papers here," Morton replied, handing them to her. She flicked through them.

"You still own forty percent—"

"You set me up," she interrupted violently. "Nobody could have done it except you."

"The board called an emergency meeting and made a decision that your services as head of the studio are no longer required," Morton stated. "You will, of course, be paid off on your contract."

"Paid off?" she said incredulously. "They're paying *me* off? Don't any of you get it? This is *my* studio. Everything that's going on here now is because *I* turned it around."

"You shouldn't worry about the studio, dear," Donna said patronizingly. "I'm bringing Mickey Stolli back to run it."

"You've *got* to be kidding?" Lucky exploded. "Mickey Stolli ran this studio into the ground."

"He's thrilled to be returning," Donna said, still savoring Lucky's fury.

"Why are you doing this?" Lucky demanded, shaking with anger. "WHY?"

Donna consulted her watch. "Ten minutes have passed. That leaves you exactly twenty more minutes to collect your personal belongings and vacate this office. I wouldn't want to have you thrown off the lot."

"Fuck you," Lucky said, her black eyes filled with rage. "Whoever you are. *Fuck you.* Because I'm going to get this studio back. Don't you doubt it for one minute. In fact, you can bet on it!"

27

"You're late," Michel Guy said sternly. "By about eight weeks."

"Excuse me?" Brigette replied; this was not the greeting she'd expected.

"You were supposed to be here two months ago, remember? When I met you at Effie's party, I told you to come and see me the next day." He leaned back in his chair, regarding her quizzically. "Y'know, an invitation from me is considered a big deal in this town."

"The reason I didn't take you up on your offer," Brigette said, "was that my stepfather died. I went to L.A. for the funeral."

"I'm sorry," Michel said. "I didn't know."

"Anyway, I'm back now."

"Yes," Nona said, joining in. "She's back, and *I'm* her manager."

"You?" Michel said, barely concealing his surprise.

"Yes, me," Nona answered defiantly. "We could have gone to any of the top agencies, but Brigette wants you to represent her. I guess she gets off on your accent."

Michel Guy's faded blue eyes crinkled with amusement. "This is a new way of persuading an agent to sign you," he said. "I thought *Brigette* was the one looking for representation, and *I* was the one supposed to be doing her the big favor."

"Things have changed," Nona said. "Brigette has a fantastic deal pending."

"And what might that be?"

"*Will* you represent me?" Brigette asked, fixing him with her blue eyes.

"I was considering it," Michel replied slowly. "Although first, I must see how you are in front of the camera. And, Brigette," he added, "models don't need managers, not until they're superstars."

"I plan on being much more than just a model," she replied confidently.

"It takes time to build a name for yourself," Michel pointed out.

"We know that," Nona interrupted. "The

thing is, we're coming to you with a fantastic shot at an immediate score." She paused for dramatic effect. "Rock 'n' Roll Jeans want Brigette to be their new spokesmodel."

Michel nodded, thinking fast. So *that's* why Rock 'n' Roll Jeans had not signed the deal with Robertson and Nature—both girls his clients.

"When did this happen?" he asked, doodling on a yellow desk pad.

"Luke Kasway photographed her before she went to L.A. The ad agency saw the photos and they're crazy for her."

Michel knew Robertson would be furious if he signed Brigette to the agency. So what? With Michel, money always came first. He addressed his next words to Brigette. "If this is true, I will make you the best deal in the business."

"That's what I want," Brigette said determinedly.

"We're on our way to see Aurora at *MONDO*," Nona offered. "I figured if we told her about the Jeans thing, she may want to put Brigette on the cover."

"No, no, no!" Michel said, almost shouting. "*You* don't do that. *I* do that. And this is *how* I do it. I throw a dinner party at my apartment. We invite Aurora, her husband, and several other interesting guests. During the course of the evening, I let it drop to Aurora that both *Allure* and *Glamour* are vying with each other to get Brigette on their cover because of the new deal that will make her bigger than any of the Guess girls. I can assure you—the next day Aurora will come to *us begging* for Brigette to appear on her cover first."

"Sounds good to me," Brigette said, smiling broadly.

"Ah!" Michel tapped his head. "The brain must always be working." His crinkly blue eyes met hers. "Am I not right, *ma cherié*?"

"Oh, yes," she said enthusiastically, quite impressed with him. "Absolutely."

★ ★ ★

"What's your background?" Alex asked. "Where are you from?"

Venus realized that Alex Woods obviously didn't know too much about her. What the hell— she'd go along with the game, humor the big filmmaker. "I'm originally a Brooklyn girl," she said amiably. "Gotta hunch half of Hollywood started off there."

"Not me," Alex replied. "I'm a local boy."

"Oh, c'mon," Venus said, flirting ever so slightly. "You can't possibly be from Los Angeles. *Nobody's* a native."

"I am."

"I'm surprised," she said. "Your work has such a New York edge."

"I spent a lot of time in New York," he said. "But let's not get off track here, *I'm* supposed to be interviewing *you*."

"It's not exactly an *interview*, Alex. I came in to see you because you've written a sensational script, and I want to play Lola. I know I can do an incredible job."

"You're pretty sure of yourself."

"Why wouldn't I be? I've accomplished a lot." She threw in some flattery to soften him up. "Kind of like you."

He looked amused. "You don't have to sell yourself. I know who you are."

"*That's* a relief!" she said mockingly, convinced he had no idea who she was.

He stood up. "Well, now we've got that straight, will you excuse me for a moment, I gotta use the john."

Oh, God, she thought. *He's a coke snorter. Can't even hold out for five minutes.*

"Sure," she said offhandedly. "Why should I mind? I've already spent the last hour hanging out here."

"Be understanding," he said, flashing the grin. "Nature's screaming." He went in the bathroom, closed the door, and immediately buzzed France.

"Yes, Alex?" she said.

"Flowers," he said. "Lucky Santangelo. Make certain the florist puts together something very special. Roses, in fact, lots of them."

"How much do you want to spend?"

"Be sure it's a big deal. In fact—make it six dozen red roses. Have them delivered to her house this afternoon so they're waiting for her when she gets home."

"What should the note say?" asked France. "The usual?"

"No, not the usual, France," he said, irritated. "I'll write my own card."

"How about Tin Lee?"

"What?"

"Flowers because you stood her up?"

"I suppose so."

He returned to his office, where Venus was lolling on the couch in a typical Lola pose. "Hi'ya, baby," she said, winking suggestively. "Wanna slide in beside me?"

It was a line from the script and she delivered it with a great deal of relish.

"We can't afford you," Alex said.

"I know, you overshot your wad on Johnny Romano."

"I don't usually work with stars."

"I don't usually work with star directors who've hardly heard of me."

"That's not true."

Venus sat up straight. "Admit it, Alex, you don't know anything about me."

"I'm not into gossip."

"Oh," she said crossly. "Is that what you think I'm about?"

"No. I didn't say that. C'mon, Venus, tell me more about yourself. You're from Brooklyn...what kind of family?"

"What is this? My biography?"

"Why're you getting so uptight?"

"I'm not."

"Then go ahead, tell me."

She plunged into a shortened version of her life story. "Hmm...let me see," she said. "Well, my father was a charming Italian chauvinist. My mom died when I was quite young. I had four older brothers, so I became their caretaker—y'know, washing, cleaning, cooking them pasta, all that housewife crap. Boy, did they get a shock when I took off with my best friend, Ron Machio. We were out for adventure—a couple of desperados—so we hitched our way to L.A. where I did everything from performing in underground clubs to nude modeling for an art class. Then I met a record producer who decided to record me. Ron put together my video. It was so outrageous that I was like...y'know, an instant hit."

"It certainly got you where you wanted to be."

"The top, Alex," she said very seriously. "That's where I wanted to be. And that's exactly where I am now."

"So why are you coming to see me about a cameo role?"

There was a determined thrust to her jaw. "Because I need to prove that I *can* act. That I'm not some freako sex machine who can't cut it on the big screen. The critics hate me. I've made four movies, and each time they've shredded my ass."

Alex said, "They do that to me all the time."

"They don't pull you to pieces physically, calling you everything from a sex machine to a vulgar, untalented whore!"

"I've been called a lot of names in my life," Alex said with a wry smile. "But vulgar, untalented whore ain't one of 'em."

"You know what I mean."

"Ignore the critics. *I* do."

"It's not that easy—but I manage. I have this

huge army of loyal fans, and in their eyes I'm always the best. They're my silent support group."

"You want to read a scene for me?" Alex said; it was possible that she did indeed have potential, and he liked her.

"I'm kind of insulted you're forcing me to read," she said, determined to let him know how she felt.

"I don't know your work, Venus," he explained. "I haven't seen any of your movies. And if what you're telling me about the reviews is true, I'd be insane if I didn't ask you to read."

She nodded, stood up, and wandered over to the window. "I'll do it if *you* read with me," she said, turning to face him.

"My casting people are waiting to join us. Lindy will read with you, she's good."

"I'm sure she is, but she's not a man," Venus said determinedly. "I need interaction, sexual tension. I gotta get it going here, Alex."

He studied her, drawn to the vulnerable streak he sensed beneath the high gloss. If he could only capture that quality on film, she'd be a perfect Lola. "What scene do you want to read?" he asked.

"I'll take a shot at the one where Lola has the breakdown, where she's really in trouble and doesn't know who's gonna help her out."

Alex picked the script up off his desk. "Good choice," he said. "Okay, Venus, go ahead and convince me."

28

Surfacing from yet another nightmare, Lennie imagined he heard a noise that was different from every other sound he knew so well. He thought he heard a woman laughing.

He sat up straight, desperately straining to hear.

Nothing—except the relentless pounding of the sea.

He had no idea of time. From the light filtering down into the cave, he assumed it was early morning.

He stood up, stretching his aching bones. Recently he'd started working out, which wasn't easy with his ankle chained. The challenge was not to lose any more of his physical strength.

He'd also realized it was important to give himself a reason for living, so he now followed a stringent routine he forced himself to adhere to.

With order, there was hope.

Without, there was nothing.

Today was one of those days he simply couldn't get it together. Instead, he sat back down on the makeshift wooden bed and began thinking about the time he and Lucky first met in Vegas. He'd been performing at her hotel as a stand-up. She'd come along, fired him, then tried to lure him into bed. He smiled at the memories.

A year later they'd bumped into each other when he was married to Olympia and she was married to Dimitri. One look and they'd both known that this time they were never going to be parted.

His wonderful, stubborn, beautiful Lucky.

What he wouldn't give to be with her now.

He wondered what she was doing. Had his kidnappers contacted her? Was the ransom demand so big that she wasn't able to pay it?

Not possible. He knew his Lucky. She would find a way to pay it even if it was a billion dollars.

He heard the noise again—a woman's soft laugh. This time he was certain he wasn't imagining it.

"Is anybody there?" he yelled out. "Anybody around?" The echo of his voice came back at him. Apart from that, there was the usual silence.

Was his mind playing cruel tricks on him? Perhaps he was truly going crazy.

If only he could get this goddamn shackle off his foot. His ankle was raw from trying.

He fell back on the so-called bed, throwing his arms across his face, covering his eyes. Despair enveloped him like a heavy cloak of unremitting gloom.

Lucky, Lucky, Lucky. Ah…my sweetheart…why aren't you saving me?

He drifted back into a light sleep, imagining he was driving a speedboat on the sea—a fast boat carving its way through the heavy waves, heading for freedom.

A girlish shriek jolted him awake. He sat up abruptly. Hovering in the entrance to the cave stood a young woman in her early twenties, with clouds of curly brown hair and a Madonna-like face.

Surely he was dreaming. She must be a vision.

The woman's hand flew to her mouth as she gasped something in Italian, a language he didn't speak.

My God, she's real, he thought. *She's flesh and blood. SHE'S MY SAVIOR.*

"Thank God you're here," he shouted. "Thank God!"

She stared at him, her eyes registering fright and surprise. Then she turned and ran, vanishing from sight.

"Come back!" he screamed after her. "Come back, whoever you are. I'm not going to hurt you. Goddamn it—COME BACK!"

She was gone.

He hoped and prayed she was going for help, because without her, he was lost.

29

The only things Lucky bothered taking were the silver picture frames on her desk containing photos of her children and Lennie. She snatched them up, and without another word marched from her office.

Kyoko ran alongside her as she headed for her car. "What happened?" he asked, almost as distressed as she was.

"That deceitful, lying sonofabitch sold me out!" Lucky seethed. "I'm going to bury him. Do you hear me, Kyoko? I'm going to *bury* that man."

"Can I help?" Kyoko asked.

"Yes. Arrange to have all my things removed from my office immediately. I want my desk out of there, my leather chair, I want every piece of furniture that belongs to me. And if that woman gives you any trouble, call my lawyer."

"It doesn't seem possible that this could happen," Kyoko fretted.

"It's very simple," Lucky said resolutely. "I was set up by my confidant and business advisor—Mr. Morton Sharkey. But don't worry, Kyoko, I'll find out why—and I'll shred his sorry ass."

"Should I inform Charlie Dollar you've left?"

"Yes, please do that," she said, trying to control her anger and think straight. "I don't want this going around the studio. Tell Charlie I had an emergency to deal with."

"Certainly, Lucky."

"You'll work for me at home, Ky, until we get this straightened out. Is that okay with you?"

"It will be an honor."

She sent him off to tell Charlie she wasn't

coming back, got in her car, and sat behind the wheel for a moment, placing the pile of silver frames on the passenger seat. Lennie's image gazed up at her. Impulsively she picked up his photo, kissing his face through the glass. "I miss you, my darling sweetheart," she murmured softly. "I miss you so very, very much."

Oh, God, what was happening to her life? First Lennie, now this. Everything was falling to pieces...everything.

She fought off tears, and drove off the lot with nowhere to go except home. Recovering her composure, she called her personal lawyer, Bruce Grey, informing him of the situation.

Bruce was as shocked as she was. "How could Morton allow this to happen?" he said.

"*Allow* it," she steamed, "somehow or other he engineered it."

"Why?" Bruce asked, puzzled.

"Beats me," she said bitterly. "However, I intend to find out. In the meantime, I'll messenger all the relevant papers over to you. Get me a complete rundown on everybody who owned the stock. Let's see if they sold, or if they merely voted in this woman's favor."

"That should be easy."

"Her name's Donna Landsman. Sound familiar?"

"Never heard of her."

"Prepare a full profile on her. Oh yes, and Bruce—get me this information before the end of the day."

The children were out when she arrived

home, everything peaceful and quiet. She walked over to the window and stared out at the spectacular ocean view.

On impulse she ran upstairs, changed into shorts and a T-shirt, and made her way down to the beach.

She loved the sea—walking along the edge of the surf was the perfect place to get her head together and think this through.

Why was this happening to her?

What had she done to deserve it?

Wasn't it enough that she'd lost Lennie?

It seemed that things were stacking up against her, but hadn't it been that way all her life?

Yes.

And hadn't she always been able to overcome?

Yes.

Okay, so this time she'd fight back and win. No question.

By the time she returned to the house, she felt better. She could deal with it. She *would* deal with it. There had to be a way.

She wished Boogie were here. Right now he was on vacation, fortunately due back tomorrow. At a time like this she needed the support of familiar faces around her—and there was nobody more loyal than Boogie.

The kids and Cee Cee were still out. Settling in the den, she phoned Abe Panther. "I hope you're sitting down," she said, wondering if he'd already heard.

"What's your problem, girlie?" he cackled hoarsely.

Automatic response: "How many times have I told you not to call me that." A beat. "Panther's been taken over. And—this is the shocker—your favorite grandson-in-law, Mickey Stolli, has been rehired to run it."

Abe began to choke on the other end of the line.

"I know it's difficult to comprehend," Lucky said. "Thought I'd drive over and see you, get your advice."

"Sounds like you need it."

"The bottom line is, I was double-crossed. I'll tell you about it when I get there."

She went upstairs and hurriedly dressed.

As she was leaving the house, a flower delivery van pulled up to the door. The driver got out and handed her a small arrangement of mixed flowers.

She tore open the card, quickly reading the scrawled message.

Sorry about last night.
Call you soon.
Alex

What was *that* all about? Ten out of ten for not being the romantic type.

Not that she wanted him to be.

Not that she needed him at all.

Throwing the card on the hall table, she left the house.

Alex got the news on the plane to Vegas. Lili informed him, via phone, that there was a rumor going around that somebody had taken over Panther Studios and dismissed Lucky Santangelo.

"No way," he said. "Who'd do that?"

"Reports are, it's a businesswoman. Nobody seems to know who."

"How could this happen so suddenly?"

"Apparently she ordered Lucky off the lot this afternoon."

Alex frowned. "She did *what*?"

"Everybody's talking about it."

"See what else you can find out, Lili, and call me at the hotel."

"Tin Lee phoned."

"What did *she* want?"

"She said she'd be delighted to see you later, and to thank you for the fantastic roses *and* the invitation."

"*What* invitation?"

"I don't know, Alex. I can't keep up with your love life *and* run your production company."

Alex hung up, puzzled. Why would Tin Lee mention an invitation when all he'd said was, *Sorry about last night. Call you soon. Alex.*

Hmm...the invitation had gone to Lucky. *Can I see you tonight? Call me.* So had the roses.

Fuck! It was obvious there'd been a mistake. Tin Lee had gotten Lucky's flowers and note, while Lucky must have received Tin Lee's.

He grabbed the phone and tried reaching Lili

again. The line was out due to turbulence.

Russell, his location manager, a cheerful man, moved over from the seat across the aisle, strapping himself in next to Alex.

"How did the Venus Maria reading go today?" Russell asked.

"Pretty damn good," Alex replied, not really in the mood for conversation.

"Are we hiring her?"

"I'm not sure."

"You should grab her," Russell said. "My kids buy every one of her CDs. They're first in line for her concerts. She's got a lock on the young audience."

Russell had worked on his last three movies, and Alex valued his opinion. "How do you think she'll come across with Johnny Romano?" he asked.

"They'll generate plenty of heat," Russell said enthusiastically.

"You could be right," Alex replied, thinking about it. "I'll call Freddie when we get to Vegas—suggest we run a test."

"Will she test?"

"She came in and read, didn't she?"

Ron Machio, Venus's best friend, arrived at Orso's—a busy Italian restaurant on Third Street—a few minutes late. Ron was tall and lanky, with straight brown hair worn back in a ponytail, and a long, bony face. "Well, madame," he said, scrutinizing Venus, who was already sitting out on the patio sipping white wine. "*Very* fifties."

She grinned, delighted he'd known immediately what period she was going for. "Sit down," she said. "I ordered for you. Wine and pasta. It's my check."

"Have we reinvented ourselves yet again?" he asked, flopping into a chair, stretching out his long legs.

"No, Ron," she said. "*This* is the me that went up for a role in Alex Woods's new movie. *This* is the me who's going to win an Oscar."

Ron's thin eyebrows shot up. *"Really?"*

"Yes, really. I believe if you want something badly enough, you can get it. Look at us—we're the perfect example. We came out to L.A. with zilch, and now I'm like Miss Superstar Big Deal and you're this hugely successful director. It's pretty amazing when you consider that neither of us graduated from college."

"Very successful people *never* graduate college," Ron said knowingly. "They're all former dropouts. All these poor schmucks who sweated their youth away in college ended up slaving in the mail room."

"*Very* philosophical, Ron. Major Mogul's influence?"

"I wish you wouldn't call him that," Ron said irritably. "If you got to know him, you'd find he's quite nice."

"I'm sure Harris Von Stepp has been called a lot of things in his time, but never nice."

"Well, he is. He's just..."

"Uptight," she offered. "Is that the word you're searching for?"

"Venus," Ron scolded, shaking a finger at her. "You can be a *very* mean little girl."

The waiter delivered two plates of linguini with clam sauce.

"Anyway," Venus said, "I read for Alex, and he seemed to like me. He's calling Freddie."

"Freddie?" Ron questioned, picking up his fork.

"Didn't I mention it? Freddie Leon represents me now."

"My, my...we *are* in the big leagues."

"It was about time I changed agents," she said, taking a mouthful of pasta.

"And naturally you had to have the best."

"But of course!"

"Minx!"

"Did I tell you about my new assistant, Anthony?"

"*Noo...*"

"He's a gorgeous blond," she teased. "Isn't that your passion, Ron—gorgeous blonds?"

"Trying to tempt me?"

"Would I do that?" she asked, all innocence.

"Yes," Ron said, curling pasta around his fork. "That's *exactly* what you'd do."

"How *old* is Major Mogul?" Venus asked, as if she didn't know.

"What has age got to do with anything?"

"'Cause you shouldn't get into that older man, younger man routine. It's so passé. And you don't need it."

"You're a *fine* one to lecture," Ron responded crisply. "Does madame recall Cooper's age? He's *at least* twenty years your senior."

"Yeah, and look where it got me," she said ruefully.

"And talking of relationships," Ron continued, "what's happening with your masseur?"

"Ah...Rodriguez," Venus sighed, twirling several thin silver bracelets enclosing her wrist.

"Is he what you expected?"

"Nobody's ever what you really expect." Venus sighed, smiling wistfully. "I guess he's okay."

"Just okay?"

"The thing is, Ron, after Cooper..."

"Oh, you mean Cooper's reputation was actually true?"

She laughed softly. "Cooper was the best lover I ever had. I'll have to go a long way to find another as good as he was."

"Ah..." Ron said. "If only he'd kept it in his pants."

"Yeah," Venus agreed, going for the joke. "Every time he unzipped 'em—his brains fell out!"

They broke up laughing.

"About this Anthony..." Ron ventured.

Venus grinned. "You're such a slut!"

"Takes one to know one."

"I think it's coffee at *my* house, right?"

"Well...if you insist."

30

Abe Panther had not left his crumbling old mansion for over ten years, ever since a major stroke had forced him out of the day-to-day machinations of the film business. When he'd sold his studio to Lucky, he'd been convinced it would be hers until his death, and long after that. The news of somebody else taking over Panther had infuriated him, especially if it was true that his thieving grandson-in-law, Mickey Stolli, was being reinstated as studio head.

Before Lucky arrived, he'd called up his granddaughter, Abigaile, to find out what was going on. Abigaile was a true Hollywood princess, pushy and grasping; she lived for entertaining and huge parties.

After Abe had sold his studio to Lucky, a bitter Abigaile hadn't spoken to him for a while. It was only when Mickey was appointed the head of Orpheus that Abigaile had finally made peace with her grandfather.

Now he was on the phone, attempting to elicit information.

Abigaile was uncooperative. "There'll be an announcement in the trades," she said crisply, unwilling to reveal more.

"I'm sure there will," Abe replied sternly. "However, *I* wish to know what's taking place now."

"It's confidential information," Abigaile said, still miffed with her grandfather for marrying his longtime companion, the obscure Swedish actress Inga Irving. "Mickey will kill me if I tell anybody."

"I'm not anybody," Abe reminded her gruffly. "I'm your grandfather."

"I'll speak to Mickey and call you later."

Abe was sitting out on his terrace, puffing on a large Havana cigar, when Lucky arrived. She kissed him on both cheeks, marveling at the tenacity of the old man.

"Sit down, girlie," he said, repeating his conversation with Abigaile.

"Typical," Lucky said, lighting a cigarette.

"Who betrayed you?" Abe asked, leaning toward her, his less-than-white dentures clenched tightly together.

"Morton Sharkey," she said, expelling a thin stream of smoke. "I intend to find out why."

"It seems inconceivable this could have happened without your knowing," Abe said, unclenching his teeth to puff on his cigar. Their smoke intermingled mid-air.

"Not really," Lucky said. "It was all done secretly. They called a board meeting, and failed to notify me."

"Nobody alerted you?"

"They wanted me out, Abe," she said forcefully. "The last thing they'd do is warn me."

"Right, right," he muttered.

"Why did I allow Morton to talk me into selling off so much of my stock?" she fretted.

"What's *wrong* with me? I should have kept fifty-one percent to protect myself."

"Why didn't you?" Abe asked, squinting at her.

"Because I needed the cash flow, and I trusted Morton."

"Never trust a lawyer."

"Don't make it worse," she snapped. "I'm burning up."

"Do you have a plan, girlie?"

She got up, pacing around the flower-bordered terrace. "I'm getting Panther back. You'll see. I'm doing it for both of us."

Abe cackled. "That's the spirit," he said, puffing on his large Havana. "If anyone can get 'em, my buck's on you!"

Inga Irving emerged from the house, greeting Lucky curtly. Inga—once a great beauty—was a big-boned woman in her late fifties, with a broad face of discontent. Long ago, when Abe was *the* Hollywood tycoon to beat all Hollywood tycoons, he'd brought her to Hollywood from her native Sweden in the hope of making her a movie star. It hadn't happened. Inga remained forever sour about her lack of success. Two years ago Abe had finally married her. It had not put a smile on her face.

"Lucky," Inga said, nodding in her usual haughty manner.

"Inga," Lucky responded, used to the Swedish woman's moody demeanor.

"Time for your nap, Abe," Inga announced in a no-nonsense voice.

"Can't you see I'm visiting with Lucky?" Abe

said crossly, stabbing his cigar in her direction.

"She'll have to come back another time," Inga said with a stern expression.

Abe continued to object, but Inga was having none of it. His ninety-year-old balls were firmly in her pocket, and that's exactly where they were staying.

"It's okay, Abe," Lucky said, kissing him on the cheek. "I've got to go anyway."

A flicker of triumph crossed Inga's face. She'd finally found a role she could excel at. Keeper of the once great Abe Panther.

Lucky got in her car and drove home. She had work to do.

"How stupid can you get!" Alex yelled over the phone.

"I'm sorry," France said, apologizing for the third time.

"*Sorry?* How could the wrong fucking note and the wrong fucking flowers go to the wrong person?" he screamed. "I went to the trouble of writing that note myself, France. What are you—a moron?"

"I'm sorry, Alex," she repeated yet again, holding the phone away from her ear.

He wondered if she'd done it purposely—even though their romance was long past, Alex knew that both she and Lili were still very possessive of him. They'd obviously assumed he'd spent the night with Lucky, and now they'd plotted to make sure she received the wrong message. Loyalty and jealousy did not mix.

"What can I do?" France wailed.

"Nothing," Alex said sourly. "Cancel Tin Lee. Tell her I had to stay in Vegas overnight. I'll call Lucky myself. Get me her home number."

Lili picked up the extension a few seconds later. "We don't have it on file, Alex."

He was sure they were making it difficult on purpose. "Call Freddie's secretary," he snapped.

"Certainly, Alex. Will you be reachable on your mobile?"

"Yeah, we're leaving the hotel now."

"I'll get right back to you."

"Wait a minute," he said, totally irritated by both his assistants. "I haven't finished."

"What is it, Alex?" said Lili, ever patient.

"Have Freddie call me."

"Is there any message if we can't reach him?"

"Yes. Set it up for Venus Maria to test with Johnny Romano tomorrow afternoon."

"It's done, Alex."

He banged the phone down and walked through the hotel to meet Russell and the rest of his crew out front. As he strode purposefully through the crowded lobby, the lure of the tables was a powerful thing. Once, he'd been a degenerate gambler. Reluctantly— with the help of his therapist—he'd given it up after he'd dropped a million dollars over a one-year period. Right now, his only addiction was work.

His team was gathered outside the hotel, watching huge water fountains erupt with fire. On the location scout were his cinematographer, line producer, first AD, set designer, and a couple of assistants.

Russell introduced him to the area location man, Clyde Lomas, a florid-faced Las Vegas native with a small snub nose that seemed out of place in his long, mournful face.

They shook hands. Clyde had sweaty palms, which put Alex in a bad mood because all he could think about was getting to a bathroom to wash Clyde's sweat off his hands.

"We got some fancy places for you to look at," Clyde announced in a loud, booming voice. "Set 'em up myself. Five houses and three hotels."

Alex glanced at his watch. "Are we going to have time to cover all this?" he said, turning to Russell.

"I hope so," Russell said. "We're booked on an eight o'clock plane back to L.A. If you feel like staying the night, I can arrange that, too."

"I wasn't planning on it," Alex said, thinking that if he could reach her, he wanted to spend the evening with Lucky.

"Let me know if you change your mind," Russell replied. "I can go either way."

They climbed into a large air-conditioned van and set off.

Lucky thought about canceling dinner with Venus at Morton's, then she reconsidered. Why should she? That's exactly what everybody would expect her to do—crawl off somewhere and vanish.

Hollywood. A town with no conscience. Just one big happy boys' club. And wouldn't they be thrilled to hear that Lucky Santangelo had been ousted.

She refused to give them that pleasure. She'd be out there, head held high for all to see. This was merely a temporary setback.

Cee Cee and the kids were home when she got back. She played with Maria awhile, then fed baby Gino his bottle. After that she handed them over to the ever cheerful Cee Cee to put to bed.

Shortly after six, a messenger delivered a large manila envelope from her lawyer. She took it into the den, ripped it open, and began studying the contents.

Donna Landsman. Businesswoman. Queen of the hostile takeover. A corporate raider with a thirst for buying small companies, stripping the assets, and then reselling them at a profit.

Lucky couldn't figure it out. If Donna Landsman was such a high-powered business tycoon, what did she want with Panther? The studio had massive debts; it would be a long while before it was in a profit-making position. There were no assets to strip, unless of course she abandoned the whole studio deal and sold off the valuable land.

Yes! That's what she planned to do. That had to be it.

As far as the other investors were concerned, on paper it showed they'd been paid twice the amount they'd purchased their original shares for. She assumed that since Morton had brought them in, it was on his advice they'd gotten out.

Hmm...Take the money and run. Why not? It was good business.

It seemed Donna Landsman had acquired thirty-nine percent of the stock. The remaining shareholders were Conquest Investments, a company based in the Bahamas—they'd retained 10 percent. And Mrs. I. Smorg, whose address was care of a lawyer in Pasadena, she owned six percent. Then there was Morton Sharkey with *his* five percent. It was a sure thing he'd pushed the remaining shareholders to vote in Donna Landsman's favor.

Screw Morton Sharkey, because *that's* what he was doing to her.

She sat back, her mind racing.

There had to be a reason he was doing this to her. There was always a reason.

Tomorrow, when Boogie returned from his vacation, she'd put him on Morton's case. Boogie had worked as her security for years, and if there was anything to find out, he'd discover it. No problem.

Until then, all she could do was wait.

3 1

Robertson had malevolent violet cat's eyes.
They followed Brigette wherever she went at
Michel Guy's dinner. They radiated *Get out
of my face and don't come back.*

"She hates me," Brigette whispered to Nona.

"Of course she hates you," Nona agreed.
"Why wouldn't she? *You're* going to be the star
now."

"Oh, c'mon," Brigette said. "She's, like, *sooo*
famous, why would *she* care?"

"Modeling careers are short," Nona said
wisely. "She's aware of that. *You're* the one on
the rise."

"Really?"

"Don't play coy with me. *You* know it.
Everyone knows it."

They'd had an interesting few days. True
to his word, Michel Guy had pulled off an
extremely lucrative deal with Rock 'n' Roll
Jeans. As soon as the company signed her to
an exclusive big-bucks contract, she was
rushed into the studio for a major photo shoot
with Luke Kasway. The ad agency had wanted her with Zandino, but Nona had vetoed his
appearance because she didn't like the idea of
her future husband modeling—in some ways,
Nona was a bit of a snob. Instead they used
Isaac—a young black model with ratted hair

and a rap attitude. Brigette thought he was cool. They'd exchanged phone numbers, but so far he hadn't called. She was contemplating phoning him.

It had taken all day to shoot the photographs; the ad agency had everyone on an accelerated schedule and the pace was frantic.

When she'd seen the finished results, Brigette was in shock. Luke Kasway was a genius who'd made her look utterly amazing.

Nona had said, "Don't get carried away, it's all lighting. Let us not forget how you look in the mornings!"

But both of them had known—along with Michel and Luke—that she was a star about to happen.

Nona had lucked into a spacious duplex apartment overlooking Central Park. It belonged to a friend of her mother's who'd taken off to live in Europe for a year. The three of them moved in immediately.

In a way, Brigette was sorry to say good-bye to Anna—she'd gotten used to the security of always having somebody around. However, she realized the time had come to be out on her own, and to stop brooding about the past.

Brigette Stanislopoulos was dead.

Brigette Brown was into a whole new deal.

She'd phoned Lucky to tell her of the move.

"As long as you're not living by yourself," Lucky had said. "And watch it—it's easier to get into trouble than out of it."

"Enjoying yourself?" Michel asked, sneaking up behind her.

"Oh, yes," she said, flattered that he was taking so much notice of her. "It's an awesome party."

"You're an awesome young lady," he murmured. *"Formidable."*

"Really, Michel?" she said, gazing up at him with crush written all over her glowingly pretty face.

He leaned down and whispered in her ear, his breath heavy with garlic. "Aurora has said yes to your cover. She wants it immediately. You're to go see Antonio—the photographer—tomorrow, and he'll shoot the next day. I'll give Nona the details."

"You're so clever!" she exclaimed.

A smile played across his face. "No need to flatter me, *ma chérie*."

She loved it when he spoke his native language, it was so sexy. "Do you and Robertson really live together?" she asked boldly.

His faded blue eyes studied her carefully. "Why do you ask?"

She hoped he didn't think she was being too inquisitive. "I just...wondered," she said vaguely.

"Sometimes we do...sometimes we don't," he replied ambiguously. "We have an...understanding."

She caught Robertson still watching her. Maybe *her* idea of an understanding and Michel's differed.

"So, my dear girl, are you happy with the way things are going?" he asked, touching her arm.

"Very happy."

"Are you glad I came into your life when I did?"

"Impeccable timing," she said, smiling.

"You know, Brigette," he said reflectively. "You're not like one of these pretty little American girls from the Midwest. You seem almost European."

"I *am* European. My mother was Greek— she died several years ago. My father was Italian."

"Ah...an interesting combination! That explains why you're so...sensual for one so young."

"Do you think I'm sensual, Michel?" she asked eagerly.

"Yes, *ma petite*. America will fall in love with you."

It had been a long time since she'd allowed herself to flirt; it was quite a heady feeling. The fact that Michel was older attracted her. Maybe a mature man was what she needed; she certainly hadn't had any luck with the young ones.

Michel took her hand, squeezing it gently. "Stay after the guests have left," he said persuasively. "We have much to discuss."

"What about Robertson?"

"She has her own apartment. Tonight she will go home."

Brigette couldn't wait to find Nona. "I'm staying after the party," she announced. "Michel wants to talk to me."

"Oh, *I* get it," Nona said, not impressed. "He's finally coming on to you, right?"

"No way," she said indignantly. "It's just...business."

"I'm telling you," Nona warned. "He's a womanizer with a fancy accent. You're just fresh meat, that's all."

"Thanks a lot."

"And what about Robertson? Is she going to sit back and watch while you two discuss...business?"

"They have an arrangement."

"Ha! You're falling for the oldest line since 'Let me just put it there.' The next thing he'll say is, 'Sorry, it was fantastic, but now I gotta go back to my girlfriend 'cause she's pissed off.'"

"You don't give me much credit, do you?" Brigette said crossly.

"I *care* about you," Nona said. "Your experience with men is limited. Tim Wealth—Mr. Rat Pack Movie Star. My brother—the hippie maniac. And that rich coke freak you were engaged to. That's about it, or am I missing someone?"

"I haven't led a normal life," Brigette admitted. "That doesn't mean I can't in the future."

"Michel Guy is *not* normal," Nona said, frowning. "Jump into bed with him and you're on a fast track to nowhere."

Brigette had no intention of being lectured to by Nona. "I'll see you later," she said, cutting her off. "Don't wait up."

"Freddie Leon called," Anthony said, surreptitiously eyeing Ron and liking what he saw.

"What did he want?" Venus asked.

"To set up a test tomorrow afternoon with you and Johnny Romano."

"A *test*," Venus said, pulling a face. "I don't test."

"You don't read either," Ron said crisply. "But for Alex Woods you did."

"Why doesn't he run film on me?"

"I presume you've read what the critics had to say about your previous performances?" Ron inquired tartly. "You're *fortunate* he wants to test you."

Venus glared at him. "Don't forget that one of those movies was *yours*."

"Mr. Machio," Anthony interrupted, trying to stave off a fight. "I'm such a fan. Your choreography and direction in *Summer Startime* was quite wonderful."

"Why, thank you," Ron said, noticing Anthony for the first time.

"*I'm* sorry, Ron," Venus said, enjoying the moment. "I haven't introduced you to my very proper English assistant—Anthony Redigio."

"Isn't Redigio an Italian name?" Ron asked with a neat little smile.

"My father's Italian," Anthony replied.

"Mine, too," Ron said. "Our Venus likes Italians."

"So do I," Anthony said boldly.

Their eyes met. Venus hid a triumphant smile. Was this a Venus match made in heaven or what?

"Did you check out that letter, Anthony?" she asked.

"I sent it over to security," he replied, busily stacking papers on the desk.

"Good. Get me Freddie on the phone, and after that, fix Ron coffee. I'll be in the other room."

Ron shook his head and half smiled. "You're such an obvious little brat," he whispered.

"Takes one to know one," she replied gleefully.

Freddie was his usual bland self. "Definitely test," he said.

"What if it gets out?" she fretted. "Doesn't that make me look *desperate*?"

"Not at all. Personally, I think you'll get the part. Alex liked you."

"He did?" she said, perking up. "What did he say?"

"He thought he could bring things out in you that nobody's seen before."

"Did he think I was unbelievably sexy?" she asked jokingly.

"What difference does it make whether he thought you were sexy or not? You're not going to fuck him, you're going to work for him."

"Oh, Freddie!" she gasped, mock-shocked. "You used the 'f' word! I've never heard you swear before."

"It's your bad influence, Venus."

She couldn't believe Freddie actually sounded human—he was usually such a cool proposition. "Okay, I'll do it," she decided. "*Only* because *you* say so."

In the office, Ron and Anthony were getting along fine. "I love *all* your work," Anthony was saying with the proper amount of deference. "I've seen everything you've done."

Ron was busy soaking up every word of praise. "Where are you from, Anthony?" he asked, sipping his coffee in a mug emblazoned with Venus's picture.

"Born in Naples," Anthony said. "My parents moved to London when I was two. I came to L.A. a year ago. Venus is my second job." He glanced over at her. "She's divine to work for."

"You *would* say that, wouldn't you," she said, grinning.

"Of course, I'm no fool!" Anthony replied archly, a touch of campiness surfacing.

"Where do you live?" Ron asked.

Venus imagined what Ron was thinking. *Where do you live, Anthony, so I can come up one afternoon and crawl all over your fine, muscular body.* He was such a randy sod.

"West Hollywood," Anthony said. "In an apartment." He paused for a moment. "Actually, I shared with a friend for a while, but he...got sick and went home."

"Sorry to hear that," Ron said, immediately sympathetic. "Are you—"

"Oh, I'm fine," Anthony interrupted quickly. "I get myself tested twice a year."

Ron nodded. "It's not like it used to be." He sighed nostalgically. "Ah...the wild times."

"Ron was *king* of the wild times, weren't you, cutie?" Venus said.

"Yes, my sweet. If my memory serves me correctly, *I* was the king and *you* were the queen."

"We shared an apartment at one time," Venus said, grinning at the memories. "It was so funny. The desk clerk would take one look at any handsome stud who walked in and automatically say, 'Venus or Ron?'"

"I'm sorry to admit I was too young to experience the wild times," Anthony said with a wistful sigh.

"How old *are* you?" Ron asked.

"Twenty-one."

"A mere puppy."

"An experienced puppy."

"Glad to hear it," Ron said, perching on the edge of Anthony's desk. "And is the...puppy currently involved?"

"No," Anthony said, batting his eyelashes in a slightly girlish way. "Are you?"

"I am," Ron admitted a tad reluctantly.

Anthony threw him a bold look. "Shame."

"Let's go, Ron," Venus said, deciding they'd had enough of each other for now. Best to let the sexual tension build. "I'm taking you to see my gym. It's *so* incredible, you'll crap!"

"Such a lady!" Ron sighed.

"Isn't that why we became friends in the first

place?" she said, grabbing his hand and dragging him off.

Clyde Lomas was driving Alex slowly crazy. The man and his loud voice were an irritating pain in the ass. Every time they entered a house, Clyde went into some kind of insane Realtor riff.

"This here's the wet bar. Over there's the entertaining area. I can assure you—this house has a wonderful flow for parties. Two barbecues, an outdoor *and* indoor Jacuzzi, a black-bottomed pool, and seven bedrooms with bathrooms en suite. The kitchen has four ovens and two dishwashers."

"I'm not *buying* the fucking house," Alex said, completely exasperated. "All I want is to walk through and take a look."

Clyde's long, mournful face became even more so. "Sorry, Alex," he said, crestfallen. "I thought I was being helpful."

"You're very helpful," Russell said, troubleshooting as usual. "It's just that Alex has his own way of doing things."

Alex strolled through the third house on their agenda, the close-knit members of his crew hovering behind him. As soon as he walked into a location, he knew if it was right or not, he didn't need any instructions. He certainly didn't need Clyde Lomas.

The third house—a large mansion situated

on the edge of a golf course—was perfect. He conferred with his cinematographer and set designer, who both agreed with him.

He turned to Russell. "Go ahead and cut a deal."

"How many days?" Russell asked.

"What's on the schedule?"

"Four. I'll be safe, and book it for five."

Alex walked outside to the pool area and called Lili on his mobile. "You were supposed to get back to me with Lucky's home number," he said irritably.

"I can't find it," Lili confessed.

"Excuse me?" Alex said, not used to being told no.

"Freddie's assistant has an embargo on her number. He's not allowed to give it out to anybody."

"Fuck Freddie's assistant. Tell *Freddie I* want it."

"Sorry, Alex, I tried. He said not without her permission."

Alex knew he couldn't push it further without coming across like an overanxious, lovesick schmuck. "What's the latest on Panther?" he asked, abruptly changing the subject.

"I found out a businesswoman bought Panther. The story is, she went into Lucky's office and ordered her off the lot."

"Does this affect *Gangsters*?"

"According to Freddie, everything will proceed as before."

"Does he know this woman?"

"Apparently not."

"Fuck!" Alex exclaimed angrily. "I've really gotta speak to Lucky. What's that guy who works for her?"

"Kyoko?"

"Yeah, get her number from him."

"I tried reaching him, he's no longer at the studio."

"Use your smarts, Lili. Call him at home."

"Yes, Alex. How's everything going there?"

"Fine. What's happening with the test?"

"All set for tomorrow afternoon. Makeup and hair are standing by. Venus will be in at one, Johnny at two. Both of them will be camera-ready by three. Does that suit you?"

"Organized as ever, Lili. Did France tell Tin Lee I'm not coming back?"

"I believe she did. And your mother's called twice."

"What does *she* want?"

"Perhaps you should phone her yourself."

"You do it, say I'm out of town."

"Will you be flying back later?"

"Get me Lucky's number and I'll let you know." He clicked off, stuffed his portable in his pocket, and rejoined his crew.

"Ready for the next location?" Russell asked.

"Take me to it," Alex said. "I definitely want to get out of here tonight."

Morton's was *the* industry hangout. It was always packed with Hollywood movers and shakers, *the* place to be seen. When Lucky entered, every head turned to stare. Today she was big news and they all knew it.

She arrived before Venus, and rather than wait at the bar, she followed the maître d' to her table, navigating her way past tables full of people she knew. She kissed Arnold Kopelson, the producer, and his smart wife, Anne. She waved at the Marvin Davises, stopped to have a word with Joanna and Sidney Poitier, greeted Mel Gibson, blew a kiss at Charlie Dollar, and finally arrived at her destination.

As soon as she sat down, Charlie got up and ambled over. "Hey—" he drawled, tucking his shirt in his pants, disheveled as usual. "The phrase—'stood up'—is not in my vocabulary."

She managed a wan grin. "Sorry, Charlie. Unforeseen circumstances."

"Yeah...I heard," he said, pulling out a chair and sitting down.

She sighed. "So did everyone else in this restaurant."

"Hey, you should've come and got me. I'm the world's greatest expert at packing up."

"It's only temporary, Charlie. I'll be back."

He leaned across the table. "Wanna give me the real scam? There has to be more to this."

"I got screwed. Let's put it this way, it won't happen again."

"Well, Lucky," he said, looking sincere for once in his life. "Don't forget, I'm always here for you."

"Thanks, Charlie, I appreciate your concern."

His stoned eyes restlessly scanned the room. "Who're you having dinner with?"

"Venus."

"Oh, yeah, Venus. Didn't'ja wanna fix me up with her?"

"You can join us for coffee if you like."

"Maybe," he said, getting up.

"Playing hard to get, Charlie?"

A crazy grin swept across his face. "Baby, the only thing hard about *me* is my head. Ain't age a bitch!"

Venus entered a few minutes later, pausing in the doorway just long enough for everybody to turn and stare. She looked her usual sexy self in a white Thierry Mugler suit and funky lace-up boots.

The maître d' led her over to Lucky. She followed him without stopping, knowing that if she paused at one table, she'd have to stop at them all. Behaving like a star gave Venus a thrill, for she never forgot her humble beginnings. If people wished to greet her, they'd pay homage when she was settled.

Lucky stood up as she approached. They hugged and kissed.

"I'm *so* glad we're doing this," Venus said enthusiastically. "I've really missed you."

"Missed you, too," Lucky responded. "Although I'd better tell you before somebody else does—this isn't the greatest night of my life."

An attentive waiter appeared at their table. Lucky ordered Perrier while Venus opted for a margarita.

"What happened?" Venus asked as soon as their waiter was out of earshot.

"Panther was taken over today," Lucky said, drumming her fingers on the table. "I was canned as head of the studio."

"You've *got* to be joking!" Venus exclaimed.

"I wish I was. But, hey—don't start sobbing in your milk and cookies, I'll get it back and then some."

"I've no doubt you will. Who took over?"

"That's the weird thing. It's not one of the big conglomerates, it's a woman with a reputation as a corporate raider. She wanted Panther big time, and somehow or other she got it."

"Will she run the studio?"

Lucky laughed humorlessly. "You'll *really* get a kick out of this one. *Guess* who she's bringing in? *Your* favorite and *mine*—Mickey Stolli."

"Get *outta* here!"

"It's true," Lucky said. "The woman is obviously deranged. Anybody with any sense would know Mickey's going to steal anything that's not nailed down. Hey," she added with a brittle laugh, "maybe that's what she deserves."

"I'm confused," Venus said. "*How* did this happen?"

"That's what I have to find out."

The waiter brought their drinks to the table. "Compliments of Mr. Dollar," he said with an *I'm an out-of-work actor hoping to get discovered* smile.

"Thank Mr. Dollar, and tell him next time it'll be a bottle of Cristal or nothing," Venus said, picking up her margarita. The waiter nodded and left. "Y'know, Lucky, I've tried calling you so many times. How come you wouldn't let your friends in?"

"Lennie's death was such a horrible shock..." Lucky said, her eyes clouding over. "I guess it was numbing...." She paused for a long moment before continuing. "I opted for work—not friends. That way I didn't have to deal with my true feelings."

"I can understand that," Venus said quietly.

"You want to know the truth?" Lucky said softly. "I miss Lennie every single moment of every single day."

"I'm sure," Venus murmured.

"Anyway," Lucky said, making a supreme effort to change the subject. "Enough about that. Tell me how it went with Alex."

"I'm testing tomorrow with Johnny Romano."

"Alex is making you test?"

"Freddie says I should."

"It's a control move. Mr. Woods is showing you who's boss."

"Oh, God!" Venus wailed. "Now that you're

not running the studio, what'll happen with *Gangsters*?"

"I'm sure this woman isn't dumb enough to mess with the schedule."

"Yeah, well, Mickey hates me," Venus ruminated, sipping her margarita. "Remember that movie where he insisted I take off my clothes when all the male actors weren't asked to show shit? We had a battle royal over *that* one."

Lucky remembered it well. "You're a big star now," she reminded her friend. "Mickey won't give you any trouble."

An agent came over to their table, an agent with a mission to get Venus to read a client's script. He greeted Lucky briefly—after all, what good was she anymore?—and zeroed in on his main prey.

Lucky allowed her mind to wander, thinking about Alex Woods for a moment. She'd had a good time with him, but that was all—he'd served his purpose. And the note he'd sent with the flowers proved she meant nothing to him. Fine with her. Over and out.

Jack Python, the talk-show host, stopped at their table. "Lucky," he said, his penetrating green eyes probing hers. "Sorry to hear the deal."

"What deal, Jack?" she said evenly.

"I understand you're not with Panther anymore."

"Isn't it strange," Lucky said. "Good news travels real slow, but bad news gets around faster than a hooker chasing a client."

"Hey—I didn't mean anything by it," Jack said. "Come on the show and we'll talk about it. I'll give you the full hour."

"What would *I* have to talk about, Jack?"

"People are fascinated by the inner workings of Hollywood, and you're one of the few women—probably the *only* woman—who owned *and* ran her own studio. We could make it an interesting program."

"How come you didn't ask me when I *had* the studio?"

"'Cause your publicist wouldn't let me within twenty feet of you."

She wasn't about to get mad at him. Jack Python was one of the good guys, his talk show was intelligent and fast-paced, far superior to the rest of the late-night mindless chat.

Jack drifted off, and Venus got rid of the agent. They ordered steaks and a bottle of red wine. Venus started telling hilarious stories about Rodriguez, mimicking his accent and his lovemaking techniques.

Lucky found herself relaxing as she listened to her friend carry on. Venus was a strong, outspoken woman. Unlike most female superstars, she had an earthy humor and a kick-ass attitude. She also refused to put up with men's crap when it came to movie-making. Directors and producers were forever trying to coerce her into doing things on-screen she deemed unacceptable. Venus always stood firm—she was never afraid of anything or anyone.

"He's really very sweet—problem is, he tries so hard it's painful!" Venus said, finishing up her Rodriguez stories.

"How about Cooper?" Lucky asked. "Do you miss him?"

"What's to miss?" Venus said dismissively, because she didn't want to get into the fact that, yes—she missed him a lot, and yet there was no going back.

Lucky scanned the room. Charlie was paying his check, which meant it wouldn't be long before he came over. "What do you think of Charlie Dollar?" she asked casually.

"Old Charlie's the greatest," Venus said, chewing on a piece of steak. "Trouble is, he's always so stoned."

"Isn't that part of his charm?"

"Coke and charm do not mix," Venus said firmly. "Although I hear he's a pretty good lay."

"Really?"

"*Not* that I'm planning on finding out," Venus added quickly.

"*Would* you go out with him?" Lucky asked.

Venus shook her head vigorously. "Dangerous territory," she said. "There's no way Charlie would be capable of sustaining a decent relationship, he's been a movie star too long. Women are easy for him—he doesn't give a shit about any of them."

Lucky agreed. "Commitment is not exactly his bag," she said. "It's not mine anymore either. The only commitment I have is to my children and to getting my studio back."

By the time Charlie ambled his way over to

312

their table, Lucky had called for the check.

"Here comes your favorite movie star," he said with his usual maniacal grin. "Ready to delight and entertain."

"You don't have to bother," Lucky said lightly. "We entertained each other."

He zoomed in on Venus. "Wanna hit the clubs? Tango the night away with a decrepit old icon?"

"Gotta get an early night, Charlie," she said apologetically. "I'm shooting tomorrow. Besides," she added wickedly, "what would you do with me—I'm over eighteen!"

He favored her with another crazed grin. "I could give you bags under your eyes you'd never forget," he offered.

"Thanks, this time I'll pass."

Much to Charlie's chagrin they departed shortly after—leaving him in the company of an aging movie star with a bad toupee, and a Lakers cheerleader with enormous silicone breasts. Charlie got along with everyone.

Outside the restaurant, they waited for their cars.

"We gotta do this again, *soon,*" Venus said. "You're more fun than a date any day!"

"Gee, thanks," Lucky said, laughing. "*And* you didn't even have to put out!"

"What a relief!"

"Call me after the test."

"I'll do that," Venus said, getting into her all-black limo, driven by an armed security guard.

The valet pulled up in Lucky's red Ferrari.

They waved their good-byes and took off into
the night.

Lucky drove home fast, taking the San
Vicente/Pacific Coast Highway route. It had
been an exhausting twenty-four hours and
she couldn't wait to collapse into bed and
get a good night's sleep. Had to get her head
straight so she could work out how she was
going to deal with this latest setback, because
that's all it was—a temporary setback.

As soon as she'd apprised Boogie of what
needed to be done, she planned on taking
the kids and staying at Gino's in Palm Springs
for a long weekend.

She picked up the car phone to warn him.

"You again." Gino sighed. "You gotta be after
somethin', kiddo. First an unexpected visit, now
the late-night phone call."

"I'm not waking you, am I?"

"No way. Paige an' I are sittin' here watchin'
The Godfather. I take a look at it once a year.
Godfather One and *Two*—forget *Three.*"

"Getting in touch with old friends, huh?"
Lucky joked.

"One of these days I'll tell you my real life
story, kiddo," he said, and chuckled. "Gino—
the early years. Whatta movie it'd make!"

"I don't doubt it. I heard stories about you
from more people than you'd care to know
about."

"So what's up now?" he asked. "Anythin' I can help with?"

She decided not to tell him the real truth. Why burden him with her problems? "I was thinking of bringing the children down for a long weekend."

"You mean I actually get to see my grand-kids?"

"Oh c'mon, Gino, you see them all the time."

"I'm teasin' you, kiddo. I'll have Paige get everythin' ready."

Gino sounded so content. He didn't seem to miss big-city life at all. It was obvious he loved living in Palm Springs in his big house with Paige to keep him company.

She wondered if that's what she should do—buy a house in Santa Barbara and forget about the film business, just veg out and be with her kids.

No way. She'd be bored within days. She needed action, and plenty of it.

She pressed in a tape and listened to Joe Cocker's raspy growl on "You Are So Beautiful." It was one of Lennie's favorites.

Recklessly, she drove faster, breaking the speed limit on the Pacific Coast Highway, racing all the way home.

Zooming into her driveway, she jumped out of the car and entered her house. Everyone was asleep. First she peeked in at the children, then she went upstairs to her bedroom and walked out onto the small terrace, remembering the times she and Lennie had made love on the sand below with only the sound of the roaring surf to keep them company.

The phone rang. She picked up the portable.

"Do you know how difficult it's been reaching you?" said a pissed-off Alex Woods.

Somehow or other he'd gotten her home number; she wasn't pleased.

"I haven't exactly been available," she said, not inclined to get into a fight with him.

"I called you at the studio this morning," he said accusingly. "Left several messages."

"I'm sure you're aware of what went on today. I wasn't exactly in a returning phone calls mood."

"Yeah, I heard." A long pause. "Are you okay?"

"I'm fine, thank you."

"Uh...about the note that came with the flowers. You got 'em, didn't you?"

"You shouldn't have bothered."

"Wrong flowers. Wrong note."

"Really?"

"Although it beats me why I sent you anything at all after you walked out on me this morning."

She took a deep breath. "Listen, Alex— let's be truthful with each other. We were a one-night fling. I needed to be with somebody, and you happened to be there."

"Oh, that's nice," he said. "How do you think that makes me feel?"

"It didn't mean anything to either of us.... I did it to get back at Lennie. I'm sorry."

There was a long silence.

"When I didn't hear from you, I stayed in Vegas," he said at last.

"What are you doing there?"

"Location scouting. I'll be back tomorrow." Another long silence. "Can we get together tomorrow night?"

She sighed. "Didn't you hear what I just said?"

"Lucky," he said persuasively, "you need me at a time like this."

"What can you do, Alex?" she said wearily. "Hold my hand while other people take control of my studio?"

"I didn't call you to argue."

"What *did* you call for?"

"To say that last night was...special."

"No, Alex," she said flatly. "Please hear what I'm saying. It was just another one-night stand on both our parts."

"You're wrong, Lucky. I've had enough one-night stands to know when it's special."

Why couldn't he just go away? She didn't need complications. "I'm sorry if I gave you a false impression."

He couldn't believe she was giving him the runaround. That he, Alex Woods, was actually getting shut out by a woman. "I can tell you're not in the mood to talk," he said abruptly. "I'll call you tomorrow."

"You're wasting your time."

"That's my problem."

She shut the phone. Alex Woods was not going to be put off easily.

Venus's long black limousine glided through the gates of her estate. As the limo passed the guardhouse, the guard emerged, waving for the car to stop.

The driver lowered his window. "Anything wrong?"

"No, no," the guard answered. "Please tell Miss Venus her brother's here."

"My *what*?" Venus said, jumping to attention in the backseat.

"Your brother Emilio, miss," the guard said, peering into the car.

"And you *let* him in my house!" she exploded, horrified.

"Well, er...yes, he had proof he was your brother," the guard said, taking a step back.

"*What* proof?" she demanded.

"Pictures of you together, his passport. I know your real name is Sierra, so I thought it was all right to allow him in."

"Well, it's *not*," Venus said angrily. "How many times have I got to tell you people, *nobody* enters my house unless I say so."

The guard took umbrage at her tone. "I was only doing my duty," he sulked.

"Your *duty* is to keep *everybody* out unless I leave *specific* instructions."

She was so furious she could scarcely breathe. Emilio Sierra. Slob brother number one. He'd sold her out to the tabloids so many times it was ridiculous. Then he'd gone off to live in

Europe, and she'd hoped and prayed he'd never come back. Recently, she'd heard he'd returned, and she'd known it was only a matter of time before he turned up again.

Goddamn it! Why did it have to be tonight?

She instructed her driver to wait while she picked up the car phone and summoned Rodriguez.

"My darling," Rodriguez said, delighted to hear from her. "I waited by the phone all day. Nobody called from casting."

Did he have to be so obvious? His eagerness to be in her video was a turnoff.

"What are you doing, Rodriguez?"

"Waiting for you, of course."

"I feel like a long, sensual massage," she murmured seductively. "Can you come over now?"

"Of course!"

"Let's go," she instructed her driver.

The limo rode smoothly up to her house, depositing her in front. She got out and marched inside.

Sitting in her living room, feet up on her marble coffee table, guzzling a bottle of beer while watching a cable porno movie on her big-screen TV was her dear brother.

Déjà vu. Hadn't this happened to her before?

"You're *not* welcome here, Emilio," she said, trying to control her fury at his nerve. "I can't believe you're back. Have you no idea what you've done to me?"

"What?" he asked, barely able to drag his eyes away from two blonds busily stroking each other's silicone implants on the TV screen.

She grabbed the remote, switching the TV off. "You sold me out," she said angrily, "time after time after time."

Emilio lumbered to his feet, placing his beer on the marble table without a coaster. Then he attempted to turn on the charm, of which he had none.

"I was in a bind, sis," he said in a whiny voice. "Had debts to pay off. Now I'm clean. I bin in AA, drug rehab, the whole bit. You gotta give me another chance."

"I don't have to give you anything," she said, outraged that he would even dare to ask.

"Look," he said, gesturing around her sumptuous living room. "You got everything. Me—I got zilch."

"I worked hard for what I've got while you sat around on your fat ass doing nothing."

Emilio's small eyes turned crafty. "If our mom was alive, what d'you think *she'd* want you to do?"

"Shove it, Emilio. Don't start with that guilt-trip shit—it doesn't work anymore."

"I'm your brother," he whined, still trying. "We're the same flesh and blood. I'm one of the few people who care about you."

Now he was going too far. "Get the fuck out of here!" she said contemptuously.

"No," he mumbled sulkily. "You want me out, call the cops."

"You think I won't?" she threatened, glancing toward the door, hoping Rodriguez would put in an appearance soon. "What happened to your big romance in Europe?"

Emilio pulled a face. "She was too old," he said. "I wasn't sittin' around for twenty years waiting for the old bag to drop."

"You really are a piece of work," Venus said, shaking her head. "What did she do—dump you when she discovered what a loser you really are?"

"I left on my own," he said resentfully.

"And you couldn't *wait* to come mooching off me again."

Fortunately, Rodriguez chose that moment to arrive. He swept in, stopping short when he spotted Emilio.

"Ah, Rodriguez," Venus said. "Meet my brother Emilio, he was just leaving."

"No, I wasn't," Emilio contradicted.

"Yes, you *are*," Venus insisted.

They glared at each other.

Rodriguez glanced from one to the other and decided it wasn't prudent to get involved.

Venus was not allowing him that privilege. She turned to him, giving a short, impassioned speech. "I don't speak to my brother," she said hotly. "I don't even *like* my brother. Now he's here in my house. How do I get rid of him?"

Rodriguez shrugged.

"How about throwing him out for me?" Venus said hopefully. "I'll have the guard help you."

"Throw me out, little sis, and you'll regret

it," Emilio warned. "If you think what I've done up until now is bad, just you wait. I'll give the tabloids somethin' that'll blow your cushy life to pieces."

She could see she was getting nowhere. "I'll tell you what, I'll give you fifty bucks— go get yourself a hotel room for the night. Then tomorrow, find yourself a job."

Emilio's expression turned cunning. "Make it a thousand and I'm outta here."

"This is *not* a negotiation," she said coldly, close to losing it.

He scratched his chin. "I don't get it, a thousand's nothin' to you. You buy shoes cost more than that."

Rodriguez drew her to one side. "Give him the money," he suggested. "Then maybe he'll go away."

"Emilio will *never* go away," she moaned.

"At least it'll get him out of your house."

He was right, getting rid of her brother was the important thing.

"You don't happen to have a thousand bucks on you, Rodriguez?" she asked.

He didn't even bother answering that one.

Leaving the two of them downstairs, she hurried up to her bedroom safe, closing the door behind her, remembering the time Emilio had gotten hold of her combination, stolen pictures of her and Martin Swanson together, and blackmailed her.

She took out a thousand dollars in cash and returned downstairs.

Emilio practically had his hand out.

She gave him the neat stack of bills. "Good-bye," she said with a cold stare. "Don't come back."

He shoved the money in his pocket, shaking his head as if *she* was the bad one. "Little sis," he said sadly. "You don't have a good memory, do you?"

"For what?"

"Our childhood. The good times."

Who was he kidding? Four brothers and a father to look after. She'd been their unwilling slave, and they'd all treated her like shit.

"Good-bye," she repeated, hustling him to the door.

She needed a good night's rest, tomorrow was her test with Johnny Romano, and she had to impress Alex Woods. But Rodriguez being there was okay—sex would give her that special glow—better than makeup any day.

When Emilio was gone, she took Rodriguez's hand, leading him upstairs to her bedroom. "Tomorrow I must look relaxed and beautiful," she said. "So...I'd like it if you made long, leisurely love to me and then went home. Can you oblige?"

"My princess," he said, passionate Latin eyes boring into hers. "You are asking the right man."

33

"More champagne?" Michel suggested.

"Thanks," Brigette said, allowing him to refill her glass.

The two of them were alone in his apartment now. All the guests had departed, including an angry Robertson. Brigette had overheard them having a heated discussion at the front door.

"You make me sick," Robertson had said in a low, furious whisper. "You remind me of a randy old dog."

"Don't say foolish things you will regret," Michel had replied, remaining calm.

"The only thing *I* regret is that I moved in with you in the first place," Robertson had said. Then she'd left, slamming the door in his face.

Brigette knew she was intruding on another female's territory, but she couldn't help herself, she found Michel hypnotically attractive even though he was old enough to be her father.

She sat on the couch in his living room, waiting to see what kind of moves an experienced older man made.

A waiter removed several used glasses from the coffee table and left the room, discreetly shutting the door behind him.

"A toast to you, Brigette," Michel said, raising his glass and clinking it with hers. "We do it the French way," he said. "Twist your arm around mine—like so." She tried to do as he asked. His arm slipped, accidentally nudging her breasts. She giggled. "Is something amusing you?" Michel asked.

"I don't know," she said, feeling the effect of several glasses of wine and now the champagne. "You, me, here. A few weeks ago I couldn't even get an interview with you. Now you're my agent, and I'm sitting in your apartment."

"I will tell you what I like about you, Brigette," Michel said, lightly touching her cheek with his fingers. "Your naiveté. It is so refreshing."

She didn't tell him that her mother had been a famous heiress, and that her stepfather was Lennie Golden. She didn't tell him about growing up surrounded by luxury and riches, or that she was also an heiress, due to inherit millions of dollars when she reached twenty-one.

She certainly didn't tell him about Tim Wealth or Santino Bonnatti. These were *her* secrets, and she was not about to reveal them to anyone.

"I'm not naive," she objected. "I've been around."

"You haven't been anywhere, my darling girl. You know nothing of life. You have no idea what will happen when your name is famous and your face is everywhere."

Bingo! He *was* the man of her dreams, sent to protect her.

"Are you a virgin, Brigette?" he asked in a fatherly, concerned voice.

She sensed he required a yes. Not that it was any of his business.

"Sort of..." she lied. Tim Wealth had taken her virginity when she was fifteen. Maybe one day, when she knew Michel better, she'd tell him the story.

"How charming you are," Michel said, moving closer. "Charming and so very sweet. Untouched by the dark side of this business."

"What's the dark side?" she asked curiously.

"A lot of the models do drugs. Uppers, downers, cocaine...even heroin."

Big secret. She knew about drugs, her coke freak fiancé had taught her plenty. Not that she'd ever indulged, she was too smart. Drugs had killed her mother.

"Does Robertson? Is that why she's so thin?"

"Too thin," Michel said without responding to her question.

"I wouldn't mind being thinner."

"No!" he said forcefully. "You are a peach ready to be split open so the right man can gently suck the virgin nectar."

She shivered as his arm enclosed her shoulders, long, sensitive fingers gently stroking her skin.

He was moving very slowly, too slowly, for she felt a sudden rush of desire. It was eighteen months since she'd broken up with her fiancé. Eighteen long months since a man had been anywhere near her. She wanted him to touch her breasts without waiting another moment.

She leaned back against the couch, feeling quite light-headed. Michel bent to kiss her neck.

"That's nice," she murmured encouragingly, smelling his strong aftershave and the faint whiff of garlic on his breath.

He reached behind her, clicking off the light. Then, without any warning, he rolled on top of her and began pulling at her skirt, attempting to push it above her waist.

"No!" she said sharply, sitting up. He was French—weren't Frenchmen supposed to be incredible, experienced lovers? Especially *old* Frenchmen. Michel was behaving no differently than any other male. Five minutes of romance—then bingo—he was on an unstoppable mission to score. She hadn't waited eighteen months for a fast roll on his couch.

"Something the matter?" he asked, his crinkly blue eyes not quite so kindly.

"I...I don't want you to do that," she said, drawing away from him.

He stood up, placing himself directly in front of her. She could see his erection straining his dark gray pants, it was practically in her face.

"Am I going too fast for you?" he asked matter-of-factly, as if there were a certain procedure they had to follow.

"Yes," she said, averting her eyes.

"Then I apologize," he said, picking up the champagne bottle and refilling her glass.

She waited patiently. The neck kissing was very pleasant, more would be acceptable.

He rubbed his erection as he sat down beside her. "Drink up," he said.

"No more, thank you," she said, thinking that maybe it was time to go home.

"I frighten you, don't I?" he said, his voice sounding strangely thick.

"No...why would you?"

"Sex...growing up...the unknown...it's always frightening. I can teach you many things...."

A warning voice sounded in her head. Michel was not the man she'd imagined; it was definitely time for a fast exit. "I think I'll be going now," she said, trying to sound casual.

She went to stand up. With one swift, unexpected move he grabbed both her wrists, pinning them together and raising them above her head. Then he lay half on top of her, crushing her body beneath his on the couch.

"What are you *doing*?" she yelled, trying to push him off.

Reaching down the side of the couch, he produced a long silk scarf with which he expertly bound her wrists together.

"Stop it!" she shrieked, truly alarmed.

"Initiation can be harsh," he said as if speaking to himself. "Later, when you realize what gratification you'll get from the things I will teach you, you'll thank me."

Oh, God! Just like Santino Bonnatti, he was some weirdo sex freak.

Stay calm.

Don't panic.

"Get...off...me..." she said, striving to shift his weight. "If you release me now, I won't tell anyone."

"Brigette," he said in a kindly tone, "surely you must be eager to learn?"

"Stop it, Michel. I'm warning you—"

"Warning me of what, *ma chérie*?" With another swift move he pulled the top of her dress down, exposing her breasts. "Ah..." he sighed. "Just as beautiful as I imagined."

Then he picked her up as if she weighed

nothing, and carried her into the bedroom where he threw her down in the center of his oversized four-poster bed. Before she had a chance to move, his strong hands clawed at her panties, ripping them off.

She attempted to kick him, but he was too fast for her. With a firm grip on her left ankle, he tied it to the bedpost. Then he did the same with her right one.

She began to scream.

"This is the penthouse, my *petite coquette*. The staff have left. There is no one to hear," he said calmly.

Except for her dress bunched around her waist she was completely naked and exposed.

Oh, God! He was going to rape her, and she was totally helpless. Tears filled her eyes, rolling silently down her cheeks.

"Don't cry," he said, his voice gentle. "You have my solemn promise I will not touch you."

"Why...are...you...doing...this?" she sobbed.

"It is better this way," he said soothingly. "You look so sweet...your furry little pussy begging for attention, so pink and ready."

"Let me go," she begged. "Please...it's not too late."

He walked to the door, throwing it open. Robertson entered the room wearing a short Roman toga and nothing else.

"Thank God!" Brigette gasped, thinking rescue was at hand.

"Now," Michel said, settling into a chair angled so he could comfortably view the bed. "You will learn what real pleasure is all about."

34

Boogie ambled into her house early in the morning.

Lucky was waiting for him. "We need to have a meeting," she said. "Immediately."

Boogie followed her into the den without saying a word.

Maria ran out from the kitchen, falling into step behind them. "Me come, too, Mommy! Me, too!" she singsonged.

"No, sweetheart," Lucky said firmly. "You stay with Cee Cee. Mommy's got business to conduct."

"Bus-a-nez," Maria said and giggled uncontrollably. "Me come, too."

"Cee Cee," Lucky called out.

Cee Cee appeared.

The little girl began kicking and yelling. "Wanna be with Mommy. WANNA BE WITH MY MOMMY."

"I promise we'll go see Grandpa later," Lucky said. "But only if you're a good girl and eat up all your breakfast."

Cee Cee scooped Maria up and carried her back to the kitchen.

"Maria's exactly like me," Lucky said ruefully, running a hand through her long dark curls. "When she wants something, she wants it now." Boogie nodded. "Nice vacation, Boog?"

He nodded again. "Okay," she said. "Let's get down to it—here's the big news. While you were away, Panther was taken over."

Boogie let out a long, low whistle.

"Yeah, I know, it was a shock to me, too." She lit up a cigarette, drew deeply, and continued. "What I need is a full report on the woman who did this—family, where she's from, information on any company she's involved with, who her business partners are, all of that. If you have to hire other people, that's okay, as long as you keep it confidential. And I want everything as soon as possible."

"Right," Boogie said, his long, thin face alert.

"And put Morton Sharkey under surveillance. Something's wrong—I don't know what. Get me stuff on his wife and kids, too—maybe his behavior has something to do with them."

"No problem," Boogie said.

"Then there's a Mrs. Smorg, whose only address is care of a lawyer in Pasadena. Find out who she is, where she lives. And everything about Conquest Investments—a company based in the Bahamas."

"You got it."

She walked over to the drinks tray and contemplated pouring herself a Scotch.

Too early. Not the answer. Besides, she still had a lingering hangover.

"Okay, I guess that's it for now."

Boogie followed her across the room. "Are you all right?" he asked.

She shrugged. "The truth is, I feel totally helpless until I get a full picture."

phone call; she was not reacting as planned. Too bad for her, there were plenty of women who'd cream at the chance to spend ten minutes in his company. Tin Lee would do anything he asked, so would a lot of other females he could think of.

He had that *I just wanna lie down and die* hungover feeling. And now he had to arrive back in L.A. ready to deal with Johnny Romano's and Venus's vast egos, because he knew it wasn't going to be Disneyland once those two got together.

When he arrived at his office, he found a stack of messages to be dealt with. In his absence, Lili could handle only so much; many things needed his personal attention.

"Johnny Romano requires a script conference," Lili informed him. "He's also insisting Armani design his clothes, and as wardrobe has quite rightly pointed out, Armani was not around during that time period."

He'd known when Freddie had talked him into using Johnny Romano that the superstar actor was going to be trouble. He'd hired him anyway, because Johnny was exactly right for the part. Thank God he'd gone with an unknown actor for the other lead role.

"I'll deal with it," he said shortly. "He's coming in to test with Venus today, right?"

"He said to be sure to tell you he's only doing it as a personal favor to you."

Alex laughed dryly. "Some thrill, huh? Dealing with stars."

"You'll handle him," Lili responded in her

usual unruffled fashion. "You always do."

"You coming to the set with me today, Lili?" he asked, feeling like some sympathetic female company.

"If you want me to," she said. She liked it when Alex was in one of his needy moods.

"What would I do without you, Lili?" He sighed, flashing a wan version of his killer smile, well aware that whatever he did, she would always be his faithful fan.

"You'd manage," she said crisply, knowing full well he wouldn't. He'd fall to pieces without her smooth organizational skills keeping everything together. Alex was not easy to work for, but she'd mastered the art of keeping him happy. She met his every need—except sexually. Lili was glad that part of their relationship was over; he'd been a selfish lover, but that was okay, she'd understood he was damaged. Alex didn't know how to give because he'd never had to. His domineering mother had ruined him in that area.

"Okay, let's go," Alex said, always on the move. "And bring the Vicodin—I'm half dead."

Every day, Leslie Kane read the trades from cover to cover. She felt it was important to know exactly what was happening in town, it gave her an edge.

Today she noted that Lucky Santangelo was out at Panther Studios. Interesting. Then she went on to read that Mickey Stolli was being reinstated as studio head. Very interesting, because it was Mickey's wife, Abigaile, who'd discovered her and made Mickey give her her first big break.

Next she read about Venus testing for the part of Lola in Alex Woods's hot new movie, *Gangsters*. She immediately grabbed the phone and called her agent.

"Why aren't I up for this role?" she demanded.

"Because it's only a cameo," her agent replied.

"I don't care. It's a cameo in an Alex Woods film. Get me a script."

"I'll talk to Alex today."

"You do that. Oh, and Quinn—in future, kindly apprise me of everything—let *me* make the decisions."

Who did he think he was dealing with? The same naive girl who'd been discovered in a beauty parlor? No, she was Leslie Kane, the current darling of the American screen and, as such, she should be treated with the right amount of respect.

She decided to play it out without using her connections as far as Mickey and Abigaile were concerned. They were her insurance—Leslie knew that if she put on the pressure, the part was hers.

Sometimes Leslie wondered what Abigaile would say if she knew about her sordid past. Mickey didn't remember her—even though he'd once attended a bachelor party for a big producer in her call-girl days. He and his friends had behaved appallingly, all they were interested in was humiliating and degrading the women, and getting their dicks sucked. A bunch of out-of-control pigs.

Thank God she'd had the strength to get out of that particular business after meeting Eddie. At least he'd done *something* for her.

Jeff Stoner entered the bedroom, a towel tied casually around his waist. He had wet hair and a big grin. He looked happy, and so he should, he was living with one of the most successful young actresses in Hollywood.

"Can we go see the new Mercedes today?" he asked.

She'd told him she wanted to buy another car, and she knew Jeff was thinking that if he helped pick it out, he'd more than likely be the one to drive it.

"Maybe," she said, keeping him hanging.

Jeff was a nice guy, but nobody could live up to Cooper.

For over two months now she'd been plotting and planning how to get Cooper back. He was ensconced in his former apartment and refused to take her calls.

What had she done? Nothing, except love him. The fact that he'd gotten caught wasn't her fault. He was blaming her, and she didn't like it.

She'd loved him, now she was beginning to hate him.

But what could she do?

★ ★ ★

Johnny Romano had the look of a true movie star with his thick, sensual lips, sly smile, and deep-set, sexually inviting brown eyes. He was Hispanic, six feet tall, and of slender build, although he'd developed his upper body enough to boast a powerful set of muscles.

Women couldn't get enough of Johnny Romano.

Johnny Romano couldn't get enough of women.

They were his addiction. Conquering them was everything. Johnny had an insatiable sexual appetite—it was not unusual for him to bed one or two women a day. Ever aware of the peril of AIDS, he protected himself with two condoms and a cavalier attitude, although he'd assured himself AIDS could never happen to *him*. He was a megastar, for God's sake, and what's more, he was a *straight* megastar. The condoms were merely a gesture in the right direction, a nod to the good Lord, because Johnny was also a devout Catholic boy.

Eighteen months previously he'd been stood up at the altar by Warner Franklin, a black lady cop. The ungrateful witch had run off with a six-foot-ten American basketball player just before they were due to wed in Europe. Johnny had never forgiven her. As far as he was concerned, Warner had given all women a bad name.

He was pleased to be testing with Venus

Maria, he'd always had a thing for her—even though, in the past, when he'd invited her out, she'd turned him down. Now that she wanted to be in *Gangsters* it could be his chance to finally score.

He strode onto the set, his entourage hovering protectively around him, ready to zip into action in case any uninvited mortal approached their star without express permission.

Alex moved over to greet him. "Johnny," he said as they exchanged a firm, macho handshake. "I appreciate you doing this, so does Venus."

"That's okay, man," Johnny said magnanimously. "Anything for you."

Yeah, sure. When it suits you.

"So..." Alex said. "What's all this crap I hear about you wanting Armani to design your clothes? We all know Armani wasn't around then. Whoever came up with that idea is just plain dumb."

Even the slightest hint of being thought of as dumb sent Johnny into a spin. "Sure, Alex," he agreed. "Armani—ha! Who the fuck thought of *that*?"

Alex said, "I know it wasn't you."

Johnny said, "No way, man."

"Wardrobe is designing special outfits for the character. You'll love 'em. This part's made for you, Johnny, you'll be great in it."

"I know," Johnny said immodestly. "And, Alex, we gotta sit down for a script conference. There's a few things I wanna change."

"Of course," Alex said pleasantly, while

thinking, *Fuck you, asshole. I'm not changing one word of my script.*

"Where's the lady?" Johnny asked, strolling behind the camera.

"On her way."

"Haven't seen Venus in a while," Johnny said casually. "Tough broad—stupid, too—she made the mistake of marrying Cooper Turner when she could've had me."

Oh, Christ! Alex thought. *She never fucked him, and he's pissed.*

"Good morning, Johnny," Lili said with a welcoming handshake.

Johnny favored her with a sleepy smile. "Hi'ya, gorgeous. How come the man let you out of the office?"

"To see you, of course," Lili replied, right on cue.

Alex smiled to himself. Lili always knew the right thing to say to keep a superstar happy.

Venus walked onto the set a few minutes later, dressed in a low-cut, clinging scarlet dress, her hair blonder than ever. She looked spectacular. Accompanying her was a smaller entourage than Johnny's. Three people—hair, makeup, and Anthony—whom she'd allowed to come along as a special treat.

"Wheeew!" Johnny whistled admiringly as he watched her approach. "Lookin' good, girl. Lookin' creamy *hot*!"

"Hi, Johnny," she said casually, knowing full well he wanted to get her into bed.

"You know what, baby?" he said, enveloping her in a crushing hug. "I gotta notion it's finally gonna be *you* an' *me*. It's time, girl."

"Let's rehearse," Alex said, anxious to get started before they got on each other's case.

"I'm ready," Venus said, moving out from Johnny's crushing hug.

She wasn't in the best of moods on account of the fact that Emilio had called this morning saying he wanted more money. And on her way out of the house, the same stupid guard who'd let Emilio in had handed her a letter that had been left in the guardhouse when the jerk was away from his post taking a leak—and it turned out to be another porno love outpouring from her number-one fan. What a weirdo! The letters made her very uneasy.

On the good side, Rodriguez had made love to her with a great deal of finesse the previous evening. She had to admit he improved every time they did it. She decided she'd definitely put him in her video, give him a thrill, he was young and eager—he deserved a reward.

Alex was a dynamo on the set. Moving fast, like a prowling black panther, he knew everything that was going on and was into everybody's business. Nobody lagged behind on an Alex Woods set, they didn't dare.

The test went smoothly. Johnny was on his best behavior, and Venus was really into it.

When they were finished, Alex said, "You both did a fine job, thanks." He was impressed with Venus's performance. If it translated onto the screen, the role was hers.

"Yeah," Johnny agreed. "My Venus here is one hot little tamale, ain't'cha, baby?" He patted her intimately on the ass.

She patted him right back, pinching his butt so he felt it. "Don't call me names, Johnny," she said pleasantly. "'Cause I got a few I can call you. Okay?"

Johnny roared with laughter. "She's something!"

It occurred to Venus that working with him would be a nightmare, his ego was probably as big as the Empire State Building.

Johnny turned to Alex, his expression turning serious. "Hey, man," he said, "when we gonna meet on the script? I need my changes."

"Tell you what, Johnny, have your notes typed up and I'll take a look. Right now I'm in the middle of preproduction—no time."

Venus knew Alex was giving Johnny the runaround. She wasn't surprised, Johnny was too stupid to get it. He was so busy being Mister Big Movie Star he didn't get anything except himself. It's a shame he wasn't more self-deprecating like Charlie Dollar—he took the whole star trip far too seriously.

She walked away from them both, proud of her performance, sure she'd done well.

Anthony was glowing with the excitement of being on a film set in such close proximity to Johnny Romano.

"You were *wonderful!*" he assured Venus on the way out. "I'm *completely* impressed."

She decided Anthony would also get a

reward. She'd lure Ron over again, all they needed was a touch of encouragement.

Smiling, she headed for her limousine. As far as she was concerned, she'd snagged the part.

35

Brigette awoke in her own bed in the bedroom of the apartment she shared with Nona and Zandino. She lay very still for a moment, gazing blankly at the ceiling. Her tears were long gone. Everything about last night was a hazy blur. She remembered Michel bundling her into a cab with the words, "Whatever you do, Brigette—this is *our* secret. It will only harm you if you tell stories. I know you wouldn't want our very private photo shoot becoming public property, would you now?"

For several endless hours Michel and Robertson had made her their plaything. True to his word, Michel hadn't touched her, but he'd watched *everything*. And Robertson had done everything, in spite of her protests.

She still felt vulnerable and exposed, even though her ordeal was over.

Why hadn't she listened to Nona? Although Nona had no idea Michel was such a pervert, she'd thought he was nothing more than just another sleazy playboy.

The sad truth was that Michel got off on watching women together—especially when one of them was an unwilling victim, bound and helpless.

When Santino Bonnatti had abused her, there'd been a weapon at hand and she'd used it, never experiencing a moment of remorse.

There'd been nothing to fight Michel with; she'd had no choice but to lie there and take it.

When she'd gotten home, Zan and Nona were asleep. She'd crept into the bathroom, standing under a long, cleansing shower before crawling miserably into bed—where she'd lain awake for hours before falling into a troubled sleep.

Now it was morning and she could hear Nona and Zan in the kitchen. She realized she'd better get up. *Be cool,* she warned herself. *Don't tell them what happened. It could spoil everything.*

She climbed out of bed and reached for her robe, noticing purple bruises on her wrists. Looking down, she was dismayed to discover more bruises on her ankles and the insides of her thighs. She wrapped the robe around herself, pulling it tight.

"Hmm..." Nona said, glancing up when Brigette entered the kitchen. "What happened to *you* last night?"

Did Nona suspect? No. It was just her way of eliciting information.

"Nothing much," she said vaguely, opening the fridge and taking out a carton of milk.

Nona was determined to find out everything. "Don't give me that nothing much bit. Did he jump you? Did the great lover get it on?"

"No..." Brigette said evasively. "He was a gentleman."

"Michel—a *gentleman*?" Nona snorted. "*Now* I've heard everything."

Brigette poured herself a cup of coffee. Although she appeared outwardly calm, inside she was shaking.

She sat down at the table and picked up a newspaper. Zan beamed at her. Nothing ever bothered him.

"Okay, so you don't want to talk," Nona said, a little bit put out. "C'mon, Zan, we've got to go over to my parents' this morning." She turned to Brigette. "Don't forget to drop by Antonio's studio today to meet the stylist, make-up, and hair people. It's all been arranged."

Brigette nodded. "Okay."

"Here's the address," Nona said, handing her a slip of paper. "Shall I meet you there?"

"I can handle it."

"We're catching the new Al Pacino movie tonight. Wanna come?"

"I...I don't think so."

"Hmm..." Nona said disapprovingly. "Seeing Michel again?"

"No, thought I'd get an early night, y'know— what with the shoot tomorrow..." She trailed off, wishing Nona would leave already.

"Good thinking," Nona said briskly, grabbing Zan's hand. "By the way, my parents are planning another one of their little bashes next Friday. Keep it free."

As soon as Nona and Zan left, she picked up the phone and called Isaac, the model from the Rock 'n' Roll Jeans shoot.

He sounded as if he were asleep. Too bad. "Remember me?" she said brightly. "Brigette Brown, your partner in jeans."

"Hey—baby," he said, rousing himself. "Gotta say I had a blast that day."

"I need a favor," she said, getting right to it.

"Like what?"

"Like I can't discuss it over the phone. Can we meet for lunch?"

"Sure," Isaac said, suggesting a small Italian restaurant on Second Avenue.

Brigette arrived first and waited outside, impatiently walking up and down the sidewalk.

Isaac pulled up five minutes later on a secondhand Harley. He parked it on the street and gave her a big embrace, as if they'd been friends for years. He looked like a rap star with his ratted hair and baggy clothes. "I was gonna call you," he said. "You got there first, girl."

"I'm good at that," she said, summoning a small smile.

A pretty young black woman greeted Isaac at the entrance with a familiar "How's it goin', man?"

"Everything's cool, Sadie," he replied.

Ignoring Brigette, Sadie led them to a window table and handed Isaac menus.

"She's got a thing for me," Isaac confided as Sadie walked away. "It's kinda dumb shit, her bein' married to the owner an' all. No use dissin' him—this bein' the best pasta in the city. I get off on their spaghetti an' clam sauce. Wanna try some?"

The thought of food made her stomach turn. She studied the menu anyway. "Maybe I'll just have a salad."

He settled back. "Did'ja see the pictures?"

"I did. You look good."

"Only good?" he said ruefully. "How 'bout *fine*, baby? Real fly an' *fine*."

She smiled again. Had to keep smiling, otherwise she'd break down and cry. "Okay—fine."

"Hey—" he said. "I heard they're takin' the big billboard in Times Square."

"Yes, I heard that, too."

Sadie returned, pencil poised. "The usual, Isaac?"

He winked at her. "Ya got it, babe. An' my friend'll have a Caesar." As soon as she walked away he said, "So what's the favor?"

Brigette leaned toward him, big blue eyes wide and appealing. "Can you get me a gun?"

"Hey—*whoa!*" he said, throwing his hands up in a defensive gesture. "What gave *you* the idea *I* can get you a gun?"

"You told me the other day if I needed anything in the city, *you* were the person to ask."

"*Sheeit!* An' I thought you were into me for my *baaad* personality."

"*Can* you get one?" she repeated.

He pulled at his ratted hair, glancing around to make sure they weren't being overheard.

"What're you gonna do with a gun?" he asked, lowering his voice.

"It's for protection."

"You carry a piece, baby, you gotta know how to use it."

"Maybe you'll teach me."

His eyes darted to a nearby table where a man and a woman sat. Satisfied they weren't listening, he mumbled, "Lemme see what I can deliver."

Sadie returned with their order, slamming Brigette's salad in front of her with a surly glare.

Isaac shoved a forkful of pasta into his mouth. "S'good," he said. "How's your salad?"

She forced herself to choke down a lettuce leaf. "Fine."

"No, baby," he joked. "*I'm* fine." Adding a cavalier, "So...you wanna go dancin' tonight? Hit the bars? Chow down on some soul food?"

"Sorry, I'm booked," she said, hoping her refusal to go out with him wouldn't come between her and a gun. "Another time would be great."

After lunch, she took a cab over to the famous Italian photographer, Antonio's, studio.

A businesslike young man ushered her into a side dressing room and in reverential tones said, "Shh...we mustn't disturb Antonio, he's shooting. I'll let everyone know you're here."

She sat down in front of a large makeup mirror studded with tiny theatrical lights and stared at her reflection. She didn't look any different. She certainly didn't look as degraded and debauched as she felt. In fact, she looked exactly the same.

Only she *wasn't* the same. She was used goods. Debased by that French pig and his vile girlfriend.

After a few minutes, Antonio's favorite makeup artist, Raoul, came in to check her out. Raoul was Puerto Rican with a thick, greased pompadour and arched eyebrows. "Antonio likes the idea of a retro look," Raoul said, studying her reflection in the mirror. "I'm into thin eyebrows. We will pluck yours out and pencil them in high and sharp. Then I shall give you beautiful cheekbones and full, ruby lips."

Norris, the hairdresser, entered next. Norris was tall, with a pale complexion and long fair hair worn in a braid down his back. "Maybe we cut your hair and dye it black," he said, standing next to Raoul, both of them thoroughly inspecting her in the mirror.

She felt like an object. "Maybe not," she said quickly.

"Excuse me?" Norris said, hands on hips, not used to an unknown girl answering back.

"I refuse to cut my hair," she said stubbornly.

"And may I ask why?" Norris asked in a *Who do you think you are?* voice.

"I have a contract with Rock 'n' Roll Jeans. They don't want me to."

"Oh," he said huffily. "In that case, *sweetie,* I'll have to put you in a black wig."

"This is my first cover and it's important I present my own image, not your idea of how

I should look," Brigette said, surprising herself.

Both men glared at her. How dare she have an opinion? She was a model. Models were supposed to look good, shut up, and listen to the experts.

"Does Michel know you have this feeling?" Raoul said with a bitchy edge.

"Michel's my agent, not my keeper," she snapped.

Raoul and Norris exchanged raised-eyebrow looks and stalked from the room—obviously to report to the great Antonio that she was a difficult little bitch.

Parker, the stylist, came in next. She was a tall woman with close-cropped gray hair and a bored smile. "I hear you're giving Tic and Tac a hard time," she said in a gravelly voice.

"I'm speaking my mind," Brigette said wearily, deciding she'd had about all she could take.

"Ignore them," Parker said breezily. "The important thing is what you're going to wear. Hmm..." She narrowed her eyes and stood back. "I see a very contemporary look. How about this?" She plucked a short white Ungaro dress off a rail packed with clothes. "And with it—these faux tiger-skin shoes," she added, sweeping down and choosing them from a box full of footwear. "*Very* now. No jewelry. Pure and simple."

"I like it," Brigette said.

"Good, I thought you'd throw me out, too."

"I'm not trying to be awkward," Brigette explained. "I simply feel I must have some say in the image I present."

"You're absolutely right," Parker replied briskly. "Although I should warn you, Antonio has *very* strong ideas, so don't be nervous tomorrow when he starts telling you *exactly* how *he* sees you. He's shooting Robertson now— do you want to take a peek?"

Brigette felt a shudder of revulsion. She never wanted to set eyes on Robertson again. "No, thank you," she said quickly. "I have another appointment."

"I'll tell Antonio. As soon as he takes a break he'll be in to see you."

"Do I *have* to wait?"

"If you want Antonio to shoot your cover tomorrow. He's *very* temperamental."

"So am I," Brigette muttered.

"What?" said Parker, not quite sure she'd heard correctly.

"Nothing."

Antonio entered five minutes later, Raoul and Norris hovering behind him. He was a short, flamboyant Italian whose big specialty was photographing major superstars. Brigette remembered coming to his studio with her mother when she was ten. He'd photographed them both for a mother/daughter photo spread in *Harper's Bazaar*. He'd fawned all over Olympia and ignored her. She was *not* about to remind him.

"You have the problem?" he asked, glaring at her with beady eyes.

She glared right back. "Only if you think it's a problem that I want to look like myself on my first cover."

Antonio shrugged; what did he care? It wasn't worth a fight for one measly cover. And this girl was naturally pretty, she'd do.

"Is okay," he said, sending Raoul and Norris into a major snit. "Ten tomorrow. You don't be late."

"He liked you," Parker said gleefully when he'd left.

"I couldn't care less," Brigette replied. And it was true—one night and all her dreams were smashed, broken into a thousand pieces. She was tired of being the helpless victim. From now on she realized she had to force herself to be as hard and unfeeling as everyone around her. No more Miss Sweetness—she was on the road to recovering her self-esteem—and if she had to be tough to do it, then so be it.

36

Palm Springs was a pleasant haven. Gino was crazy about his grandkids and spent every moment with them while his wife, Paige, sat back with an indulgent smile. Paige, who was in her fifties, was still an extremely attractive and very sexy woman.

On Sunday she and Lucky sat out by the pool, watching Gino splash with little Maria in the shallow end while baby Gino kicked his legs on a blanket under a striped beach umbrella.

"You should bring them here more often, Lucky," Paige said, sipping a piña colada through a straw. "Gino loves spending time with them."

Lucky gazed out at the world through black Porsche shades. "You're right, I will."

"It'll make him so happy."

Lucky picked up a Diet Coke. "Y'know, Paige," she said reflectively, "seeing you and Gino together makes me feel good, you're really great for him. You keep him in line, and that ain't easy!"

Paige smiled softly. "Gino's the love of my life," she said simply. "I can't imagine why it took me so long to make a decision."

"Well, you did have a husband in the way," Lucky pointed out.

"Yes...that was a touch difficult. However, your father is a *very* persistent man."

"*Nooo?*" Lucky joked.

"I wish I'd known him when he was young," Paige continued. "Or maybe not, I'd probably never have lived to tell the tale."

Lucky agreed. "He told me the other day I should make a movie of his life. I said there wasn't a rating that would cover it."

They both laughed.

Gino walked over, holding Maria's hand. "The kid an' me, we're goin' shoppin'," he announced.

"Shopping? It's ninety-two degrees," Paige said, her copper-colored hair hidden beneath a large straw hat. "Why not wait until later?"

Gino patted her on the thigh—a move not

lost on Lucky. Ah...Gino the Ram—he'd probably still be at it when he was ninety!

"The kid an' I are gonna buy a puppy," Gino said, fixing Lucky with an accusing look. "It seems you promised."

"I forgot," Lucky said with a sudden flash of guilt.

"Gonna get a doggie, Mommy," Maria singsonged proudly.

"Shall I come, too?" Lucky asked.

"No, kid, stay here with Paige—discuss girl things. Maria an' me—we got a lot to talk about."

Maria giggled uncontrollably.

"Okay, honey, let Cee Cee put you in your shorts and top, then you can go with Grandpa."

"Doggie!" Maria screamed excitedly, jumping up and down. "We go get doggie!"

Lucky watched Maria run off to change. She was trying hard to relax and clear her mind. It was difficult letting go, but she was determined to have these few days of peace before battle. And there *would* be a battle—for she had no intention of allowing her studio to be taken over without a fight.

Before leaving L.A. she'd tried calling Morton Sharkey at home *and* his office. He'd changed his home number, and an embarrassed secretary in his office informed her that Mr. Sharkey was unavailable.

Yeah. Sure.

Morton Sharkey was behaving like a very naughty boy. And naughty boys got punished. Big time.

When Maria was dressed, Lucky walked out to the car with her and Gino. "Don't choose a large dog," she warned Gino as he lifted Maria into his blue station wagon, securing her in her own special car seat. "I can't deal with some giant monster roaming around my house."

Gino cocked his head to one side. "What's the matter, kid—you don't trust me?"

She laughed and hugged him. "Of course I do," she said, feeling sentimental.

"Then leave it to us, we got good sense."

When she returned to the pool, Paige asked if she wanted to go to the golf club for lunch. She declined. Much as she liked Paige and found her amusing company, sitting around at a golf club eating lunch with the ladies was not exactly her idea of a good time.

Besides, she had too much on her mind.

Nobody was getting away with taking Panther from her. Nobody.

Venus was rehearsing. Clad in a white leotard, her hair piled on top of her head, and wearing no makeup, she sweated along with her talented troupe of dancers. She loved shooting her videos—discovering the right moves, creating a mini scenario. She regarded her videos as three-minute movies. It was always a challenge coming up with something new, raw, and exciting.

This time she was using Dorian Loui, a

Venus commandeered a corner table with Ron, Anthony, and Dorian. "Three fags and a superstar," she joked. "Who's the odd one out?"

"It's always you," Ron remarked sagely.

"Talking of odd ones out," she said, "guess who turned up at my house last night?"

"Let me see," Ron said, waspishly. "Pacino? Stallone? De Niro? Stop me when I'm getting warm."

"Try Emilio."

"He's back?"

"Unfortunately. I had to give him a thousand bucks to get rid of him."

"Mistake."

"He wouldn't have left otherwise. I told him I was calling the police, and he said, 'Go ahead.' I didn't know what to do."

Ron nodded. "The truth is, you're screwed. If you let him back in, he sells everything about you to the tabloids, and if you shut him out, he's still got a story."

"Maybe my lawyer can get him to sign a release saying he can't sell anything to the press if I pay him a couple of thousand bucks a month. What do you think?" she asked hopefully.

"I think Emilio is about as trustworthy as a rabid dog."

Rodriguez appeared at the door of the restaurant, pausing for effect.

"Take a look at *that*," Ron said, staring admiringly.

"That, my dear," Venus said with a possessive smile, "is Rodriguez. *My* Rodriguez."

Lucky awoke with a start. She'd fallen asleep by the pool. Gino was still out with Maria, Cee Cee had taken baby Gino inside for his nap, and Paige had gone off to the golf club for lunch.

God! Falling asleep in the middle of the day. What was happening to her?

The sun was impossibly hot. She stood up, feeling slightly dizzy, and dove into the pool, swimming several lengths before surfacing.

This was insane. Her life was falling to pieces and she was sitting around a pool in Palm Springs getting a tan. When Gino arrived home, she'd tell him she'd been summoned to an urgent meeting in L.A. and had to leave immediately. The children could stay, there was no need for them to rush back.

Boogie hadn't called. It was unlike him to lag behind on an assignment. He'd better have plenty to tell her tomorrow, because she was getting extremely restless.

She got out of the pool and went over to the bar where she fixed herself a Scotch on the rocks.

Great! Now she was drinking in the middle of the day. Could things get any worse?

Picking up her purse, she extracted a cigarette, and without really thinking, opened the zippered compartment where she kept the photographs of Lennie she'd found in his hotel room.

She took them out and stared at them.

Why torture yourself? a little voice screamed in her head. *Why not tear them up and throw them away?*

No. There was something about the pictures. Something not quite right...

She kept staring at them. What was it that bothered her? Was it the blond? The way Lennie was standing? He seemed almost startled as the blond wrapped her naked body around him.

It was time to find out exactly what Lennie had done on the day before the accident. She had a feeling it was important to know.

Alex sat at an outdoor patio table at The Four Seasons with Dominique and Tin Lee. He didn't know how he'd gotten there. Somehow it all seemed to have been arranged without him. "You're taking your mother to lunch on Sunday," Lili had informed him. "With Tin Lee."

If he was forced to see Dominique, he may as well have Tin Lee along, so he'd agreed.

When he'd arrived, both women were already sitting at a table, chatting away. His mother appeared quite cheerful for a change.

Tin Lee was positively glowing. "Alex," she said, jumping up and kissing him on the cheek.

"You look tired," Dominique said, her critical eye sweeping over him.

Ah, yes, that was his mother—quick with the compliments as usual.

"I'm in preproduction," he pointed out. "There's always too much to do. I need another ten hours a day."

"I've left several messages over the last few days," Dominique said, concerned only with herself.

Didn't she listen to him? "Been busy," he explained again, signaling the waiter and ordering a vodka martini.

"It's lunchtime," Dominique pointed out, crimson lips pressed together in silent disapproval.

"Hey—guess what?" he said dryly. "I'm over twenty-one."

"And you look it," she responded.

Tin Lee placed her hand on his arm. "Alex, it is so good to be here with you," she said. "I've missed you."

"You see," said Dominique as if she were personally responsible for Tin Lee's feelings. "The poor girl has missed you."

"Thank you for the beautiful roses," Tin Lee said. "And your nice note. I'm sorry you had to stay in Las Vegas. If you had asked me, Alex, I would have flown up there to keep you company."

He wasn't impressed that his mother and transient girlfriend were obviously bonding.

"Tin Lee and I have been talking," Dominique said. "Did you know, Alex, that she comes from a very good family in Saigon? Her father was a surgeon."

"Before the troubles," Tin Lee said quickly. "I was a baby when the troubles began."

"That's irrelevant, dear," Dominique said, quieting her with a look. "The point is, you are well bred."

Tin Lee nodded. The waiter came over with menus. Alex ordered eggs, potato pancakes, and smoked salmon.

"Fattening," Dominique said disapprovingly. "You're putting on weight, Alex. You should be on a diet, you're of an age where you could get heart disease."

Jesus Christ! Why did he have to put up with this shit?

Somehow or other he managed to get through lunch.

When the waiter served coffee, Tin Lee stood up and said, "I'm going to the little girls' room."

As soon as she left the table, his mother started. He was expecting the usual complaints. Instead, she said, "Alex, you've finally made an excellent choice."

"Excuse me?" he said, by this time on his third martini.

She patted her lips with a napkin, leaving a deep crimson stain. "Tin Lee is an extremely smart girl from a good family."

Was he hearing right? "Huh?"

"It's time you were married. This is the girl for you."

Was she fucking *crazy*?

"I've no intention of getting married," he said, almost choking on his martini.

"You're forty-seven," Dominique admonished. "People are starting to talk."

"Yeah? What're they talking about?" he asked belligerently.

"A woman at my bridge club asked me the other day if you were gay."

"Gay!" he exclaimed. "Are you fucking out of your mind?"

"Kindly do not use foul language in front of me," she said haughtily. "I do not appreciate it."

"Listen," he said, endeavoring to remain calm. "I am *not* getting married, so banish that thought. Besides, what happened to 'All Asian women are hookers'?"

"Tin Lee is a *very* nice girl," Dominique repeated. "You could do a lot worse."

"I've met an American woman I like," he muttered.

Now why had he told her that? She didn't deserve any information about his life.

"Who is she?" Dominique asked, quick to pounce.

"Nobody you know," he responded vaguely.

"I'm fond of Tin Lee. She's young and pretty. She'll make a good mother for your children. I'm ready for grandchildren, Alex. You're depriving me."

It was always about her. "Hey, Ma," he said roughly. "I got news for you. Tin Lee ain't in the running."

Dominique gave him a crushing look. "It's time you grew up, Alex."

"No," he exploded. "It's time you minded your own fucking business and left me alone."

And with that he got up and walked out.

Lucky was on her way inside from the pool, when Inca, the housekeeper, ran from the house, flapping her hands in the air.

"Miss Lucky! Miss Lucky!" she yelled hysterically. "Important telephone!"

"Calm down, Inca. What is it?"

"Miss Lucky—come quick! Come quick! The man on the phone—he say Mr. Gino—he's been shot."

37

Ever since the night at Michel's apartment, Brigette had managed to avoid seeing him or Robertson. It hadn't been easy, but somehow or other she'd done it.

The photo session for the cover of *MONDO* had gone well. Antonio had behaved himself—in fact, he was quite charming in a "gay Italian star photographer" way. Score one for Brigette.

Parker had been most impressed. "He sees stardom in your future," she'd informed her. "Otherwise he'd shred you with his Cuisinart tongue—adorable little queen that he is."

After the Antonio session she'd spent several days doing a series of promotional photos for the Rock 'n' Roll Jeans campaign with Luke. He was a delight to work with; the more she got to know him, the more comfortable she felt in his presence.

Nona kept on mentioning that Michel wanted to get together. She'd nodded and said, "Yeah, sure, we'll do it." But she never allowed Nona to pin her down to a date.

She refused to attend Nona's parents' party. Instead, she stayed with her grandmother, Charlotte, for a few days in her Park Avenue apartment.

It was not an enjoyable experience. Charlotte was a social shark. All she did was attend numerous parties, luncheons, and spend the rest of her time shopping for an even more extensive wardrobe. It wasn't Brigette's scene.

Without telling anyone, she found a Realtor and rented her own apartment. "I'm moving out," she informed Nona over breakfast the next day.

Nona put down the *New York Times*. "You're doing *what*?"

"It doesn't work—you, me, and Zan living together."

"Why not?"

"I need to be by myself."

"If that's what you want..." Nona said unsurely, thinking that since Brigette had signed the big jeans contract, she'd changed.

Brigette was disappointed that Isaac hadn't come through with a gun. She called him.

365

"Well?" she demanded aggressively. "What's happening?"

"Hey—girl, cool it—I'm tryin'...."

"Either you can get it or you can't," she said flatly.

"I might have somethin' by tonight. Wanna meet?"

"Okay," she agreed, surprising herself.

There was no reason for her to sit alone in her apartment when she could go out and have a good time.

She was ruined goods anyway. Whatever she did—it didn't matter anymore.

School made Santo physically sick. He hated everything about it—the students, the teachers, the work; as far as he was concerned, everybody was shit. Whenever possible, he cut class and roamed around Westwood, visiting the movie theaters, catching all the latest films. What did grades matter anyway? He had plenty of money—one of these days when his mother dropped, he'd inherit everything.

Sometimes he fantasized about what life would be like after Donna was gone. He'd have the big house, the cars, the money. He'd be able to do whatever he liked.

Of course, if George was still around, he'd be a problem. The ideal situation would be for the two of them to go together. In fact, he wouldn't mind blowing them away himself—

taking a shotgun and zooming the two of them into oblivion.

He had a gun—a Luger pistol he'd bought from a boy at school who was desperate for money. He kept it hidden under his mattress along with a box of bullets. Anything was available at school, at lunch break the school yard was a virtual bazaar of drugs, weapons, porno magazines, and videos.

Mohammed, the nephew of an Arab potentate, was a one-man pharmacy. He could supply anything—Quaaludes, Valium, Librium, Halcion, coke, speedballs, grass. Another boy, son of an action-movie star, was into weapons—Uzis, pistols, semiautomatics. He was capable of filling any order.

"I wanna buy a shotgun," Santo told him.

"You got it," the boy said. "Gimme a coupla days."

A shotgun would be useful to have, then maybe one night, when George came home late from one of his business trips, he'd go downstairs and blow the miserable old bastard away.

Jeez, Ma—sorry. Mistook him for an intruder.

That would settle George—get him out of the way permanently.

Mohammed was busy doling out drugs in a corner of the yard. Santo sidled over, scoring his weekly supply of grass. "Gimme some coke, too," he requested.

"Didn't know you were into coke,"

Mohammed said, his Middle-Eastern face impassive. He didn't do drugs himself, only sold them.

"Figured I'd try something stronger."

"Something stronger?" Mohammed said, stroking his chin. "Smoke heroin, s'better than crack."

"Never tried either."

"Then it's time. Girls get off on it."

"I'm buying a Ferrari," Santo boasted, hoping to impress.

Mohammed nodded. "Nice wheels. Got one myself."

Santo said, "Yeah. Beats the shit outta my Corvette."

Mohammed said, "We gotta go drag racing one day."

"Yeah," Santo agreed.

His first friend. It felt good.

Once a week, at a prearranged time, Donna's brother, Bruno, phoned to assure her everything was all right. This week he hadn't called, and Donna was nervous.

The thought of Lennie escaping always lurked in the back of her mind. Even though she knew it was unlikely, because the caves were like a maze—impossible to get out of if you didn't know the way. And even if he *did* escape, he was too far from anywhere to summon help.

Still...Bruno not calling was worrisome.

Just as she was beginning to panic, Furio phoned to inform her that Bruno had been in a car accident, but she was not to worry, that he, Furio, was taking care of everything while Bruno was in the hospital with a broken arm and leg.

Talking to her lost love was strange. She remembered him so vividly, and yet he had no connection to the woman she was today.

She had an empire. Furio had nothing. The love they'd once shared no longer existed.

She was still flush from her triumph over Lucky Santangelo. Sitting in Lucky's office and firing her had been one of the best moments she'd ever experienced.

Lucky, who considered herself such a winner, was a winner no more. Donna had reduced her to a loser in every way.

She'd taken her husband.

She'd taken her studio.

And today she was taking her father.

Yes, revenge—Sicilian style—was extremely sweet.

38

It was unbelievable. Gino had been shot.

As soon as Lucky established what had happened, and found out that Maria was unhurt and safely in police custody, she raced to the hospital, desperately trying to contact Paige on the car phone—reaching her at last and telling her to get to the hospital as fast as possible.

When she arrived, Gino was being wheeled into surgery. "Ohmigod!" she exclaimed, leaning over the gurney taking him into the emergency operating room. "Daddy...Daddy..."

Gino had the strength of a horse; he was still alive and talking. "The bastards...finally...got...me," he gasped in a strange, gurgly voice.

She clutched his hand, running alongside the gurney. "*Who* finally got you?" she asked urgently. "Tell me who?"

"Dunno," he mumbled. "I'm an old man. Thought the wars were long over..." He trailed off, unable to continue. Blood bubbled from a corner of his mouth, trickling down his chin.

She tried to remain calm. "Where was he hit?" she asked the doctor.

"Missed his heart by a fraction of an inch," the doctor replied. "The other bullet's in his thigh."

Her throat was dry with the fear of losing him, but she said it anyway. "Will he make it?"

"We'll do our best."

What if their best wasn't good enough?

What if her father died?

It was unthinkable.

She left the hospital and broke all records driving to the police station to fetch Maria. Her little daughter was sitting forlornly in a corner of the precinct room, thumb stuck firmly in her mouth, eyes wide with fright, clutching the leash of a frisky Labrador puppy. "Mommy, Mommy!" she cried, jumping up when she spotted Lucky. "Bad man shot Grandpa! Baaad!"

"I know, sweetie, I know," she said, picking Maria up and hugging her tight. "How did it happen?" she said, turning to the policeman on duty.

"Our report says Mr. Santangelo was walking to his car in the open parking lot of the shopping mall. According to eye witnesses, a man came from out of nowhere and fired two shots at him. Then the perpetrator took off in an unmarked car and a shopkeeper called the police."

"Was it a robbery?"

"This kind of random crime happens all the time."

"Was it a robbery?" she repeated, her voice rising slightly.

"Doesn't look like it."

She turned to leave.

"Uh, ma'am," the cop called after her. "Detective Rollins would like to speak to you."

"Not now," she said. "I'm on my way back to the hospital. Have him contact me tomorrow."

Her mind was considering all possibilities. First Lennie's death, then the loss of her studio, now Gino getting shot. This was starting to look like more than just a run of bad luck. Something was going on, and she was determined to find out what.

She drove Maria back to the house, made sure she was all right, then left her and the new puppy with Cee Cee and immediately rushed back to the hospital, where Gino was still in surgery.

Paige was huddled on a seat in the corridor, her face streaked with tears. She stood up as soon as she saw Lucky and clung to her. "Why would anyone shoot my Gino?" she sobbed.

"Nobody seems to know, Paige." She hesitated before continuing. "Uh...was he involved in any new business dealings?"

Paige shook her head.

"Do you know if he has any enemies?"

"The police were here asking the same thing."

"What did you tell them?"

"That he's an old man who loves his garden."

"Right," Lucky said thoughtfully. She knew what Gino would say if he were around. *You heard of criminal justice, kiddo? You know what that means? Justice for the freakin' criminals. You gotta keep the cops out of it. We'll deal with it ourselves.*

Ah, yes, he'd taught her well. The police would never catch the man who'd shot him; therefore, it was up to her to track him down.

If he lived, she'd have the strength.

If he didn't...

After what seemed like an eternity, the doctor emerged from surgery. He had gray hair and hangdog bushy eyebrows. At least he looked capable, not like some slick-haired TV actor.

Lucky tried to read his face as he approached.

Was it good news? Bad? She couldn't tell. Taking a deep breath, she composed herself and stood up to greet him, for Paige was immobile.

"We were able to remove both bullets," the doctor said in a deep, sonorous voice. "However, there was considerable loss of blood, and due to your father's age..."

Her stomach dropped. She was icy cold with the fear of losing him.

Gino...Daddy...I love you so much....

Paige suddenly sprang into action. "Is he alive?" she cried, jumping to her feet.

"Yes," the doctor said. "Depending on his constitution, there's a possibility he'll pull through. I advise you not to get your hopes up. We'll do our best."

Their best might not be good enough, then what? Lucky knew Gino couldn't live forever, but she'd never imagined the end would come with an assassin's bullet.

"He'll make it," she said, a determined thrust to her jaw. "Gino's strong."

"I hope so," the doctor said, his eyes revealing that he didn't think so.

"When can we see him?" Lucky asked.

"He's in recovery now. We'll keep him there for a few hours. If all goes well, we'll transfer him to intensive care later. You can visit him then."

Lucky took her stepmother's arm. "C'mon," she said, noticing how pale Paige looked. "I'm taking you home for an hour."

Paige shook her head. "I'm not leaving," she

said stubbornly. "I have to stay close to Gino in case he needs me."

Lucky understood. "Okay, I'll be back soon. Is there anything I can get you?"

"No, nothing."

Lucky hurried from the hospital, her mind in overdrive. As soon as she got in her car, she picked up the phone and called Cee Cee. "I'm on my way home," she said. "Try to reach Boogie on his pager. When he calls back, keep him on hold until I get there."

Gino's words repeated in her head. *Thought the wars were long over*...

What did he mean? *What* wars? He'd made a certain amount of enemies over the years, but that was long ago. Gino had been a legitimate businessman for at least thirty years. They'd had a lifelong battle with the Bonnatti family, but when Carlos Bonnatti had fallen from the nineteenth floor of his Century City penthouse, the battle was finally over, for Carlos was the last of the Bonnattis.

She couldn't get a handle on it. Who would want to shoot an old man?

Hmm...she thought, maybe the police were right and it *was* a random crime, a robbery gone wrong.

Only what were they robbing Gino of? He was an old man driving a station wagon, accompanied by a child and a puppy. He was hardly a potential victim dressed the way he was, in casual shorts and a shirt. He wasn't even wearing a watch.

As she drove toward the house, it occurred

to her that Gino might not be safe in the hospital. Should she put a guard on him? If it *wasn't* a random crime, and somebody *had* been out to get him, they'd be monitoring his progress. Yes, it would be prudent to have somebody at the hospital and another armed guard at the house, especially as her children were alone with only Cee Cee and Inca to protect them.

She shuddered when she thought of what could have happened. If Maria had gotten in the line of fire...If the bullet had smashed into her little girl...

It didn't bear thinking about.

Cee Cee greeted her at the door. "I gave Maria a mild sedative and put her to bed."

"How's she been?" Lucky asked anxiously.

"The puppy kept her distracted."

Lucky sighed. "I guess she's too young to understand what really happened." Cee Cee agreed. "Did Boogie call back yet?"

"He's waiting on the line."

Lucky hurried into the library, sat behind Gino's desk, and picked up the phone.

"I had to be sure of my facts before I contacted you," Boogie said.

"Forget it, Boog, Gino's been shot."

"What?"

"He's in recovery. They removed two bullets. I want guards at the hospital and at the house. Arrange it immediately."

"It's done, Lucky. I'm on my way there. I have a lot to tell you."

"Everything else can wait," she said. What

did her studio matter when her father was lying in the hospital battling for his life?

She put down the phone and methodically began opening the drawers of Gino's desk, searching for a clue—some indication that he was involved in any kind of business venture.

There was nothing to be found except a pile of betting sheets. She picked one up and studied it. Gino enjoyed betting on basketball, two hundred here, three hundred there—he'd never been a big gambler; after all, he'd owned hotels in Vegas and seen how recklessly people could lose their money.

So...it wasn't like they were after him for an unpaid gambling debt, this was minor stuff.

Inca knocked on the door. "Miss Lucky," she said hesitantly, "there's a Detective Rollins here."

"Show him in."

Detective Rollins was a balding middle-aged man with an unfortunate smirk. He spoke in a gruff voice. "Sorry about your father," he said, not sounding sorry at all. "You *are* Lucky Santangelo?"

"That's right," she replied, wondering how he knew her name.

"I've been looking up the family history," he said with a smug little sneer. "Thought there might be something you wanna share with me."

"Like what?" she said blankly, drumming her fingers on the desk.

Detective Rollins shrugged. "You know..."

"*What?*" she repeated, fast losing patience with this jerk.

He managed to wipe the smirk off his face long enough to say, "If this is a mob hit, we don't appreciate it around here. This is a quiet community."

"What the hell are you talking about?" she said sharply, black eyes flashing.

He moved closer, leaning across the desk, his big, fat fingers splayed across the dark wood.

"I'm talking about your family's reputation. I got a file on the Santangelos from the FBI."

She was outraged. "My father's lying in the hospital, and all you can do is get files from the FBI. Why aren't you out finding the man who shot him?"

The sneer was back. "I was hoping you'd be able to tell me who that might be."

She jumped up. "I don't believe this!" she exclaimed angrily. "My father isn't *connected* in any way, if that's what you're implying."

"C'mon, Lucky," he said, like she was the biggest liar he'd ever come across.

"Miz Santangelo to you," she said icily.

The detective shifted his weight and glared at her. "Okay, *Miz* Santangelo, your father has a rap sheet. He fled the country on tax avoidance. He's done jail time for murder. You wanna tell me this wasn't mob related?"

She hated this man, he was a moron. "If you were doing your job, you'd be telling *me* what happened. Not making dumb assumptions."

He backed off. "Okay, okay, I know you people went legit years ago, but that doesn't mean you don't have enemies."

Yeah, right, like she'd tell *him*. "Detective Rollins, if that's all you have to say, I suggest you leave."

He walked to the door and stopped. "If Gino comes out of this, we'll be watching him," he said, wagging a warning finger at her.

"Fuck you," she said.

"Yeah, you're a Santangelo, all right," he sneered.

She slammed the door behind him. She didn't need some moronic detective poking his long nose into their affairs. Everything was legitimate, and had been for years. It wasn't fair that Gino got shot and the cops regarded *him* as the criminal. *We'll be watching him.* What kind of shit was *that*?

"I'm going back to the hospital," she informed Cee Cee. "When Boogie gets here, send him over."

She stopped in Gino and Paige's bedroom and grabbed a sweater for Paige. On the way out, she went by the bar and took a swig of Scotch from the bottle. She needed something to keep her going.

At the hospital, there was no change in Gino's condition. "He's fighting," Paige said, her eyes puffy and red-ringed.

"He'll win," Lucky assured her, putting a comforting arm around her stepmother's shoulders. "Here, I brought you a sweater. Put it on, you're shivering."

"Will he be all right?" Paige asked hopefully. "Will he, Lucky?"

"Of course," she said, more confident than she felt. "You know Gino, he's not going out this way. Gino will go in his own bed, most likely making love to you."

"That's a cheerful thought," Paige said, summoning a weak smile.

"And he'll probably be around ninety-eight at the time," Lucky added. "Yeah, ninety-eight and as feisty as hell."

She used her influence and commandeered a small office with a phone. Then she sent out for food and forced Paige to eat. Around seven o'clock Boogie arrived, accompanied by two men, both in their early thirties.

"This is Dean, and Enrico," Boogie said. "Dean will stay here, Enrico's gonna cover the house. They're both aware of the situation."

Lucky nodded her approval.

"We must talk," Boogie said.

"Drive Enrico over to the house," Lucky instructed. "When you get back, we'll sit down."

"Who were those men with Boogie?" Paige asked as soon as they'd left.

"I'm putting a little protection in our lives," Lucky explained, trying not to alarm her. "Y'know, Paige, we're both aware of my father's uh...colorful past. This is called taking precautions."

Paige plucked a Kleenex from her purse and blew her nose. "I don't understand any of this."

"I'm being extra careful," Lucky continued. "Gino would do the same if it were me lying in that bed."

When Boogie returned, he and Lucky took the elevator down to the hospital cafeteria. Lucky sat at a Formica-topped table while Boogie went up to the counter and got two cups of coffee. He came back and handed one to her.

She sipped the hot liquid. "I'm anxious to know about Donna Landsman," she said. "Only I'm not sure if this is the time for you to fill me in. It's more important that you find out who shot Gino, and why."

"They could be connected," Boogie said.

She frowned. "Connected? How?"

"When you hear what I have to say, you'll understand."

She felt a shudder of apprehension. "Go ahead."

"I found out about Donna Landsman—the companies she's involved with, the takeovers she attempted and didn't succeed at. The ones she won. I also have information about her personal life."

"Yes?"

"She's married to George Landsman."

Lucky took another gulp of hot black coffee. "Is he an active business partner?"

"Very active. He manages the money. He's also a former accountant with a surprising history."

She leaned across the table. "Like what?"

"Like he was Santino Bonnatti's accountant."
A long, silent pause. "Lucky—Donna
Landsman is Santino Bonnatti's widow,
Donatella."

A chill pervaded her body. "Oh, my God!"
she exclaimed.

And suddenly, everything became startlingly clear.

39

After walking out on his mother, Alex drove
directly to his beach house. This house was
his private domain—pristine and modern.
He never allowed anybody to visit. Women,
he took to his apartment; business meetings
were office affairs; and since he never entertained, the house was his—no intruders.

He'd made the mistake of bringing his
mother here once. That was enough. "It's
cold," she'd said, inspecting everything with
a critical eye. "You need a woman's touch."

What did she know? She lived in an
apartment that was so overdecorated it was
ridiculous. The minimalist style he'd settled
on suited him. He liked clean-cut lines and
flowing rooms.

He employed a Japanese couple who lived
on the property. They never disturbed him
unless he requested their presence.

The house stood on a high bluff overlooking
the ocean. It was spacious, with a huge terrace

that swept around in a half circle incorporating two waterfalls, lush greenery, and a pond full of exotic fish. When he had time to meditate— which wasn't often—this was where he came.

Alex considered his house to be the most peaceful place on earth. It was his private retreat, where he could not be touched by the outside world.

Although he'd had several martinis at lunch, he'd promised himself to never drink at the beach house. Today he made an exception, pouring himself a large vodka. Then he picked up a copy of his script, and strolled out to the terrace.

He hadn't realized it before he got her private number, but Lucky also lived at the beach. This did not exactly make them neighbors, as he'd found out her house was in Malibu. His was farther along the coastline, at Point Dume. Still...it was nice to know that she probably enjoyed the ocean as much as he did.

He'd left several messages on her answering machine; so far, she'd failed to call back.

He pulled out a lounger, took off his shirt, and began going through his *Gangsters* script with a red pencil. He drove his production people crazy. Every day he made changes, and he'd continue to do so throughout the movie.

At around five o'clock, the doorbell rang. He let it ring three times before he got up, put on his shirt, and went to the door.

Standing there was Tin Lee.

"What the *hell* are you doing here?" he asked, frowning ferociously.

"Alex," she said, standing her ground. "Your mother was worried about you. She insisted I come."

"What *is* this shit?" he roared, furious at her intrusion. "That woman doesn't run my life. She has no right to tell you where I live. *Fuck!*"

Tin Lee stood up for herself. "What do you mean, Alex—no right? We have been lovers. How can you be so cold toward me?"

Goddamn it! This was just what he didn't need.

"Sorry," he muttered, realizing it wasn't her fault. "My mother drives me insane—you know that—you've seen what she's like when she's in action."

Tin Lee stretched out her hand. "Alex, this is a tense time for you. Your movie is starting, everything is happening. Please...may I come in for a moment?"

He did not want his house invaded. Yet how could he send her away? She'd driven over an hour to get here. "Sure, come in," he said reluctantly.

She stepped into the front hall, pretty and petite in her white sundress and strappy sandals. "This is wonderful!" she exclaimed, looking around. "Why do you not live here all the time?"

"It's my weekend retreat," he said. "I come here to think, to work."

"I'm sorry if I'm intruding."

"Hey, listen—it's not you. I'm fucked up because Dominique drives me so goddamn crazy."

Tin Lee was sympathetic. "Why do you let her drive you crazy, Alex?"

"Because she's my mother. Don't you understand, it's like a conundrum. There's no rhyme or reason for it."

He walked out onto the terrace. Tin Lee followed him.

"Do you want a drink?" he asked, thinking about another vodka for himself.

"No, Alex," she said boldly. "I would like you to make love to me."

It was the last thing he felt like doing.

Before he could stop her she unzipped the back of her white sundress. It fell in a heap at her feet.

"No!" he said.

"Yes, Alex," she said persuasively. "Why shut me out, when you *know* you want me?"

She moved toward him—a perfectly formed, exquisite creature in white bikini panties and nothing else, her small breasts bouncing only slightly, the dark brown nipples startlingly erect.

He shouldn't have drunk so much. He felt himself becoming aroused.

Her hand reached for the zipper on his pants, quickly pulling it down.

What was that famous expression? Ah yes... *A standing prick has no conscience.*

Hey—he was free, white, and over twenty-one—he could do what he liked. He didn't have anyone to be faithful to.

Tin Lee sank to her knees, grappled with his belt, and pulled his trousers and underwear down around his ankles.

He placed his hands on the back of her glossy black hair, driving himself hard into her petite mouth.

She almost gagged, managed not to, pulled back, and said, "Please, Alex, can we go in the bedroom?"

"No," he said, as hard as the proverbial rock. "I like it out here."

She'd come to him, he hadn't invited her. Now she could take the consequences.

The music was loud, throbbing and sensual, the set smoky and dark, with moody lighting creating just the right decadent atmosphere.

Venus was high on the adrenaline of performing, she loved what she did. The only problem was, this was their eighth take, and Rodriguez was blowing it every time. He simply wasn't a professional.

"Honey," she said, drawing him to one side, thinking she had only herself to blame for including him. "You've *got* to relax. All you have to do is stand at the bar while I slither down your body, rip off your shirt, and kiss you. Now, we've done that enough times in real life, so what's the big deal?"

He was embarrassed. Rodriguez liked to excel at everything, and this was not turning out well. "I'm sorry," he said, eyes downcast, long lashes casting a faint shadow.

"Think of me, baby," she purred seductively. "Forget about the camera and concentrate on *me.*"

"I will," he assured her.

"Oh, and Rodriguez. Whatever you do—*don't* stare into the camera lens. Okay?"

"Yes, my darling," he said. "Next time will be perfection."

"It better be, 'cause you're wearing me out." She muttered under her breath as she went over and conferred with Dorian.

"We can't replace him now," Dorian said. "We have to finish shooting this setup today."

"I know."

"When *are* you girls going to learn?" Dorian sighed, pursing his lips. "There's only one place for a hard cock—and that's at home."

Venus couldn't help giggling. "Maybe I should take him to my trailer and fuck him," she mused. "That'll relax him!"

Dorian raised a startled brow. "Ooh, you've got a mouth on you, girl!"

"And I suppose *you* don't," she retorted sharply.

Finally, after another two hours, Rodriguez got it. Everyone sighed with relief.

As soon as they were finished, Venus rushed to the phone and spoke to Freddie. "I was supposed to hear from you today," she said accusingly.

"I'm waiting to get a call from Alex," he said. "With the changes at Panther, everything's chaos."

"I know, Freddie, but *Gangsters* starts shooting any minute. I have a schedule to work out."

"As soon as I reach Alex, I'll contact you."

She wasn't satisfied with his reply. "Is it Mickey Stolli?" she demanded. "Is *he* against using me?"

"I haven't discussed it with Mickey."

She wasn't sure she believed him. "Okay, okay—call me when you hear."

One of the background dancers passed by. "Just wanna say it was a pleasure working with you, Venus," the guy said with exactly the right amount of reverence in his voice.

"Thanks," she replied, checking him out. He was almost as good-looking as Rodriguez.

What was this thing she had about handsome men? *All package and no calories*—that's what Ron said. She stifled a giggle, observed Rodriguez chatting up the makeup girl, and beat a hasty retreat.

Her car and driver were waiting outside the studio. "Home!" she exclaimed, collapsing on the backseat. She wasn't in the mood for sex or conversation. Every muscle in her body ached—all she wanted to do was soak in a hot tub.

As they entered her driveway, the same guard who'd stopped them before waved the limo to a halt.

Venus wound down her window. "What now?" she asked impatiently.

"Your husband, Cooper Turner, is here."

"Where?"

"I thought it was all right, since he's your husband, to let him in the house."

Her green eyes narrowed with fury. Was this guy the moron of the century or what? "You're fired," she said.

"You havin' a good time?" Isaac asked.

"I'm having a *great* time," Brigette said, and giggled.

And, yes, she was having a good time. Sitting in a crowded restaurant with Isaac, eating soul food, surrounded by his friends. She'd downed a couple of vodkas and shared a joint with one of the girls in the ladies' room.

She'd started off the evening uptight, but the drinks had relaxed her, and the joint had made her feel a lot more at ease with this new group of friends.

"Hey, you gotta get down," Isaac said. "You got this uptight thing goin'."

"That's 'cause I usually mix with uptight people."

"Yeah, well, now you gotta hang loose, y'know what I'm sayin'?" He handed her a sparerib. "Chew down on it, girl, get your hands good an' greasy. Y'know how to do that, doncha?"

"I know how to do that," she replied, picking up a sparerib, suggestively sucking off the meat.

"That's more like it," Isaac said, laughing.

An hour later they piled out of the restaurant and made their way to a private club. Brigette had been to several of the more upscale Manhattan discotheques, but the one Isaac took her to was down in the Village, dark, smoky, and very funky.

He had not gotten her a gun. "I'm workin' on it," he'd assured her.

By this time she didn't care.

The group they were with consisted of Isaac, two anorexic black models, one spaced-out white guy, one overexcited Puerto Rican, and a gay Chinese dancer in drag. Nona wouldn't approve. Nona liked to run with the more successful crowd. This group was on the edge—exactly where Brigette had decided she belonged.

They stayed at the first discotheque until three in the morning, then they moved on to another place in Manhattan, which didn't start until dawn. On the way they stopped at a coffee shop, devouring pastrami sandwiches and cheesecake all around. "We need our strength," Isaac joked. "You're gonna be dancin' all night, girl—an' then some!"

He was very cute and friendly. When he kissed her on the dance floor, it seemed totally natural. She responded with plenty of heat.

"Wanna come back to my place?" he whispered in her ear.

She didn't know what time it was. She didn't care. "Yes," she said.

They took a cab back to his one room in the Village. As soon as he closed the door, he began kissing her. Starting with her mouth, quickly moving down to her neck. His hands were all over her, and she could feel his urgent desire.

She responded eagerly.

She wanted to be with a man.

She wanted to be with Isaac.

It was the only way to block out all memories of Michel and the humiliating things he'd forced her to do.

Isaac began peeling her dress off. She didn't mind at all. In fact, she was into it.

They fell on the bed, and he was on top of her, his hands on her breasts, luring her to the point of no return.

Just as he was about to enter her, she had a hazy thought. "Do you have...protection?" she gasped.

"Sure, baby," he responded, not stopping what he was doing for one moment. "Around here there's a dude with a gun on every street corner."

He laughed. She giggled.

Who cared anyway?

She gave herself up to the night.

40

Gino was released from the hospital a week after being shot. His doctor remarked that he had the constitution of an ox. *Yeah,* Lucky thought, *he should only know. It would take a lot more than a couple of lousy bullets to finish Gino Santangelo.*

Lucky hadn't wanted to tell Gino what was going on while he was in the hospital, but as soon as they got him home and settled in his own bed, she laid out the facts.

"Santino Bonnatti left a widow," she said, restlessly pacing up and down next to his bed. "Donatella."

"So?" Gino said.

"So," Lucky continued, "Donatella resurrected herself. After Santino died, she married his accountant, got herself an education and a makeover, and today she's a successful businesswoman going by the name of Donna Landsman."

"What're you tellin' me?" Gino said, struggling to sit up.

"It's Donna who's carrying on the vendetta against the Santangelo family."

"A goddamn *woman*?" he bellowed, his face grim.

"Yes, Gino, a woman."

"Are you sayin' the bitch put a hit on me?" he said heatedly.

"I'm certain she did," Lucky replied. "It was her who plotted to take over my studio. And somehow she arranged to have Lennie killed." A beat. "That car crash was no accident."

"What're we gonna do about it?" Gino said furiously. "What the fuck we gonna do?"

Lucky's eyes were black and deadly. "There's

no *we*, Gino. You're eighty-one years old. You've just been through a very traumatic experience. You can't be involved."

Gino clenched his jaw. "Says who?" he demanded.

"Says me, Gino."

Their eyes locked. Once he would've tried to control his willful daughter. Now he had no chance.

"I've sent Maria, the baby, and Cee Cee to stay with Bobby and his relatives in Greece," Lucky continued matter-of-factly. "This time I'm dealing with things *my* way."

"What's your way?" he asked warily, knowing full well what a wild one his daughter was.

She laughed mirthlessly. "Remember the family motto—'Don't fuck with a Santangelo.'"

He shook his head. "Whaddya think you're gonna do, Lucky? Blow this fuckin' bitch away?"

"No...not yet, anyway. Right now I'm working on regaining control of enough shares so I can throw her out the same way she did me."

"Listen t'me, Lucky," he said warningly. "Things are not like they used to be. This ain't the old days when violence ruled."

"I know," she said, thinking to herself that he was finally growing old.

"Paige tells me there's some detective poking his dick into our business, tryin' to find out things. In your position, you gotta be careful."

"Detective Rollins," she said dismissively.

"Don't worry about him, he's an asshole. He's under the impression this was a mob hit."

"In a way it was, huh?" Gino shook his head disbelievingly. "How *about* that?"

"The main thing is that you're protected. I've arranged for round-the-clock guards. Now that you're safely home, I'm leaving for L.A. this afternoon. You still have your gun, don't you?"

"Does the Pope keep a Bible?"

She smiled in spite of everything. "You take it easy, Gino. Remember, you're not as young as you used to be, even though you *think* you are."

He laughed ruefully. "In my mind I kinda stopped at thirty-five. Hey—kid—I was pretty hot at thirty-five."

"You're pretty hot now," she said, going over to the bed and kissing him.

"Listen," he said, his tone suddenly serious. "One phone call an' this bitch is taken care of. Not one fuckin' problem."

"No, Gino. That's not the way I want to handle it."

"It's the clean way."

"It's not my way."

"Okay, okay."

She stood back from the bed and repeated a phrase from her childhood. "So I'll see ya, Gino."

He grinned, remembering. Then his black eyes met her black eyes, a match in every way, and he said, "So I'll see ya, kid. Don't do nothin' *I* wouldn't do."

She grinned back at him. "That's what I like—plenty of leeway."

Boogie was waiting downstairs. He already had her luggage loaded in the trunk of the car and was ready to go. Lucky slid into the passenger seat. "You drive," she said, impatient to get back to L.A.

Boogie had put together an excellent team of security. Two armed men were on alternate duty at the Palm Springs estate; Enrico had accompanied the children and Cee Cee to Greece; and Dean was staking out her beach house.

On the ride back, she tried to sleep—a useless exercise, for she had too many thoughts buzzing around in her head.

Donna Landsman née Donatella Bonnatti. The woman had waited four years to exact revenge for her low-life, child-molesting husband's death, and she'd done it in a clever and devious fashion. As far as Lucky was concerned, Donna was a far more dangerous adversary than the male Bonnattis had ever been.

However, clever as she was, she had no idea how swift and deadly Santangelo justice could be.

Lucky relived the scene in her office. She should have known, she should have seen it in Donna's eyes. Why hadn't she noticed the hate there? Why hadn't she realized before?

She killed Lennie. My Lennie. My love.

Donna Landsman doesn't deserve to live.

Lucky knew she was going to have to take care of her personally. Whatever Gino said, there was no other way.

First she'd get her studio back. *Then* she'd exact the appropriate revenge for the shooting of Gino, and Lennie's death.

Boogie drove fast, respecting her silence. She reflected that in times of trouble, Boogie always came through, he'd proven himself so many times in the past. He was also the best investigator in the business; within forty-eight hours he'd discovered everything there was to know about Donna Landsman. He'd accessed her tax returns, bank statements, credit lines. He knew who her doctors were, her dress size, where she lived, what cars she drove. He even came up with a full record of all the plastic surgery she'd undergone. "You know me," he'd said with a modest shrug. "Once I start digging, it's all over."

He'd also found out that Morton Sharkey kept a very young girlfriend. Her name was Sara Durbon, and she lived in an apartment Morton paid for.

The lawyer in Pasadena who looked after Mrs. Smorg's shares had refused to give up the address of his client. "Don't sweat it," Boogie assured Lucky. "I've got someone on it. We'll be into his files any moment."

As far as Conquest Investments were concerned, Boogie's contacts were still digging through reams of red tape, trying to find out exactly who controlled the company.

They arrived at the Malibu house just past noon. Boogie followed her into the front hallway. "What's our first move?"

"When I have all the information in front

395

his ankle. For several hours a day he worked on the rusty chain, praying for results.

Yeah. Who was he kidding? Maybe in another six months.

For the last few days only one of the men had appeared with his food. Nobody told him why. Nobody spoke to him and it was driving him FUCKING CRAZY!

What would happen if they both dropped dead? Would he be left to starve to death? Did anyone else know he was there?

Over the weeks, months, he'd tried to communicate with them. They refused to listen. They were robots, fucking robots.

Today he was putting into operation a plan he'd been thinking about for a while. When the man came in with his food, he was going to grab him and hold the jagged piece of rock to his throat. Then he'd threaten to slit the bastard's jugular unless they released him.

Desperate people did desperate things.

"HEY, LUCKY," he yelled in a loud voice. "HOW YA DOIN' TODAY, KIDDO?"

No, mustn't call her kiddo—that's what Gino calls her. Mustn't get between her and Daddy.

She had a strong bond with her father. Lennie wasn't jealous, he knew how much they'd gone through together.

"You love me even more, don't you, babe?" he muttered feverishly. "You an' me—we're soul mates." Then he began yelling again, "WHERE ARE YOU, LUCKY? WHAT ARE YOU DOING? WHY AREN'T YOU GETTING ME THE FUCK OUT OF HERE?"

Sometime in the late afternoon, he heard someone approaching. Whenever his captors came, he could make out the echo of their footsteps long before they appeared. He braced himself—ready for anything. This was it. This was the day he was either going to die or escape.

Fuck! He could feel his heart pounding in his chest—bouncing around like a Ping-Pong ball—as he waited.

He hovered in the shadows, listening as the footsteps drew closer. Tensing up, he prepared for action. All the working out he'd done had paid off—in spite of his meager diet, he was stronger than he'd been at the beginning. Stronger, and determined to survive.

When the man entered, he jumped him, taking the bastard by surprise, grabbing him around the neck with a blood-curdling scream.

Only it wasn't the man, it was a girl, and she began screaming too. *"Aiuto mi! Aiuto mi!"* The plate of food she was carrying smashed to the ground. *"Aiuto mi!"* she shrieked again.

She was speaking Italian, of which he knew very little—although he understood enough to know she was yelling "Help me." He had a firm lock around her neck. "Who are you?" he demanded savagely. "WHO THE FUCK ARE YOU?"

She struggled, trying to kick back and throw him off balance. She succeeded. They fell to the ground, knocking over the pail of water that was his washing facility.

Now they were rolling in the mud, struggling

for position. She was like a frightened deer, whimpering with fear.

He managed to get on top of her, pinning her arms above her head.

When he had her in position, he stared into her face, soon realizing it was the same girl he'd seen before.

She cried out in Italian. It sounded as if she were praying. *"Mi lasci in pace!"*

"Speak English," he said harshly. *"Parla inglese."*

"Who...who are you?" she whispered in broken English, her pretty face a mask of sheer panic.

"Who are *you*?" he responded.

"Furio a...a...away," she stammered. "He say I bring food."

"You bring me fucking food, huh? Who is Furio anyway?"

Tears welled up in her eyes.

"Who is Furio?" he repeated.

"My papa," she whispered.

"Are you alone?" he asked.

She nodded, petrified.

"I'm a prisoner here—did you know that? *Prigione.*"

She tried to wriggle out from under him. The softness of her body, the smell of her, was like ripe nectar, luring him with all the comforts he'd missed.

"Do you have a key to get this off my ankle?" he demanded.

She shook her head blankly.

What was he going to do? Right now he

had her in his power. But how long before he had to let go?

"You have to help me," he said, very slowly to make sure she understood. "I'm desperate."

"My poppa...he say you bad man," she said. *"Cattivo uomo."*

"No. Not me. Your father's the bad man. He kidnapped me. KIDNAPPED. *Capisce?*"

She nodded silently.

"I can't let you go," he said, "not until you figure a way to get me out of here. Can you do that?"

She gazed up at him.

"Can you?" he demanded. *"Puo lei?"*

"I try..." she said at last.

There was no way he could trust her.

Unfortunately, he had no choice.

4 2

The fact that Mickey Stolli was a major prick was not lost on Alex. There were dozens of men like Mickey running around Hollywood. Short, unattractive guys with a shitload of power. Guys who never got laid in high school. Guys with no fucking talent who leeched onto the true filmmakers and took credit for all the successful movies that got made.

Alex called them the Hollywood executives who didn't know their ass from a hole in the ground. Mickey Stolli was one of them.

What happened when these guys acquired

power was, they made up for all their short-comings. The movies they greenlighted were always about hookers, strippers, and beautiful girls searching for the right man to come along and save them.

Fantasy time in Hollywood. Put all your hang-ups on the screen for every poor jerk to identify with.

Some of the guys used their power to sleep with as many famous women as possible. There was one particular producer who made a lot of big-budget movies. His casting sessions were legendary—and they always took place in his home. He interviewed many important actresses. When they came to his house, he had a hidden video camera running, and if they *really* wanted the part in his latest epic, he ended up screwing them on film.

Saturday afternoons he entertained his male friends with his library of videos. Their wives thought they were over at his house watching football.

Other guys got power by marrying it. Mickey Stolli had married Abigaile—the granddaughter of the once big Hollywood mogul, Abe Panther. From his relationship with Abigaile, Mickey was able to parlay himself into a studio head. Not bad going.

Alex knew that to survive as a filmmaker in Hollywood he had to keep cordial relationships with these guys, otherwise he was screwed. So when Mickey Stolli came to him and announced how pleased he was that Panther was making *Gangsters,* Alex was sure there would be a price.

"You got an estimated budget of twenty-two million dollars," Mickey pointed out. "That's major, Alex."

Alex said, "You'll see every dime on the screen."

"Yeah, yeah, I understand that. You're a great filmmaker, Alex. Not good—*great*. I'm proud t'be associated with you."

What the fuck does the little prick want?

"Thanks, Mickey."

"Uh, I gotta favor t'ask."

Here it comes. "Yes?"

"The role of Lola...put Leslie Kane in it."

"Leslie *who*?" Alex said.

"She's starred in a couple of hit movies. America loves her. Leslie's the girl every guy wants to take home to meet Dad."

"I was planning on casting Venus Maria."

"Venus?" Mickey snorted. "She's movie poison. Believe me—I should know, I've had her in a couple of flops."

"She tested with Johnny, she was dynamite—this could be her breakthrough movie."

Mickey ran a chubby hand over his bald head. "Breakthrough, schmakedo—who cares? Do me this favor with Leslie and there'll be no grief with your budget. Are we reading each other?"

Alex didn't say yes immediately, he told Mickey he'd think about it.

Lili got on his case big-time. "Mickey Stolli will cause us nothing but problems," she said. "You'd better use Leslie Kane, it's not a big role."

"Have you ever seen her act?" Alex asked.

"She'll be fine. It's too late to go to another studio with *Gangsters*, we're almost at our start date. You have to do this."

Finally, he'd said yes. Now all he had to do was meet Leslie Kane and see what a big mistake he'd made.

"*What?*" Venus yelled. "Alex Woods cannot do this to me. The sonofabitch simply can't do it."

She sat in Freddie's office, cheeks flushed with fury. Freddie had just informed her that Leslie Kane would be playing the role of Lola in *Gangsters*.

"I'm sorry," Freddie said, his bland features perfectly composed. "Alex wanted you, but the studio insisted on Leslie. There's nothing he can do."

"Nothing he can do!" she shouted, filled with frustration. "It's *his* movie, Freddie. *He* calls the shots. Leslie is completely wrong for the part. She's the boring girl next door for crissake!"

Freddie shrugged. "I have three other scripts for you to read. You'll find something you like better."

"Oh, yeah, *what?*" she said sarcastically. "A Scorsese film? Something with Oliver Stone? I'm sure they can't *wait* to hire me. I wanted *this* role."

She left his office in a state, muttering to herself. Leslie Kane indeed. First she went after

Cooper, now she had *her* role in *Gangsters.* It wasn't fair. Mickey Stolli had screwed her again.

It hadn't been a good week. Emilio driving her crazy with his insane demands, phoning several times a day. Then Cooper turning up at her house, begging her forgiveness. Fortunately, just when she'd begun to weaken, Rodriguez had arrived, and she'd bid Cooper a fast good-bye.

Cooper was not used to competition—especially younger, equally good-looking competition. He'd been furious.

She slumped in the back of her limo and made an impulsive decision. "Take me to Panther Studios," she instructed her driver.

Mickey Stolli was on the phone in his office when she burst in. "Remember me?" she said, standing in front of his desk, hands on hips, glaring at him.

He glanced up, covering the mouthpiece of the phone. "Hey, Venus, baby—what're *you* doing here?"

A flustered secretary followed her in. "I'm sorry, Mr. Stolli," the secretary said. "I couldn't stop her."

"That's all right, Marguerite, we're old friends," Mickey said, gracious for once in his life.

Mickey was fifty years old, short, bald, with a permanent suntan, all his own teeth, and a hard body thanks to daily tennis—his passion. He had a rough-edged voice tinged with memories of the Bronx only when he was angry. Recently he'd been running Orpheus Studios, but he hadn't gotten along with the Japanese who owned it, so when Donna Landsman had approached him about returning to Panther, he'd quit immediately. Panther was his prize. His studio. Coming back was like coming home.

"I'll call you later, Charlie," he said into the receiver. Slamming the phone down, he gave Venus his full attention. "What can I do for you, sweetie?"

"Alex Woods *wants* me in *Gangsters*," she said agitatedly. "I want to be in *Gangsters*. I did a great test, and now you're casting that wimpy little Leslie Kane. What's *wrong* with you, Mickey?"

"Leslie Kane brings 'em into the theaters. There are times Alex Woods keeps 'em out."

"Don't talk crap," she snapped. "Alex is a brilliant filmmaker, and you know it."

Mickey shrugged. "He wants Leslie. What can I tell you?"

"You're lying, Mickey. Just because we've had our outs—"

"Does Freddie know you're here?" Mickey interrupted.

"No," Venus replied. "I figured since we had such a convoluted past together, I should come see you myself." She leaned across his desk. His eyes feasted hungrily on her cleavage. "This role means a lot to me, Mickey. How about reconsidering?"

"What's in it for me?" he asked, sweat

beading his bald head as he watched the platinum-haired superstar show off her big tits.

She licked her full, pink lips. "What do you *want* to be in it for you?"

"A blow job."

She laughed mockingly. "A blow job, Mickey? Is that all?"

He could feel the hard-on springing to life in his pants. "Do I hear a yes?" he said hopefully.

"Show me a signed contract and we'll see."

Mickey watched her sashay her delectable ass out the door. She was something, Venus Maria. He'd always had a hot nut for her—even when he was banging Warner Franklin, the black cop, and she'd been no slouch in the getting it up department.

Mickey fantasized about Venus on her knees in front of him, his legs spread while her blond head dipped between them, licking and sucking—doing all the things he knew she'd excel at. He got off on the picture.

He wouldn't get anything out of Leslie. She was Abigaile's friend, and even though he'd heard the rumors that she used to be a hooker, he wasn't sure he believed it. Leslie was too straight.

Venus was right, Leslie *was* completely wrong for Alex's film. He'd had to put the screws to Alex to get him to use her, now he could reverse them.

Hey—as the new head of Panther, he had complete autonomy. If he wanted to hire

Venus Maria, he could do so. And if she wanted to give him a blow job, well...she just might get lucky.

Abigaile Stolli and Leslie lunched at the Ivy.

Leslie was her usual fresh-faced self, long red hair swept back into a girlish ponytail, a simple paisley granny dress covering her killer body. The look suited her; in spite of past indiscretions, she was still only twenty-three and had kept her innocently sexy demeanor.

Abigaile Stolli was in her early forties—a short woman with shoulder-length auburn hair and snubbed features. She was not a beauty, but Abigaile had no need to be; she was a powerful Hollywood wife with a pure bloodline. Abigaile was true Hollywood royalty.

Everyone fussed around Leslie, calling her "Miss Kane" this and "Miss Kane" that. She enjoyed every moment, and why shouldn't she? She'd had to struggle to get where she was today.

"Thanks for your help, Abbey," she said, raising her glass of freshly squeezed orange juice toward Abigaile, toasting her friend.

"Here's to *Gangsters,*" Abigaile responded. "You'll be wonderful in it, dear."

"I hope I'll get along with Alex Woods," Leslie worried. "He has quite a reputation."

"Any problems, go right to Mickey," Abigaile said expansively, enjoying herself because she liked to be seen lunching with a star.

"*He'll* take care of Mr. Woods. Mickey runs the studio with an iron hand."

"I'm glad to hear that," Leslie said. "I'm sure I'll enjoy working for him again."

"Above all—Mickey's a professional," Abigaile said.

A professional what? That was Leslie's question. When she'd been married to Eddie, he'd had plenty to say about Mickey Stolli— who, at the time, was his boss at Panther. "The guy's a thievin', no-good, two-timing rat bastard," Eddie had often fumed. "And he's getting me in big trouble."

Leslie had never found out exactly what the big trouble was, all she knew was that it had something to do with skimming money and drugs.

"By the way, dear," Abigaile said. "We're giving a small dinner for Donna and George Landsman tomorrow night. Just a few people. Alex Woods, Cooper Turner, Johnny Romano. We'd love you to come. And bring..." She trailed off, unable to remember the name of Leslie's live-in—even though she'd met him on several occasions.

"Jeff," Leslie filled in.

"Ah, yes, Jeff—of course. Can you make it?"

As if there was any way she'd miss it. "We'd be delighted," she said.

Jeff picked her up from the restaurant in her new bronze Mercedes, happy in his role as resident stud and glorified chauffeur. It was better than going on endless auditions for pilots that never got made. Leslie didn't feel sorry for him; if he ever became a star, Abigaile would remember his name.

"We're going to dinner at Mickey Stolli's tomorrow," she informed him.

"Okay with me, hon," he said, maneuvering the Mercedes into the flow of traffic.

I'm sure, she thought. And began planning what she'd wear to win Cooper back.

Mickey called Alex late on Monday night. "I changed my mind. If you wanna use Venus, y'can."

"What happened?"

"It's kind of involved—it's gotta do with my wife and her friendship with Leslie. Listen, don't mention to Venus or Freddie she's got the part until I tell you. Let it hang for a few days. I'm givin' Leslie a script she'll like better. That way we'll ease her out of *Gangsters*—no sweat."

Alex couldn't believe he was putting up with this shit. "I'm not used to working like this, Mickey," he said tightly.

"Aw, c'mon, Alex," Mickey cajoled. "Bend a little. You're gettin' what you want."

"Sure, Mickey," he said, hating himself for kissing up. It wasn't his style.

"Good. Oh, an' Abigaile told me to remind you—you're having dinner at our house tomorrow night. Leslie will be there. Act as if she's doing *Gangsters,* okay?"

Alex complained to Lili, who shook her head wisely. "You have taught me much about

Hollywood, Alex," she said. "One of the things you impressed upon me was never to ask a question when you already know the answer."

"Okay, Lili, okay." He went into his office and shut the door. Every day he interviewed dozens of actors for minor roles. His casting people made recommendations, then they'd bring five or six actors in to try out for each role. Alex saw them all personally. It was time-consuming, but he refused to work any other way.

He had a few minutes before the casting calls started, so he picked up the phone and tried Lucky again. He'd been calling her constantly, getting nothing but her answering machine. He'd heard about Gino being shot, and he was anxious to find out more. He also wanted to make sure she was all right, and to let her know that he was there for her. Even if she didn't want a relationship, he could still be her friend.

This time an actual human being answered the phone.

"Alex Woods calling for Lucky Santangelo," he said.

"I'm sorry, Mr. Woods, she's stepped out."

"Who's this?"

"Kyoko, her assistant."

He cleared his throat, feeling foolish. "Hey, Kyoko, I've been trying to reach her for a week now. Have her call me back."

"Yes, Mr. Woods."

"She can find me at my office or my house." He put the phone down. What was it about Lucky that he found so attractive?

Her spirit. She was a wild one, just like him.

And he yearned to get to know her better.

★ ★ ★

They were in Brigette's apartment, arguing. Nona had turned up unexpectedly, and Brigette wasn't pleased.

"What?" she said irritably.

"I'd like to know what your problem is?" Nona repeated. "You've become a total pain in the ass."

"Why am I a pain in the ass?" Brigette said. "Just because I don't do everything you want me to?"

"You don't do a *thing* I suggest. I'm supposed to be your manager, Michel's your agent, and you refuse to have anything to do with either of us."

"I have my reasons," Brigette said mysteriously, not wanting to get into it on account of a lousy hangover.

"*What* reasons?" Nona demanded. "Isaac— whom you can't seem to live without any-more? You're out every morning 'til four or five, then you sleep all day. Your career is just getting started, Brigette. Now's the time to work it."

"I can do whatever I want," Brigette replied truculently. "Nobody owns me."

"What does *that* mean?"

"I don't need this modeling crap if I don't want to do it."

Nona sighed her displeasure. "Oh, that's nice, isn't it? Coming from the girl who was all starry-eyed and would do anything to get on the cover of *MONDO*. Now you're suddenly into 'I don't need this modeling crap' bit. Hey—I can walk away from it, too, if that's what you'd like."

"Okay, walk," Brigette said. All she wanted to do was crash into bed and sleep for a week—maybe forever.

"I don't get it," Nona said, shaking her head. "Did something happen I don't know about?"

Brigette turned away from her and went into the kitchen.

"I'm right, aren't I?" Nona said, following her.

As each day passed, Brigette was becoming increasingly unhappy. She couldn't keep it to herself any longer. "Look," she said, turning back to Nona, speaking furiously. "Nothing happened that you didn't warn me about."

"So something *did* happen—I'm right. Is it Isaac?"

"Michel," Brigette muttered, sitting down at the counter.

"What did *he* do?"

"I can't tell you," Brigette said, laying her head on her arms.

Nona went over to her and put her arm around her shoulders. "C'mon, Brig, it can't be *that* bad."

"You warned me he was a sleaze."

"So? He made a pass at you? Big deal. I'm sure you handled it."

413

"It's worse than that," Brigette said, her eyes downcast. "He tied me up—spread-eagled like a chicken, and then brought Robertson in to do all these things to me while he watched and took photographs. It was the most degrading thing I've ever experienced. Why do you think I don't want anything to do with him?"

"Oh, God, Brigette. How come you didn't tell me about this before? We could've reported him to the police."

"Oh, yeah—I can see the headlines now. Heiress tied up and forced to experience lesbian sex. Don't you understand—it would ruin my life if this got out."

"I'm so sorry...I had no clue..."

"I guess I'm just unlucky with men."

"What a fucking *bastard*!"

"Nona," Brigette said urgently. "You've got to promise me you won't tell anybody, not even Zan."

"You know I'm your friend, but we've got to do *something*. We can't let him get away with it."

"What?" Brigette asked despairingly. "He's got photos..."

"You know who we *should* tell?" Nona said.

"Who?"

"Lucky. You've always said she can deal with anything. She'll know what to do."

"I can't tell Lucky."

"Why?"

"Lucky's got her own problems right now— what with Gino getting shot, and losing the studio....I can't lay this on her."

"Lennie would want you to. Listen, we could fly to L.A. immediately."

"It's too humiliating."

"Surely you feel better now you've told me?"

"Yes..."

"Well, think how you'll feel when you tell Lucky, and she does something about it."

"Oh, God, Nona, why did he do it?"

"Because he's a sick pervert who deserves to get his. Now you've got to listen to me, my idea's the right one. We go to Lucky. I'll fly to L.A. with you."

Brigette nodded. "Maybe you're right."

"I *know* I'm right. We're getting on a plane first thing tomorrow."

43

While Kyoko was taking care of the mail, Lucky studied the call sheet from Lennie's movie, ticking off the people she wished to talk to. Dealing with Lennie's death was private business, something she had to look after on her own.

First she called Ross Vendors, the Australian director. He was at home in Bel Air, between jobs. Ross told her how sorry he was about Lennie, that he'd been so great in his movie—and any time she wanted to view the half-finished assemblage of film, it was fine with him.

"I was wondering," she said tentatively.

"How did Lennie spend the day before the accident?"

"He was in great shape, Lucky," Ross said in his booming "one of the boys" Australian twang. "All he could talk about was you flying in the next day, he couldn't wait. In fact, he drove us all nutty—'Lucky will be here tomorrow...love her so much...never thought marriage would be like this....' I'm telling you—the man wouldn't shut up."

She smiled softly. "Really?"

"I would've told you this before, only I didn't like to disturb you in your time of grief."

"That was thoughtful of you, Ross." She paused for a moment before continuing. "Uh...maybe you can tell me—who did Lennie hang out with on the set?"

"Lennie didn't really hang out. He dropped by the hotel bar a few times after work, but mostly he went to his room and studied his script. Jennifer was the only one who had a lot of contact with him."

"Jennifer?" she asked, sounding casual, although her heart began pounding uncontrollably.

"Our second AD," Ross said. "Great kid. She fussed over Lennie. Made sure he got to the set on time, that his car was there whenever he needed it. In fact, on the day before you arrived, she got his call changed so he could go to the airport to meet you."

"Oh, yes...Jennifer, I think I *do* know her." Another pause. "She's a pretty blond, right?"

"That's our Jennifer. Cute girl."

Yeah. Especially naked, in my husband's arms.

She scanned the crew list until she found the name Jennifer Barron. Then she called the number listed.

An answering machine picked up. "Hi, this is Jennifer. If you need to reach me, I'm working on *The Marriage* at Star Studios for the next six weeks. Leave a message and I'll get back to you."

Lucky phoned Star Studios, got through to the production office of *The Marriage*, and spoke to an assistant.

"The whole crew's on location," the assistant said. "They're shooting down at Paradise Cove."

Paradise Cove was ten minutes away from her house. She told Kyoko she had to run out, informed the guard she would not be needing him, jumped in her car, and drove there.

The huge parking area above Paradise Cove beach was filled with enormous location trucks and luxurious trailers. She parked her Ferrari, got out, and walked around. "Where is everyone?" she asked a passing extra.

"They're on the beach, shooting the wedding scene."

She made her way down toward the beach, going by the Kraft service setup and a gaggle of extras stuffing their faces with free snacks.

What if Jennifer was the blond from the photographs? What was she going to say to her? What was she going to do?

You bitch, you were fucking my husband!

No. All she wanted to ask was why—nothing more.

The crew were up ahead on the sand—everyone running around preparing for the next shot, everyone except the actors, who were sitting in a row in their personal director's chairs—makeup, hair, and various assistants hovering in attendance.

"Excuse me," she said, stopping a grip. "Can you point me in the direction of Jennifer Barron? I think she's one of the ADs."

He gestured to the lineup of actors. "She's over there, talking to Sammy Albert."

"Thanks."

Thirteen years ago, Sammy Albert had been the hottest actor in town, now he was king of the second-rate features—a faded star with a bad hairpiece and bleached teeth. Lucky had never met him, although she certainly knew who he was.

More important to her was the blond standing next to his chair. The girl was in disguise. Baseball cap, dark shades, an L.A. hard body in brief shorts and a T-shirt. Lucky had no idea if it was the woman from the photographs or not.

She strode over and tapped the girl on the shoulder. "Jennifer?"

"Yes."

"I'm Lucky Santangelo. You were working on my husband's movie in Corsica. Lennie Golden."

"That's right."

418

"Can we go somewhere and talk?"

"Sure."

They sat on the sand under a shady palm tree.

"Jennifer," Lucky said, choosing her words carefully. "Everyone's told me how...close you and Lennie were on the location. Well...what I need to know is—exactly *how* close?"

Jennifer was startled. "You think there was something going on between me and Lennie?" she exclaimed. "All he ever spoke about was you, Lucky." She hesitated. "Is it okay if I call you Lucky?"

"Go ahead."

The girl was obviously flustered. "Where did you get the idea Lennie and I had something going?"

"I uh...saw the pictures," Lucky said.

Jennifer looked puzzled. "*What* pictures?"

Reaching into her purse, Lucky undid the zippered compartment and produced the photo of Lennie with the blond on the set. "This is you without the hat and glasses, right?" she said, handing it to Jennifer.

Jennifer studied the photo and burst out with relieved laughter. "*That* silicone babe—are you kidding me?"

"It's not you?" Lucky asked.

"No way," Jennifer said vehemently. "It's some dumb bimbo who kept trailing Lennie around the set."

"Was she working on the movie?"

"She was an extra," Jennifer said, adding a thoughtful, "Y'know, a funny thing—Lennie called me to find out her name the night before he was killed."

"Why?"

"Don't know. I was joking with him—I said something like, 'Sure you don't want her measurements and diaphragm size, too?' Uh...just my sense of humor, Lucky. Lennie got it."

"What did he say?"

"As far as I remember, he said, 'It's not what you think.'" Jennifer took the picture and looked at it again. "Where's her boyfriend? He was there when it was taken. Somebody's cut him out." She shook her head. "I'm telling you, Lennie didn't even *know* her."

"But he *did* ask you her name?"

"She was on his case," Jennifer said. "Earlier in the evening he said she'd called him in his room."

"And?"

"And nothing. He told her to get lost."

"Do you think he could've changed his mind later?"

"I doubt it. You know your husband—he wasn't into anyone except you. And if he *was* planning a one-night stand with this blond, he'd hardly ask *me* for her name and number. He must have had another reason for doing so."

Lucky reached into her purse and took out the other photographs. "These were in his room," she said, handing them to Jennifer. "When I arrived, it looked as if a woman had spent the night."

Jennifer stared at the photos for a moment. "I don't get it," she said, puzzled. "Why would he be with a naked woman in the doorway of his hotel room? It seems more like he's trying to push her away."

"Do you think so?"

"Take another look."

Jennifer was right. It did seem as if Lennie was trying to push her away. Why hadn't she noticed before?

Because you were too busy getting pissed off.

"How can I find out who she is?"

"My friend Ricco was responsible for hiring the extras. I heard he's working on a movie in Rome now, I'll call him—maybe he can help." She paused a moment before continuing. "Y'know, Lucky, your husband was my favorite. I'm so used to movie stars hitting on me—it's always, 'Come on, baby, how about a blow job?' I used to joke with Lennie that he was the only one who never came on to me."

"You've been a big help, Jennifer. Here's my home number, as soon as you find out anything, call me."

"I will." She glanced up. "Oh, God! Watch out. Here comes Sammy Albert. When he heard your name, he was in heat."

"Surely he knows I'm not the head of a studio anymore?" Lucky said dryly.

"Guess not," Jennifer said with a sly smile. "And *I'm* not telling him!"

"Lucky Santangelo," Sammy said, clapping his hand on her shoulder. "You're some gutsy gal. I've always had a thing about meeting you."

"Sammy Albert," she said, copying his tone. "I'm a big fan."

"Of course you are," he joked. "To what do we owe the honor of your visiting our humble set?"

"I live nearby."

"Does that mean lunch at your house?" he said with a knowing wink.

Sometimes she *hated* actors! They honestly believed that all women were theirs for the taking. "You'll have to excuse me, Sammy, I'm late for an appointment."

"Shame."

"It was a pleasure meeting you."

"*My* pleasure, babe," he said with another knowing wink.

Back at the house, she checked on Gino in Palm Springs. "What are you doing?" she asked.

"Bettin' the ball games, what else?"

"Are you bored?"

"Naw...bored is for chickenshits," he said, chuckling. "What's happenin' there? Anythin' I should know about?"

"I'm waiting for Boogie to get me all the information."

His tone became serious. "Remember what I said, kiddo—ya gotta be careful."

Boogie arrived promptly at six. "Come out to the garage, Lucky," he said.

"What's going on, Boog?"

"You'll see."

She followed him through the house, out a side door to the garage.

Tied to a chair, his arms and legs bound, a gag in his mouth, was a small, weasel-faced man with a bad case of the out-of-control sweats. He wore a mud-brown suit, black shoes, and a grubby yellow T-shirt. His hair, what there was of it, lingered around his shoulders in greasy ringlets.

"Meet Sami the Mutt," Boogie said. "He's the fuckhead responsible for pumping two bullets into Gino. Here"—Boogie reached into his belt and handed Lucky his gun—"in case you feel like using it."

Sami's eyes almost popped out of his head.

Lucky knew the game Boogie was playing. She weighed the gun in her hands, staring threateningly at Sami the Mutt. "Maybe I should put one right between your shriveled-up balls," she said, as cool as ice. "What do you think, Sami? Retribution for my father?"

Sami struggled in the chair, making panicked gurgling noises.

Boogie strolled over to him, slid a knife from his pocket, and cut the gag from Sami's mouth.

"I was doin' a job, I was hired t'do a job," Sami said, his words tumbling over each other in his haste to explain. "If I'd known the mark was Gino Santangelo, I wouldn't have touched him."

Lucky continued to stare at him, lacerating him with her deadly black eyes. "Who hired you?" she said.

"I dunno...some guy in a bar gave me cash. Din't know the hit was Gino Santangelo."

"You're full of crap," Lucky said. "You knew who it was. You went out and shot my father for money. What kind of a dumb shit are you?" She lifted the gun, pointing it directly at his crotch.

He peed in his pants.

"Not such a big man now, huh?" Lucky said. "How much were you paid?"

"Four thou—cash," Sami muttered, hanging his head.

"And who did you say hired you?" Lucky repeated, not lowering the gun.

"Some guy in a bar."

"In L.A.?" Boogie said.

"Yeah, there's this strip joint near the airport. This guy—he comes in there sometimes."

"What's his name?"

"Dunno." He looked at Boogie pleadingly. "Can you get her t'put the gun down?"

"I suggest you find out," Lucky said, deliberately calm. "Because if I don't have his name by tomorrow, I'm shooting your scrawny little balls all the way to Cuba. And believe me— I've done it before."

"You and I—we're leaving now," Boogie said, going over and putting a blindfold on Sami. "Miz Santangelo is giving you twenty-four hours to come up with a name. I'm driving you back to town and letting you loose. I'll bring you back here tomorrow—same time. And you *will* have a name for her."

Lucky returned to the house. She felt nauseated. So many memories drifting back to haunt her. Memories of her childhood, men coming to the house, Gino in whispered conversations, the knowledge that she was different from other little girls because her daddy spent half his life on a plane back and forth to Las Vegas. And then her mother's brutal murder. Gino was in Vegas when it happened. She was at home.

Was there anything she could have done to save her beautiful mother?

No.

At times the guilt was so overwhelming it almost suffocated her.

She'd gotten revenge years later.

Now she'd have to do it again.

It was a grim thought.

4 4

Abigaile set a good table. She loved entertaining stars, it was her favorite pastime—a pastime at which she excelled. Giving a dinner party for Donna and George Landsman seemed appropriate, since Donna was technically Mickey's new boss. Not that Abigaile had ever heard of the Landsmans, but so what? In Hollywood, if you had money, you could rise to the top extremely quickly.

Her guest list was stellar. It included Cooper Turner, who had not revealed whom he was bringing, and Johnny Romano, who'd told her secretary he'd be accompanied by a date but had not supplied her with a name.

What did these men do—call a woman half an hour before they left their house, and tell her to put on a dress? Whatever happened to social niceties?

Alex Woods was bringing someone by the name of Tin Lee, and Leslie Kane would be with her live-in boyfriend.

Donna Landsman's secretary had called yesterday to say that Donna would have her sixteen-year-old son with her. This absolutely infuriated Abigaile, she certainly didn't want some unknown teenager sitting at her table. Besides, it ruined her table placement.

Graciously she'd said it was okay, then told her own daughter, Tabitha, who was also sixteen, that she would have to attend the dinner with them.

Tabitha, home on vacation from her Swiss boarding school, pulled an uncooperative face. "C'mon, Mom," she complained, "have I really gotta sit down with a bunch of boring old farts?"

"I would hardly call Cooper Turner, Alex Woods, and Johnny Romano boring old farts," Abigaile said frostily, annoyed by her daughter's lack of respect.

"*I* would," Tabitha groaned. "Why can't you invite Sean Penn instead?"

Tabitha was a problem. At fourteen she'd run off with an eighteen-year-old Hispanic waiter; at fifteen she'd accidentally set the house on fire during a wild party while her parents were on vacation; and at sixteen she'd insisted on having her nose fixed, her hair streaked magenta, and several unspeakable body piercings. Quite frankly, Abigaile didn't know what to do with her.

It was only ten A.M., but Abigaile insisted her maids prepare everything early just to make sure there were no mistakes. She personally inspected her diningroom table—a perfect fantasy of crisp beige linens, expensive crystal, and fine old Victorian silver. "Very nice, Consuela," she told her housekeeper.

Abigaile considered herself one of the great Hollywood hostesses. Her dinner parties were legendary, and a ticket to the Stollis was a much sought after invitation. She recalled with a small triumphant smile the party she'd thrown a couple of years ago, when a certain black politician and an extremely famous feminist had gotten into a screaming match across the table.

"Cunt!" the black politician had screamed at the feminist.

"What did you call me, you black prick?" the feminist had screamed back at him.

And from there it had turned into a wild free-for-all. The two of them had run from the Stollis's house, yelling at each other all the way. According to the servants, they'd then proceeded to make out in the back of the politician's limo. That particular dinner party was the talk of L.A. for months.

Yes...Abigaile certainly knew how to throw a party.

She continued smiling to herself at the memory and left the dining room. She had much to do before sitting down with her guests. Manicure, waxing, pedicure, facial, hairdresser, yoga, Pilatus, a fitting at Nolan's... Abigaile didn't know how she managed to fit it all in.

★ ★ ★

"How about stepping out with me tonight?"

"Who is this?" Venus mumbled into the phone, barely awake. She'd kill Anthony for putting a call through to her this early.

"It's Johnny, baby."

Her mind refused to function. "Johnny?"

"He*llo*—Johnny Romano. What planet are you zoomin' on today?"

"Oh, Johnny, sorry, it's early....I was asleep."

"It's past noon, baby."

"Impossible!"

"Check it out."

She groped for her bedside clock and was amazed to see that it was indeed twelve-fifteen. She must have needed the sleep, usually she was up at seven.

"Whaddya say, baby?" Johnny persisted. "Dinner at Mickey Stolli's? There's no one I'd sooner take than you."

"Who'll be there?" she said sleepily.

"It's a dinner for the broad who took over

Panther," Johnny said. "Got no idea who's invited. Maybe Alex."

It occurred to Venus that he hadn't heard she wasn't playing Lola. She decided not to tell him, although it might be a good idea to elicit his support. She could always tell him later, if she agreed to go.

"I'm not sure if I can make it," she said, giving herself time to think.

"Hey—c'mon, babycakes," he urged. "You an' me—we're an explosion waitin' to happen. Let's do it."

"If I go with you, it's a strictly platonic deal—get that straight up front. I'm not one of your legion of open-legged starlets begging for action."

"Hey, why d'you think I'm into you?" he said indignantly. "You ain't easy. I go for that in a woman. It's an unusual thing." He paused. "'Course, it beats me how you're able to resist me."

"Y'know what, Johnny?" she said caustically. "I'll try my hardest."

"Is that a yes, baby?"

She yawned. "It's a maybe. Call back in an hour."

"Venus, Venus," he sighed. "You're a difficult one."

Why was she even considering it?

Because she wanted to see Mickey again, and if Alex was there, that would be even better.

She buzzed Anthony. "How come nobody woke me?"

"You left a note last night," Anthony said. "'Not to be disturbed before noon.'"

"I did?"

"You certainly did. Rodriguez called three times. He wants to know when you'll be viewing your video, said he'd like to see it with you."

"I bet," she replied, deciding that Rodriguez was getting to be too much of a good thing. "Do I have any appointments, Anthony?"

"Yes, you do."

"Cancel everything. I'm taking today off. My plan is to sit by my pool, eat whatever I want, and do absolutely nothing. Wait a couple of hours, then call Johnny Romano and tell him I'll go to the Stollis's dinner tonight. Find out what the dress is, and what time he'll pick me up."

Yes, she decided, it would be good to confront Alex Woods and Mickey Stolli in the flesh. Remind them that she *was* Lola, and that they were making a big mistake by casting anyone else.

45

"Hi," said Lucky.

"Hi," said the girl in the revealing bra top and ripped denim shorts, barely glancing at her.

They stood side by side at the makeup counter in the Dart drugstore on La Cienega.

"You tried this color?" Lucky asked, holding up a bronze lipstick.

Sara gave it a perfunctory glance. "No, but it looks kinda interestin'."

"I think so, too," Lucky said, putting down the lipstick. "Hey," she said, staring at her, "aren't you Sara Durbon?"

This got Sara's attention. "Well, yeah, I am," she said, tugging at her shorts, which were caught in the curve of her butt. "Do I know you?"

"Not really," Lucky said, picking up another lipstick. "We have a mutual friend."

"Mutual friend?" Sara said, rubbing her chin with a skinny index finger. "Like who?"

"Morton Sharkey."

"Morton's a friend of yours?" Sara said, wrinkling her nose.

"That's right."

"I've never met any of Morty's friends," Sara said, and giggled. "Howdja know me?"

"He talks about you a lot. I've seen your photo."

"He talks about *me*?" Sara said in surprise. "I thought I was his dirty little secret. Y'know, on account of the fact that he's married an' all."

"He must really be fond of you."

"I don't get it," Sara said, creasing her forehead. "I'm, like, *never* supposed to say nothin' to nobody."

"What do you do, Sara?" Lucky asked. "Are you an actress, a model—what?"

"Oh, I get it," Sara said, nodding knowingly. "His wife sent you, didn't she? The old bat found out 'bout me, an' now you're here to tell me to get lost, or pay me off or somethin'."

"*Could* I pay you off?" Lucky asked, wondering what the hell Morton saw in this raggedy teenager.

"*Did* his hag wife send you?" Sara demanded belligerently.

"No, she didn't. However, I *am* interested in exchanging money for information. How do you feel about that?"

Sara narrowed her eyes. "What's with this Morton Sharkey guy?" she said. "First I get all that money..."

"What money?" Lucky asked quickly.

"It don't matter," Sara said, censoring herself before she got into trouble.

"Sara, you and I should sit down and talk. I can be very useful to you."

"Like how?" she asked suspiciously.

"Well, if you're an actress, maybe I can get you a job. If you're a model, same thing."

Mistrust filled Sara's eyes. "Why'd ya do that for me? I'm nobody."

"I have my reasons. How old are you?"

"Twenty-one," she lied.

"The truth?"

Sara shrugged. "Seventeen," she admitted with a giggle. "Goin' on seventy!"

"What did you do—run away from home?"

"Howdja know?"

"I'll be truthful with you, Sara. I have a personal score to settle with Morton Sharkey, and I'm ready to pay anything to do so. Tell me what you want, and I promise you—it's yours."

"Anything?" Sara said, a touch of greed creeping into her voice as she considered the possibilities.

"Name it."

"Lady—you got yourself one big deal."

★ ★ ★

"She never called me back, Kyoko."

"I'm sorry, Mr. Woods. I gave her your messages."

"Yeah, yeah." Alex was starting to feel like a fool. Lovesick movie director in hot pursuit of woman who obviously didn't give a damn. "Is she in town?"

"Yes, Mr. Woods."

"I'll call later."

"She'll be home by four," said Kyoko, feeling sorry for him.

Alex put the phone down. He was about to start a twenty-two-million-dollar movie, and all he could think about was Lucky Santangelo. Wasn't she at least interested in knowing what was going on at her former studio?

Lili buzzed him on the intercom. "Alex."

"What is it?"

"Everyone's waiting downstairs."

"Tell 'em I'll be right there."

"Don't forget you have a dinner at Mickey Stolli's. Tin Lee will be at your apartment at seven-thirty."

"Christ! Why did I say yes?"

"I don't know, Alex, but you did."

"Okay, okay." He marched out of his office annoyed with himself; social dinners were not his thing.

Lili stopped him at the door. "Johnny Romano called about the script changes again."

"Stall him, Lili. You know how to do that better than anybody."

Russell greeted him downstairs. All their locations were in place, except one, and today was their last opportunity to find it.

"You got some good things lined up, Russell?" he asked.

"You won't be disappointed," Russell said.

They got into the van, where the other members of the crew waited, and set off.

Luck was on his side. The second location they visited was exactly what he was looking for. "A done deal," he told Russell. "No need to see anything else."

The van dropped him back at his car early. He glanced at his watch; it was around three-thirty. For a moment he considered going back up to his office, he had plenty to do. Instead, he got in his Porsche and drove directly to Lucky's house at the beach.

If Lucky Santangelo wouldn't speak to him on the phone, he'd be there to greet her when she got home.

Too bad if she didn't like it.

Lucky sat with Sara at a corner table in the Hard Rock Cafe. Loud rock music blared out—

instinctively, Lucky had known the noise would make Sara feel comfortable and, therefore, more talkative.

She'd already given her two thousand dollars in cash, now she was waiting for the payoff.

"Okay, Sara," Lucky said, watching the girl devour a double-size cheeseburger. "Tell me everything, and after you've done that, there's another two thousand in it for you."

Sara, who liked money better than anything in the world, was quick to spill the goods as she gobbled down her cheeseburger. "I met Morty when I was workin' in a massage parlor on Hollywood Boulevard," she began. "He came in one day—like, he was all sneaky an' desperate to get it on. Only I was smart, told him I din't do that kind of thing." A sly smile. "'Course I did, but when you work in that business, you kinda learn what the guy's trip is. You can tell if they're gonna give you money or trouble. I knew he was the money kind, so I played it all innocent. An' before I knew it, he'd slipped me five hundred bucks for a hand job." She rolled her eyes as if she couldn't believe anyone would be that stupid. "Five hundred freakin' bucks for a sixty-second jerk-off! After that, he kept on coming back." She stopped to take another large bite of her cheeseburger. Tomato ketchup dribbled down her chin, a few red spots landing on her top. She didn't seem to notice. "Okay, then he was after me t'see him outta business hours, so I had him over to my place. He took one look

435

an' said he was gonna set me up in my own apartment. This dude is puttin' me on, I thought. But *nooo*—Morty was serious. Then I get, like, a visit from this woman."

"What woman?" Lucky asked.

"She was, like, this fancy-dressed woman. She turned up at my door with some guy. They offered me a lot of money if I let them set up a hidden movie camera. Big freakin' deal. I said yes."

"What was her name?"

"Dunno."

It had to be Donna. "What happened then?"

"They set the camera up in my bedroom closet, an' told me how to angle myself so they could get some hot shots of Morty in action." Sara giggled. "Morty was *always* in action. Guess his wife never gave him any, 'cause he's the horniest old man *I've* ever been with."

Lucky sighed. A horny old man with a hard-on. Guaranteed to betray you every time. "Did he know there was a camera?"

"'Course not," Sara scoffed, taking another bite of her burger. "So I get the videotape of him, give it to them, an' they paid me mucho bucks like they promised. Then Morty found out what I'd done."

"How did he find out?"

"The woman started blackmailin' him. Boy, was he pissed! Beat the crap outta me—didn't think he was that tough." She grabbed a handful of french fries, stuffing them in her already full mouth.

"He hit you?"

"I s'pose I deserved it. But like I told him, I *needed* that money. Where else was I gonna score like that?"

"What happened next?"

"Well," she said, and screwed up her face, "after a few days, he forgave me. Moved me out of my place 'cause he din't trust me no more. Now I'm, like, in this 'spensive apartment, an' he gives me an allowance. Truth is— if a better deal came along, I'd grab it."

"Am *I* a better deal?"

"Depends on what you're offering."

Lucky sat back, laying out her rules. "First, this meeting is confidential. That means you can't tell anyone. Second, I want a copy of the videotape."

"Don't have it."

"Quit with the lying."

Sara giggled; lying was a natural way of life to her. "Howdja know?"

"You had a copy made, didn't you?"

"It'll cost you big," Sara said with another sly smile.

"How big?"

Sara sucked in her cheeks and blew out air. "Ten thousand," she said, making up an amount on the spot. "Yeah, ten thousand— cash—that'll do it."

★ ★ ★

As soon as he saw Lucky's red Ferrari driving down the private road, Alex jumped out of his car and stood in the middle of the road, waving her to stop.

"What the hell are you *doing*?" she said, swerving to an abrupt halt. "I could've killed you."

"What does it look like I'm doing?" he said, strolling over to her window. "Obviously, I had to take drastic measures to speak to you since you never return my calls."

She ran a hand through her long dark hair. "You're crazy," she said, shaking her head.

"Yeah, yeah. Did you know we're almost neighbors? I live down the street."

"Really?" she said, unimpressed.

"How about coming to my house for a drink?"

"Alex," she said patiently, "I thought I explained how I felt on the phone."

"I know," he said. "You only slept with me to get back at Lennie. That made me feel really good about myself. But, okay, if that's the way you want it, I can live with that. Come see my house."

"Why?" she said, still thinking about her meeting with Sara.

"Because I'd like you to," he said persuasively, flashing the smile that always got him his own way.

She didn't want to encourage him, yet she couldn't help liking him. Hey—if Alex wanted to be friends—fine with her, as long as he realized there was no romance. "I can only stay ten minutes," she said firmly. "I'll follow your car."

"Drive with me, you know how much you like my driving."

"I said I'll follow you, Alex. That's the only way I'm coming there."

"Don't lose me."

"Wouldn't think of it."

He got in his Porsche and set off, checking his rearview mirror. She was right behind him in her Ferrari.

Fifteen minutes later they arrived at his house.

"Down the street?" she questioned with an arched eyebrow.

"We share an ocean," he said, grinning, ridiculously happy to see her.

She got out of her car, checking out his house from the outside. "Hmm...very nice," she said, admiring the clean architectural lines.

"I built it," he said.

"In your spare time?"

"Very funny."

They walked toward the house. "Aren't you about to begin shooting?" she asked.

"Next week."

"And you're wandering around Malibu trying to kill yourself in front of my car."

"Unfinished business plays on my mind." He regarded her silently for a moment. "I had to see you, Lucky."

"So you're seeing me," she said, trying to avoid direct eye contact.

He opened the front door and led her inside.

She stood in the enormous, soaring hallway with the huge skylights and let out a long, low whistle. "Magnificent," she said admiringly.

"And I thought all you could do was direct."

"This house is very special to me," he said, gesturing around the open space. "Very private. I never bring anyone here."

Lucky walked through the hallway, into the living room, and out onto the terrace. "Breathtaking," she exclaimed. "My house is a shack compared to this." She turned to him with a smile. "Wanna sell?"

He smiled back at her. "Nope."

"Don't blame you."

"Can I get you a drink?"

"Water."

"With Scotch?"

"Water," she repeated, remembering their last encounter.

He went into the house and fixed himself a vodka and her a glass of ice-cold Perrier. When he returned outside, she was sitting down. "I'm pleased you came," he said, handing her the drink.

"I guess you're right, Alex," she said thoughtfully. "We *are* unfinished business."

"Glad you realize it."

"Y'know," she said reflectively, "if we do continue to see each other as friends, you have to respect the way I feel."

"I can do that."

"It'll be a long time before I'm over Lennie."

"That's understandable."

"The truth is—I really regret what happened between us the other night."

"Was it that bad?" he asked ruefully.

"You know what I mean, Alex. It was hot and exciting and we were both in the mood. But my reasons for doing it were wrong. I can't forget Lennie that quickly."

"What you're saying is—if I play the good friend role and stay around long enough, things could change?"

"I have no idea what the future will bring, Alex."

They held a long, intimate look. "I was upset to hear about your father," he said, breaking the silence. "What happened?"

"I'm in the process of finding out," she said. "It's more complicated than I thought."

"Is he doing okay?"

"Gino's strong. He'll recover."

He felt totally at ease having her in his house. "How about staying for dinner?" he suggested. "My cook'll fix us anything you like. We can sit out here—watch the sunset...."

"Sounds tempting, only I'm busy tonight," she said, standing up.

Hey, he wanted to say, *so am I, but I'm prepared to break my date.*

Then he started thinking—was she seeing someone else? Did he have competition?

"I have to get back," she said.

He had a sudden insane desire to take her in his arms, hold her, and kiss her. He'd never felt like this about any woman. Before Lucky, he'd considered they were only there to put a smile on his face. Now he had this juvenile crush.

She walked inside. "By the way," she said over her shoulder, "anything going on at my studio I should know about?"

He liked the way she still called it her studio. The woman had a no-defeat attitude he truly admired.

"I haven't met Donna Landsman yet," he said, following her into the house. "I have that pleasure in store tonight."

She looked at him quizzically. "Didn't you just invite me to dinner?"

"Hey—come with me."

"Where?"

"Mickey Stolli's having a dinner for Donna at his house."

"Jesus!" Lucky said. "Trust Mickey to be right in there, kissing ass."

"So like I said—come with me."

Lucky considered the possibilities. Face-to-face with Donna Landsman in a social situation. Donna unaware that she knew her true identity. Mickey would shit himself if she turned up at his house. It was a tempting prospect. "Who else is going?"

"I can have my secretary find out." Now it was his turn to look at her quizzically. "I thought you had other plans."

"I can always change my mind."

So can I, he thought. Once more, Tin Lee would be left at the altar. "So," he said, "dinner here, watching the sunset, wasn't good enough. But you'll consider coming to Mickey's?"

She laughed. "The only reason I *might* consider it is because I wouldn't mind sitting across the table from Donna Landsman—seeing what she has to say. And as for Mickey—well, he and I are deadly enemies. Just to see his face when I walk in...the kicker being he can't do a damn thing about it because I'll be with you."

"You know, Lucky, you have a way of making a guy feel really good about himself. First of all, you sleep with me, then tell me it doesn't mean anything. Now you'll go to a dinner party with me only to get back at the people who're there. Thanks, babe, my ego's in overdrive."

"You want me to come or not?"

His eyes met hers. There was electricity in the air. "Yeah, I want you to come."

"Then call me in half an hour." She laughed softly. "I promise I'll take the call."

He walked her out to her car. She got in her red Ferrari and drove home.

Things were shaping up.

46

Being the majority shareholder of a big Hollywood studio was far more rewarding than Donna Landsman had imagined. The day her takeover of Panther Studios was announced in the trades, she'd received flowers from dozens of people she didn't know—including several movie stars, and many important executives in the film industry.

Donna had never met anyone famous in her life, so when Abigaile Stolli called, informing her she'd like to throw a dinner party in her honor, Donna was delighted—especially when Abigaile revealed the stellar guest list. It was an impressive lineup.

Donna had her secretary call to get Santo invited. When she told him, he immediately sulked. "Don't *wanna* go," he complained.

"Of course, you do," she replied in her *I'm taking no nonsense from you* voice. "You'll meet all those famous people. They might do you some good in the future, connections are everything."

On reflection, he'd decided it wouldn't be such a bad idea. At least he'd get a decent meal for a change. He hated his mother's cooking, and the cook she employed was even worse. The old bag made nothing but dried-up pasta and unappetizing tomato sauce with dull salads. Hint, hint—his mother wanted him to lose weight. Well, screw her, before all the dieting and plastic surgery she was no beauty. He remembered when she was his father's wife— the old Donatella. It was like that woman had died and this over-made-up cow had come to take her place.

"Is George going?" he asked.

"Of course he is," Donna replied. "I wish you'd try to get along with George. You make no attempt."

"Maybe if he stopped pretending like he's my father," Santo said with a surly glare. "The way he acts sucks."

"George has *never* tried to take the place of your father," Donna admonished.

"Yes he has," Santo mumbled. "He's always on my case."

He knew George had disapproved when she'd informed him about the Ferrari, he'd heard them screaming from his room. Well, Donna was screaming—George never raised his voice. Donna, of course, had won.

Santo considered George to be an ineffectual worm. Donna kicked him around good. Santo couldn't understand why she kept him when it was quite obvious she'd be better off divorcing the spineless creep. Maybe if she was going to meet movie stars, she'd find somebody she liked better. Arnold Schwarzenegger or Sylvester Stallone. Yeah! That was the ticket! A stepfather he could respect.

"You have to wear a suit and a tie," Donna informed him.

"Why? Are we going to church?" Santo replied with a rude smirk.

"It's only proper," Donna said, concerned about her own outfit. She was not used to mixing with movie stars, it made her feel insecure.

Santo was aware he could get away with almost anything, but tonight he knew she'd force him to put on a dumb suit. He went to his room and sulked. Didn't she realize he looked even fatter in the one suit he possessed?

Locking his bedroom door, he crossed the room and opened his closet. Hidden in the back was the shotgun he'd recently purchased from the movie star's son at school. Yeah! He'd gotten himself a shotgun and two boxes of bullets. Shit! Talk about a power trip! Anytime he wanted, he could blow them both away.

Donna first.

George second.

POW! Just like that.

The fact that he owned the gun made him so psyched that he decided to write another letter to Venus. In his mind, they were getting closer every day, bonding, exactly like people in love should.

He imagined her reading his letters, wondering who he was, wishing and hoping they'd meet soon and be together forever.

He'd started delivering his letters personally—choosing the early hours of the morning to do so. He'd creep down the hillside above her estate, and force his way through the brush with not much effort. Then he'd scale the wall and deliver his latest offering. The stupid guard was always asleep. Her security sucked, big-time.

He had a favorite routine. Write Venus a letter. Jerk off.

Write another one. Jerk off again.

Life wasn't so bad after all.

Venus had the best day doing nothing. In the afternoon, Ron came over and sat by the pool with her. She'd noticed that lately he was spending more and more time at her house.

"Have you and Anthony closed the deal yet?" she inquired with a mischievous smile.

"Don't ask things like that," Ron replied testily. "You're just a nasty, curious, little girl."

"Why? 'Cause I want you to move out of that mausoleum you're living in?"

"No, because it's none of your business."

"I tell *you* all about Rodriguez," she said, sipping a Diet Coke through a straw.

"Where is he today?"

"Driving me crazy. I mean, he's under the false impression that he and I are a couple. He thinks that after a few great lays, we're Mr. and Mrs. America. Poor Anthony's running interference on the phone."

"I notice you've hired a new guard."

"Yeah, that other one was a moron. Every time I came home, there was somebody else waiting in my house. This one seems more together. I'm hoping he can catch the crazy who keeps on hand-delivering letters to my house."

"What letters?"

"Didn't I tell you? I've been receiving porno crap from some nutcase who thinks we're gonna be married and run off into the sunset. I mean this guy is *really* out there."

"I presume you've handed them over to the authorities?"

She removed her sunglasses and threw her head back, catching rays. "I will when I get around to it. Anthony's keeping a file."

"It only takes one deranged fan to shoot a bullet into you."

"Thanks, Ron. That's very encouraging. You've made me feel much safer!"

Late in the afternoon, after Ron had left, Anthony buzzed to inform her that Rodriguez was at the front door, practically in tears.

"Okay," she said, relenting. "Send him over to the house."

Rodriguez burst through the front door carrying flowers. "Have I offended you, my princess?" he asked, liquid eyes full of love.

"No, Rodriguez," she said firmly. "Only you must realize we're not *living* together. We're not even girlfriend/boyfriend. I need my space."

"What are we then?" he asked, looking hurt.

"You're my masseur," she said, deciding to go the honest route. "And I pay you for your services."

He was crestfallen. "Is that all I am?" he asked mournfully.

She figured it was better to let him down sooner than later. "Yes, Rodriguez, that's all you are."

She knew she probably sounded cold and unfeeling, but surely it was best to end it this way before he got too caught up in the whole scene?

"I'm sorry if I disturbed you," he said tightly.

"That's okay," she said, glancing at her watch. It was around five. "Do you have time to give me a massage now?" she asked, attempting to soften the blow.

"Of course," he said stiffly.

"I'll meet you in there."

She went upstairs, took a shower, wrapped a towel around herself toga style, and strolled into the massage room.

Rodriguez had changed into white cotton chinos and a short-sleeved T-shirt—his working clothes.

She observed, as she always did, that he was incredibly good-looking. Maybe someone would discover him and make him into a star.

She got onto the table, lying on her stomach. Rodriguez whisked the towel from under her. She didn't have any false modesty—he'd seen it all, and then some.

"Use the lemon oil today," she suggested. "I love the smell."

"Certainly," Rodriguez replied obligingly, pouring a small puddle of oil in the center of her back and rubbing it in with his firm fingers. He began humming a Latin song under his breath. A good sign; at least she hadn't broken his heart.

She closed her eyes and let go, thinking about Cooper. The other night he'd been so convincing in his quest to win her back. "I've changed," he'd told her. "We can get back together any time you say. I'll never stray again, it's not worth it."

Sure, Coop, she'd thought. *You've been doing it for thirty years. Why would you change for me?*

Fortunately, she was not naive.

Rodriguez's hands were on her ass, kneading, moving in circles, creeping closer and closer to the crack.

"Rodriguez," she murmured sleepily. "Remember, this is a business arrangement. I can't be your girlfriend."

"I understand," he said, hands still working it, spreading the cheeks of her ass.

"No, don't do that," she said not too convincingly.

"In Argentina," he said, "when a woman says no...sometimes it is safe to assume she means yes."

She felt the tip of his insistent tongue.

Oh, God! One more time. After that she would never encourage him again.

47

"He's here," Boogie said.

"How did you get him to come back?" Lucky said.

"He tried to skip town. I persuaded him not to."

"Does he have an answer for us?"

"Listen for yourself."

She followed Boogie to the garage. Same scenario. There was Sami the Mutt trapped in a chair, red-rimmed eyes darting furtively around the closed space like a trapped animal searching for a way out.

This time she carried her own gun—a small silver automatic she'd owned for several years. She had no intention of using it on this pathetic excuse for a man. However, there was nothing wrong with scaring the crap out of him.

He'd shot her father, narrowly missing little Maria by inches. His intention had been to kill Gino for money. If it had happened, she'd have blown him away without another thought—this worthless piece of human excrement.

She stood in front of him, casually holding her gun down in front of her so he couldn't miss seeing it. "Do you have a name for me, Sami?" she asked, her voice echoing around the empty garage. "I hope you do, because today I'm not in the mood to fuck around."

Sami glanced first at the gun, then over at Boogie, who'd propped himself against the wall. "Go ahead," Boogie said easily. "Tell her."

"John Fardo, he hired me," Sami mumbled, sweat bubbling on his forehead.

"Tell her who that is," Boogie encouraged.

"John's a limo driver. One of his clients had him set up the job."

"What client?" Lucky asked, her black eyes deadly and watchful.

"Dunno," Sami said in a strained voice. "John works at Galaxy Star Limo—it's on Sepulveda." Sweat dripped down his ratlike face as he squirmed in the chair. "You gonna let me go now?"

"Get this piece of shit out of here, Boogie," she said, walking to the door. "And make sure he takes the money he was paid and gives it all to charity. Every cent."

She returned to the house, thinking that they didn't make hit men like they used to. Fortunately for Gino, Sami the Mutt was a blundering amateur with no balls.

She sat in the den, dialed information, and got the number of the limo company. Then she called them. "You have a John Fardo working there," she said, very businesslike. "He usually drives Mrs. Landsman…Mrs. Donna Landsman…is that correct?"

The receptionist asked her to hold a moment, came back, and said, "That's right, ma'am."

"Fine. I need to contact Mrs. Landsman later. Will John be driving her tonight?"

"Yes, ma'am. He drives her every night."

Big surprise.

Alex was delighted when Lucky called and said she could make it. He told her he'd pick her up at seven, then immediately tried reaching Tin Lee to cancel. She wasn't home.

This made him very nervous, as Tin Lee knew the dinner was at Mickey Stolli's. He phoned Lili at home.

"How did the location scout go?" Lili asked.

He could hear her TV playing in the background and wondered if she was alone. "Fine," he said. "Uh, listen…I've had a change of plans, I can't take Tin Lee to the Stollis's."

"Did you call her?"

"I tried, she's not home. What can I do?"

Lili turned her TV down. "You'll have to meet her at your apartment and tell her the bad news."

"I was planning on staying at the beach."

"Shall I call the Stollis to cancel?"

"No, don't do that," he said quickly. "I'm still going."

"*You're* still going," Lili repeated patiently, "only you're not taking Tin Lee."

"You got it."

"Do you have another date?"

"As a matter of fact, I do."

"Then I suggest you reach Tin Lee as fast as possible."

"That's smart of you, Lili, but I thought I just told you, I can't fucking reach her."

"I'm sorry, Alex," she said, unfazed by his growing anger. "There's nothing *I* can do."

He had a sneaking suspicion Lili quite enjoyed his romantic screwups. "Okay, okay," he said, pissed off that she wouldn't help. "*Don't* come up with a solution."

He called the hall porter at his apartment building on Wilshire. "I'm expecting a guest at seven. When she arrives, tell her I've been held up on business and can't make dinner tonight. She's to go home and wait for me to call her. Have you got that?"

"Yes, Mr. Woods," said the desk porter.

"You're *sure*?"

"Absolutely, Mr. Woods."

Alex didn't know what else he could do. If he drove back into town to take care of it himself, he'd be late picking Lucky up. The smart thing was to stay at the beach.

He went into his bathroom and tried to decide what to wear. Black, of course, because he never wore anything else. A black silk shirt, black Armani jacket, black pants. It was a look.

Christ! He was as nervous as a teenager going on a first date. This was a joke.

After dressing, he went to his bar, stared at a bottle of vodka, and decided against it. Half a joint would take the edge off. Had to be alert.

He consulted his watch, nearly seven.

One joint and he'd be ready for anything.

Mickey got in his car and left the studio. He hadn't heard from Venus since her surprise visit. He didn't know if this was good or bad. What the hell? She'd come around. Now he was head of Panther again, anything could happen. And he wanted it to happen desperately, because Venus was one hot babe, and it was time for him to get a piece of that juicy action.

Being back at Panther was a relief. Running Orpheus Studios had never been his kind of deal—answering to the Japanese, keeping everything above board and respectable. Mickey was used to doing things his way, he did not enjoy kowtowing to anyone.

He called Abigaile from the car to check on their party. She immediately started bitching because she didn't know the names of Cooper Turner's or Johnny Romano's dates.

"Who gives a shit?" Mickey said, eyeing a blond in a black Mercedes who'd pulled up alongside.

"What am I to write on their place cards?" Abigaile wailed.

"Write it when they arrive," he said

impatiently. The blond zoomed past. He didn't give chase.

"Calligraphy is not one of my talents," Abigaile snapped. "I have a person who writes my cards."

His wife could be a real pain in the ass, although he had to admit that since they'd reconciled, things were better than they'd been before the split. Two years ago she'd thrown him out after she'd caught him with Warner. Being out on his own was no fun. Hotel life was a drag, he'd yearned for the comforts of home. In fact, to his amazement, he'd even missed Abigaile.

Yes, Abigaile, who gave great party *and* organized his social life, was a definite asset.

But that didn't mean he couldn't screw around when the feeling hit him.

Abigaile hung up on Mickey, annoyed because he didn't understand. "Consuela," she called, summoning her housekeeper. "We do not have the names for these two place cards."

Consuela shook her head—like it mattered. These American women worried about the craziest things.

Abigaile held up the card with Mickey's name on. "Can you copy this calligraphy?"

Consuela stared at her blankly.

"The *writing*," Abigaile said, raising her voice. "Can you *copy* it?"

"Sure, Mrs.," Consuela said with a *What do you think I am, an idiot?* shrug.

"Divine enough for them to cast me as Lola?"

Anthony nodded respectfully. "There *is* no other actress for the role."

He certainly knew the correct things to say.

Johnny's limo arrived shortly after. It was a double stretch—bigger than any she'd ever seen.

She wondered if his dick was as big as his limo. Ha, ha! She was *not* about to find out.

Johnny whistled at her dress. She complimented him on his gray sharkskin suit and black gangster-type shirt. He helped her into the car, copping a surreptitious feel. She pretended she didn't notice.

Johnny's limo driver was a beautiful black woman. Two female bodyguards sat ramrod straight up front.

"Do you really need all this?" Venus asked, settling in the backseat.

"Sure, babe, an' you should have the same," he said with a sly smile. "It's tax deductible."

My—what big teeth you have, she thought as he reached for a bottle of Cristal and poured her a glass. Rap music serenaded them on low volume.

She accepted the glass of champagne and thought about the letters she'd been receiving. "Who deals with your fan mail?" she asked.

"Never read it—don't wanna see it," he replied, gulping the champagne as if it were water. "I get a lotta crazy letters."

"Me, too. Lately I've had obscene letters

arriving at my house. The envelopes turn up on my doorstep."

He refilled his glass. "How does your guard let this happen?"

She shrugged. "It's a mystery."

"You gotta deal with it. Beef up security, put a couple more guards on your property."

"You're right."

"I'll recommend some people to you," Johnny said, his hand falling casually onto her thigh. "When we're working together, we both gotta be surrounded at all times."

"I've been meaning to talk to you about that," she said, casually removing his hand. "Alex has decided to go with Leslie Kane. I'm out of the movie."

"No way!" Johnny exclaimed, frowning.

"'Fraid so."

"Impossible. Who told you this?"

"Freddie Leon."

"You want I should do something about it?"

"If you like," Venus said. "Only don't expect any favors in return."

"Don't worry, babe," Johnny said, swigging more champagne. "When Johnny says he'll do somethin'—consider it done."

"Thank you," Venus answered demurely.

"It's late," Leslie said as Jeff ran into the house. "Where were you?"

"Jeez! I got held up at the gym, didn't realize the time," he said, totally out of breath.

"I'm dressed and ready to go," Leslie pointed out. "We have to leave at seven-fifteen."

"Sorry," he said. "I'll throw myself in the shower and be out in a minute." He raced into the bathroom.

What did he think she was? A moron? He'd been with another woman, she could smell it all over him. And even if she couldn't, his wife had phoned to gloat. Yes, Jeff was married. Somehow hc seemed to have developed a mild case of amnesia when it came to telling her. "I'm Amber," the woman had said on the phone. "Jeff's wife. If you don't believe me, look in the back of his photo book—our marriage license is concealed behind the last photo."

"Why are you calling?" Leslie had asked blankly.

"Thought you should know."

"Thanks. Now I know."

That had been several days ago. She had no idea why the wife had called and, quite frankly, she didn't care, because Jeff wasn't around to stay. Jeff was merely a convenience until she got Cooper back.

She'd checked out his photo book. He *was* a married man. A *lying* married man.

How foolish of him to pick tonight to liaise with his wife. How foolish of him to pick any night when he was with her.

She followed him into the bathroom. He was already in the shower, scrubbing his body with a soapy washcloth.

"Who was at the gym?" she asked. "Anybody I know?"

"No, it was kinda quiet," he shouted over the noise of the running water.

God, he was a bad actor, no wonder he hadn't gotten a break.

She picked up a bottle of scent from the countertop, spraying a generous amount behind her ears and between her cleavage. Cooper loved scent, smells turned him on.

She wondered who Cooper was bringing tonight. She'd read in the gossip columns he'd been seen out with several women. One, the divorced wife of a sports star; another, a TV talk-show hostess; and the third, a German supermodel.

She hoped it was the first one—less competition.

Jeff emerged from the shower and began vigorously toweling his balls.

"Your hair's wet," she said.

"It'll take me two minutes if I borrow your hair dryer."

"You know where it is."

She walked out of the bathroom. He was dumb. Plain dumb.

What was it with men?

Obviously, brains and a hard-on did not mix.

Cooper's date, Veronica, was a famous runway and catalogue model specializing in sexy but respectable lingerie. He'd met her on a plane, taken her out a few times, and found her to be attractive and quite intelligent for a model. She didn't cling. He liked that in a woman. The one thing he *didn't* like was her deep, guttural voice—she sounded like a man.

"Hi, Cooper," she said when he buzzed her apartment. "I'll be right down."

Veronica traveled a lot, from New York to Paris to London, she was always on the move. She had apartments in L.A. and New York.

"Sure you don't want me to come up?" he asked through the speaker, automatically thinking that maybe a blow job wouldn't be a bad idea. Up until now, he'd been behaving like a gentleman. Tonight he planned on closing the deal.

"Okay," she said, not exactly enthusiastic.

He took the elevator to the fourteenth floor.

"Come in," she said, greeting him at the door, chicly clad in a cream-colored sleeveless dress, her long arms faintly tanned and muscled. She was almost six feet tall, with shoulder-length streaked hair, cat eyes, an intriguing overbite, and a slightly too long nose. It all worked.

Cooper walked into her apartment, hard-on firmly in place.

"Cooper," she said, noticing immediately. "You're incorrigible! I've never met anyone like you."

"Can I help it if I'm pleased to see you?" he said, taking her hand and placing it on his erection.

"Save it," she said, chuckling hoarsely. "For later."

If he'd done that with Venus Maria, she would have whipped it out and given him what he wanted. Veronica was a little too cool for his liking. She was a star in her own field, maybe too much of a star. Although like every other successful model, she harbored the dream of becoming a famous actress. That was her weakness.

He changed tactics, snaking his hand down her neckline, taking her by surprise. She was not wearing a bra. "Beautiful tits," he said.

"I know," she said, smiling confidently. "Shall we go?"

Tea with Dominique was an enlightening experience. Tin Lee sat stiffly on the heavy damask-covered couch perusing Dominique's photograph albums—observing Alex as a child. In the beginning of the book there were pictures of him with his dad, playing on the beach, riding horses, swimming. Then came the birthday photos in which Alex was surrounded by both parents—all three of them carefree and laughing. Morbidly, Dominique had devoted three pages to Alex's father's funeral. The photographs of Alex were heartbreaking—his little face a solemn mask of grief as he stood next to the casket. After that, the smiling stopped, and Alex was serious in all the photos. There he was sitting with his grandparents, staring out a window, standing awkwardly in the yard. At the back of the album there were several pictures of Alex in his military academy uniform. A forlorn figure in the austere gray uniform, his face sad and lonely.

"Alex needed the discipline," Dominique said, a touch defensively. "*I* couldn't look after him, I had my own life to lead. I was a young woman when my husband dicd. I had certain...needs. I'm sure nobody expected me to give up everything."

"I understand," Tin Lee said quietly, not understanding at all.

"Alex doesn't," Dominique said bitterly. "He blames me for everything."

"What does he blame you for?" Tin Lee asked curiously.

"The death of his father," Dominique said, her scarlet mouth turning down. "Alex thinks I nagged Gordon to death. He doesn't know the real story. Gordon was a hopeless drunk and a worthless womanizer. I had every reason to nag."

"Have the two of you ever discussed it?" Tin Lee asked, sipping tea from a fragile china cup.

Dominique shook her head. "No, Alex refuses to talk about anything personal. He only sees me because his guilt tells him it's his duty to do so."

"If I may say something," Tin Lee interjected. "Perhaps the two of you fail to get along as well as you should because you're always criticizing him."

"I criticize him to get his attention," Dominique said sharply. "If *I* didn't criticize him, who would?"

"I think it makes Alex unhappy," Tin Lee ventured tentatively, hoping she wasn't going too far.

"Don't become an expert on him, dear," Dominique said caustically. "What takes place between me and my son is no business of yours."

Duly chastised, Tin Lee stood up. "I have to go," she said. "Alex hates being kept waiting."

"Come with me before you leave," Dominique commanded, leading her into her bedroom.

Tin Lee followed obediently. Dominique went over to her bureau and opened an old velvet jewel box standing on top. She picked out an exquisite diamond cross hanging from a thin platinum chain. "You see this?" she said. "It belonged to Alex's grandmother. I want you to have it. Wear it tonight."

"Oh, I can't accept it," Tin Lee said, startled. "It's too expensive."

"No, dear, go ahead," Dominique said, handing it to her. "It's comforting to know Alex has someone who cares for him, a girl who's not after his money."

Tin Lee stood in front of the mirror, placing the diamond cross around her delicate neck. "Beautiful!" she gasped.

"Enjoy it," Dominique said. "And enjoy tonight. Alex taking you to an industry party is a good sign."

"I hope we can all have dinner later this week," Tin Lee said.

"Yes," Dominique said. "I'd like that. I don't have many friends. I get lonely by myself."

"I'll make sure Alex arranges it."

Tin Lee hurried downstairs and waited for the valet to bring her car.

Anxiously she glanced at her watch. She was running late. She hoped Alex wouldn't be too annoyed.

48

Alex picked a yellow rose from his garden and took it with him on his way to meet Lucky. When he emerged from his car outside her house, he held it gingerly by the prickly stem, not used to making romantic gestures.

Lucky answered the door herself, looking stunning in a black Yves Saint Laurent evening suit, plunging-neckline white blouse, and diamond hoop earrings, her dark hair framing her beautiful face with wild jet curls. Alex noticed a security guard hovering in the background. Idly, he wondered why she needed security.

"Come in," she said. "My place is a dump compared to yours."

"No, it's not," he said, looking around. "It's very comfortable."

"Yours is the *Architectural Digest* version of

mine," she said ruefully. "But then, I've got kids, and you don't, because you never married, right?"

"You can remember what we discussed the other night?"

She nodded. "Of course."

"You were blasted, you know that."

"Hey—I can hold my liquor. I might have been bombed, but I know exactly what happened." She laughed softly, "Remember...what was her name? Ah, yes—Driving Miss Daisy, that's it."

"How could I ever forget?"

"Will you put her in *Gangsters*?"

"Maybe," he said, handing her the yellow rose. "By the way—you look beautiful tonight."

"Thank you," she said, placing the rose on a table. "I didn't know you were a horticulturist."

"Thank my gardener. I just go out and pick 'em."

"Do we have time for a drink?"

"Only if you have one, too."

"I don't plan on a repeat performance."

"One drink, Lucky. We're both grown-ups."

Their eyes met for an intimate moment. Lucky looked away first, a sign of weakness. "What'll it be?" she said pleasantly, refusing to allow herself to be sucked in. Alex was an extremely charismatic man, but as she kept telling herself, it was far too soon for her to consider a relationship.

"Vodka martini."

The phone rang.

"You get your phone, I'll make the drinks," he said, heading for the bar.

She reached for the phone. It was Jennifer.

"My friend Ricco, the guy I said was working in Rome, is in L.A., staying at the Chateau Marmont," Jennifer said, sounding out of breath. "I think you should hear what he has to say. We can meet him in half an hour."

"How about later?" Lucky suggested.

"No. He's on a midnight plane back to Italy and he has dinner plans, so it's got to be now."

Lucky glanced over at Alex, busily mixing martinis. "Okay, now," she said, making a fast decision.

"Meet me in the hotel lobby as soon as possible."

"I'll be there," Lucky said, replacing the receiver.

Alex walked toward her, carrying her drink. "I'm good at this," he said, uncharacteristically happy. "Used to be a bartender."

"How would you feel if I met you at the Stollis's?" she said. "Something important just came up. I have to stop somewhere first."

"You're kidding, right?" he said.

"Sorry, no."

"Then I'll come with you."

She was silent for a moment, trying to decide if she wanted him along. "It'll make us late for the Stollis," she said at last.

"Big deal," he responded.

"Okay, let's split. I'll fill you in while we drive."

He gulped his drink.

Why was it every time he saw Lucky it turned out to be an adventure?

The American Airlines plane took off from Kennedy Airport on time.

"Are you sure we're doing the right thing?" Brigette asked.

"Yes," Nona said firmly. "Neither of us is equipped to deal with Michel. He's a sick psycho. Lucky will know how to handle him."

"I feel so bad about screwing up," Brigette said worriedly. "Every time I screw up, Lucky has to come and rescue me."

"What do you mean?"

"Well, last time with the kidnapping and everything..." She trailed off. "Lucky took the blame when I shot Santino Bonnatti. She spent time in jail for something she didn't do."

"Yeah, but you stood up at her trial and told the truth. Shit happens, Brigette. You have to learn how to cope."

"So why am I running to Lucky?"

"'Cause you're strung out. Every night it's you and Isaac out on the town, getting stoned and drunk. Is that what you want your life to be?"

"Not really."

"So it's time to stop running. Besides, I want you straight so you can help me plan my wedding."

"I asked Isaac to get me a gun."

"You *didn't*!"

"Oh, yes, I did."

"And what were you planning on doing if he'd gotten you one?"

"I dunno. Blow Michel away."

"I don't think so. You're in enough trouble as it is."

"I suppose I am."

"It's not too late to straighten things out," Nona said comfortingly. "When we're rid of Michel, we'll find a reputable agent. Your career is only just beginning."

"I know you're right—Lucky's my only chance."

After dinner and a movie they both fell asleep until the steward announced it was time to prepare for landing.

"Great flight," Nona said, buckling her seat belt and nudging Brigette awake. "I booked us into the Hilton. I didn't think it was wise for us to descend on Lucky unannounced."

"I want you to be there when I tell her," Brigette said anxiously.

"'Course I will."

Brigette put her hand over Nona's. "Thanks for being such a good friend."

"Hey," Nona replied lightly. "All I'm doing is protecting my ten percent!"

Leslie and Jeff were the first to arrive at the Stollis's. Jeff in his one and only suit—an

Armani, purchased for him by Leslie. And Leslie in a white silk dress.

Abigaile greeted them at the door. The women exchanged air kisses and compliments. Jeff beamed happily—how did he get so lucky? Mixing in this company was a major plus. Thank God he had an understanding wife who was letting him do his thing for the benefit of their future.

"Mickey will be down in a minute," Abigaile said, leading them through the spacious front hallway to the bar.

A handsome barman sprang to attention.

"White wine," Leslie requested, nervously smoothing down the skirt of her dress.

"Tequila on the rocks," Jeff said, feeling insecure.

Leslie threw him a warning look; he did not hold his liquor well and they both knew it.

"Just one, cutie," Jeff said, catching her look.

She hated it when he called her "cutie."

Abigaile wished somebody else would arrive fast, or that Mickey would get his ass downstairs. She didn't relish being in sole charge of the guests. It was okay when there were lots of them and they could mingle. Now she had to entertain these two until somebody else arrived, when all she really wanted to do was be free to supervise. Not to mention checking on Tabitha, who'd refused to come out of her room to show off what she was wearing. Little Madame.

Abigaile heard the doorbell in the background. A few moments later, Johnny Romano strolled in accompanied by Venus Maria.

Abigaile frowned. How *dare* Johnny not announce who his guest was when she was as famous as Venus? The man had no manners, but then, what could you expect from an actor? Especially a Latin actor who happened to have gotten rich in a string of disgustingly raunchy movies. Abigaile conveniently forgot that Mickey had been responsible for most of them.

"Abbey, baby," Johnny purred, favoring her with the famous Latin-lover leer and a quick pinch on the butt. "Who's my favorite Hollywood wife?" He bent to kiss her.

"Johnny, dear," Abigaile responded, wrinkling her nose as she breathed in a strong whiff of his strangely exotic aftershave. "You look *wonderful*. And, Venus, it's been ages! *So* good to see you again."

"Thanks, Abbey," Venus said calmly, although inside she was seething because she'd spotted Leslie, and Johnny hadn't mentioned *she* was going to be there.

Abigaile led them over to the bar. "Do you know Leslie and..." She blanked on Jeff's name again.

Leslie, wide-eyed with shock, managed to stammer out, "J...Jeff." She had not seen Venus since the dreaded night at her house. This was a disaster. Now she'd have no chance with Cooper.

"Hi, Leslie," Venus said coolly.

For a moment, Leslie considered ignoring the tramp. Instead, she mumbled an uptight "Hello."

Jeff seemed to have forgotten where his loyalty should lie. "Venus!" he exclaimed with a big *I'm your greatest fan* grin. "We met at Leslie's, remember? Some night *that* was!"

Both women shared the same thought: *What an asshole!*

Johnny, who as far as he knew hadn't encountered Leslie before, shook her hand, holding it a few seconds too long. "Been readin' a lotta good things about you," he said. "Welcome to the stratosphere."

Leslie managed a strained smile. "Thank you."

She guessed he didn't recall their one night of unadulterated lust in a bungalow at the Beverly Hills Hotel—her and two other girls. He'd paid ten thousand dollars for the three of them and behaved like a greedy pig.

"No, thank *you*," Johnny replied, putting in some heavy-duty eye contact. If he didn't score with Venus, this red-headed lovely could be a definite contender.

At which point Mickey put in an appearance—showered and shaved, bald head glistening, Turnbull & Asser shirt, Doug Hayward English suit, and red Brioni tie. "Welcome, everyone," he said, beaming at his guests, doing a classic double take when he spotted Venus. "Good evening, my dear," he said, turning on as much suave charm as he could muster. "We weren't expecting you."

"I know how you like surprises, Mickey," she said, automatically flirting. "So here I am."

"Yeah," Johnny added. "Me an' Venus, we're an item."

"An item?" Abigaile chimed in, thinking Venus's dress was ridiculously low cut.

Johnny squeezed Venus's arm. "Hey—Mickey—we figured since we're makin' *Gangsters* together, we'd give you some extra PR. The tabloids are gonna cream over *this*."

Mickey quickly glanced at Leslie. She was talking to Jeff and didn't seem to have heard. Thank God.

Abigaile, however, *had* heard. She took Mickey's arm and said, "Excuse us a moment," whereupon she led him over to the other side of the room and said a sharp, "What's Johnny talking about? Hasn't anybody *told* Venus she's out of *Gangsters*?"

Mickey nodded. "Yeah, yeah, honey, it's all taken care of. Don't worry your little head about it."

"My *little head*?" she said haughtily. "Who do you think you're talking to—one of your brain-dead starlets?"

"There's been a change of plan," Mickey said, scowling. He couldn't stand it when Abigaile got uppity.

"What do you mean—a change of plan?" Abigaile snapped.

"I found a better movie for Leslie. Figured I'd send the script to her first, get her excited. She'll be starring with Gere."

"Richard?"

"No, *Maxie*," he said, raising his eyebrows. "What do you think? Of course, Richard."

Big change of attitude from Abigaile, who imagined Richard Gere attending one of her future dinners. "Oh, that's nice. She'll be thrilled."

"I told ya, didn't I? Alex is too tough for Leslie. He'll give her nothin' but grief. I'm doin' the kid a favor. We won't announce it tonight."

"Why not?"

"'Cause I don't want Venus finding out. She's probably pissed at me. So is Alex. They're all pissed at me. I run a studio, nobody likes me."

"That's ridiculous, Mickey—everybody loves you."

He had *her* back on track. "Thanks, honey. Now let's relax and have a nice evening. Keep your mouth closed, that way we won't get into trouble."

"No, Mickey," Abigaile said grandly. "*You* keep *your* mouth closed. *Yours* is the big one."

She hurried back to their guests. Venus and Johnny had wandered outside by the pool. Leslie and Jeff were having a heated conversation at the bar. And Cooper Turner and his date were making an entrance.

"Abigaile, sweetheart," Cooper said, kissing her on both cheeks. "This is Veronica."

"Hello, dear," Abigaile said, craning her neck to greet the tall model.

Leslie, who had been secretly haranguing Jeff for being so nice to Venus, glanced up and

saw Cooper approaching. Her attitude immediately changed. "Cooper," she said with a welcoming smile, "how lovely to see you."

"Hi, Leslie," he said. "Meet Veronica."

Leslie nodded, continuing to smile while
thinking to herself, *Oh, God, he's with that trashy
model who poses in those sexist lingerie catalogues that get dropped in your mailbox whether
you want them or not. She's not so hot in real life.
Too tall and horsey, with enormous teeth!*

"Veronica," Cooper said easily, "say hello
to Leslie Kane and her boyfriend, Jeff."

"Hi'ya, Cooper," said Jeff, extending his
hand, completely unconcerned that Leslie
and Cooper had once been lovers.

Venus and Johnny strolled in from outside. Perfect timing, as the guests of honor—
Donna and George Landsman—entered the
room, a sulking Santo trailing behind them.

Abigaile went into hostess overdrive.
"Donna," she gushed. "I'm *thrilled* to meet you.
Mickey has told me *so* much about you.
Welcome to Hollywood! We're *delighted*
Mickey is back at Panther."

An alert Mickey jumped into action.
"Donna," he said, unwittingly ignoring George,
"welcome to my house."

Donna had already spotted Cooper Turner,
Johnny Romano, and Venus Maria, and was
completely intimidated. She could deal with
anything businesswise, but mixing with these
famous people was a new experience. She
grabbed Santo, lurking behind her, and pushed

him to the forefront. "This is my son, Santo," she said.

"Hello, Santo, dear," Abigaile said, wondering why they'd allowed the boy to get so fat.

Santo spotted Venus across the room and his heart began pounding uncontrollably.

Venus. *His* Venus. In the flesh, only a few yards away from him. A dull red flush spread over his face.

"Gotta use the bathroom," he mumbled.

"Now?" Donna hissed, not pleased.

"Yeah, now."

Graciously, Abigaile said, "It's to the left of the hallway, dear."

Santo rushed from the room. Had Venus noticed him? Oh, jeez! He hadn't planned on them meeting like this.

He darted into the john, slamming the door behind him. Fortunately he'd brought a joint with him. Groping in his pocket, he lit up and inhaled deeply, frantically trying to compose himself.

Tabitha, on her way downstairs, saw the fat boy enter the guest bathroom. She chuckled to herself. This was a good one, she'd burst in and embarrass him. Ha! That would teach her mother to force her to attend one of her moronic dinner parties.

She reached the door of the guest bathroom and flung it open. Santo, who'd forgotten to lock it, nearly jumped ten feet in the air. He was caught with a joint half an inch from his lips.

Tabitha took in the scene. Quick as a flash, she closed the door. "You must be that Donna person's son," she said.

"Yeah," he mumbled. "Santo."

"I'm Tabitha—the Stollis's daughter. I notice you've got a nice, fat roach. Give me a drag and I won't tell anybody."

Aaron Kolinsky, the desk porter on duty at Alex's apartment building, had a bad stomach ache. Some of the tenants were enough to make any man ill with their stupid demands: "Walk my dog"; "Get my car waxed"; "Run to the market for me."

What did they think he was? A one-man service? The other guy working the shift was a young punk who knew nothing. He didn't know shit. Aaron found that he had to take care of everything.

At seven o'clock, he quit for the night. He'd had enough. Seven o'clock in the morning until seven o'clock at night was enough for anybody to have to put up with these rich people and their constant demands.

He left long before Tin Lee put in an appearance. It didn't matter anyway, he'd completely forgotten Alex's instructions.

Tin Lee walked up to the desk, announced she was going to Alex's apartment, took the elevator upstairs, and rang his bell.

No answer.

After five minutes, she came downstairs

478

again. She was running over half an hour late, Alex was probably furious and had gone on ahead.

"Did Mr. Woods leave a message for me?" she asked.

"No, ma'am," said the new desk clerk, more interested in reading his hidden copy of *Playboy*.

"Are you sure?"

"Nope. Nothing here."

"Do you have a phone book?"

He handed over a big, fat, L.A. phone book. Fortunately, Mickey Stolli was listed. She copied down the Beverly Hills address and collected her car from the valet, thinking she'd arrive at the dinner in time to be seated. Alex would be delighted she was so resourceful.

Somehow she felt their relationship was about to step up to another level. And not a moment too soon. Tin Lee felt it was time she asserted herself.

49

Sitting in Alex's Porsche on the way to the Chateau Marmont, Lucky started talking and found she couldn't stop. "I don't know why I'm telling you this," she said. "It's family history."

"So what you're saying is that the Bonnattis always held a grudge against the Santangelos, and Donna is carrying on the tradition?" Alex said.

She nodded. "It goes way back to Gino, and

Enzio Bonnatti, in the twenties. They were business partners in the beginning, bootlegging, speakeasies—they made a lot of money. Then Enzio got an urge to move into hookers and drugs, and Gino wasn't into that, so they split their partnership. Gino went to Vegas, where he built hotels. Enzio took a different road." She paused for a moment, lighting a cigarette. "Enzio was my godfather. I was over at his house all the time. In a way, I was closer to Enzio than I was to Gino. Until one day I discovered that Enzio was responsible for my mother's murder *and* my brother's. It was a shattering revelation."

"Jesus!"

"I was devastated. But there was absolutely no doubt I had to do something about it."

"Why you?" Alex questioned, his eyes fixed firmly on the road.

"Gino was in the hospital, he'd had a heart attack." She pushed back her long dark hair, remembering the experience in vivid detail. "I went to Enzio's house, lured him upstairs and...I shot him." She took a long, deep breath. "Everybody thought it was self-defense. I told the cops he was trying to rape me." Another beat. "It wasn't self-defense, Alex. It was pure revenge."

"And they never arrested you?"

"Nope. Gino had connections. Plus, I really made it look like I was defending myself."

Alex took his time before answering. "That's some story," he said at last.

"Y'know, Alex," she said thoughtfully, "if

you wait for the law to take action, you may as well forget it. If somebody close to you was murdered, would you sit in a courtroom watching them pussyfoot around for a year or two? Or would you deal with it yourself and get real justice?"

He stopped at a red light and turned to look at her. "I don't know what I'd do, Lucky."

"The Arabs have it right—an eye for an eye."

"Maybe..." he said slowly.

"Hey—you want the murderer locked up in jail working on his appeal while *we* pay the bills?"

"Not me."

"And how about hearing how he's found God, what a changed person he is—all that shit. Because we both know that's what happens. Believe me, Alex, if somebody does something to me or my family, they're going to get it back in spades."

"I agree the death penalty *is* a deterrent, and they should put it into effect more often. But taking the law into your own hands..."

"Why not?" she demanded angrily. "The law is so fucking clever? I don't think so."

They drove in silence for a while until they reached the hotel. Lucky stubbed out her cigarette and got out of the car. The Chateau Marmont had a history of Hollywood scandals and was much beloved by actors and the artistic community.

"I'm crazy about this place," she said as they walked through the hotel entrance. "I always expect to see Errol Flynn or Clark Gable in the lobby."

"I didn't know you were an old-movie fan," he said, surprised.

"I *love* old movies. That's all I ever watch on television. Old movies and soul music are my two passions."

"You like soul music?"

"Crazy about it. Marvin Gaye, Smokey Robinson—"

"David Ruffin, Otis Redding..."

"Hey—you're into it, too," she said, smiling.

"I have a large collection of original records."

"Me, too!"

"So," Alex said, "what are we trying to find out tonight?"

"This guy, Ricco, was in charge of the extras. Jennifer said the blond in the photos was hanging around the set. She probably got herself hired purely to set Lennie up."

"And you think Ricco can help you?"

"He did all the hiring. With unions and stuff, it's not that easy to get into a movie."

"Even in Corsica?"

"It was still an American production."

"And if you find out Donna Landsman *was* responsible, what then?"

She gave him a long, mocking look. "Now, c'mon, Alex, you wouldn't want to be an accessory, would you?"

He felt like he'd wandered into a scene from one of his own movies. Lucky's rules were different from everyone else's.

Jennifer was waiting in the lobby. "Glad you

could make it," she said, hurrying toward them.

"Meet Alex Woods," Lucky said.

"A pleasure," Jennifer said, her pretty face flushed. "Ricco wants us to go straight up to his room. I'll call and tell him you're here." She went over to the desk and picked up the house phone.

"Pretty girl," Alex remarked.

"Your type?" Lucky asked.

"No, Lucky, *you're* my type."

"Hmm...not into California blonds, huh? That makes you unusual."

Jennifer returned and the three of them got in the elevator.

In a way, Lucky was glad Alex was with her. It was hard discovering how Lennie had been set up, and gut instinct told her it *was* a setup. Not only had they taken Lennie from her, but they'd wanted her to think he'd betrayed her, too. Donna Landsman was a cold and devious bitch.

Ricco flung open the door to his hotel room. He was a short, dark, Spanish man with an animated expression, a pencil-thin moustache, and a way of speaking rapid English—repeating words twice while waving his arms wildly in the air.

"Jennifer, my Jennifer," he greeted her, giving her a big hug. "Is she not the most gorgeous girl you've ever seen?"

"Ricco," Jennifer said, embarrassed by the compliment. "This is Lucky Santangelo, and Alex Woods."

"I think perhaps I have died and gone to the heaven of the filmmakers," Ricco exclaimed, rolling his expressive eyes. "Mr. Woods, an honor to meet you. I have worshiped every one of your movies. One day, perhaps you let me work on them. And Miss Santangelo, you have made some fine films at Panther."

"Thanks," Lucky said. "I guess Jennifer told you what this is about."

"Exactly, exactly," said Ricco. "Jennifer has told me and I do recall...yes, I recall the blond very well indeed, very well indeed. A beauty. She come to me and say, 'Ricco, put me in the movie.' I tell her no lines. She says fine, fine. I cannot understand why a beautiful woman like this want to be an extra, but I obliged."

"Where can I contact her?" Lucky asked.

"Yes, yes. My assistant has gone to my files, and we give you an address in Paris. I have it for you—here." He handed her a slip of paper.

"I appreciate it," Lucky said.

"For you, madame, anything."

They left his room.

"I thought it was important you spoke to him yourself," Jennifer said.

Lucky nodded. "I'm glad I did."

"It looks like somebody wanted you to think Lennie was playing around on you," Jennifer said. "Although they couldn't have known he was going to be in a terrible accident the next day."

"Don't be so sure about that."

"What do you mean?"

"I mean this was planned," Lucky said

slowly. "I can assure you, Jennifer, Lennie's death was no accident."

Tin Lee drove directly to the Stollis's mansion. When she arrived, she gave her car to a parking valet and entered the front door. A butler looked her over. "Can I help you, madame?"

"I'm Mr. Woods's guest," she said, giving the man her name.

He consulted his list. "Ah, yes...please go in."

She walked through the spacious front hall into the living room. Abigaile saw her coming. "You must be with Alex, dear," she said. "I'm Abigaile Stolli."

"Yes, Mrs. Stolli," Tin Lee said, feeling slightly uncomfortable arriving on her own.

"Where's Alex?" Abigaile asked, peering behind her.

"Isn't he here?"

"Oh, I see...he told you to meet him. Don't worry, dear, I'm sure he'll arrive any moment. Go to the bar and have a drink."

Tin Lee went over to the bar, where she was immediately pounced upon by a slightly inebriated Jeff.

"Well, well, well," he exclaimed with a sloppy grin. "If it isn't Tin Lee. How'ya doin'?"

Jeff and she had attended the same acting class. "I'm fine, Jeff," she said, relieved to see a familiar face. "How are you? It must be a year since we've seen each other."

"You're as pretty as ever," he said, slurring his words as he pawed her arm.

"Who are you here with?" Tin Lee asked, surreptitiously backing away from his touch.

"I'm living with Leslie Kane," he said proudly. "She's my gal."

"*The* Leslie Kane?"

"You bet your cute little Japanese ass."

"I'm not Japanese, Jeff," she said stiffly.

"Whatever," he said vaguely, unaware he was being offensive. "Who're *you* with?"

"Alex Woods."

"Holy shit!" He laughed too loudly. "Didn't *we* do well?"

★ ★ ★

Leslie had gone over to Cooper and was trying to engage him in conversation. Unfortunately, Veronica was sticking to his side like superglue; plus, he had one eye on Venus, who was busy talking to Mickey.

"I've been asked to do a press junket for our movie," Leslie said. "They want me to fly to London and Paris. Will you be going?"

"Hadn't really thought about it," Cooper said, still watching Venus.

"I'm sure it would help the movie."

"You'll do a good job on your own."

She was bitter about his attitude. When their affair was secret and he could bang her whenever he wanted, he'd been all over her.

Now that they'd been found out, he was treating her badly and she didn't appreciate it.

"Are we allowed to smoke in this house?" Veronica asked, looking bored.

"Smoking's bad for you," Cooper admonished.

"I do *everything* that's bad for me," Veronica retorted, displaying horse teeth in a nasty smile.

Cooper laughed.

"I'll have a smoke by the pool," Veronica said, perfectly secure that she could do whatever she liked.

"I'll come with you," Cooper offered.

"No, wait a minute," Leslie said, placing a restraining hand on his arm. "I have to talk to you."

"Don't worry, Cooper," Veronica said, her deep voice jarring his nerves. "I'll see you in a minute." She strolled out to the terrace.

Cooper stared at Leslie as if they were no more than casual acquaintances. "What?" he said, aggravated.

"I need to ask you a question," she said.

"Go ahead."

"What have I done to you to make you behave so coldly toward me?"

"Nothing," Cooper said restlessly, feeling trapped.

"We used to make love every day until your wife found out. Now you act as if you hardly know me. It's not as though you're with her anymore."

Cooper was silent for a moment. He knew

he hadn't treated Leslie fairly, but that didn't mean she could hang on forever. After all, the girl was an ex-hooker—not exactly a sweet little virgin. "Listen, honey," he said, hoping to get rid of her permanently. "Consider it a movie fuck."

Her eyes filled up. "What?"

"It lasted while we were making the movie. This happens a lot in the business."

"Are you telling me I didn't mean anything to you?"

"At the time, Leslie. Not now."

She was filled with mixed emotions. She hated him. She loved him. There was a lump in her throat, and she wanted to scream aloud.

"Don't make a big thing of this," Cooper warned. "You broke up my marriage, Leslie. That's why we can't be together again, because—and maybe I'm being unfair—I blame you."

"You blame *me*?" she gasped.

"Yes," he replied. "So stay away from me, Leslie. It's better for everyone."

★ ★ ★

"I need a drink before we go to the Stollis's," Lucky said. "Can we stop somewhere?"

"We're late anyway," Alex replied. "May as well."

"One drink, that's all. I don't plan on doing what I did the other night."

"Why not?" he said lightly. "I enjoyed every minute of our adventure."

They went into the bar at Le Dôme. He ordered a vodka and Lucky requested a Pernod and water.

"So now what you're telling me is that you think Donna Landsman was responsible for Lennie's death?" Alex said when their drinks came.

Lucky nodded. "Exactly."

"Even with no proof?"

"Oh, come on, Alex. Who needs proof? I know for sure she hired a hit man to take care of Gino—her driver was the go-between."

"*How* do you know?"

"'Cause I had the hit man at my house earlier, tied to a chair in my garage. Fortunately, the jerk was a total amateur. He confessed. She may have business smarts, only she certainly doesn't know what she's doing when it comes to hiring muscle."

He was shocked. "You had him at your house?"

"That's right."

"Why didn't you hand him over to the police?"

"Get serious, Alex—what was I going to say? 'Oh, hi, Mr. Detective. Please arrest this man. Oh, yes, and I think Donna Landsman is responsible for setting up an accident in which my husband was killed. And she also hired a guy to shoot my father—this guy, in fact. She's been a very bad girl and needs to be put in jail.' I don't think so!"

"Guess you're right."

"I *know* I am."

"Jesus—you really say what's on your mind."

"You do the same thing in your movies."

He downed a shot of vodka, clicking his fingers for another one. "Yeah—I put the feelings I'm unable to express in real life up there on the screen. A lot of my anger comes out in my movies. My theory is that's why I never won an Oscar. Sure, my films get nominated because I know how to make a hell of a powerful statement, but the anger in them turns some Academy members off. Result—they don't vote for me."

"Is this a recent revelation, or are you in therapy?"

"Had a shrink. The guy told me plenty. Listening to you is better. I *do* know I have to take control of my own life. That's the key to inner peace."

"You've got that right. Look at me—I haven't exactly led a peaceful life, but I've learned to go with it. You can bet I'll never have an ulcer."

"You're a fortunate woman, Lucky. You were married to a man you loved, you've got three beautiful children." He paused for a moment. "You know, I've never been in love with anyone, never had a meaningful relationship, or even wanted to. My only close relationship is with my mother, and that's about as fucked up as you can get."

"Take control," Lucky said. "The power's within you. Use it."

"Maybe you're right."

He looked at her for a long moment. She suddenly felt very close to him. It took every ounce of willpower she possessed to finally break the look.

She realized Alex was right—they were unfinished business, but now was not the time.

5 0

"I'm stoned," Tabitha said and giggled. "This is, like, real heavy shit, where'd you score?"

"School," Santo replied, thinking she was really weird-looking in her orange spandex microskirt that barely covered her crotch, and cut-off skimpy top revealing most of her midriff. His eyes rested on the gold ring attached to her belly button. He controlled an insane urge to rip it out. Would she scream? Would her ripped flesh bleed? He wouldn't mind giving it a try.

"Hey—what school you go to?" she said, running a hand through her spiked magenta hair.

"Why?" he asked suspiciously.

"S' not polite to answer a question with a question."

"Where do *you* to go school?" he asked, noticing her fingernails were painted a creepy, dull black—like she was out of some vampire movie.

"Boarding school," she said. "Switzerland. Here"—she snatched the joint from him again, jamming it between her lips— "more for me.

Otherwise, I'll tell 'em you were in here jerking off."

"You wouldn't do that," Santo said, still trying to recover from the shock of seeing Venus in the flesh, more gorgeous and sexy than in her photos.

"I can do anything I want," Tabitha boasted. "*I'm* the daughter of the house."

He'd seen girls who looked like her hanging around the Strip on Saturday nights. Usually they were sitting on a curbside throwing up, or fighting with each other before crowding in to see some sleazy rock band. Rich punks. He'd never been into that scene. He preferred the gold Rolex, unlimited credit, and a very expensive car.

"So," Tabitha said, sucking on the joint. "Your mom's the one who kicked Lucky Santangelo out at Panther, right?"

"I guess so," he mumbled.

"My dad hates Lucky Santangelo," Tabitha said matter-of-factly. "She threw *him* out at Panther. I've never met her, but *I* think she sounds cool. And my great-granddad says she's the best."

"You've got a great-granddad?"

"Yeah, doesn't everyone? Do you know who he is?"

"Who?"

"Abe Panther," she boasted. "He founded Panther Studios."

"Yeah, well, *my* father was murdered," Santo said, scoring points.

Tabitha ignored that pertinent piece of

information. "Why are you so fat?" she demanded.

"Why are *you* so rude?" he countered, hating her and her stupid outfit and her ugly hair. Who was she to call him fat? She was a total freak.

"S'pose we gotta join the party," Tabitha grumbled. "Okay, fat boy, let's go."

"Don't call me that," he said, hating her even more.

She giggled. "Give me another joint and I won't."

Abigaile looked around. To her relief, everyone appeared to be having a good time. She glanced at the clock. It was eight-thirty. Where was Alex Woods? He was the only guest missing. She didn't think it was polite to summon everyone to the dining table until he was present.

"Tin Lee, dear," she said, going over to the bar. "Did Alex give you any indication of what time he was arriving?"

"I thought he'd be here before me," Tin Lee replied. "He must have gotten held up. As you know, he's starting production on Monday, he's very busy."

"He could've phoned if he was going to be late," Abigaile said, hardly able to conceal her aggravation.

"I'm sure he wouldn't mind if you went ahead without him."

"Hmm..." Abigaile said, not pleased.

She was on her way to the kitchen when she spotted Tabitha, dragging Santo behind her. Oh God, the outfit! Mickey would have a heart attack when he saw it. She swooped into her daughter's path, blocking her way. "Tabitha," she said, quietly seething. "May I see you for a moment?"

"Mom," Tabitha said, her orange spandex microskirt riding up. "Have you met Santo?"

"Yes, I've met Santo," Abigaile said through clenched teeth. "Come, dear, I wish to speak with you."

Tabitha, who was feeling the effects of the grass, giggled stupidly. "What're we gonna talk about, Mom? Sex? Do you and Dad still do it?"

Abigaile gripped her daughter's arm and was on her way to maneuvering her out of the hall when in walked Alex Woods, accompanied by Lucky Santangelo.

Abigaile stopped short. Tabitha took the opportunity to wriggle from her grasp and escape.

"Sorry, Abbey," Alex said, not sounding sorry at all. "Got held up in a meeting." And before she could say a word, he and Lucky were on their way into the living room.

She hurried behind them, desperately trying to catch Mickey's eye. He was in such an intimate conversation with Venus that he didn't notice.

Tin Lee jumped down from her bar stool and ran to greet Alex. "I was late getting to your apartment," she started to explain, then she saw Lucky and stopped.

Alex's worst nightmare was coming true. "What are *you* doing here?" he said, completely exasperated. "Didn't you get my message?"

"What message?"

"You must be Alex's date," Lucky said, getting the picture, and feeling sorry for the poor girl who—pretty as she was—was way out of her depth. "I'm sorry I kept him. Alex and I had a business meeting. He asked me to come here for a drink."

"I'm sure it's okay if you stay for dinner," Alex said quickly. "I'll tell Abigaile." He made his way over to Abigaile, who was still trying to get Mickey's attention. "Abbey," he said. "Lucky's staying for dinner."

"Lucky Santangelo is not Mickey's favorite person," Abigaile responded tartly. "They have a history."

"She happens to be my date."

"No, Alex," Abigaile responded. "Your *date* is Tin Lee—who, I might add, has been here for half an hour without you."

"My *date* is Lucky Santangelo," he said, refusing to back down. "Tin Lee is the one you're fitting in."

"There's no room at the table, Alex."

"Pull up another chair, Abigaile."

They glared at each other.

"I'll see what I can do," she said crossly.

Lucky assessed the situation. She knew all the players except George, Donna Landsman's husband. Without hesitating, she walked right up to the woman and said, "So, we meet again."

Donna was shocked to see her. She tried to compose herself, aware that it would be unwise to make a scene. Mickey inviting Lucky was a big mistake, one he would pay for. "How are you?" she said coldly.

"Pretty good, as a matter of fact," Lucky replied, staring at Donna, trying to reconcile the new image with the old Donatella. There wasn't the slightest resemblance. "Thing is, I've had time to reflect, get myself organized, consider the way things have been going."

Cooper snuck up and grabbed her from behind. "Hi, gorgeous! Great to see you."

"Cooper—have you met Donna Landsman?"

"Sure."

"Isn't it nice to know we have such an *experienced* woman at Panther—you *are* experienced in the film industry, aren't you, Donna?"

George answered for her. "Mickey Stolli will do an excellent job."

Lucky raked George with a look, summing him up instantly. Worshiped his wife, probably never got laid before, a whiz with finances, had no idea what Donna was up to.

She turned back to Cooper. "Are you making any deals with Panther?" she inquired.

"You'll have to ask my agent," Cooper said with a smooth smile.

"Oh, I'm sure Donna will pursue you. She probably has all the agents and managers crawling up her ass *begging* for deals. And, Donna, I must say—it certainly looks like it could accommodate them."

Before Donna could respond, Lucky moved away, leaving Donna fuming. She was not fat. How dare the skinny Santangelo bitch make a comment like that. And why was Lucky walking around so cool and collected? Wasn't it enough that she'd lost her husband, her studio, and almost lost her father? What else would it take to bring her down?

"Did you hear that?" Donna said to George, her face red with anger. "Did you?"

George tried to calm her. "No scenes," he said quietly. "You mustn't let these people see she's upset you."

"What's she doing here?" Donna seethed. "I thought Mickey hated her."

"I'll find out."

"You'd better," Donna snarled, her triumphant entry into Hollywood society ruined.

★ ★ ★

Abigaile finally managed to pry Mickey away from Venus. "Have you seen who's here?" she said, amazed that he hadn't noticed.

"Everything's going great, honey," he said, a stupid smile spread across his face. "What's your problem?"

"My *problem* is Lucky Santangelo."

"What about her?"

"She's over there! Alex brought her. *And* he has a date here." She glared at her husband as if it were his fault. "What are you going to do about it?"

Mickey shrugged. "There's nothing we *can* do. What did Alex say?"

"He told me to lay another place at the table."

"Go ahead and do it."

"I don't *want* that woman in my house. She *fired* you from Panther."

"True, but in this town you gotta get along with everyone—you never know when you'll need 'em. So, Abbey—go tell your maid to set another place. It's no big deal."

"It *is* a big deal," Abigaile fretted. "It'll ruin my placement."

"Honey," Mickey said mildly, "take your goddamn placement and shove it up your ass! Now do as I say."

Still glaring, Abbey retreated.

Mickey headed straight for Lucky. "I see Lucky Santangelo has decided to honor us with her presence."

"Hi, Mickey," she said coolly. "How's everything?"

"Pretty damn good. I'm back at Panther, where I belong. Now all I gotta do is dump that lineup of crappy movies on your schedule. The only good one is *Gangsters*."

"I'm sure you'll turn things around, Mickey. Only *you* can put Panther back where it was before." A meaningful beat. "In the crapper."

Johnny strolled over, joining in the conversation. "Lucky, baby," he said. "No shit—you are my favorite."

"*Everybody's* your favorite, Johnny," she said. "Do yourself a big one and get a new line."

"Why?" he said, grinning. "The old one's always worked for me."

Jeff stumbled and almost fell off a bar stool on his way over to join the illustrious group. This was an opportunity too good to miss. "I've always wanted to meet you," he said to Lucky, slurring his words. "You're beautiful, rich, and powerful. There should be more of your kind of woman in Hollywood. I'm Jeff, I'm an actor."

"Big surprise, Jeff."

He grinned at her, swaying slightly. "An' you're as beautiful as everybody said."

Alex walked over and took Lucky's arm. "Come here, Lucky—talk to Venus for me."

"What now?"

"Here's the deal," he said quietly. "Mickey wanted Leslie to play Lola, then changed his mind—now he wants Venus, only she's under the impression she didn't get the part. You'll tell her she did, and not to mention anything tonight."

"What am I—the mediator around here?"

"Do this for me, Lucky. Please."

She sighed. "Yeah, sure, like I have nothing else on my mind."

Tabitha sat Santo on a couch and proceeded to give him a brief rundown of the players.

"You see the woman with the long red hair? She's Leslie Kane, used to be a hooker. My father doesn't believe it, neither does my mother. I *know*."

"How do you know?" Santo asked.

"My mom's manicurist told me, she's into everything. And the guy with her—he's some freeloader out-of-work actor who's living with her. That's Lucky Santangelo over there, the one with the black hair. The dude with her is Alex Woods. You know who he is?"

"'Course I do," Santo said, thinking that this girl wasn't treating him very nicely.

"Okay, so he's meant to only like slit eyes. I guess that's his date—the one with the funny name."

"How do you know all this?"

"I *observe*," Tabitha said, twirling the gold ring in her navel. "See Cooper Turner—he fucks anything that moves. And Venus Maria—so does she."

"What did you say?" Santo said, his face reddening.

"You heard. Venus is a *major* slut. Fucks everyone."

"Don't say that about Venus," he said furiously.

"Why? Do you know her?"

"Yes. She's a wonderful person."

"Ha! Shows how much *you* know. Right

now she's fucking her masseur 'cause she can't find anybody else since she booted Cooper Turner out. Tonight she's hitting on Johnny Romano—he screws all his girlfriends in the back of his limo. Bet he gets it on with her tonight."

"You've got a dirty mouth," Santo said.

"Yeah?" Tabitha jeered. "And I bet you'd give anything to have it wrapped around your tiny little dick."

★ ★ ★

"What are we doing here?" Lucky said to Venus. "And *what* are you doing with Johnny Romano?"

"Okay, okay—you caught me—this is pretty low," Venus said, grinning sheepishly. "I wanted to come tonight—if only to see Mickey's face when I walked in. He's under the impression I'll blow him if he gives me the role in *Gangsters*. I'm kind of stringing him along, then maybe I'll slap him with a sexual harassment suit."

"Great idea," Lucky said. "You slapping Mickey Stolli with a sexual harassment suit is *definitely* a *Newsweek* cover."

Venus laughed. "Yeah, but nobody would believe it. They'd say *I* was the one harassing *him*."

"I've got good news for you," Lucky said. "There's some complicated thing going on here involving Mickey. However, according to Alex—*you* are Lola, and Leslie's *out,* but you're not supposed to say anything tonight."

"Are you *sure?*" Venus said.

"Alex told me himself."

"Oh, God—what a relief! Now I don't have to blow Mickey!"

"You weren't seriously considering it?"

Venus laughed. "What do *you* think? And by the way, how come you're with Alex Woods?"

"He's...a friend."

"Oh, c'mon, Lucky, it's *me* you're talking to. Alex is following you around with that look. You know the look I mean."

"Let me ask you something?"

"What?"

"Am I an Alex Woods type?"

"Honey, you're so cool, you'd be anybody's type."

They both laughed.

Alex walked over.

"Done," Lucky said.

He smiled at Venus. "How are you?"

"Better since I heard the news."

"Let's keep it to ourselves. We'll talk tomorrow."

"I'll have to put a muzzle on Johnny—he's decided to defend my honor and get me the role."

"Don't tell him why."

"Of course not."

"And talking of muzzles," Lucky said, "what do you plan on doing with him on the way home?"

"Not a damn thing," Venus said, smiling. "Exactly *nada!*"

Abigaile did as Mickey asked, and had the maid set another place at the table. She hated it when things didn't go the way she wanted them to. Her daughter looked like a refugee from a bad Madonna video; the Landsmans's son was fat and unattractive; Lucky Santangelo was making everyone uncomfortable; and Mickey was behaving like a horny schoolboy, lusting after Venus as if he'd never seen a pair of tits before.

However, Abigaile refused to let anything ruin her perfect evening. Putting on a proper smile, she clapped her hands together. "Dinner is served, everyone," she trilled. "Shall we make our way into the dining room?"

5 1

Her name was Claudia, and as far as Lennie was concerned, she was an angel. She'd given him back the will to live, and that meant everything, it gave him hope that there *was* a future.

He'd found out he was in Sicily. How he'd gotten there or why was still a mystery. Claudia had told him everything she knew. She'd discovered that her father, Furio, and his friend Bruno were being paid to keep him in the cave. Someone in America had hired them to do so; she suspected it was Bruno's sister.

"Who's she?" he'd asked.

Claudia said she was a very rich woman

who lived in Los Angeles. As far as Claudia knew, nobody was aware of his existence except Bruno and Furio. Recently Bruno had been involved in a car accident and was in the hospital with a broken leg. Furio was away from the village on business, which was why she'd been entrusted to bring him food.

Claudia was twenty-one, and worked as a seamstress in a neighboring village. She'd learned English at school, and lived at home with her five brothers and sisters.

"My father...he trusts me," she said in broken English. "He no trust others. Now I hear your story...I am not sure what I think."

Several hours after capturing her that first day, Lennie had been forced to let her go—but only after they'd talked for a long while. He'd tried to explain to her who he was, that he'd been kidnapped, and exactly who she should contact in America. He'd even given her Lucky's number to call.

"Not possible," she'd said.

"Why?" he'd demanded.

"Not possible," she'd repeated.

Before she'd left the cave he'd made her promise to return, to help him. "You *have* to find a way to get this chain off my ankle. You must, Claudia, otherwise they're going to let me die here."

She'd returned the next day with two cigarettes, an apple, and a box of matches. Precious treasures.

Now she visited him every day, bringing whatever she could and talking to him. He learned about her life in the tiny village where there was not even a movie theater; her boyfriend—whom her father hated; and her abusive older brother, whom—according to her—everybody hated.

"You've got to get to a phone," he begged her. "Summon help…"

"No," she refused, shaking her head. "My papa would know it was me. I must help you my way."

"When's that going to be?" he said roughly. "I'm going insane trapped here."

"Be patient, Lennie. I will help you. That is my promise."

"When, Claudia, *when*?"

"One day I want to go to America," she said, her eyes shining at the thought.

"Help me, and you will," Lennie assured her.

The next day she brought him a crudely drawn map.

"When I get the key, I bring it. You leave immediately. I replace key before papa finds it missing. You follow map."

"Why can't you lead me out of here?"

"No." She shook her head, her long hair swirling around her beautiful, innocent face. "I go to my village. You travel other way. They come after you."

"When can we do this?"

"On the weekend my papa drinks beer…he sleeps. I try to get key."

Only a few more days. He couldn't believe it.

Only a few more days and maybe he'd be free.

52

As the guests trooped into the Stollis's dining room, Mickey grabbed Abigaile. "I've handled it," he said, pleased with himself. "Gave that Santo kid a hundred bucks and told him to take Tabitha out to a movie and get a hamburger."

Abigaile frowned. "What will Donna say?"

"Who gives a shit? If you think my daughter's sitting at our dinner table dressed like that, think again."

"Was Santo all right with this?"

"He took the money, didn't he?"

"If you say so," Abigaile said with a put-upon sigh. "I'd better remove their places."

"I've already had the maid do it."

"Thank you, Mickey."

He winked. "I deliver in a squeeze."

"Yes, you do," Abigaile agreed, nodding. It was quite possible that Mickey was right, with Tabitha out of the way she'd be more relaxed, although tonight's gathering was not her ideal group.

She considered her seating plan. She'd placed herself between Cooper and Johnny Romano—the best seat in the house; Mickey was flanked by Leslie and Donna Landsman; she'd squeezed Lucky in between Venus and Alex, placing Tin Lee on his other side—

let's see how he'd deal with *that*; George was next to Tin Lee; and on the other side of Leslie was Jeff, then Veronica.

All in all, she thought she'd done a masterful job. Seating was never easy, but Abigaile liked to think she excelled.

★　★　★

Alex took Lucky's arm as they entered the dining room, Tin Lee trailing behind them.

"I don't want to be here," Lucky whispered. "Not one little bit."

"You're here—accept it," Alex said.

"Nobody forces me to do anything I don't want to."

"This is a favor for me," he said persuasively. "After all—I went with you to see Ricco."

"Nobody had a gun to your dick," she said flippantly. "You *wanted* to."

He steered her in another direction. "How are you planning on dealing with that situation?"

"Maybe I'll fly to Paris," she said casually. "And *no,* Alex, you can't come with me. This will be a solo trip."

"You'd fly all that way on spec?"

"Not on spec. I've already called Boogie, he's put people on the case."

"And Boogie is...?"

"My private investigator. He's a pretty sharp guy—he can find out anything about anybody."

"You employ your own private investigator?"

"I have to meet this woman face-to-face. We all know money can buy most things—I'm positive it can buy her."

"Why not wait until your man has some credible information?"

"I have to do this now."

"You're *very* impulsive."

"Look at her," Lucky said, nodding scornfully toward Donna as she entered the dining room. "I remember when Santino had her shipped in from Sicily. She was a peasant who couldn't speak a word of English. Do you know that I went to their wedding?"

"Whatever else, you have to admire what she's achieved."

"Fuck you, Alex!" Lucky said, turning on him. "She's a murderer. I don't admire anything about her, and neither should you."

"I didn't mean—"

"I don't care *what* you meant. Go look after your girlfriend, she's feeling neglected."

Mickey caught up with Lucky before she sat down at the dinner table. "You got a lotta balls coming here," he said, his voice low and rough-edged.

Lucky stared at him. "Wasn't it Abigaile who used to go around wearing yours for earrings?"

"Once a cunt, always a cunt."

"Hey—throw me out," she challenged. "It'll make for good dinner conversation."

"I wish I could," he said hoarsely.

Her black eyes narrowed. "You think I *want* to be here? I promise you, Mickey, I'm only staying to piss you off."

★ ★ ★

Tabitha and Santo sat in Tabitha's BMW, with the engine running, outside the Stollis's.

"I hate my freaking parents," Tabitha said glumly.

"I hate mine, too," Santo agreed.

She bit at a hangnail. "At least we've got *something* in common."

"Your dad gave me a hundred bucks—like I need *his* money—I got plenty of my own."

"I have to drive this boring car 'cause *Mommy* thinks it's *safe*," Tabitha sneered. "What do you drive?"

"I'm getting a Ferrari," he boasted.

"Not bad."

"My mother buys me anything I want 'cause she feels guilty."

"About what?"

"That she married this dweeb George after my father was murdered."

Finally he had her attention. "Really, honestly—murdered?" she said excitedly. "Like, *how*?"

"Shot," he said, knowing he sounded real cool.

"Like, *ambushed*?"

"No. The cops said he was molesting some kids. One of them put a bullet through him."

"*That's* a weirdo story."

"It's not true."

"So, like, what *is* the truth?"

"It had something to do with my mother catching my dad with another woman."

"Who shot him? Your mom?"

"I wouldn't be surprised. They were always screaming at each other. Yeah...I think the old cow could've done it."

"Wow!" said Tabitha, completely impressed.

"Did you see what my mother looks like?"

"Like every other Hollywood old bag—a face full of plastic."

"She used to be fat."

"Like you?"

"Bag the insults."

"You could work out. Look at me, I'm real skinny 'cause I throw up a lot. I'll teach you how t'do that if you like. It's pretty gross at first. After a while you get used to it."

"As soon as she got rid of my dad, she made herself real thin and stuff. Then she married the geek. I hate 'em both."

"Don't blame you," Tabitha said, shifting restlessly.

"We could go to my house and pick up my Corvette," Santo suggested, trying to hold her attention.

"You got more dope there?" she asked hopefully.

He nodded.

"What are we waiting for?"

"Weren't we supposed to go to a movie?"

Tabitha threw him a scornful look. "Get a

life, Santo. We'll smoke a little weed, then come back later. They don't give a crap *what* we do."

"And so," Veronica said, guttural voice too loud for the table, "there I was on the runway in Paris wearing nothing but a bra and panties, and this Japanese dignitary is staring at my crotch when I tripped and fell right into his lap. I nearly crushed the poor little man."

Jeff roared with laughter. Cooper smiled politely. Veronica's harsh voice was starting to drive him completely crazy.

He glanced across the table at Venus. She was busy talking to Lucky. He tried to attract her attention. She refused to acknowledge him. What a fool he'd been to cheat on someone as loyal as Venus. He missed her desperately and would do anything to win her back.

Leaning past George and ignoring Tin Lee, Donna said to Alex, "I'm delighted we're making your movie at my studio."

Alex gave her a stony look, wondering if everything Lucky suspected was true. "Where are you from originally?" he asked.

"Italy," Donna replied. "Why?"

"I thought I detected a slight accent."

"No," she said fiercely, "I have no accent."

George interjected, "Your *parents* are from Italy, Donna. *You* were born in America."

"Yes, that's right, I was," she lied.

"Really?" said Lucky, who had the uncanny ability to tune in to several conversations at once. "What part of Italy were *they* from?"

"Milan," Donna lied.

Lucky fixed her with a steely look. "My grandparents came from Bari. The Santangelos." A meaningful pause. "Perhaps you've heard of them?"

"No," Donna muttered, furious that she had to put up with this. She loathed being out of control, sitting with these Hollywood people who thought they were better than everyone else. She especially loathed having to deal with Lucky Santangelo face-to-face. This was *not* part of her plan.

It seemed Lucky Santangelo was indestructible. What else could she possibly do to bring the bitch to her knees?

Donna began considering the possibilities.

53

Lucky left the table on the pretext of visiting the ladies' room. Once she was out of the dining room, she walked through the front door, gave the valet parker twenty bucks to drop her at the nearby Beverly Hills Hotel, and from there took a cab back to her house.

She knew she should have told Alex she was leaving; she also knew he would have insisted she stay, and she was not in the mood. Sitting in the same room as Donna Landsman was sickening, breathing the same air was beginning to stifle her.

Donna Landsman had killed Lennie.

She didn't deserve to live.

Earlier, when she'd spoken to Boogie, he'd told her he had news on the shareholders. She'd arranged to meet him later, at her house.

Driving down the highway, she found herself thinking about Alex. He was interesting and talented and attractive and a challenge. The more time she spent with him, the more she felt herself being sucked in.

It was no good, she was not ready for an involvement.

She wondered what her children were doing. It broke her heart that they'd never see Lennie again. Even though she knew it was safer for them to be out of the country, she couldn't help missing them. Kids were so resilient, they got through every day no matter what. They were probably having a wonderful time.

Back at the house, the guard waved to her as the car drove up to the garage.

Boogie was already there, sitting in the kitchen watching CNN. He clicked off the TV and jumped up when she walked in.

"Let's go in the living room," she said, impatient to hear what he had to say.

They sat on the couch and Boogie started talking. "It's taken a while," he said, "but we finally discovered who Mrs. Smorg is."

"Yes?" Lucky said, tapping her fingers on the coffee table.

Boogie's long face was impassive. "Inga Smorg—alias Inga Irving—is currently Mrs. Abe Panther."

Lucky was shocked. Inga. Abe's wife. This was a big surprise.

Abe would have a fit if he found out Inga had helped oust her. She must have bought the stock as an insurance policy behind Abe's back. The stoic Swede had always been jealous of Lucky's closeness with Abe, so when the opportunity arose to vote, Inga had elected not to support her.

"What about Conquest Investments?" she asked, reaching for a cigarette from a pack on the table, her addiction totally out of control.

"Another of Mrs. Smorg's little secrets," Boogie said. "She and Morton Sharkey are in partnership. Conquest belongs to them—fifty-fifty."

"Are you telling me they control an off-shore company together? One that Abe doesn't know about?"

"That's right. She operates under the same name that was on her passport before she married Abe."

"So," Lucky said thoughtfully, "if I can get Inga *and* Morton to vote in my favor, I'll have enough stock to regain control?"

"That's the way it is."

"This is easy, Boogie. All I have to do is tell Abe what's going on."

"Be careful, Lucky—Abe's an old man. You don't want to get him excited."

"I'll speak to Inga first. Maybe the *threat* of my telling Abe she owns stock in Panther will be enough to make her change her mind." She stood up and walked over to the window. "Okay, now fill me in on the blond in Paris."

"Her name's Daniella Dion. She's a very expensive call girl who works for an infamous French madam, Madame Pomeranz—a woman known for supplying beautiful girls to politicians and visiting VIPs."

"That figures."

"Daniella is a real pro. She's been doing this since she was fifteen—eight years. For a while, until he died, she was the mistress of an octogenarian industrialist. He left her money—the wife contested his will, Daniella ended up with nothing—and she went back into the business two years ago."

"When can I see her?"

"For twenty thousand dollars a day and all

515

expenses, she'll fly to Los Angeles for an 'appointment.'"

"Arrange it."

"I already have. She'll be here in two days. She's under the impression a friend is buying her time as a birthday present for Johnny Romano."

"*Very* inventive, Boog."

"I had to make sure she came."

Lucky laughed dryly. "For twenty thou a day, it's hardly likely she'd hang back. That's the most expensive fuck I've ever heard of."

"There're women who go for higher," Boogie said knowledgeably.

Lucky blew a stream of smoke toward the ceiling. "Since when did you become an expert?"

★ ★ ★

Nona and Brigette sat in their hotel room debating whether to hire a car, drive over to Lucky's and surprise her, or telephone first.

"I vote we phone," Brigette said. "It's too late to go running over there."

The truth was, she was reluctant to tell Lucky her story. She felt embarrassed and foolish, and, quite frankly, she didn't know how Lucky *could* deal with it.

Nona handed her the phone. "Go ahead," she urged. "I bet she's up."

Reluctantly, she dialed Lucky's number. "Guess where I am?" she said brightly when Lucky came to the phone.

"Here?"

"How did you know?"

"Because when somebody says, 'Guess where I am,' you can guarantee they're around the corner. What are you doing here?"

"Uh...I had to come out for a modeling assignment. I'm staying at the Hilton with Nona."

"Why are you at a hotel when you could've stayed here?"

"We didn't want to bother you. Anyway, your house, with the kids and everything, is full."

"The children are in Europe with Bobby."

"I didn't know that."

"Perhaps if you kept in touch, you would."

"Lucky, um...Nona and I were thinking—can we have lunch tomorrow?"

"This is not the greatest time for me. How about dinner at the house tomorrow night?"

"Sure."

"And if you change your mind," Lucky added, "come stay. Spend the weekend."

"We kind of, like, only came for a day."

"I'll send a car. It'll be outside your hotel at five-thirty."

"Don't use my real name. Brigette Brown's my name now."

"I understand," Lucky said, wondering why Brigette sounded so edgy. "See you tomorrow, sweetheart."

"She wanted us to stay with her," Brigette said, hanging up the phone.

"Why didn't you say yes?" Nona said. "We could have spent tomorrow at the beach."

"I thought we'd go shopping, drop some money."

"Oh, Brigette, Brigette—what am I gonna do with you?"

"Shopping is therapy, Nona."

"Sure."

"Should I phone Isaac?" Brigette asked, feeling better now that she'd spoken to Lucky. "He'll be wondering what's happened to me."

"Why would you want to be with a guy who's only interested in getting high?"

"What's wrong with that?"

"You're at the start of a big career. Don't mess it up."

"You sound like my *mother*."

"Oh, great. Just 'cause I'm trying to be the sensible one around here."

"No. You're right. My mother would never say anything like that. She'd be too busy out screwing rock stars."

"We all know you didn't have a normal childhood," Nona said, and sighed. "Neither did I."

"I guess if we can survive our parents we're pretty fortunate, right?" Brigette said.

"Right," Nona agreed. "Let's go to bed."

"Bed?" Brigette exclaimed. "It's only eleven-fifteen."

"Brigette—"

"Okay, okay."

Alex watched the door, waiting for Lucky to reappear. After five minutes, he knew she wasn't coming back. "Excuse me," he said, getting up from the table. He walked outside, found a waiter, and said, "Where's Miss Santangelo?"

"Don't know, Mr. Woods."

He went to the front door and asked a valet parker, "Did Miss Santangelo leave? Did she take my car?"

"No, Mr. Woods, she ordered a cab."

He had half a mind to make a quick exit, but Abigaile and Mickey would never forgive him, not to mention Tin Lee, who was sitting beside him with a frozen smile on her face. God, how had he gotten himself into this position?

Lucky did what she wanted to do. He'd been like that once. Now he was a typical Hollywood player, toeing the line so he could get his fucking movie made, and Lucky had run out on him yet again.

He returned to the dining room. "Abigaile," he said, "Lucky wasn't feeling well, she went home."

Abigaile exchanged a look with Mickey.

Donna smiled, bitterly triumphant. She'd won. She'd driven the bitch away.

Now all she had to do was figure out how to get rid of her permanently.

54

The Stollis's dinner dragged on.

Jeff got drunker; Leslie got sulkier; Mickey got bolder; Abigaile got fussier; Alex got angrier; Tin Lee got tenser; Johnny got hornier;

Venus got flirtier; George got quieter; Donna got gloomier; Veronica got louder; and Cooper got more detached.

As soon as coffee was served, Alex was on his feet. "C'mon," he said to Tin Lee, roughly pulling her to her feet. "Say good-bye."

They stood outside the house next to their respective cars.

"Would you like me to come home with you?" Tin Lee asked, tentatively placing her hand on his arm.

"Y'know, Tin Lee," he said, realizing it was not fair to string her along any further. "This isn't working out for either of us."

"Excuse me, Alex?" she said, removing her hand.

"I can't make you happy."

Oh, she thought miserably. The *"I can't make you happy"* speech, which, roughly translated, means *"You can't make me happy."*

Her eyes filled with tears. Over the months, she'd grown attached to Alex, and even though he was not the world's greatest lover, she had a need to be with him. Deep down she felt he needed her, too, because she was a calming influence on his otherwise turbulent life. Surely he realized it?

"Alex—" she began.

He cut her off. "I don't want to talk now," he said abruptly.

"If we don't talk now, when will we?"

"Look, I'm starting my movie, I'm very busy. I shouldn't even be out."

"I visited your mother tonight," she said quietly. "We had an interesting talk. I saw your family photo albums. You were a sweet little boy, Alex."

"Why did you do that?" he asked, mad at Dominique for allowing such intimacy.

"Your mother is lonely, Alex. She loves you very much."

"I'm not interested in hearing what you think about me and my mother," he said angrily. "Dominique is *not* your friend, okay?"

Tin Lee sighed. "What do you want from a woman, Alex?" she asked. "What would make you happy?"

He didn't answer immediately, he considered her question. "Peace," he said at last. "That's what I want, peace."

★ ★ ★

Venus and Johnny Romano made their exit shortly after Alex. Comfortably lounging in the back of his limo, Johnny stretched out his long legs and poured Venus more champagne. "Really boring, babe," he announced. "Those people got no clue how to get down."

"Maybe that *is* their idea of getting down," Venus remarked.

Johnny smoothed back his Latin-lover heavily greased black hair. "Well, they got one dull life."

"Abigaile doesn't think so."

He swigged from the champagne bottle. "So how come you told me not to say anything about the movie?"

She gave a small, triumphant smile. "Because...I've got the role."

He smiled broadly. "Hey, baby—must've been something I said."

"I'm sure it was, Johnny."

"We gotta celebrate," he said. "Wanna stop by my place?"

"What kind of celebration is that?"

"Don't put it down till you've seen it." He leered. "*Wanna* see it, babe?"

"See what?" she asked, as if she didn't get his double entendre.

He grinned lasciviously, patting his immediate erection, quite obvious in his tight-fitting black pants.

Venus averted her eyes, feigning a yawn. "I'm more interested in getting a good night's sleep...by myself."

"Hey—baby, Johnny Romano *never* forced himself on anyone. Never had to. But I'm telling you," he added boastingly, "you got no idea the goodies you're missing."

"My—what a big ego you have," she drawled.

"Yeah, all the better to eat you up with."

She couldn't help laughing. Johnny's lines were outrageously corny.

"Hey—" he said, reaching for more champagne. "Did you catch the face on that fat kid when he saw you?"

"What fat kid?"

"The Landsmans's son. He took one look at you and nearly came in his pants!"

"Johnny!"

"Maybe he's your number-one fan, baby-cakes."

"I didn't notice him."

"You're so cool. He's gonna be talking about you for months, and *you* didn't notice the poor kid."

"I saw the Stollis's daughter twirling her little navel ring in your direction."

"Sixteen? Too young."

"What?" she said, amused. "By about three months?"

He laughed. "You're funny. We're gonna have good times on this movie."

"You bet we are, Johnny. First we'll work *very* hard, *then* we'll have good times."

"I'm renting a house in Vegas. There's room for one more."

"Thanks, Johnny, I'll get my own house. That's the nice thing about being a star—I can afford to do whatever I want. And what *I* want right now is to be left alone."

★ ★ ★

"I have an early photo shoot tomorrow," Veronica said, glancing meaningfully at Cooper.

He took the hint and stood up.

"I enjoy those catalogues you appear in," Mickey said, absently rubbing his bald head.

"Very sexy, Veronica. Very sexy indeed."

"Thank you, Mickey," Veronica replied, towering over him.

Mickey moved a little closer. He liked tall women, they gave a whole new meaning to going down. "You ever thought about being in a movie?" he asked.

"As a matter of fact, I have. Last week I signed with William Morris for film and commercial representation."

"Good move."

She favored him with a horsey smile. "I'm glad you think so."

He licked his fleshy lips, this one was a definite turn-on. He'd like to squeeze his cock between her big tits and come all over her. "Give me a call at the studio sometime. Maybe I can help."

"I'll do that, Mickey."

Cooper kissed Abigaile on both cheeks. "Nice dinner, Abbey, thanks," he said, not meaning it.

"We must do this again," Abigaile gushed, always delighted to have Cooper as a guest.

"Absolutely," Cooper said, thinking, *No way!* He took Veronica's arm and led her out the front door. "Sorry about that," he said in a low voice as they waited for his car.

"I'm sure you're planning on compensating me," Veronica purred provocatively.

"Definitely," he answered, on automatic pilot, although his mind was on Venus. Seeing her with Johnny Romano had really upset him.

He drove to Veronica's apartment, got out of the car, and escorted her inside.

In the elevator, she suddenly pounced, pinning his shoulders up against the wall, kissing him with the most inventive tongue he'd ever come across. God, she was strong!

This was a switch, *he* was the one usually calling the shots.

"Hey," he objected as her hands traveled intimately down his body, rubbing his penis. "Let's not get carried away."

"Don't be a tease, Cooper," she said, exploring his left ear with her probing tongue. "I've heard about your reputation. The girls are all dying to know."

"What girls?"

A low, throaty laugh. "We have a little supermodel club. Y'know, see who can fuck the most billionaires and movie stars."

"That's really impressive," he said sarcastically.

"No," she said, her hand pressed firmly against his dick. "*This* is what *I* call impressive."

And before he could say anything, she reached for the Stop button, and as the elevator lurched to a halt, urgently began unbuckling his belt.

Cooper felt like a girl with a guy who was coming on too strong. Was this date rape? *Oh God, Venus, where are you when I need you?*

Before he knew it, Veronica had his pants down around his ankles and was busily working on removing his undershorts.

It occurred to him that any moment somebody could buzz for the elevator, the doors would open, and he'd be exposed for all to see.

"Let's go to your apartment," he said.

"I want to do it here," she countered, breathing heavily as she unzipped the back of her dress, allowing it to fall from her long, lean body.

The most famous underwear model in the world didn't wear any. She was tall and smooth-skinned, with a shaved pussy and prominent nipples. She was also very, very naked. "Kiss this," she said, shoving one of her boobs toward his mouth. "Kiss it, suck it—c'mon, lover boy, show me what you can do."

"Am I about to make your list of billionaires and movie stars?" he groaned, chewing on a nipple.

"Maybe you'll be top of the list," she promised, throwing a long leg around his waist, deftly trying to maneuver him inside her.

"Are you sure they don't have security cameras in these elevators?" he said, feeling his erection slipping away.

"Get with the program, baby," Veronica encouraged in her guttural voice. "Do it to me—do it to me good."

A standing-up fuck—just what he felt like.

He wondered what Venus was doing now. Was she in Johnny's infamous limo? Was he plying her with champagne while telling her she was the sexiest woman in the world?

Johnny was too obvious, Venus wouldn't fall for his corny crap.

As he thought about Venus, his erection completely deserted him, and he slipped out of Veronica, who was not pleased. "What's the matter?" she said sternly, sounding like a drill sergeant.

Oh, God, he didn't want her running back to the supermodel squad, reporting that he was a dud.

"Can't do it in an elevator—too public," he explained. "It's not my thing."

"Public sex excites *me*," Veronica said, flicking out her extra-long tongue and wriggling it at him, kind of a snakelike come-on. "I once did it in a bathroom at the White House. Nobody knew."

"Except the President," he joked.

She didn't get it.

"Let me see if I can persuade you to overcome your fear of elevators," she said, falling to her knees and taking his penis into her mouth, ramming in his balls along with it.

This little move made him nervous, not horny. She had the biggest mouth he'd ever come across. He felt himself shrinking more as each moment passed.

"This isn't going to work," he said, attempting to remove himself from her mouth before she crushed his precious balls to pieces.

"Don't I turn you on, Cooper?" she said in her deep, brown voice. "Every man in America wants to fuck me. They leaf through my catalogue, then look at their fat wives, and go— 'Ah...Veronica...my fantasy woman. I want her tits in my mouth, my tongue in her pussy.'"

"The problem is that I don't have a fat wife at home," Cooper said, groping for his pants on the elevator floor and hurriedly pulling them on. "I need a drink," he added tersely.

"Oh, you have to drink to get it up, is that it?" she said nastily.

He was beginning to dislike her more and more; in spite of her outward appearance, there was nothing feminine about her.

"I was married to Venus Maria," he said. "In fact, I still *am*. We're separated."

"She's shorter than I expected."

"She's a very special woman."

"Then why are you separated?"

Good question.

Someone yelled down the elevator shaft. "Are you stuck?"

Calmly Veronica stepped into her dress. "Zip me up," she commanded.

He did as she asked and flipped the On switch. The elevator rumbled into action.

Veronica smoothed down her dress. "How old are you, Cooper?" she asked.

"It's public record," he said with an unperturbed smile, secretly livid she would ask such an intimate question.

"Hmm..." she said knowledgeably. "Perhaps you need a shot of testosterone."

Bitch! "Not when I'm with my wife I don't," he said, wiping the smile off her horsey face.

The only people left at the dinner party were Abigaile and Mickey, Donna and George, a drunken Jeff and an uptight Leslie. She'd been dying to go for the past half hour, but it was impossible to get Jeff to move. He sprawled on a couch with a sloppy smile stuck on his face. "Y'know, Mickey," he said, "one of these days I'd like to produce."

You'd better learn to act first, Mickey thought sourly. There was nothing he hated more than the slew of good-looking guys who came to Hollywood figuring they could be actors, producers, directors. This Jeff guy was an out-and-out loser. Somebody had to talk some sense into Leslie.

"Where do you think the children are?" Donna said, her lips pressed into a thin, disapproving line.

"Dunno," Mickey said, not too concerned. "Maybe the movie ran longer than they expected."

"I'm disappointed," Donna said, ignoring George's warning look.

"How's that?" Mickey said.

"You invited Santo here for dinner, then sent him out to a movie. That's not very polite."

"The kids didn't want to sit around with a bunch of old people like us," Mickey said expansively. "Tabitha will take care of your boy."

"He doesn't need taking care of," Donna said frostily. "He also doesn't need to be led astray."

"What do you mean by that?" Abigaile said, quickly joining in. Nobody was going to criticize *her* daughter.

"Santo is a good boy," Donna said.

"Are you implying that Tabitha is a bad influence?" Abigaile said, bristling.

"Maybe I should call our house," George suggested.

"Yes," Donna said, trying to control her aggravation.

"Use the phone behind the bar," Mickey offered.

Leslie got up to go to the guest bathroom.

"May I have a word with you, dear?" Mickey said, following her into the hall.

"Sure, Mickey," Leslie said, listless since Cooper had left with the skinny six-foot model with the phony tits.

"You're looking tired," he said.

"Do you think so?"

"Y'know, Leslie," Mickey continued, putting his arm around her shoulders. "Leading ladies—they gotta be sparkling at all times. Who *is* this schmuck you're with?"

"You mean Jeff?"

"What are you doing with a loser like him? Is he a great fuck? 'Cause I can find you another guy who's better in bed, *and* has brains to go with it."

"I really don't appreciate your interfering in my personal life, Mickey," she said huffily. "I might be doing a movie for you, but that doesn't give you the right to comment on who I see."

"Honey," he said patiently, "I'm trying to

teach you street smarts. *Never* live with an actor. They're ego-inflated pricks. Surely you've worked that out by now?"

"Look, I admit Jeff is a little, um...happy tonight, but that's only because he's glad to be here."

"I bet he is," Mickey snorted.

"Anyway, Mickey, don't worry—he's not around permanently. I'm using him, the way you guys use women."

"I've never used a woman in my life," Mickey said indignantly.

No, of course not, she thought. *How about that bachelor party where you had a girl spread-eagled on the buffet table while you ate the celebration cake out of her pussy for the boys' amusement?*

"Anyway, I'm taking him home now," Leslie said. "By the way, Mickey, I had an idea."

"What?"

"Wouldn't Cooper be great in *Gangsters*?"

"The movie's cast, Leslie."

"I know," she said, her eyes gleaming. "But can you imagine? Cooper Turner in *Gangsters,* with Johnny Romano and me—what a combination!"

"Didn't you just finish a movie with Cooper?"

"Yes, and it's going to be big. Why don't you find another script for us to do together? We have sensational screen chemistry."

"Yeah," he said, thinking that this was exactly the out he was looking for. "That's not a bad idea. If I come up with something, would you sooner do that than *Gangsters*?"

"Yes," she said, "as long as it's with Cooper."

"A nice romantic comedy—right?"

"Perfect."

"I'll definitely get into it, baby. Come by the studio for lunch."

"My pleasure, Mickey."

"Meanwhile, take the loser home. I don't want him throwing up on my couch."

"I can hear a phone ringing," Tabitha singsonged, completely out of it. They were both lolling in the middle of Santo's bed in a drugged-out stupor.

When they'd gotten back to his house they'd shared another joint, then Tabitha started exploring his room, begging for something stronger.

He remembered the heroin Mohammed had sold him. "Girls get off on it," Mohammed had said. Tabitha was a girl. She had perky little tits almost exposed by her flimsy top. He wouldn't mind touching them; he'd never touched a real girl. So they smoked the heroin and ended up floating on a beautiful blue cloud above the world, watching everyone.

Santo was overcome with a feeling of goodness. Everything was so nice, and he was filled with joy. Wow! Tabitha felt the same way.

They were both so mellow and calm that it seemed only natural they should take their clothes off and fling them at each other, screaming with laughter.

Santo kept thinking about Venus at the party, her blue eyes, blond hair, and the way she looked in her daring red dress.

He got naked, glanced down, and couldn't believe how hard he was. His cock resembled a rocket ready for takeoff.

Before he knew it, Tabitha was sitting astride him and they were making out.

She moved fast, riding him like a show horse. All he could see were her perky little tits and her belly button with the gold ring bouncing up and down. It was a mind-blowing experience.

When she fell off him, they both started laughing uncontrollably and rolling around on the bed.

He wondered if he should show her his collection, maybe read her some of the letters he'd sent to Venus, which he'd dutifully copied.

Something warned him she might be jealous. It wouldn't do to have her and Venus fighting over him.

"You're not bad, Santo," Tabitha said grudgingly, stretching out her arms. "We should do this again."

"Anytime you say."

"I'm starving," she said, jumping off the bed.

Naked, they ran downstairs and raided the fridge in the kitchen. Fortunately, the servants had retired for the night to their own separate quarters behind the pool house.

"Where's your *parents*' bedroom?"

He took her into Donna's room. She threw herself onto the middle of the huge old-fashioned four-poster bed, flinging the velvet embroidered cushions at Santo, screaming with high-pitched laughter.

"How we gonna clear this up?" he said, worried for only an instant. "My mom'll know we were in her room."

"Who cares?" Tabitha said carelessly. "Come over here. Let's do it again on her bed."

He hadn't taken much persuading.

Now they were back in *his* room and the phone was ringing.

"Ignore it," he said, grabbing her pointy little tits.

"You sure?"

"Wanna show you something."

"What?"

He got off the bed and went to his locked closet.

"*What?*" Tabitha repeated impatiently.

Unlocking the closet, he reached in the back, pulling out his new prized possession.

"Holy shit!" she exclaimed. "That's a *big* gun."

"All the better to kill them with," Santo replied, laughing like a maniac.

"Huh?" Tabitha said, blinking rapidly.

"One of these days," Santo boasted, "I'm gonna blow their fucking heads off!"

55

Johnny Romano was not as pushy as Venus had thought. When she turned down his invitation to go back to his place, he accepted her refusal in a good-natured way. His limo was now parked outside her house.

"Gotta say I'm buzzed you're doing the movie," he said, flexing his long, surprisingly elegant fingers.

"So am I," she said, noticing his huge diamond pinkie ring and diamond-studded identity bracelet. He had to be wearing at least half a million bucks' worth of diamonds. "The script's brilliant, you'll be terrific."

As big a star as he was, Johnny still enjoyed receiving praise. "You think so?" he asked anxiously.

"Absolutely."

"I got me this acting coach," he said, his voice filled with boyish enthusiasm. "Don't laugh— the guy comes to my house twice a week. He used to work with De Niro."

"That's smart, Johnny. You can never know enough about your craft."

"I got Lucky to thank for gettin' my career back on the straight."

"How come?"

"Remember when she first took over Panther?"

"How could I ever forget? From undercover secretary to studio mogul in one quick move."

"I was doin' a lot of shit movies then. Violence. Sex. She called 'em my 'motherfucka movies'—'cause that's all I ever said! They made me a fortune—but Lucky pointed out I was never the hero. 'Be a hero,' she told me, 'that's what the audience wanna see.' An', goddamn it—she was right."

"Good for you, Johnny. There's nothing like moving on."

He edged across the seat, getting closer. "Did you enjoy tonight, baby?"

"It was okay."

"Didn't bother you seein' your old man with that luscious piece?"

"Cooper and I are history."

"Shame for him." His thigh was now pressed up against hers. "Fortunate for me."

"Don't bet on it, Johnny," she said, moving away.

"I got somethin' funny to tell you."

"What?"

"Veronica used to be a man."

"Get *outta* here!"

"I met her in Sweden years ago, when I was workin' as a waiter. She'd just had the operation."

"Come *on*."

He laughed. "Cooper'll never know the difference."

"You're bad, you know that. Why didn't you *tell* him?"

"And spoil a beautiful romance? No way." He laughed again. "So...I saw you bending Mickey's ear all night."

"He's got a hot dick for me—what can I do?"

"Oh, baby, baby—you got a way of sayin' it the way it really is."

"Secret of my success," Venus said with a confident smile. "And now, Johnny, I'd appreciate it if you'd let me out of the car."

He did as she asked and said good night without pushing it.

She was relieved, not being in the mood to fight off an overly amorous Latin movie star.

The first thing she did was play back her answering machine. There was a plaintive message from Rodriguez begging to see her, and a happy one from Ron.

"Taking your advice, sweet thing," Ron said. "I'm moving out."

He didn't say where he was moving, otherwise she would have called him.

She went into her all-white dressing room, stepping out of her red dress on the way.

The phone rang. Hoping it was Ron, she ran to pick it up in the bedroom.

"Hi, it's Cooper."

"Oh...hi."

"You looked *veree* sexy tonight."

"What do you want, Coop?" she said, sitting on the edge of the bed, wondering if he'd discovered the truth about Veronica.

"Just wanted to say hello."

"That's not very original."

"I'm fresh out of lines."

"You? *Never!*"

"I was thinking..." he said.

"What?"

"Oh, about what a great marriage we had."

"How can you say that when your mission was to screw as many other women as possible?"

"I know," he said, sounding repentant. "All my life I did exactly what I wanted, and women came along for the ride. Then I met you, fell in love, and got married. I didn't think

I *had* to change. I was selfish and incredibly dumb. Now I realize I made a big mistake."

"What happened? You strike out with the model? Didn't get any, huh?"

"I got plenty; problem was, I didn't want it."

"Really," she said, not about to ruin his evening with Johnny's story.

"How 'bout you? Was Romano all over you in the car? You know, he jokes about it to his pals—tells everybody that once he gets a girl in the back of his limo, a blow job goes with the territory."

"You should know me better than that."

"Can I come over?"

"What for?"

"To talk...that's all, I promise."

She knew she should say no, but she felt herself weakening.

He took advantage of her silence. "Strange coincidence," he said. "Right now I happen to be on your block."

"Okay," she said, against her better judgment. "Come on over."

Johnny Romano's limo cruised down Sunset. He sat back, chatting on the car phone to Leslie.

She cradled her portable while taking a good look at Jeff. He was sprawled in the middle of her bed, still in his clothes, snoring like a stuffed-up hog. Mr. Romance strikes again.

"You gave me your number, an' I'm usin'

it," Johnny said. "An' this man is wonderin' what you are doin' right now."

"Where's Venus?"

"Why would I be with Venus when I've got *your* number, baby?" he said, putting on the sexy, macho voice he used for imminent seduction. "How 'bout havin' a drink with me?"

Jeff burped and rolled over on the bed, reeking of booze.

Leslie thought of Cooper. He was probably real cozy with that big horse model and her big horse teeth. She felt sad, she'd loved Cooper all her life, and for a few magical weeks she'd had him to herself—now he didn't want her anymore. It wasn't fair.

"I can pick you up in five minutes," Johnny said. "Just tell me where I gotta point my limo, an' baby—believe me—I'm there."

★ ★ ★

Alex drove directly to Lucky's house at the beach.

A security guard stopped him at the door. "Good evening, Mr. Woods," the guard said politely. "Ms. Santangelo mentioned you might drop by."

"She did? Good."

"She also said she doesn't wish to be disturbed."

"She left me that message?"

"Ms. Santangelo said she'd talk to you tomorrow, Mr. Woods, and to please not call her tonight."

"Oh...fine...okay."

Alex got back in his car, furious with Lucky for playing games. One moment she was confiding in him. The next she was treating him like a total stranger. He understood that she had problems, but why wouldn't she let him help her?

He drove home experiencing a feeling he'd never had before. Was this love? Because if it was, then love was a crock.

He decided he had to get himself together, forget about Lucky Santangelo and concentrate on what he did best. Making movies.

The guard waited until Alex drove off, then buzzed Lucky. "Mr. Woods was here. I told him you'd speak to him tomorrow."

"Thanks, Enrico," she said.

You're doing the right thing, she told herself. *Mustn't encourage him. Alex is getting too close, and it's not what I want.*

She sat on her bed and reached for Lennie's photograph, in a silver frame. She missed him so much. His smile, his company, his lovemaking, his conversation.

There could be no substitute.

Not yet anyway.

"There's no reply at our house," George said,

replacing the receiver. "Perhaps we should wait for Santo at home."

"I agree," Donna replied, glaring at Mickey. "I wish you'd consulted me before you sent my son off with your daughter."

Mickey shrugged. "Thought I was doing the kids a favor. How was I to know they wouldn't get back on time?"

"They'll be here soon," Abigaile said. "Tabitha's a very reliable girl."

"Yes, from her appearance I would judge her to be *really* reliable," Donna said sarcastically.

"Excuse me?" Abigaile said, not liking Donna's tone at all.

"Do you actually let your daughter walk around dressed like that?" Donna said.

"At least she's not bloated and overweight," Abigaile responded, not caring if Mickey got mad.

Mickey quickly moved in, nudging his wife to shut up. "I'm sure they'll be here any moment," he said. "As soon as they arrive, I'll personally drive Santo home. He'll be fine."

Donna glared at him. How dare they send her son off just because they didn't want him sitting at their boring dinner table? She hated the Stollis. She had a good mind to fire Mickey as soon as she found somebody else to take his place. In fact, the entire evening had been a disaster.

Their limousine was parked in the driveway. Donna marched over, waiting for her driver to spring out and open the door.

The man didn't move; he was slumped over the steering wheel, obviously asleep. Donna tut-tutted her annoyance while George tapped on the glass.

No response. George opened the door and the driver, John Fardo, fell out onto the concrete driveway.

"Oh, my God!" Donna shrieked.

George bent over the man, feeling for his pulse. "Get help," he said tersely.

Donna hurried back to the Stollis's front door and rang the bell. Mickey opened the door. "Our driver's sick," Donna said. "Call the paramedics."

Mickey walked outside. "He looks drunk to me," he said, staring at the man on the ground.

John Fardo groaned, gradually regaining consciousness.

"Are you all right, John?" Donna asked.

"Yeah, yeah, I'm fine...fine," he muttered, embarrassed about the incident.

All he could remember was somebody dragging him out of the car, beating the shit out of him, and shoving him back behind the wheel with the curt warning, "Don't ever fuck with the Santangelos again." After that, he must have passed out.

Making a supreme effort, he pulled himself together and staggered up off the ground. "Sorry, Mrs. Landsman...dunno what happened. I, uh...guess I musta fallen."

"Fallen?" she said imperiously.

He hoped they wouldn't notice his swollen

face in the dim light. "I'm okay now. Lemme drive you home."

The Landsmans got in the car.

Mickey shrugged and went back in the house. "Their driver was drunk," he informed Abigaile, who was already on her way upstairs.

"What did you think of the party?" she asked over her shoulder.

"Your usual success," he said, following her up the stairs.

"How would *you* know?" she said tartly. "You spent the entire evening drooling down Venus's neckline."

"Honey, you can't possibly be jealous of me and Venus. She works for my studio."

"You paid her too much attention, Mickey. It's disrespectful to me."

"Gotta keep the actresses happy."

"Ha!" Abigaile snorted, stopping for a moment.

Mickey grabbed her ass. "Come here, hon," he cajoled. "You know you're the only one for me."

The first thing Donna noticed as they approached their house was Tabitha's BMW parked in the driveway. "Thank God they're here," she said to George. "I was beginning to worry."

"He's sixteen, Donna. You worry about him too much. Santo needs discipline, not coddling."

543

"Why would he bring Tabitha here?" Donna mused. "*I* know. It's probably because those stupid Stolli people made out he wasn't a welcome dinner guest. Santo was upset."

That'll be the day, George thought. Donna had no idea what a spoiled monster she was raising.

They entered the house.

"Santo!" Donna called out in the dark hallway, reaching for the light switch.

"They must be up in his room," George said.

"Why would he take her up there?" Donna said.

Why do you think? George thought, following his wife to their private elevator.

"I can't believe they invited Lucky Santangelo tonight," Donna grumbled. "A true lack of judgment on Mickey's part. I shall be watching him very closely from now on."

"Yes, dear," George said, standing next to her in the small but luxurious elevator.

The door to Santo's room was closed.

"Knock," George said.

"Why should I?" Donna said, flinging open the door. "This is my house."

Santo was sprawled on his bed, passed out. Lying across him was a half-naked Tabitha, also in a drugged stupor. Loud rap music blared from the CD player in the messy room. On the bedside table was a half-eaten pizza, a spilled bowl of popcorn, half a joint, and an empty bottle of Scotch precariously balanced on its side.

"Oh, my God!" Donna wailed. "What has she done to my baby?"

5 6

Lucky took Boogie with her to meet Sara and deliver the money. They met at the Hard Rock Cafe, a milieu in which Sara had seemed comfortable the last time. Sara ran in, sat down, and immediately ordered a double cheeseburger.

"Is this the only time you eat?" Lucky inquired.

"I got me a healthy appetite," Sara replied, grabbing her burger as soon as it arrived, taking huge bites, stuffing her mouth until she couldn't jam anything else in. "Okay, how we gonna do this?" she asked as soon as she'd finished. "I gotta get the money before I hand over the tape."

"You'll come with me to my car, where I have a VCR," Lucky said. "We'll play the tape, and if it contains what you say it does, you'll get your money. It's as easy as that."

"Oh, yeah—like, really easy," Sara sneered, eyeing Lucky with deep suspicion. "How'd I know you won't kidnap me? Sell me into white slavery, that kinda shit?"

"You have to trust me," Lucky replied calmly, wondering if the girl was on drugs—she was certainly manic enough.

"Me—I don't trust no one," Sara said,

proud of her spiky attitude. "Everyone's out for their own thing."

"If you want your money, you'll *have* to," Lucky said coolly.

"Who's he?" Sara said, rudely gesturing toward Boogie.

"My associate."

Sara squinted her eyes. "How do I know *he* ain't gonna do something to me?"

Lucky was starting to lose patience. "Either you want the money or you don't," she said curtly.

"Okay, okay," Sara answered quickly, not wanting to blow such a windfall. "Where's your car?"

"Outside."

"I may as well tell you," Sara said, her expression turning crafty. "My friend knows where I am, an' if I'm not home in an hour, she'll call the cops."

"Very sensible," Lucky said dryly. "I'm glad you've figured out how to protect yourself."

They walked outside to the waiting limousine.

"Cool," Sara said, liking the fact it was a limo. "Y'know," she continued chattily as she climbed in, "I had this customer...uh, I mean, like, *friend*. He'd arrive at the massage parlor in his big, freakin' limo, an' then he'd wanna get a very *personal* massage in the backseat while his driver took us around town. This big old car had black windows so nobody could peek in. Sometimes he opened that glass thing so's his driver could get himself an eyeful. I din't go for that, but the old lech paid good."

Why had Morton picked this sad little girl to get himself in trouble with? They were a total mismatch. "Does Morton know you had all these adventures before you met him?"

Sara giggled hysterically. "Morty thinks I was workin' the massage parlor thing like a *good* girl."

Lucky leaned over and inserted the tape in the VCR. The picture was scrambled for a moment before becoming clear.

She stared at the screen. There was Morton in Sarah's bedroom, sitting on the side of her bed, fully dressed, in a three-piece suit. Enter Sara in a schoolgirl outfit.

SARA: "Hi, Daddykins."

MORTON: "Were you a good girl at school today?"

SARA: "*Very* good, Daddy."

MORTON: "Are you sure?"

SARA: "Yes, Daddy."

MORTON: "Come sit on my knee and tell me all about it."

SARA: "I did do *something* bad...."

MORTON: "Am I going to have to spank you?"

SARA: "I don't know, Daddy. Were you a good boy at the office today?"

MORTON: "No, I did something bad, too."

SARA: "Then I think *I'll* spank *you.*"

And so it went on. Lucky watched, in a trancelike state. She knew some people could only get off by indulging in their fantasies, but as far as she was concerned, it was kind of a sick obsession. What was wrong with normal sex? Who needed fantasies and props?

As soon as Morton began to divest himself of his clothes, she clicked off the machine and said, "Okay, I've seen enough." Opening the window, she spoke to Boogie, who waited outside. "Give her the money and let's go."

Sara climbed out of the car and stood awkwardly on the sidewalk. Boogie handed her a paper shopping bag. "Here," he said. "You want to count it?"

Sara grabbed the bag and peered inside, barely concealing her excitement. "Is this all I havta do?"

"That's it," Lucky said. "Put the money in a safety-deposit box and go home. Not a word to Morton."

"Won't he find out?" Sara asked.

"Maybe," Lucky said. "It didn't bother you last time—or him. He's still paying your rent."

"I'm usin' the money to get outta town with my girlfriend," Sara confided. "I've had it with L.A. You should've *seen* some of the weirdos who came into the massage parlor. Games, games, games—that's all they were into. An' most of 'em wished I was ten!"

"Spare me the details," Lucky said.

"Well," Sara said, clutching the shopping bag to her side. "We're gonna try our luck in Vegas. Me and my friend. If there's anything else I can do...you got a phone?"

"Don't worry, Sara, if we need anything, we'll contact you."

Boogie got into the car, and the limo sped off.

Santo blamed George. His mother would never have punished him in such a vicious fashion if George hadn't encouraged her. He was sixteen, for Crissakes. If he couldn't make out with a girl in his own room, what *could* he do?

George suggested a list of punishments and Donna agreed. Santo had never seen her so angry. Her face was white and pinched; she could barely look at him.

1. No Ferrari.
2. No allowance for six weeks.
3. No going out after school.
4. No credit cards.

Shit! He'd been caught having sex, not murdering the freaking president.

Donna didn't say a word while George confronted him with his punishments.

"C'mon, Mom," he whined, turning to her. "It wasn't so bad."

"Drugs are very bad," George said ominously, like it was a federal offense—which, of course, it probably was. "Your mother and I will not tolerate them in our house."

"Her house," Santo muttered sourly.

"No," Donna said, appalled by her son's

behavior. "It's George's house, too. And he's taking care of this problem until you learn to behave."

He couldn't believe that she was siding with George. It was unthinkable. What a freaking cow!

He wondered what kind of punishment Tabitha had gotten after her father had come to fetch her. "I never want to see her with my son again," he'd heard Donna say as Mickey whisked Tabitha off.

After George had finished yelling at him, and Donna had refused to intervene, he went to his room and sat glumly in front of his computer, staring blankly at the screen.

No Ferrari.
No allowance for six weeks.
No going out after school.
No credit cards.

What a sack of shit.

He was confused. He hadn't meant to do it with Tabitha, when all along he'd been saving himself for Venus. Now freaky Tabitha had gone and spoiled everything.

What if the things she'd said about Venus were true? That Venus was nothing but a slut and a whore.

It suddenly occurred to him that all this wasn't Tabitha's fault at all. *Venus* was to blame. If he hadn't seen her at the Stollis's party, and if Tabitha hadn't told him all those things about her, he wouldn't have gotten so stoned that he'd ended up not knowing what he was doing.

Yes. *Venus* was responsible for him not getting a Ferrari. It was *her* fault. She'd ruined his life, and he was going to make sure she paid for it.

★ ★ ★

"This is for you," Cooper said, standing over Venus.

She rolled over in bed, stretching lazily. "What?" she mumbled, half asleep.

"Orange juice, raisin toast, coffee, the trades, and this..."

She struggled to sit up. Cooper held a silver tray with all of the things he'd mentioned on it. He was also stark naked, and carefully balanced on the edge of the tray was his erect penis.

She began to laugh hysterically. "What are you *doing?*" she exclaimed, sitting up.

"Nothing," he deadpanned.

"What am *I* doing?" she groaned, realizing she'd spent the night with the husband she was about to divorce.

"Falling in love with your husband again?" he suggested, charming her with his handsome smile.

"Oh, no...once was enough, thank you, Cooper. You're a lot of fun, but I've finally realized—you are *not* husband material."

"How many other guys make you breakfast?" he asked plaintively. "Where else can you get this kind of service?"

"Mmm..." she said, still smiling. "Orange juice, raisin toast, coffee, a hard-on...maybe I should reconsider."

"Look, you," he said, removing his dick from the tray and sitting on the side of the bed, "I know what I did was unforgivable. If you'd done the same to me, I probably would've walked. Truth is, I learned my lesson, and now I want us to get back together."

"Hmm..." she murmured languorously.

"Last night I was with one of the most desired women in America. And you know what? I left her, and came running over to be with you."

"Ha!" she exclaimed, sitting up further.

"What does 'ha' mean?"

"According to Mr. Romano—who knows about such things—Veronica is a sex change."

"Jesus, Venus! That's ridiculous. And not true."

She giggled. "Guess you made the right decision, Coop."

He frowned. Could that explain his lack of interest? His survival instinct must have kicked in, saving him from...what?

"We belong together, Venus," he said persuasively, refusing to allow her to get him off track. "You know that."

"Cooper," she replied, her face serious. "This new movie I'm about to start is very important to me, and—"

"Wasn't last night special?" he interrupted, fixing her with his ice-blue eyes. "Wasn't it

552

the greatest? We really are something together, everyone says so."

She smiled at the memory of his incredible lovemaking. "I must admit, Coop, you certainly do have a technique like nobody else..."

"And let me assure you, from now on I'm saving it all for you."

She wanted to believe him. However, this was Cooper Turner speaking—a man with a lifelong reputation for screwing around. She'd taken a chance with him once...was she foolish enough to do it again?

He was right in there with a fresh pitch. "All I'm asking for is another shot. C'mon, honey, you *know* it's right."

She felt herself weakening. "Well...maybe we *could* see each other—kind of get reacquainted."

"I thought we got reacquainted last night."

She giggled again. "Oh, yeah, and I'd like more of that tonight, tomorrow, and...if things work out...well...eventually, we could talk about moving back in together."

"Deal," he said, smiling broadly.

"Now you'll have to excuse me," she said, jumping out of bed. "I must speak to my agent."

"I love it when you get serious," he said, grabbing her arm and pulling her back on the bed.

She smiled...what the hell...one more chance wouldn't kill her.

Lucky stepped out from behind a marble pillar, accosting Morton Sharkey in the lobby of his Century City office building. "Hi, Morton," she said, removing her Porsche shades and fixing him with her black eyes.

He stepped back, startled.

"Surprised to see me?"

"Uh…Lucky." He was almost stammering. "This uh… *is* a surprise. What are you doing here?"

"I came to see you."

"You did?" he said, agitated.

She moved closer. "Ever since you pulled your little stunt at Panther, I've been unable to reach you even though I've left messages every day, told your secretary it was urgent, and repeatedly faxed you. Didn't your mother teach you it's very rude not to respond?"

"I'm sorry, Lucky, I've been extremely busy."

"You sold me out, Morton," she said flatly. "And I don't like that."

He adopted a defensive attitude. "I did what was best."

"For whom?" she said coldly. "You were my business advisor. You helped me gain control of Panther, then you went behind my back and screwed me." A pause. "I don't get it, Morton. Unless, of course, somebody was *forcing* you to behave in such an unethical way."

He began edging toward the elevator, trying to distance himself from her. "Uh, Lucky— you still have forty percent of Panther. I'm sure with Mickey running it again, it'll go into profit...."

She moved in front of him, blocking his way. "Just like before, huh? You—better than anyone—know he ran the studio into the ground."

"These things happen," he muttered, too ashamed to look at her. "Business is business."

"Mistake number one, Morton, you sided with Donna Landsman."

"Mrs. Landsman is a respected business-woman."

"No. For your information, Mrs. Landsman is the widow of Santino Bonnatti."

Alarm spread across his face. "What are you talking about?"

"Remember the Bonnattis? I'm sure I must have told you the story many times."

He stared at her silently, thinking, *So that's why Donna Landsman had been so anxious to gain control of Panther.*

"Fortunately for you, I'm in a good mood," Lucky continued pleasantly. "Therefore, I'm giving you a chance to redeem yourself. My lawyer will immediately arrange for you to sell me your five percent of Panther, plus your half of the Panther shares you have in Conquest Investments. That'll give me back a control-ling interest. Then I want you to set up the same scenario—just like you did for Donna. I'll be sitting in my office when you bring her in and *I* tell her *she's* out. Oh, yes, and make sure Mickey Stolli is with her. I want to personal-ly fire his fat ass."

Morton's voice faltered. "I...I can't do that."

"Oh, yes, Morton, you certainly can." A long pause. "By the way, how's your wife? And children?" Another long pause. "I guess Donna hasn't shown them the tape yet."

The color drained from his face. "What tape?"

"Morton, you're a good businessman; however, you have to realize that when you're dealing with somebody like Donna—or, in fact, someone like me—you're out of your league. Not only does Donna still have your balls in a vise, but now I also have a copy of the tape."

"Oh, God!" he groaned. "Please don't do this to me."

"Cooperate, Morton," she said coolly. "And I'll see that every copy of the tape—including the original—is destroyed. And if you *don't*, well...I'll *personally* make sure your wife views it, because you've been a *very* bad boy and you deserve to be punished."

His shoulders slumped and he looked ready to collapse. "Jesus! What have I done?" he muttered.

Lucky sighed and shook her head. "Don't you get it? Nice guys aren't supposed to screw around on their wives—especially with a teenage hooker. It's not proper. Marriage is a contract. And in my world, a contract means something."

She turned and walked away, leaving an ashen-faced Morton standing alone.

Leslie spent the night with Johnny Romano, not bothering to return to her own house until early in the morning. She entered her bedroom and was annoyed to see that Jeff was exactly where she'd left him, fully clothed and snoring. The idiot wasn't even aware she'd been out all night.

She went into her bathroom, took a shower, dressed, and applied fresh makeup. Then she hurried into Jeff's closet and packed all his clothes into a suitcase that she dragged to the front door.

That done, she sat down and wrote him a short note.

Dear Jeff:
This isn't working for me. I will be out until three. When I get home, I would like you to be gone. Please leave my keys on the kitchen table.
Leslie

She left the note on top of the suitcase and drove to the Four Seasons, where she checked in for the day.

If there was one thing Leslie hated, it was confrontations.

★ ★ ★

Alex hit his office like a dynamo—energized and full of vigor. He'd woken up early and decided he'd better forget about Lucky for now and get back to concentrating on his movie. Once he'd made that decision, he'd started feeling good.

"What's goin' on?" he asked as he burst in, slapping France on the ass as he passed.

"Alex!" France said. It wasn't an objection—more another way of saying *Thanks!*

Lili was delighted to see him in such good form. "Do we have our old Alex back?" she asked, following him into his office.

"What do you mean?" he responded.

"You've hardly been yourself lately," Lili said crisply.

"Don't talk crap," Alex said.

"I'm merely being truthful."

"Okay," he said briskly, moving on to more important things. "This is the deal. Leslie's out. Venus is in. Talk to her agent, confirm with Mickey, and arrange for her to come in at four. I want to check out Johnny's clothes today. Then put together a full read-through with the entire cast on Thursday. Got it?"

"Yes," Lili said, smiling happily. "Are we sending flowers to anyone?"

"Absolutely not," Alex said firmly. "It's back to business, Lili. We're making a movie here. Let's get it together."

After seeing Morton, Lucky met with Inga. She'd called her early in the morning and suggested they should talk.

"What about?" Inga had asked suspiciously.

"Something I'm sure you don't want Abe to hear."

That was enough to spur Inga into action. She'd agreed to meet Lucky for lunch in the dining room at the Beverly Wilshire Hotel.

When Lucky walked in, Inga was already sitting at a table. "Hi," Lucky said, settling into a chair, her back to the window so she could view the room.

Inga nodded, her broad, unlined Swedish face impassive as usual.

"I could have come to the house," Lucky said, "only I didn't think you'd want Abe to hear our conversation."

"Is it *about* Abe?" Inga asked, her strong jawline thrust forward.

"No," Lucky replied, wondering if Inga would object to her smoking at the table. "Well, I say no, but in a way it *does* have to do with him."

"How?" Inga asked.

Yes. Inga would definitely be put out if she smoked. "Shall we order?" she said, waving to the captain. He hurried over with menus.

"I usually don't eat lunch," Inga said. "Perhaps an apple and a piece of cheese."

"How frugal of you," said Lucky, consulting the menu and ordering a steak and french fries. "I need my strength," she said with a small smile. "So many people have been stabbing me in the back lately, I'm positively weak. This afternoon I might lift weights—have you ever done that? It's great therapy. Makes me feel sensational."

"No," Inga said. "For exercise I swim ten lengths in the pool every day."

"*Very* good for you," Lucky said, imagining Abe sitting poolside, watching.

Inga ordered a salad, waiting impatiently to see what Lucky had to say.

"How well do you know Morton Sharkey?" Lucky asked at last, leaning her elbows on the table.

Inga shrugged. "Not very well at all," she said warily.

"Tell me how you met him. Through Abe?"

"Yes."

Lucky nodded. "I remember when I was looking to buy Panther. Abe recommended Morton. He'd used him for a couple of deals and trusted him. I must say, I trusted him, too. Silly me. I even trusted him when he persuaded me to privately sell off a large block of shares. He suggested I diversify, sell sixty percent of Panther and use the money for other investments. I agreed. Of course, I should have kept fifty-one percent, but...I went with Morton's advice. He said he had investors in place who were controllable, nothing could ever go wrong...."

Inga was starting to look uncomfortable. "What's your point?"

"You know what my point is, Inga," Lucky said, her voice hardening. "You're not a stupid woman....Or should I call you Mrs. Smorg?"

"Abe is ninety," Inga said brusquely. "I've lived with him for the last forty years. By obtaining a piece of Panther Studios, I protected my future."

"Fine with me," Lucky said calmly. "But why did you side with Donna Landsman?"

"Morton advised me to do so."

"Oh, you mean your *partner*, Morton Sharkey, the person you own Conquest Investments with?"

"Abe has never done anything for me," Inga said bitterly. "I have no money, nothing in my name. I know when he dies his great-grandchildren inherit everything."

"You're married to him, Inga," Lucky said evenly. "California law states you get half of his estate."

Inga stared into space. "Abe made several irrevocable trusts before we were married. I signed a prenuptial *and* a quit claim on his estate. In his will he has left me a hundred thousand dollars. That's it." She gave a heavy sigh. "I am not a young woman anymore. I have a certain lifestyle to maintain."

"By protecting yourself, you screwed me," Lucky said tersely. "By siding with Morton, you gave me no chance."

"I had to do what he said, he takes care of my investments."

Lucky laid out her terms. "This is the deal, Inga—if you don't want Abe to know about your outside activities, sell me your shares immediately. You hold six percent personally and half of Conquest is another five. That'll give me back eleven percent." She paused for breath. "My lawyer has drawn up the papers. You'll get top dollar—be smart—buy yourself IBM with the money."

Inga realized she had no choice. "Very well," she said stiffly. "I will do as you say."

★ ★ ★

"I've a bitch of a headache," Mickey grumbled.

"I'm sorry to hear that," Leslie replied sympathetically.

They sat together in the commissary at Panther Studios.

"Not exactly a hangover," Mickey said, hunching his shoulders. "Although I *was* drinking."

"Your party was very nice," Leslie said, not meaning it, but what the hell—may as well make Mickey feel good.

"It might have been nice for you," he said vehemently. "But *I* had a situation where my daughter ended up fucking that Santo kid in his house—and *I* had to go get her."

"No?" Leslie said, suitably shocked.

"What is it with kids today, Leslie?" he asked mournfully. "They treat sex and drugs like it's no big deal. When I was sixteen, buying *condoms* was a big deal."

"I'm sorry to hear Tabitha's giving you trouble," Leslie said. Obviously the kid took after her father.

He drank half a glass of Evian water.

"Trouble, schmuble...I suppose the kid's gotta do her own thing. She goes back to boarding school in a couple of weeks."

Leslie picked at her salad. It was time to talk about *her*. "Well, you'll be pleased to know I took your advice."

"What advice, sweetie?"

"Jeff is history."

Mickey nodded his approval. "Smart move. A girl like you can have anybody you want." He jabbed his finger at her. "You gotta work the stardom thing, Leslie. Work it."

"I'm sure you're right," she murmured.

"An' talking of working it...have *I* found a script for *you*."

"Really?"

"I've been thinkin' about your career. *Gangsters* is not right, you're too nice to pull off that kind of sleazy role."

"What script, Mickey?" she asked eagerly.

"It's about a guy and a gal who meet in Paris, fall in love, fall out of love, then fall back in love. Hokey shit—the public'll eat it up."

"It sounds wonderful. Are you sending it to Cooper?"

"Yeah, yeah, I'll send it to him. But, Leslie, you gotta realize Cooper's like an old whore—give him the right amount of money and he'll stand on his head and recite the alphabet. He does it for the loot."

"That's not a very nice thing to say," Leslie said, springing to her former lover's defense.

"I keep on telling you—ya gotta wise up to actors."

563

"I'll read the script," she said sweetly, ignoring his criticism. "If I like it, I'll do it."

"Honey." He laughed rudely. "*I* like it, *you'll* do it. Have I ever given you bad advice?"

It wasn't worth arguing. Better he was on her side. "No, Mickey, you and Abigaile have been very good to me."

"Okay, sweetie—remember that," he said, squinting across the table at her. "You look better today—not so pinched. Throwing Jeff out agrees with you."

"Thank you, Mickey," she said demurely.

And she did not tell him about her night's adventure with Johnny Romano. It was a one-shot deal to get over her disappointment with Cooper. And not a very exciting one. Johnny Romano was still a greedy pig, only interested in his own satisfaction.

It would never happen again.

"Outfit—sensational. Attitude—just right," Alex said.

"Thanks," Venus said, and smiled. She was sitting in his office, enjoying their meeting. "Coming from you, that's a big compliment."

"I spoke to Freddie."

"So did I."

"Everything's under control," Alex said. "Contracts are on their way."

"You don't know how thrilled I am to be doing *Gangsters*," Venus said. "I guess I told

you before—the critics hate me. This time I
don't want them seeing Venus on the screen,
I want to *be* Lola." She looked at him intently. "I *know* you can bring the performance out
in me that I've never been able to give before."

"If I can't get it out of you, nobody can,"
Alex said, never modest about what he knew
he could achieve. "I'll personally work on
the script with you. Today you'll do clothes,
hair, and makeup tests. Tomorrow there'll be
a read-through with the rest of the cast."

"This is such a special day for me," Venus
said, brimming with enthusiasm. "Not only
have I gotten the part of my career, but I've
decided to give my husband another chance."

"Cooper?" Alex said, raising an eyebrow.

She laughed happily. "He's the only husband
I've got."

"Taking him back, huh?"

"The truth is," she said, grinning sheepishly,
"he's irresistible."

"That's what *you're* gonna be in *Gangsters,*"
Alex said, killer smile at full force. "Irresistible."

On the drive back to her house, Lucky had plenty of time to think. Finally, it was all coming
together.

She would get her studio back.

She would never get her husband back.

After she regained control of Panther, she
knew she'd eventually have to deal with Donna
Landsman. There was no way she could allow

Donna to get away with murdering Lennie.

She'd been keeping the thought in the back of her mind. Soon she'd have to face it.

She sighed—a deep sigh. When would the Bonnatti family learn?

57

"My papa is back," Claudia said, nervously clasping her hands together. "He say I no come here again."

"Jesus, Claudia," Lennie said, desperately trying to control his frustration. "When are you getting the key?"

"This weekend...when my papa sleeps."

"Why can't you call the American Embassy? Get help. Get me *out* of this fucking place?"

Her pretty face was serene. "Lennie," she said seriously. "My life is here—in my village....I help you escape, my papa cannot know. No one can. We must do it my way."

Sometimes he felt he was in the middle of an Italian movie, acting out scenes. Beautiful peasant girl with incredible, voluptuous breasts and sturdy thighs rescues handsome American stranger from a life in captivity. Shit! Universal would make it in a minute!

"Claudia," he said, purposely speaking very slowly so as not to frighten her away. "Isn't there a way to get me out of here today? What about your boyfriend? Can't he help?"

She turned on him with a ferocious "No!"

He'd upset her. Had to be careful. He

566

sensed she was in two minds about betraying her father. Now he realized she hadn't even told her boyfriend.

"Okay, okay," he said soothingly. "You can't blame me for being impatient."

"Where is the map I gave you?" she asked. "If my papa sees it..."

"Don't worry. I've hidden it."

She was edgy today, full of fear. What if she changed her mind and left him here to rot?

No. She wouldn't do that. They'd forged a connection, a bond. She had a little crush on him, and he felt the same about her. Not that it lessened his love for Lucky. This was merely circumstances.

"Claudia." He held out his arms. "Come here."

Warily she walked toward him. Today she had on a dress like Sophia Loren had worn in the movie *Two Women*. A clingy cotton dress that buttoned all the way down the front, exposing her bare legs and lightly tanned skin. On her feet were simple sandals. She wore no makeup except a soft pink lipstick. Her long auburn hair fell to below her waist. He noticed she had a little scar on her left cheek, and her eyelashes were impossibly long.

She stood close to him. He could see she was near tears. He breathed in her scent and asked her what was wrong.

Her lower lip began to tremble. "I...I am confused..." she stammered.

"I know this is difficult for you," he said, trying desperately to reassure her. "You feel you're betraying your father, and yet you know that what he's doing is very wrong. Criminal, in fact."

She nodded silently.

He reached out his hand, touching her arm. "When I'm free, Claudia, I won't forget you. I want you to come visit me in America."

"Not possible," she said, shaking her head. "No one can know I helped you."

"Look," he said, "if you bring me a paper and pencil, I'll write down my address and phone number. Anytime you want anything, I'll be there for you...or I'll send you money. Whatever you want."

"I know what Papa has done is bad," she said, her face serious. "This is why I help you."

"Is that the only reason?"

"Lennie," she said, confused. "I feel...close to you. So very close."

He pulled her to him, kissing her passionately. She struggled, but only for a second, then she gave herself up to his kiss, throwing back her head, her lips soft and giving and so very sweet.

Forgive me, Lucky, but I have to make sure she comes back, and this is the only way I know how.

Besides, the touch of another human being, the feel of her body, filled him with hope. There was a future. He wasn't dead yet.

She explored his face with her hands, stroking, caressing. "My American prisoner," she murmured lovingly. "I will set you free. I will."

Automatically he began undoing the buttons of her dress, exposing her full breasts.

She was truly one of the most luscious women he'd ever seen, her skin smooth, her nipples ripe and inviting as he bent to kiss them. She tasted so sweet he couldn't stop himself.

She lay down on the damp ground and threw her arms above her head in a gesture of pure abandonment. Her underarm hair was thick and somehow very sexy. He teased her nipples with his tongue.

"We shouldn't be doing this," she said, breathing heavily. "It is not right."

He noticed she didn't move away.

"No one will ever know, this is between us," he said, quickly unbuttoning the rest of her dress, his fingers fumbling on the material.

She wore old-fashioned underpants that reached up to her waist. Recklessly he plunged his hand down them, feeling his way through a thick forest of pubic hair to reach the warm moistness of her desire.

She caught her breath, gasping with passion. She was his last chance at freedom.

"This weekend…you'll come back, you'll help me," he said, plunging into her welcoming softness.

"Oh, yes, Lennie, oh, yes—you have my promise."

58

"So," Brigette said, nervously pulling at her hair. "That's the story. I'm sorry, I don't know how

I get caught up in these things..." She bit her lip, anxiously awaiting Lucky's reaction.

Lucky stood up from the outdoor table where they were finishing dinner. "There's no need for you to apologize," she said soothingly. "You've been very unfortunate. Not all men are like Santino Bonnatti and Michel Guy. Although you do seem to have a way of attracting the worst elements."

"Michel seemed so nice," Brigette said miserably. "I mean, I *trusted* him. He was older and gentle, and...maybe I even encouraged him."

"He took advantage of you, Brigette," Lucky said vehemently. "Any man who ties a woman up and forces her to have sex against her will with another woman...well, this is definitely a bad guy."

"I tried to warn her," Nona said, joining in. "Although I had no idea he was such a sicko."

"And Robertson...did she go along with it?" Lucky asked.

Brigette shrugged. "He told her what to do and she did it. I guess she was stoned."

"Yeah," Nona agreed. "A lot of those models think of nothing else except getting stoned and laid. It's all one big kick."

"It might be a kick," Lucky said curtly, "but Michel Guy's not getting away with it, I can promise you that."

"I told you," Nona said, shooting Brigette a triumphant look.

"What'll you do?" Brigette asked.

"I'll make time to visit Mr. Guy in New York."

"He'll deny it," Brigette said. "He'll say I encouraged him—I know he will."

"Who do *you* think I'll believe?" Lucky asked softly. "You or him?"

"Me?" Brigette said in a small voice.

"Of course, you, sweetheart."

Brigette jumped to her feet and hugged Lucky. "Thank you," she said. "You're the best!"

"Y'know, if Lennie were alive, he'd break this Michel prick's balls," Lucky said.

"I miss Lennie so much," Brigette murmured sadly. "I miss him every day."

Lucky nodded, her eyes misting over. "So do I," she said quietly. "We all do."

★ ★ ★

Early the next morning Lucky chartered a plane and flew to New York.

She'd instructed Brigette and Nona to stay at her house in L.A. until she got back, which, if all went according to plan, would be later that same day. Daniella Dion was coming to town, and she was next on Lucky's list of people to deal with.

In the meantime, her personal lawyer was finalizing the details of getting her studio back.

Morton had called late last night, sounding panicked. "What if Donna Landsman shows the tape to my wife?" he'd asked. "How can I stop her?"

"That's something you'll have to work out with Donna," she'd replied, not really concerned with his problems after what he'd done to her.

"Jesus, Lucky, if this gets out, I'll be ruined."

"You should have come to me in the first place," she'd said, in a way, feeling sorry for him. "I could've taken care of it."

"I made a mistake," he'd said miserably.

Big mistake, Morton.

Today she felt invigorated, invincible. Sometimes the power within her was so strong she was convinced she could do anything.

The plane came in for a smooth landing. There was a car at the airport to meet her. The driver took the freeway to the city, riding the potholed streets to the center of Manhattan where Michel Guy's office was located. Lucky marched in without an appointment, bypassing two secretaries.

"You can't see Mr. Guy without arranging it first," one of the flustered secretaries said, dashing after her.

"Let me correct you," Lucky said. "I can do whatever the hell I like."

Michel Guy was sitting in his office, legs propped on his desk, smoking a big fat Havana cigar.

Lucky took him completely by surprise. His legs came off the desk, the cigar came out of his mouth, and he said a startled "*Oui?* What can I do for you?"

"Do you know who I am?" Lucky said, staring him down.

He stared back at her. She certainly wasn't a model, but she was an extremely beautiful woman with a vaguely familiar face. "No," he said at last. "Should I?"

"Maybe you'll recognize my name—Lucky Santangelo?"

Ah—now he knew exactly who she was, he'd recently read an interview with her in *Newstime*. "You own a studio in Hollywood," he said, wondering what the hell she was doing in his office. "How can I help you?"

"I thought you might be interested to know the identity of my stepdaughter."

"Your stepdaughter," he said blankly.

The secretary stood by the door, glaring at Lucky.

"Okay, Monica, you can leave us," Michel said, waving her away.

Lucky sat down uninvited and lit a cigarette. "It seems she didn't tell you."

"Who didn't tell me what?" Michel said, irritated and intrigued at the same time.

Lucky's voice was suddenly cold and hard as she stood up and leaned over his desk. "You know something, Michel? You're a mean fuckhead with a small dick."

"Excuse me," he said, becoming alarmed at her behavior.

"*Schifoso*. You know what that means in English?"

"I'm French," he said.

"Piece of filthy garbage," she said, blowing smoke in his face. "*That's* what it means."

"What do you want?" he said, deciding

he'd better summon help.

"I want to tell you a little story," Lucky said, sitting down again. "Pay attention, Michel— it's short and simple."

This intrusion had gone on long enough. "I'm busy right now," he said. "I suggest you make an appointment and come back another time."

"I built hotels in Vegas—two of them," she said, ignoring his request. "During construction, one of my investors balked at putting up the balance of the money he owed— even though we had a firm agreement. That night I broke into his apartment with a couple of friends to assist me in case he was foolish enough to get out of line. He awoke to find a nice, sharp knife poised at the base of his penis." A long, meaningful pause. "Now...what do *you* think he did?"

"I don't know," Michel said, realizing she was totally crazy.

"He put up the money, plus, of course, *he* kept his precious cock and *I* kept my hotel." A short silence. "In the end, everyone was happy."

He stood up, one eye on the door. "What do you want from me?"

"My stepdaughter's name is Brigette Stanislopoulos. Perhaps you know her better as Brigette Brown."

The color drained from his face. "Oh," he said blankly. "I had no idea who she was."

"I bet you didn't. I bet you thought she was some little girl you could fuck with. Blackmail, perhaps? Use as your toy?" Her voice

574

cut into him like a knife. "She's only nineteen, Michel. Aren't you ashamed of yourself?"

He'd read all about Lucky Santangelo. She was powerful. She had connections. He didn't want to find himself on a plane back to Paris with his balls in his mouth.

"I'm telling you," he said, speaking fast. "I had no idea. When that woman asked me to get the pictures…"

"*What* woman?" Lucky asked, knowing exactly who he meant.

"She paid me a fortune," Michel said, his words tumbling over each other. "If I'd known Brigette was related to you, I'd never have done it."

"*What woman?*" Lucky repeated icily.

"Donna Landsman. She paid me to get compromising pictures of Brigette. I…I feel bad."

"Really? Bad, huh?" Lucky said calmly, picking up an ivory-handled magnifying glass from his desk. "You see this, you fucking pervert," she said, her tone changing. "I should shove this right up your French ass, because that's exactly what you deserve. But instead, you and I are going to get the pictures."

"I sent them to Mrs. Landsman," he said quickly.

"I'm sure you kept the negatives and a set for yourself."

"No."

She turned the magnifying glass in her hands, examining the sturdy ivory handle. "Were you listening to the story I just told you?

I can promise you, Michel—a knife at your cock is *nothing* compared to what I have planned for you if I don't get everything immediately. So let's go to your apartment, or wherever you have them. And let's not waste any more time. *Capisce*?"

The look in her deadly black eyes convinced him to do exactly as she said.

Lucky didn't linger; she was on her way back to L.A. as soon as she'd obtained the photos *and* negatives from Michel Guy. She'd also made him sign a letter relinquishing all rights as Brigette's agent.

"Believe me, Michel," Lucky had told him. "You're getting off easy."

He believed her. Fucking with Lucky would be a big mistake, and Michel was too smart to make that kind of mistake.

Boogie met her at LAX. They drove in silence to her house. Brigette was asleep when she got there. Lucky slipped the envelope containing the incriminating photos and negatives under her door, then she went to bed herself.

In the morning she awoke early and switched on the TV, watching while she dressed.

Morton Sharkey and Sara Durbon were on the morning news.

At eleven P.M. the previous evening, he'd blown both their brains out.

The news of Morton Sharkey's demise was a big shock to Lucky, she hadn't realized he was in such an unbalanced state. According to the police report, Morton had walked in on Sara when she was preparing to split for Vegas. They'd had a big fight, overheard by the woman in the next apartment. The fight had culminated in two gunshots. The neighbor had called the police. Before they could get there, Sara's girlfriend had arrived to fetch her, and discovered the bodies. She'd run screaming from the building.

Lucky felt sad, because whatever Morton had done, he didn't deserve to die for it. It was especially tragic that he'd taken Sara with him— poor little Sara, who'd only wanted to eat hamburgers and make money.

Lucky immediately tried to contact Morton's wife. Candice was too distraught to come to the phone. Instead, Lucky spoke to his daughter, who accepted her condolences.

There was only one person to blame for his death—Donna Landsman.

Lucky realized she must get hold of Donna's set of photographs of Brigette, and also the incriminating tape of Morton with Sara. At least let the man rest with dignity. He'd had the decency to transfer his shares back to her, and her lawyer assured her that everything would be cleared with Inga by the end of the day. Tomorrow, Panther would be hers again.

Through Kyoko's studio connection she found out Mickey Stolli's movements for the next day. He was lunching with Freddie Leon at the Palm.

"As soon as he leaves the studio," Lucky instructed Boogie, "arrange to have his furniture cleared out, and mine put back in. When he returns from lunch, I'll be waiting to greet him. Make sure Donna Landsman is there, too."

Boogie nodded. "There shouldn't be a problem."

Brigette was ecstatic when she'd found the photographs under her door. "I promise I'll *never* do anything to make you ashamed of me again," she said fervently. "I'm going to do nothing but work, work, work; you'll be really proud of me."

"It wasn't your fault," Lucky said. "Don't ever think it was."

"Did you uh...look at the photos?" Brigette asked, embarrassed.

"No," Lucky lied. She'd had to check them out to make sure they were the right ones; she didn't mention that there was another set. Boogie was already arranging for a professional safecracker to stage a raid on Donna's house.

"What did Michel *say*?" Brigette asked.

"Forget about that lowlife," Lucky replied. "The good news is that your contract with him is null and void, he collects no commissions on the Jeans deal, and I'm setting you up with another top agency."

"Thanks, Lucky," Brigette said, relieved and happy. "Nobody could have done it but you."

Later in the day Lucky called Johnny Romano. "Have you got ten minutes if I drop by?"

"For you—baby—anything."

She drove over to his house, a neoclassic mansion in Bel Air with more marble than a mausoleum. A stunning black girl, dressed in a tight white suit and extremely high stiletto heels, led her into the games room where Johnny was playing pool with a couple of gofers. He greeted her with a hug and a kiss.

"I need a favor," she said. "It's kind of a weird one..."

"Nothing's too weird for me," Johnny said, leading her over to a futuristic pinball machine.

"Well..." she said, watching Johnny play with his new toy. "There's this very expensive French call girl..."

"Tell me more," he said, intrigued.

"She's flying to L.A. from Paris because she's under the impression she's been bought as a birthday gift for you."

He laughed. "For me?"

"That's right."

"Baby—it ain't even my birthday!"

"I know that."

His sleepy eyes lit up. "Is this some kind of kinky sex thing you're into? 'Cause if it is, y'know I'm into it, too."

"It's more complicated than that—it's to do with Lennie," she said, proceeding to tell him of her suspicions. "While you're with her, I'll be in the other room with a listening device."

"Detective work," he said, nodding to himself. "I like it! When we do this?"

"She's arriving tonight, I've booked her into a bungalow at the Beverly Hills Hotel. Boogie will pick her up at the airport and take her straight there. Will you do it for me?"

"Baby, you can count on Johnny Romano—he's your man!"

The immigration officer eyed the delectable blond in the Chanel suit reeking of some incredible, exotic scent, and decided she was worth his full attention.

"How long do you plan on staying in America?" he asked, eyes dropping to her rounded breasts with the prominent nipples straining the material of her blouse.

"Maybe a few days," Daniella Dion said vaguely.

"Is your trip business or pleasure?" he inquired, craning over his desk to get a better look at her sensational legs, showcased in an extremely short skirt.

"A little bit of both."

"And what business are you in?"

"Lingerie," she said.

"Lingerie," he repeated, his throat suddenly dry.

"That's right," she said with a small, provocative smile.

He stamped her passport and reluctantly watched her step away from his desk. He couldn't wait to get home and make love to his overweight wife, this blond definitely had him revved.

Daniella sauntered through customs and located the driver standing outside with her name printed on a large white card.

"Please follow me, Miss Dion," Boogie said politely, taking her carry-on bag. "Is this your only luggage?"

She nodded.

"Then we can go straight to the car," he said, leading her down the escalator and through the doors to where the limousine was parked.

Holding open the back door, he watched her slide onto the shiny leather seat. She was spectacular. Even Boogie was impressed.

He got behind the wheel of the limo and took off. "We'll go straight to the Beverly Hills Hotel," he said, keeping an eye on her in the rearview mirror. "Unless you wish to stop somewhere first?"

"No," she said. "You may take me to the hotel directly."

"There's Evian, Scotch, or vodka in the back. Please help yourself."

"Nothing, thank you."

"Your first trip to L.A.?" he asked conversationally.

"I'm tired," she said, a touch petulantly. "I don't wish to talk. Please close the partition."

He shut the dark-glass partition and called Lucky at the hotel. "We're on our way," he said.

"Hey, baby—I want you to know I broke a date to accommodate you tonight," Johnny said, prowling around the luxurious bungalow at the Beverly Hills Hotel.

"So, I owe you one," Lucky said. "After I get the studio back, you can come to me with any script you want to make, and we're in business. That's a promise."

"You don't owe me anythin', Lucky. You're the one who turned my career around."

"You'd have worked it out eventually."

"Yeah, but you *made* me change."

"No. All I did was make you realize the smart way. Why do you think Clint Eastwood has lasted all these years? And Robert Redford? They won't play guys who beat up on women. They're the hero everybody loves; I knew you could be that guy, too. And now you are."

"You bet your fine ass," he said, grinning.

His sexism didn't bother her, she was used to Johnny, he reminded her of a boisterous puppy.

"Can we go over the questions again?" she asked.

"Go ahead, baby," Johnny said.

"Okay. When you've got her in bed, you say, 'I know about you and Lennie in Corsica.'

Then she'll probably say, 'What are you talking about?' Then *you* say, 'You were paid to set him up.'"

"And after that?"

"Well, you'll have her naked in bed—vulnerable—in a strange country. I guess, depending on what *she* says, I'll come into the room and ask her myself."

"Hey, Lucky," he said, grinning slyly. "You're payin' all this money—you want I should do the deed?"

"Whatever turns you on."

He shook his head and laughed. "I never paid for pussy, an' baby—I *ain't* startin' now."

"Let me remind you, *I'm* paying, and she's *very* expensive. Maybe you *should* get our money's worth."

"There's not a condom big enough for me to stick Romano—the magic eye—into a hooker."

Romano—the magic eye! Was he kidding! "Very delicately put," she said, trying to keep from laughing.

"Just tellin' you the way it is."

"Okay," Lucky said, hoping Johnny could handle it. "Just remember—she's *your* birthday present; when I've got my answers, you can do whatever you like."

★　★　★

Daniella sat in the back of the limo, blankly gazing out of the window. She wasn't fond of traveling and the plane journey had been long and tiring, although she should be used to long hours on a plane because her business often took her out of Paris. One of her regular clients was a Saudi prince who paid an enormous amount of money for her to visit him at his palace in Saudi Arabia once a month; another client was an Indian maharaja who sent for her to come to Bombay several times a year; then there was the Australian media king who summoned her to Sydney twice a year to entertain him and his wife on their birthdays.

She'd made up her mind that the day her bank balance reached a certain level, she would quit altogether and vanish. She'd take her small daughter and buy a quaint old farmhouse in Tuscany where they could live in peace.

Daniella didn't care if she never saw another man again. They were animals, all of them. They paid for sex and then imagined they owned her. Stupid fools. They never owned her, they merely borrowed her body for the time it took.

She opened her purse, removed an elaborate solid-gold compact—a gift from the prince—and inspected her face. *I am beautiful,* she thought, *but is that all they see?*

Yes, she told herself, *that's all they see.*

She took a Valium from her purse, and popped it in her mouth, washing it down with a bottle of Evian. Then she reached beneath her blouse, touching her breasts with the tips of her fingers, twisting her nipples until they began to harden.

As soon as she'd aroused herself, she reached

under her skirt, parted her legs, and methodically began rubbing her pussy.

She was so practiced in the art of self-gratification that it took only seconds before she reached a satisfying orgasm.

Gasping aloud, she fell back on the seat, closing her eyes, allowing the sweet sensation to wash over her.

Early on in her career she'd decided that no man would ever be allowed the privilege of making her come. She wanted the power over them, not the other way around. Since then she'd always taken care of herself before an appointment. That way she made sure that whatever they did to her, she was always in control of her feelings.

Adjusting her skirt, she sat up straight, preparing herself for the evening ahead with Johnny Romano. He might be a movie star, but that was not an unusual client for Daniella. She'd had many other movie stars before him. She'd had kings and princes. She'd had politicians. She'd once had a president.

Tonight was going to be no different from any other night. Business as usual.

60

Daniella drank Pernod and water.
Johnny drank Cristal champagne.
Daniella smoked a strong French cigarette.
Johnny smoked a joint.
And he stared at her...and couldn't stop star-

ing, because she was the classiest blond he'd ever seen. Like a young Catherine Deneuve, she sat opposite him, cool and collected, legs crossed, expression attentive, everything about her perfect.

They'd exchanged a few pleasantries—things like "How was your trip," "This is a lovely hotel," etc. Now she waited patiently for him to make the first move. And even though he knew Lucky was impatiently prowling around in the second bedroom with a radio device, picking up everything they said, he wasn't inclined to rush this little scene.

Daniella realized she'd better initiate the action. "What do you like, Johnny?" she asked in her low, throaty voice. "What *really* turns you on?"

I like the look of you, he wanted to say. *I like your accent. ...I like your smooth, creamy skin...your legs...your face. ...I like the whole classy package.*

He couldn't believe she was a hooker, there had to be some mistake. "You seen any of my movies, baby?" he asked, snapping his fingers— a nervous habit he'd acquired after Warner had dumped him. "Am I big in Paris?"

"Oh, yes, Johnny," she replied, not sure if he was or wasn't. "Very big."

The truth was that she'd barely heard of him, and she'd certainly never seen any of his movies. Although she did remember a cover story in *Paris Match*, where he was photographed at the Playboy mansion draped in blonds. Typical.

"I guess they dub me in French over there, huh?" he asked, desperately trying to impress.

"I'm sure," she murmured.

"I hope they hire the right actor," he said anxiously. "What do *you* think of the voice they use?"

"Excellent," she said, although she had no idea what he was talking about.

★ ★ ★

Sitting in the other bedroom, Lucky couldn't believe it. What was Johnny after—a review?

Maybe she should have met with Daniella by herself and asked the questions. Too late now.

While she was at the hotel, Boogie was organizing a raid on Donna's safe. He'd paid off one of the Landsmans's servants to get a map of her house and knew exactly where the safe was located. The Landsmans were out to dinner, and the man they'd hired to do the job was an expert who could get into the safe, remove the items Lucky wanted, close it, and Donna would never know anything was missing until she went looking.

Lucky took a deep breath. Tomorrow she'd get Panther back. She couldn't wait to see Donna's face. Mickey's, too. Those two deserved each other.

Johnny was still droning on about his movie career in France. What was the matter with him? She'd picked Johnny because he was supposedly the stud of the century. Apparently he was a slow starter—either that, or this woman didn't turn him on.

Daniella stood up, sensually slipping off the jacket of her pink Chanel suit. Underneath, she wore a white sleeveless blouse. "I'm hot," she murmured, fanning herself with her hands.

"Yeah, it is hot in here," Johnny agreed. "Should I put on the air-conditioning?"

American idiot, Daniella thought. *He might be a movie star, but he is an idiot. Why doesn't he make a move?*

Ah, well…it was obvious the seduction was up to her. She hoped he wasn't going to be like her last American movie star…Lennie Golden. Lennie had been completely resistant to her charms.

Daniella had never had that happen to her before. At the time, she'd been quite shocked, then impressed, because there was nothing more attractive than an incorruptible man.

She slowly unbuttoned her blouse, shrugging it off, revealing a white-lace nippleless bra. Her breasts were enclosed, the nipples bursting free. Johnny gave a low groan of appreciation. Next, she unzipped her skirt and stepped out of it. Underneath, she wore an old-fashioned white garter belt, sheer stockings, and a white lace thong.

She leisurely sashayed over to Johnny, standing in front of him, legs apart so that her crotch was eye level. "Your move," she purred provocatively.

He was immediately aroused. This woman was his all-time fantasy. A lady in the living room; a whore in the bedroom. He wondered if she cooked, too.

"Have you ever thought about being in movies?" he asked, squeezing the insides of her creamy thighs.

"No," she replied, "I never have."

"You could be. You're gorgeous, baby."

"Thank you," she said, hitching his fingers into the edge of her thong, slowly helping him pull it down until her blond, fluffy pubic hair was only inches from his face.

He stared at her bush, then gazed up at her nipples—so rosy and erect. Jesus! Enough was enough. He could only take so much. He stood up. "Put your arms around my neck," he commanded. She did as he asked. "Now wrap your legs around my waist."

She did that also.

He carried her into the bedroom, placing her on the edge of the bed.

She lay back, gazing up at him expectantly. He gripped her ankles, spreading her legs.

"Shall I undress you?" she asked, noting his bulging erection.

"Later," he said. "Right now I'm gonna eat your pussy."

"No!" she said quickly, knowing it was foolish to object to anything a client required, but too tired to care.

Johnny was not to be put off. "Baby, most women are *beggin'* for a little mouth action."

"Why don't *I* eat *you*?" she suggested, attempting to sit up.

He pushed her back down. "You're *my* present—*I* get to choose. So close your eyes an' have yourself a *good* time."

Johnny had completely forgotten that Lucky was in the other room, waiting. And even if he'd remembered, it wouldn't have mattered. This was something he had to do *now*!

★ ★ ★

It occurred to Lucky she'd definitely picked the wrong guy. Was Johnny trying to turn her on? What was the matter with him?

Her cell phone rang. She grabbed it.

"Mission accomplished," Boogie said.

"Both items?"

"Everything."

"Lock them in your safe. I don't want them in my house. Once she finds out, she may retaliate. Oh, and Boog—job well done."

She clicked off the phone and continued listening to the noises coming from the bedroom.

Groaning and sighing. Gasping and moaning. Somebody was having a good time on her dime.

Twenty minutes must have passed before the grunts and groans stopped and Johnny finally got down to business. "Uh...Daniella," she heard him say.

"Yes?"

"I know what happened between you and Lennie Golden."

Lucky held her breath. *Here we go*, she thought, *this is where I find out the real truth*.

"Excuse me?"

"Lennie was my good friend," Johnny said. "He was in Corsica making a movie, you came on to him...set him up."

A long pause. "How do you know this?" Daniella said at last.

"I saw the photographs."

Another long pause. "I do what I'm paid to do. With Lennie, I was paid to seduce him. It did not work out."

"You mean you didn't fuck him?"

"No. He kept on talking about his wife."

"No shit?"

"He would have nothing to do with me."

Lucky was listening intently. *Lennie...her Lennie...* Oh, how she'd misjudged him.

Johnny was into it now. "Who paid you?" he asked.

"I can't reveal that."

"Sure you can."

Daniella went to get out of bed. Johnny grabbed her arm, keeping her there. "I really like you," he said.

"Rule number one," Daniella said. "Never be nice to the whore who services you."

"You're no whore. You're a beautiful woman who happens to charge for what most babes in this town give away for free. The way I see it, you got a moral edge. You also got the best set of tits I ever seen."

"They're yours, Johnny—for the night. Tomorrow I return to Paris."

"I could pay more for you to stay."

"Why would you?"

"'Cause I kinda like bein' with you. You could stay at my house for a week."

"I'm sure you can afford me; however, I'm not sure you'll have such a good time."

"Why not?"

She shrugged.

"So...you don't wanna be in a movie, you're not gettin' off on my fame, which means you're not with me 'cause I'm Johnny Romano—you're here 'cause you got paid. That's okay. A nice, clean business arrangement. You know what—you're the first broad I ever fucked for money—only it's not my money."

"How interesting," she said, concealing a bored yawn.

He jumped off the bed. "You gotta meet a friend of mine."

"I charge extra for *ménage à trois*."

"No sex, baby—only conversation. Wait here."

"Jesus!" Lucky said when he entered the room. "You took your time."

"I thought you wanted me to get our money's worth."

"You sure did that and then some. I'm not thrilled I had to listen."

"You *should* be thrilled with what she said. You heard—Lennie didn't screw her."

"Can you put on something other than your Jockeys? I know you're well endowed,

Johnny—you don't have to shove it in my face."

"Daniella's really something," he said dreamily. "Wait till you see her. Lennie must have loved you a lot to have resisted *her*."

"We loved each other, Johnny," she said quietly.

"You got any idea what it's like on location? By the third week you'd fuck a sheep, you're so bored."

"How eloquent," Lucky said, following him into the bedroom.

Daniella was sitting up in bed, a sheet covering her nudity.

"This is Lucky Santangelo," Johnny said. "Lennie Golden's wife. You might wanna repeat what you told me. I'll leave you two alone." He left the room.

Lucky stared at the French call girl. She was very lovely—much more so than in her pictures. "Uh...I'm sure you know that after the night Lennie supposedly spent with you, he was in a car accident," she said awkwardly.

"I am very sorry," Daniella said, lowering her eyes. "There are two things I should assure you of—one, he did not spend the night with me. And two, I had no idea they were planning to kill him."

"So you're aware he was murdered?" Lucky said, her heart starting to beat erratically.

"I am not a fool," Daniella said. "I realized they were setting him up in some way. My job was to seduce him. The photographer was to capture us in bed. However, your husband had no desire to make love to me." A short pause. "I've never had a man turn me down if the situation was right, and the situation with your husband was exactly right." Daniella let the sheet drop, revealing her perfect breasts. "Look at me, Lucky, I am not modest, my beauty is all I have. I exist to service men."

Lucky took a deep breath. "Who hired you, Daniella?"

"My madam in Paris set it up. She was contacted by a woman in America. I was told to go to Corsica, see this man who could get me on the film, and seduce your husband."

"What about the photos of you and Lennie together?"

"They removed my so-called boyfriend from the picture taken on the set. I was acting like a naive fan, Lennie was extremely gracious."

"And the other photo?"

"I went to his hotel room at night, stood at his door and dropped my robe, begging him to invite me in. The photographer caught us in the hallway."

"Why are you being so honest with me?"

Daniella shrugged. "I have no reason not to be. It cost you plenty to fly me here, so it must mean a lot to you. Your husband is dead. I'm sure it soothes you to know he was not unfaithful."

"I appreciate your honesty."

"Sometimes honesty is all we have."

Lucky went back into the living room.

Johnny was smoking a thin cigar and watching wrestling on TV.

"I'm leaving," she said. "Thanks, I owe you one."

She got in her car and drove to her house.

Lennie, my darling Lennie, what did I do? I slept with Alex to get revenge. Now I realize I had nothing to get revenge for.

I betrayed you and I feel so bad, because I should have known you would never betray me.

Forgive me, sweetheart. I will always love you.

61

"I'm getting my studio back today," Lucky announced.

"That's so cool," Brigette exclaimed. "How did you pull *that* off?"

"Don't you know?" Lucky said with a self-deprecating grin. "I can do anything."

"I'm beginning to realize that," Brigette said, and giggled.

She and Nona stood in the front hallway, their suitcases packed.

"I wish you'd stay longer," Lucky said.

"We would," Nona replied, "only Brigette's billboard goes up any moment, and there's all kinds of press things planned. Plus, we're meeting with the new agent you arranged."

Lucky pulled Brigette to one side. "What about that guy you were seeing?" she asked.

"Isaac's fun," Brigette said, "but now I understand he's not for me."

"Don't go off men just because you've come across a few bad ones," Lucky warned.

"I won't. I promise."

"Lennie's watching over you—he'll make sure you find the right one."

Brigette hugged her. "Thanks, Lucky. I'm going to miss you *so* much."

"You, too," Lucky said, hugging her back. "Plan on visiting again soon."

She saw them into the limo, then returned to the house and checked in with Gino, who sounded like his old self. Nothing kept Gino down, he was a true survivor.

When was her life going to return to normal? Sadly she realized that, without Lennie, things could never be the same.

At one-thirty she was sitting behind her desk at Panther, with her own furniture and Kyoko stationed at his desk in the outer office, just like old times.

"Donna Landsman will arrive at two-thirty," Boogie said. "She thinks she's attending a meeting with the heads of production."

"Good," Lucky said. "That's exactly the way I want it."

"Mickey has a two-thirty here with one of his overseas distributors. The timing should be right on."

Boogie was correct. Mickey drove onto the lot exactly one minute behind Donna Landsman. They ran into each other as Donna was getting out of her limousine, entering the building together. It couldn't be more perfect.

Mickey saw Kyoko in the outer office and frowned. "Where's Isabel?" he asked irritably.

"She'll be right back, Mr. Stolli."

Grumbling to himself about secretaries, Mickey led Donna Landsman into his office and stopped short.

Lucky swiveled around in her chair to greet them. "Surprise!" she said. "Isn't this just like old times?"

Mickey's jaw dropped.

Donna Landsman's face hardened.

"What *is* this?" Mickey shouted. "What the hell is going on?"

"I'm back," Lucky said calmly, enjoying their frustrated rage. "Exactly like I said I'd be."

"How is this possible?" Donna said, her pinched face white with anger.

"Simple," Lucky replied easily. "I acquired another eleven percent of Panther shares and voted myself back in. And you know what, Donna? You'll *never* get control again, so you may as well start selling your shares back to me." A short pause while Donna digested the news. "Of course," Lucky continued, "you may have to take a substantial loss, but hey—it's only money."

"What the *fuck*..." Mickey fumed. "I have a frigging contract."

"Sue me," Lucky said evenly. "I'd love to meet you in court."

"Where's my furniture? My files? My god-damn awards?" he yelled.

"I had everything delivered to your house, Mickey. I'm sure it's all sitting safely in your driveway. Abigaile will be *very* happy."

"You won't get away with this," Mickey fumed, blue veins bulging in his forehead.

"Hey—whoever wins, right? Sorry, Mickey, this time you backed a loser."

Donna glared at Lucky, her arch-enemy. "You will live to regret this," she said through clenched teeth. "Nobody crosses me. Nobody."

"Oh," said Lucky, "I'm shaking in my boots."

Donna turned and swept out, Mickey close behind her.

"Kyoko," Lucky called out, feeling pretty high. "Bring in the champagne. We're celebrating."

"Who's that with Johnny?" Alex asked France as Johnny Romano walked into the big banquet room where the read-through was taking place.

"No idea," France said. "Maybe it's his girlfriend."

"I didn't know he had one."

"One a day according to Alex," France said impishly.

A few moments later Venus ran in and sat down next to Johnny.

"Meet a very good friend of mine from Paris," Johnny said. "Daniella, this is Venus."

"Hi, Daniella," Venus said, smiling warmly.

Daniella nodded warily. Her job did not usually include attending the read-through of a movie, but Johnny was paying, so what did she care? She'd phoned Paris and told her baby-sitter she would not be back for a few days. Johnny had walked in while she was on the phone. "Who you speaking to?" he'd asked.

"I'm telling my sitter I won't be back as promised."

He'd looked surprised. "You have a kid?"

"She will be fine. She's used to my being away."

"How old is she?"

"Eight."

"You must've been a baby when you had her."

"Sixteen."

"So I guess you were by yourself, had to support her. Is that why you started...uh...in the profession?"

"That is correct."

Alex entered the room and settled at the head of the table, his first assistant on one side, line producer on the other. After a few minutes he stood up to address his actors. "Now I don't expect anybody to give a brilliant performance today," he said, looking along the table. "Remember, this is just a read-through to see how the lines run, what kind of interaction we get. In fact, it's a working experience you should all enjoy." He pushed back a rogue lock of black hair and flashed the killer smile. "If anyone has any objection to their dialogue, make a note of it and come to me. I'm very open to other ideas. Okay, any questions? If not, let's get started, and let's have fun, because that's what moviemaking *should* be."

Venus nudged Johnny, her face glowing. "This is the first time I've done this on a movie. They usually just throw you into makeup and hair and shove you in front of the camera."

"Yeah," Johnny said. "It's cool." He turned around and checked out Daniella, sitting behind him, then he turned back to Venus. "You ever been into that kind of soul-mate thing?" he asked. "Like when you meet somebody, an' you know that's *it*, man, you're fuckin' *dead*."

Venus smiled. "Is she the one?"

"Could be," Johnny said.

"Congratulations," Venus said, squeezing his arm. "Another stud laid to rest."

"I've got one regret though," he said, grinning broadly.

"Tell me."

"That you an' I never got it together."

"Too late now."

"Baby, it's *never* too late."

Donna sat in her limousine, her stomach churning with fury. Lucky Santangelo had won again. This could not be happening. And Morton—the coward—had killed himself. If he was still around, Lucky could never have wrested control.

Why was it that everything she'd done to punish Lucky had failed?

Even the hit man she'd hired had not managed to kill Gino, he'd merely wounded him.

Her plan had been to return Lennie to Lucky eventually, but in her mind she started writing a different scenario. Why *should* Lucky get him back? Why not kill him and deliver his body parts one by one to the bitch? That would wipe the smile off her face once and for all.

She wondered if either Bruno or Furio were man enough to do it. Or would they expect her to hire somebody?

She had to think about this, it was not a casual decision.

And then it came to her, she'd do it herself. *She'd* go to the cave and shoot Lennie, then she'd photograph his dead body and send the photographs to Lucky.

Yes, she'd let the bitch know her husband had been alive all this time, and if she'd had any brains, she might have figured it out and saved *him* instead of concentrating on getting her damn studio back.

Donna was pleased with her solution. She couldn't tell George, he knew nothing about Lennie. She'd say her father was sick and that she had to go to Sicily for a couple of days. Then she'd stay in a hotel, hire a car, drive to the caves, and do the deed.

Lucky Santangelo thought she was so smart. She'd regained her studio, but she'd lost her husband forever.

It served her right.

Congratulations started coming in immediately; news traveled fast in Hollywood.

Freddie was one of the first people to phone. "I couldn't be more pleased," he said. "What happened?"

"An aberration," Lucky said. "A power play by a woman who didn't know anything about the movie business…"

"All I can say is I'm delighted you're back."

"Thanks, Freddie."

"Does Alex know?"

"I don't think so."

"He's having a read-through of the movie. Go tell him yourself."

"Maybe I will," she said thoughtfully.

Alex was pleased with the way things were going. Sometimes readings could be a disaster—there'd been times he'd realized he'd cast the wrong people, and changes had to be made before filming could start.

This time everything clicked. Venus was quite wonderful as Lola, and Johnny was really into his role. The rest of the cast of mostly unknowns were excellent.

When they broke for lunch, Alex sat with Venus and Johnny—and his new girlfriend, Daniella, who seemed nice, although quiet. She was certainly a beauty.

Everyone reconvened at two-thirty. Shortly

after that, Lili whispered in his ear that she'd just heard Lucky Santangelo had regained power at Panther.

"You're kidding," Alex said. "Where did you hear this?"

"It came from a very reliable source," Lili assured him.

"So," he said, "we're back in business with Miss Santangelo."

He'd decided that since Lucky had made it clear she wanted space and time, he'd give it to her. Right now he had his movie to keep him busy, and making movies was the most demanding mistress of all.

At four-thirty they were finished. Johnny shot out of there, with Daniella in tow.

Venus stood up and hugged Alex. "This is the greatest week of my life," she said happily. "I know things'll work out with Cooper, and making *Gangsters* with you is the breakthrough I've always dreamed of."

"You're a good actress," Alex said. "It's clear to me that nobody bothered bringing it out in you before."

"Thanks," she said, thrilled at such extravagant praise.

"Did you hear that Lucky got the studio back?" he said.

"Fantastic!" Venus exclaimed. "When?"

"Today. Lili heard about it before it happened!"

"Wow—that's great! And *guess* who's walking through the door?"

He turned to stare. It was Lucky herself.

"Hey—" Alex said, thinking how beautiful she was. "We were just talking about you."

Lucky smiled. "All good or all bad?"

"Always good," he said, returning her smile.

"Well, I figured as your new boss, I should pay you a visit."

"Hey—Lucky," Venus said with a big grin. "You pull it off every time. Anybody else would, like, creep away...you just kind of got it together and turned it around. *How* did you do it?"

"I have my ways," Lucky said mysteriously.

"Okay, I'm outta here," Venus said. "Got a husband waiting at home."

Lucky raised an eyebrow. "A husband?"

Venus continued to grin. "It's second-chance time. See ya!" And she was gone.

"Alex," Lucky said, "now that I'm back *in* control, I think I should mention that your projected budget is totally *out* of control. Can we talk?"

He laughed. "There's nobody I'd sooner talk to than you. Only you're a little difficult to get hold of."

"Hmm...trust me, I'll be watching your budget big-time. In fact, you can bet on it."

"I hope you'll visit the set sometimes, too."

"I'm here today."

"Maybe a weekend in Vegas?"

"Who knows...when do you leave?"

"Three days shooting in Malibu, then Vegas the end of next week."

"Don't be surprised if I turn up."

"Lucky," he said, giving her a long, meaningful look. "It would be the best surprise you could possibly give me."

"Well," she said, slightly flustered. "This was a quick visit. I have to go."

He took her arm and walked her to the door. "You like my new attitude?"

"What attitude is that?" she asked.

He smiled, high because the reading had gone so well. "I'm into my concentrated moviemaking mode. That means I'll leave you alone for six months."

"Is that a threat or a promise?"

"Take it any way you like."

They smiled at each other, and she got in her car and drove off, thinking about all the events of the past few weeks.

Donna Landsman.

No more delays.

It was time.

62

"It's been three days—I thought you'd deserted me," Lennie said, so relieved to see Claudia he could barely stand it.

"I'm sorry, my papa—he returned," Claudia apologized.

"Yeah, I know," he said bitterly. "Mr. Cheerful's back. He dumps food in here like he's feeding a dog. I gotta tell you, I hate your father, Claudia. You should get away from him, he's full of bad karma."

"What is...karma?"

"I hope you never have to find out."

"Tonight my papa will drink too much *vino*. When he sleeps, I steal the key, and bring it to you. You have the map?"

He patted his pocket. "It's safe."

She handed him a small flashlight. "Here—we will need this."

"Thanks," he said.

"If they discover you're gone, they will come after you. But they will not know until tomorrow, when Furio brings food."

"How'll you get here late at night?"

"I shall be careful, too."

"Shouldn't your boyfriend come with you?"

"No!" she said sharply. "If he knew, he would not allow me to help you." She hesitated, obviously distressed. "If he found out about us..."

"There's nothing to find out, Claudia," he reassured her. "You were here for me, that's all. I'll never tell anybody what happened between us."

She nodded, satisfied he would not betray her. "As soon as I get the key, I will be here. You must be ready to leave at once."

He didn't know how he was going to get through the next few hours until she returned. Somehow, he knew he'd find the strength.

6 3

Donna arrived home from the studio seething. She screamed at the maid, who promptly quit. She marched into the kitchen and screamed at the cook, who wanted to quit but needed the job.

George was still at the office. She phoned him and spewed venom. "Do you realize our lawyers are incompetent fools?" she yelled. "Somehow or other, Lucky Santangelo has gained back control of Panther. I want to know how this happened, George. I *demand* to know."

"It was never a good business proposition," George said, not sounding upset at all. "And you have to admit, Donna, you know nothing about the film business. This could be a good thing."

"Good!" she screamed, infuriated by his stupidity. "Good! Whatta kinda moron are you? *Stupido!*"

"Excuse me?" George said.

"Our lawyers are stupid," she said, embarrassed, realizing she'd inadvertently slipped back into her former accent.

"I'll look into it," George said.

"You do that."

She suddenly thought about the pictures she had of Brigette Stanislopoulos—the true murderer of Santino. It had taken time and money to track her down, but she'd done so, just after the girl had signed with a modeling agency. A small investigation of Michel Guy had revealed his predilections. A large sum of money had assured his cooperation.

What a stroke of genius! Now that she had

the pictures, she'd sell them to every porno magazine in the world. How would Lucky Santangelo like *that*? Her former stepdaughter exposed for all the world to ogle.

A small, cold smile. *You can't control everything, Lucky. You're not invincible.*

She was on the way to her safe to get the photographs when Santo arrived home from school.

"Why are you home early?" she demanded, catching him in the front hall.

"Why are *you*?" he retorted, seemingly unrepentant about the incident with Tabitha.

Lately they hadn't been speaking much. She yearned for her little boy back, the innocent boy she'd fussed over and raised. Now he was this big, hulking lout with a smart mouth who did unspeakable things with dirty little girls. He'd betrayed her and she didn't like it one bit.

"Where are you going?" she said as he tried to dodge past her.

"Upstairs," he said sullenly. "Locked up in my room." He threw her a filthy look. "That's what you want, isn't it?"

"It's your own fault, Santo," she said, her voice rising. "What you did was disgraceful."

"No," he said, scowling. "What I did was normal."

It infuriated Donna that he was still trying to justify his actions. "If your father knew you'd turned into a sex-crazed drug addict— he'd kill you rather than have you as his son," she said darkly.

"I'm no drug addict," he sneered. "Get with it, Mom. Everybody smokes pot."

She had the last word. "*My* son doesn't. Not anymore."

He ran up the stairs, slamming his way into his room, convinced his mother was the most hateful woman on earth.

Donna waited until he was gone, then went into the library, closed the door, and moved quickly to her private safe, concealed behind a tasteful Picasso.

She entered the combination, flinging open the small safe that contained important documents and a modest amount of jewelry—her good jewelry was locked safely in the bank.

She rummaged around, searching for the videotape of Morton Sharkey, and the pictures of Brigette.

This was ridiculous, she'd put them there herself, now she couldn't find them. Surely she wasn't losing her mind?

Methodically, she removed everything from the safe.

No tape. No pictures.

Was it possible that George had gotten hold of the combination?

No. George wouldn't dare invade her private safe.

She had to stay calm, and deal with this in a rational way. They were misplaced, and she *would* find them.

Santo went straight to his computer. He'd gotten out of school early because there was no one to stop him. What did he care about math or history? He didn't need to know any of that shit because one of these days *he* was inheriting the Bonnatti fortune. His father had left him money in trust, and when Donna dropped, he'd get her money, too. So screw school. Right now he was more interested in settling the score with that tramp, Venus Maria.

He sat down at his computer and began composing a new letter. A letter of hate.

The bitch had it coming.

6 4

Lennie waited impatiently, the hours crawling by at an interminably slow pace.

He wondered if Claudia was ever coming back. The thought of freedom was so intoxicating he could barely keep still, but he knew he had to reserve his strength for the escape— if it ever happened.

The man he now knew was Claudia's father arrived with his food, practically threw it at him, and vanished.

He stuffed a chunk of bread in his pocket for the journey. Then he sat on the edge of his makeshift bed, studying the crudely drawn map Claudia had given him. She'd promised she would lead him out of the maze of caves. After that, he was on his own, they each had to go in different directions.

Freedom. What a beautiful word. He said it aloud a few times simply to reassure himself.

He thought about his children. If it were up to him, he'd never leave them again. He'd take his movie career and shove it up the studio's ass, because from now on he was staying with his family. *Nothing* would separate him from Lucky.

After a long while he reached the conclusion that something must have gone wrong, Claudia wasn't coming back.

His head began to ache until he thought it would split open. He lay down on his so-called bed, overwhelmed with disappointment.

Eventually he must have drifted off to sleep, because when Claudia finally arrived she had to shake him awake. "Lennie," she said tensely. "Get up, hurry."

He opened his eyes, dazed for a moment. Was this another dream? No, Claudia was actually standing over him.

"We must leave immediately," she said, handing him the key. "If my papa wakes..."

She didn't have to say more. He sat up, and with fumbling hands inserted the key into the rusty lock enclosing his swollen ankle.

The lock was so stiff and corroded it refused to open. "Jesus!" he said, panicked. "This isn't the right key."

"It is," she insisted, bending down to help.

They both struggled with it, until somehow he managed to force the key in and wrench the lock apart.

At last he was free! He picked up the chain, and flung it violently across the cave.

Claudia slipped the key into her pocket. "Come, we must go," she said. "It is already late."

For a moment he was overcome with trepidation. He'd been a prisoner for so long he didn't know if he could handle freedom.

Claudia grabbed his hand. "Follow me," she said. "When we leave the caves, we must climb the side of the cliff."

"What cliff?" he said, alarmed.

"It is not dangerous," she assured him. "I do it all the time in the light. Now it is dark, it might be more difficult."

"Are you telling me that when we get out of here we've got to climb a cliff?"

"Yes, Lennie," she said steadily. "If I can do it, so can you. Come." She took the flashlight from him and began moving swiftly through the pitch-black labyrinth of cavernous caves.

He stuck close behind her, with only the slim flashlight to guide them, trying to ignore the slime and the scurrying rats as they made their way through.

As they progressed, the sound of the sea started getting louder. Jesus! How close *was* the ocean?

"The tide is in," Claudia said matter-of-factly. "We have to walk through water—don't be nervous."

As they emerged from the maze of caves, moonlight lit their way. The sea was lapping at the entrance and the night wind was howling.

Lennie shuddered as the realization hit him that he'd been hidden deep beneath the ground. He could have fucking drowned and nobody would ever have known.

Now they were knee-deep in the swirling sea and he was freezing cold.

"Hold on to me," Claudia shouted over the wind.

"I am," he yelled back.

She shone the flashlight toward some rocks.

"Over there," she said. "Hurry, the tide...it's still coming in."

This was more frightening than his incarceration.

They fought their way through the breaking waves to the rocks—by the time they reached them, they were soaked through and numb with cold.

Claudia was as agile as a gazelle. She leaped onto the rocks, then leaned behind her and grabbed Lennie's hand, helping him up.

As he started to clamber over the sharp-edged clusters, a jagged piece ripped his foot. "Shit!" he exclaimed, his foot dripping blood.

"Come on!" Claudia encouraged.

Finally they reached the bottom of a rugged cliff.

Lennie looked up and his stomach turned. Climbing it was a daunting prospect.

"Follow me," Claudia urged.

He did as she said, and they began slowly clawing their way up the side of the cliff, clinging to vines and trees until after a few feet they reached a rocky, man-made path.

Lennie almost slipped and fell a couple of times. The nightmare was getting worse. If it weren't for Claudia's strength and bravery, he'd have had no chance.

When they got to the top, they both collapsed onto the ground.

After a few minutes Lennie got up and took the flashlight from her, shining it on the sea below.

Realization hit hard. He'd been buried somewhere within the bowels of the earth. Hidden in a place nobody could ever find. It was a miracle he'd survived, and it was only thanks to Claudia.

"You must hurry, Lennie," she said anxiously. "Be safe. Take the path to the right and keep moving fast."

"How am I ever going to thank you, Claudia?"

"You don't have to," she said. "Go home to your wife and children. Be happy, Lennie."

And before he could say anything, she kissed him softly on the lips, then slipped off in the other direction, vanishing into the darkness.

Once more, he was all alone.

65

Saturday morning was one of those beautiful days, the kind of day that makes everybody aware of why they live in L.A.—in spite of earthquakes, riots, floods, and fires. This day was what L.A. was all about—crystal-clear blue skies, balmy sunshine, a city surrounded by palm trees, grassy hills, lush greenery, and magnificent mountains.

Lucky couldn't sleep. She got up early and wandered out onto her bedroom terrace, gazing out at the ocean. After a few minutes, she decided to jog along the seashore. She put on shorts and a T-shirt, ran downstairs, and set off along the shoreline.

Half an hour later she found herself below Alex's house. She stood still, jogging in place, wondering what he was doing.

A steep stone stairway led up the bluff to where his house stood. She considered visiting him. It was early, maybe he was still asleep, or perhaps Tin Lee had stayed the night.

What the hell, the gate to the bottom of the stairs was unlocked, surely it was a sign he wouldn't mind visitors?

She headed up the stone steps, taking them two at a time until she ran out of breath.

She stopped for a moment. *What are you doing?* she thought. *Why are you encouraging him? You pushed him away and he went, now what are you trying to do? Get him back?*

No way. I simply like his company and conversation. It doesn't have to be sexual. What's wrong with having a platonic male friend?

Platonic. Bullshit. You like him.

Wrong.

Yeah, sure.

At the top of the steps was another gate; she threw the catch and stepped onto his property.

Alex was sitting out on his terrace surrounded by a laptop computer, his script, newspapers, a pot of coffee, orange juice, toast, and cereal.

"Hey—" She waved, heading toward him. "Surprise visitor."

He glanced up, startled. "Lucky," he said, breaking into a big smile. "What a *nice* surprise."

"Jogged down the beach and happened to

find myself outside your house," she said casually. "Is that coffee for one, or can I get a cup, too?"

"Sit down. I'll call my housekeeper." He pressed a buzzer and a moody-looking Japanese woman appeared. "One more cup, Yuki."

Lucky flopped into a chair beside him, stretching out her long, tanned legs.

"Didn't know you were so athletic," he remarked, delighted she was visiting. As soon as he'd drawn back, she'd come to him.

She laughed. "I'm not. I needed to release a whole bunch of pent-up tension."

"I can think of better ways to do that," he said, putting down his script.

Yuki returned with another cup and filled it with coffee. Lucky took a sip. "I can't wait to get back to the studio on Monday," she said, removing her sunglasses and placing them on the table.

"And I can't wait to start *Gangsters,*" Alex said. "I have more fun making my movies than at any other time."

"That's because it's your escape."

"You're right," he said wryly. "Sometimes I wonder what I'm escaping from. I have no relationship with my mother, no wife, no children, in fact, no connections at all. "

"Making movies *is* your life," Lucky pointed out. "The actors and the crew are your family."

"Yeah, right again," he said, biting into a thin slice of toast. "Y'know, I'm one of the few directors who actually *likes* actors. I worked with a producer once who came up to me after I'd had lunch with the talent, and said in a pissed-off voice, 'You gonna eat with the actors?' as if they were some form of repellent underlife."

"I like actors, too," Lucky said. "In fact, I married one. Thing is—I see them as slightly damaged and incredibly needy."

"You see everybody as damaged," he remarked. "You should've been a psychoanalyst."

"I would have been good," she said, stealing a piece of his toast.

"So," he said. "Are you going to tell me what happened with the French hooker?"

"Well...she assured me she never slept with Lennie."

"Oh."

"I believe her. She had no reason to lie. She thought she was getting paid to set Lennie up for a magazine. Actually, she was surprised he didn't succumb to her charms, and let me tell you—her charms are plenty. She's gorgeous."

He regarded her curiously. "How did you find this out?"

"I flew her in as a birthday present for Johnny Romano."

Lucky never failed to amaze him. "You did *what*?"

"Johnny owed me a favor, so he went along with it."

"Is she a luscious blond?"

"That's right."

"He brought her with him to the reading. Didn't you see her?"

"No, Johnny was gone by the time I got there."

"She was definitely with him."

Lucky grinned. "They must've clicked. Trust Johnny to fall for a hooker. Daniella was supposed to fly back to Paris the next morning."

"Guess she didn't."

"How's your mother?" Lucky asked, pouring more coffee.

"Haven't spoken to her lately."

"Why not?"

"When you and I talked the other day, you made me see things more clearly. You're right—if I don't choose to see her, it shouldn't make me feel guilty."

"*Now* you're getting it."

"Dominique wasn't exactly the greatest mother in the world," he added, thinking about his fucked-up childhood.

"Understanding people's weaknesses is the key to a healthy relationship," Lucky said wisely. "Accept her for what she is, and she'll cease bothering you."

"Her latest ploy was to push Tin Lee on me. The result was that she pushed her right out of my life."

"Tin Lee seemed sweet," Lucky said, helping herself to more toast. "And she obviously adores you."

"Yes, she's very sweet and patient. However, according to my shrink—whom I haven't seen in six months—there was a reason I only went out with Asian women."

"Oh, yes. What reason was that?"

"It doesn't matter, because you came into my life and made me realize there's nothing wrong with a good old American."

She threw him a quizzical look. *"Old?"*

He laughed. "You know what I mean."

"In that case, I'm flattered."

They sat in companionable silence for a few minutes. "What about you, Lucky—how are you feeling?"

She picked up her sunglasses and put them back on, hiding behind the dark lenses. "Pretty lousy about us. I slept with you to get even with Lennie—now I find out I had nothing to get even about."

He was getting fed up with her excuses—it didn't make him feel good. "You weren't planning on becoming a nun, were you?" he asked, a touch sharply.

She refused to get mad. "It was too soon, Alex," she said quietly.

He stood up, changing the subject. "What are you doing today?"

She shrugged vaguely. "No plans—how about you?"

"I'll work on my script, maybe go down to the gym, do a little kick boxing. I used to be into that on a regular basis."

"I'd love to try it."

"Come with me."

"I wouldn't mind."

"I'll pick you up in an hour."

She jumped up. "I've got a better idea—drive me home and wait. I don't feel like jogging all the way back."

He shook his head disapprovingly. "Low stamina."

"You can say that again."

They looked at each other and burst out laughing.

Venus woke up, reached out, and was ridiculously pleased to discover Cooper asleep beside her. She rolled over, snuggling cozily against his broad back. "Y'know," she murmured. "You're a great lover...did anybody ever tell you you're a great cuddle, too?"

"Can you believe this?" he said sleepily, turning around and holding her warm body close.

"What?" she asked, delightfully comfortable.

"You've got me off other women. I'm cured! It's like getting a drunk off booze!"

"One drink and I'll shoot your balls off," she threatened jokingly.

He struggled to sit up. "You've been spending too much time with Lucky," he said disapprovingly. "You're beginning to sound just like her."

"Wouldn't mind that, I think Lucky's great."

"So do I. Only her language is out of control."

"Coop! For a world-famous womanizer—there are times you can be such a prude!"

"Women should be seen and not swear."

"Veree funny." She threw her leg over him, cuddling even closer. "You know what I'd like?" she murmured.

"What, baby?" he said, stroking her platinum hair.

"That's it," she said triumphantly. "I'd like to have a baby—*our* baby."

"*You* were the one who always said—"

"I know," she interrupted. "I said I didn't want to. But I've been thinking—after I've finished *Gangsters,* let's get pregnant."

"It might be nice," he said unsurely.

"Nice!" she exclaimed, sitting up. "Cooper, get *with* it. You and I will have the cutest little babies in the world!"

"Are we talking baby or babies?" he asked wryly.

"I was thinking one or two might do it."

"Oh, one or two, huh?" he said, playfully grabbing her breasts. "And when the baby is feasting on *these,* what am I supposed to do?"

"You'll take turns."

"I want my turn now," he said, putting a nipple in his mouth and sucking vigorously.

The intercom buzzed. "You get it, Coop," she said, extracting herself.

"It's *your* house."

"*Our* house," she corrected, reaching for a robe. "From where I sit, you've definitely moved back in."

"Wise woman," he said, picking up the phone. "Yeah?"

"Oh...uh, Mr. Turner...Miss Venus's brother is here. He says it's urgent he sees her."

"It's your brother," Cooper said, covering the mouthpiece. "When did *Emilio* creep back into town?"

"What does he want?" she asked, frowning.

"The guard said it's urgent."

"Will you see him with me?"

"Prepare yourself. I'm likely to throw his fat ass out."

"That's *exactly* what Emilio needs—somebody to boot him out of my life forever."

★ ★ ★

Santo awoke with a nagging toothache. He informed his mother, expecting her to be sympathetic. She was not.

"I'm in agony," he whined, rubbing his cheek.

She called the dentist and made an emergency appointment.

"Drive me there, Mom?"

"No," she answered brusquely. "It's time you learned what punishment is. When you treat *me* with respect, I'll treat *you* the same way."

Stupid old hag. How could he respect her when she was married to a loser jerk like George?

"So you won't take me?" he said accusingly.

"No, Santo," she replied, not even looking at him.

Screw her. At least it gave him an opportunity to get out of the house.

He ran upstairs, grabbed his jacket and a printout of the letter he'd composed to Venus last night. He'd spent three hours hunched over the computer, trying to decide exactly what to say. In the end, it was short and to the point.

His mother buzzed on the house intercom, telling him he had to leave immediately as the dentist was coming into his office especially to see him.

He checked his closet to make sure it was locked, then hurried back downstairs.

"'Bye," he yelled, passing the open door to the breakfast room.

Nobody answered.

Fuck 'em. One of these days he'd *force* them to pay attention.

George removed his spectacles, peered through the window, and watched Santo drive off. "What does he do all day?" he said.

"Works on his computer," Donna replied.

"At what?"

"I've never asked him," she said, sipping her coffee.

"It's obvious he needs help."

"I know."

George nodded to himself. "I'll find out the name of a capable psychiatrist."

Donna wasn't sure if she liked that idea— Santo talking to a stranger, revealing family business. For now she decided to agree with

George. When she came back from Sicily, she'd make her own decision.

"Oh, yes," she said. "I almost forgot to tell you. One of my brothers called. My father is sick, I have to make a trip to Sicily. I thought I'd leave Monday. It's his heart."

"Should I come with you?"

"No, you stay here and watch the business."

"If you're sure?"

"Yes, I'm sure." A pause. "By the way," she added casually, "did you happen to take something from my safe?"

"I wouldn't dream of going to your safe, Donna. Why? Is something missing?"

"Not missing...misplaced. I'm sure I'll find it."

George picked up the newspaper and started reading.

"I'll be upstairs," Donna said.

If George hadn't invaded her safe, who had? Could it be Santo? Could *he* have taken the photos and the tape?

No. He didn't even know she *had* a safe.

Still...it wouldn't hurt to check out his room.

As soon as Santo left the dentist's office, he drove over to Venus Maria's house, cruising past a couple of times before parking across the street. He sat in his car, watching the house for a few minutes.

The guard's station was close to the entrance of the property. He could see a middle-aged man sitting inside the small wooden structure, reading a magazine and eating an apple.

Very alert. Venus should get herself better security. This jerk was useless.

He knew a place around the back of the property where he could sneak onto the grounds without anyone spotting him. It was risky during the day, but so what? He'd do it anyway because it was about time the whore knew who she was dealing with. Once she read his letter, she'd realize he'd busted her cheating ass.

Venus deserved to be punished just as he'd been punished.

And who better to do it than him?

Santo's room was certainly tidier than the other night. For a teenage boy, he was really quite neat—there were no horrible posters of half-naked women on the walls, no dirty clothes lying around the floor, no drugs—thank God!

Donna sat on the edge of his bed, thinking about her other three children, all of whom had left home. She didn't want Santo leaving, too. Deep down, he was still her baby, her sweet little boy. The truth was, he was all she had, and she loved him.

She wondered if George was forcing her to be too hard on him. He said they had to be tough, but not if it was going to drive Santo away. The last thing she wanted was to lose her son.

She noticed he'd left his computer on. She crossed the room to switch it off.

There was a message printed on the screen. She bent to look.

> Whore.
> Cunt.
> You lick everybody's cock.
> I fucking hate you.

Oh, my God! Who was this message for? Was it meant for her?

A cold chill swept over her.

Santo—her own flesh and blood—had finally turned against her.

66

"Why do you keep on bothering me?" Venus demanded.

Emilio glared at her accusingly. "You could be nicer to me," he said defensively. "I *am* your brother."

Didn't he *ever* get it? "No, Emilio, you're not," she said, her temper heating up. "When you sold me out to the media, you *ceased* being my brother."

"I'm gonna havta write a book," he said, his expression turning crafty because he knew she'd hate that more than anything.

"Go ahead and write it—there's nothing else you can say about me that will hurt me any more than the things you've already told the press."

"How about leaving your sister alone?" Cooper suggested, joining in.

"How about butting out?" Emilio replied nastily.

"Get smart with me, Emilio, and you're heading for a broken leg."

"You *threatening* me, Cooper?" Emilio said disdainfully. "'Cause that'll make *really* good copy."

"I gave you a thousand bucks last time—what do you want now?" Venus wailed.

"I blew it."

"On what?"

"Had a bad night...got mugged."

"Mugged, my ass."

"It happens to people in L.A. all the time."

"I wish I hadn't given you the money," Venus said. "I felt sorry for you, now I realize nothing helps. This time I'm leaving instructions that you *do not* get in here again."

"Listen to your sister," Cooper said. "Do yourself a favor and stay away."

"You rich bastards make me puke," Emilio sneered. "You got no fuckin' clue what it's like bein' me."

"Deal with him, Cooper, I've had it," Venus said, completely exasperated.

Cooper grabbed Emilio's arm.

Emilio pulled roughly away. "Don't fuckin' touch me, man," he snarled. "I'm leavin'." He marched out, slamming the door behind him.

"Jesus!" Cooper said. "Are you *sure* you have the same parents?"

"Unfortunately, yes."

"He's a dumb prick."

"The worst kind."

"Well, let's not spoil our day."

"Whatever you say...husband."

Cooper smiled, lazily pulling her toward him. "Come here, wife."

She smiled back. "You don't have to ask twice."

Emilio stood outside the front door, burning up. Why *should* he leave—simply to please them? They treated him like a piece of shit. As her brother, surely he deserved more?

He glared at his beat-up old rental car parked in the driveway. She had three frigging cars sitting in her garage, a Mercedes, a Corvette, and a Jeep. Would it kill her to give one to him?

He made his way around the side of the house, contemplating climbing up to her bedroom and relieving her of some of her jewelry. She had plenty, she wouldn't miss a diamond bracelet or two.

Just as he was edging around the back of the house, he noticed a fat boy lurking in the bushes, acting suspiciously.

"Hey—" Emilio called out. "Whatcha think *you're* doin'?"

Santo took one look at Emilio and started to run.

Emilio saw his chance to be a hero. Without thinking of the consequences, he raced off in pursuit, tackling Santo to the ground when they were only a few yards from the surrounding wall.

Santo struggled ferociously, but even though Emilio was not as fit as he should be, he was able to keep him pinned down. He sat on top of the fat boy, yelling for assistance.

A neighbor's dog started to bark. A maid darted out of the kitchen door, saw what was going on, and scurried back into the house to summon help. A few seconds later Cooper emerged, followed by Venus.

"What's happening?" Venus shrieked.

"Caught this asshole sneakin' around," Emilio puffed, out of breath. "I'm lookin' out for you, little sis."

Cooper grabbed his cell phone and called for the guard. "What are you doing here?" he said, walking over to Santo.

"Got lost," Santo mumbled. "Didn't know this was private property."

"Lost? You had to have climbed the wall to have gotten in," Venus said angrily. Then she noticed the envelope clutched in his hand. She took a closer look, immediately recognizing the scrawly writing on the front. "Oh, God!" she exclaimed. "It's you, isn't it? You're the sick little fuck who's been writing me all those filthy letters."

"What letters?" Cooper said.

"Porno letters," she said, snatching the envelope out of Santo's hand.

The guard ran up, gun drawn.

"You're too late," Emilio said, shooting an *I saved your butt* look at his sister. "Good thing *I* was around."

Venus began scanning the letter. "Read *this*!" she said, handing it to Cooper.

He studied the letter, then took another look at Santo, sprawled on the ground. "Wait a minute—" he said. "Aren't you the Landsmans's son? Weren't you at the Stollis's house? What the *fuck* are you doing here?"

Lucky and Alex were in the gym, practicing kick boxing. "Where did you learn to do this?" Lucky asked, her eyes shining, face flushed.

"Is this great, or what?" Alex said enthusiastically. "Learned it in Vietnam—one of the few good things I got out of that place."

"Wow!" she exclaimed. "It sure beats the treadmill."

"That's why I do it."

"I'm sweating."

"Let's go home and take a shower."

"Alex," she said, frowning. "Please, remember what I said—just friends."

"Hey—I didn't mean together." He shook his finger at her. "You and your dirty mind, Miz Santangelo."

She laughed; being with Alex made her feel good. "Drop me home. I've a ton of paperwork to go over."

"Can we have a platonic dinner tonight?"

"Nope."

"How about lunch then? I'll buy you a hot dog."

"I don't eat hot dogs."

"You're an American, aren't you?"

"Have you any idea what they put in them?"

"Don't tell me," he groaned. "Can I interest you in a pasta salad?"

"A pasta salad—are you *crazy*?" she exclaimed. "I have Italian blood. Let's go get a big dish of spaghetti bolognese. Then we'll both go home and work—good plan?"

"You in your house, me in mine?"

"What's wrong with that?"

"Can I ask you a question?"

"Go ahead."

He stared at her. "When *will* you be ready for a relationship?"

She took her time before replying. "That's not a question I can answer right now," she said at last. "But when I am—you'll be the first to know."

"I beg your pardon?" George said into the phone, his plain face reddening.

"Who is it?" Donna asked impatiently.

"We'll be right there," George said, slamming down the receiver, which was unlike him. "Well," he said, shaking his head as if he didn't believe what he'd just heard. "That letter you were telling me about on Santo's computer was not meant for you."

"How do *you* know?"

"Apparently he's been writing porno letters to the singer, Venus Maria. He's been caught on her grounds trying to deliver his latest effort."

"No!" Donna said, shocked.

"Oh, yes," George replied. "We'd better get over there before they call the police."

★ ★ ★

"I've got a surprise," Nona said. "We're taking a cab to Times Square."

"My billboard is up!" Brigette said excitedly.

"Yup."

"Does Isaac know?"

"He's probably been gaping at it ever since it appeared!"

"Should I call him?" she asked eagerly.

"Don't start that again," Nona warned. "Isaac is not for you."

"Okay, okay, he's history."

They went downstairs, hailed a cab, and fifteen minutes later they were there.

Nona paid the cabdriver while Brigette leaped out, shrieking with delight. "Oh, my God!" she said. "It's fantastic!"

"You look incredible!" Nona said, joining her on the sidewalk. "Boy, is Michel Guy gonna be sorry he blew *your* career!"

They stared up at the giant billboard of

Brigette and Isaac clad in nothing but tight blue jeans and big, wide smiles.

A camera crew from *Entertainment Tonight* passed by and began filming the huge billboard.

Nona nudged Brigette. "If they only knew you're standing right here...Hmm...I think I should tell them."

"No way," Brigette said, panicking. "I look awful."

"You don't, you look fantastic. Let's start the publicity machine rolling. Girl, prepare yourself—'cause you're going to be the biggest." Nona sauntered over to the camera crew. "Excuse me," she said. "Are you shooting the jeans billboard?"

The cameraman turned to her. "Yeah, it's a hot campaign—there's sure to be a lot of talk about this one."

"What do you think of the model?"

"She's a beauty."

"I'm Nona, her manager. And she's standing right over there. Her name's Brigette Brown. Remember it—she's going to be the next big supermodel."

The cameraman couldn't believe his luck. "Can we talk to her?"

"Absolutely," Nona said. "Come this way."

They stopped for lunch at a little Italian restaurant situated on the beach. Lucky ordered the spaghetti she craved, and Alex went for a steak. They shared a bottle of red wine.

"I'm really happy everything worked out for you," Alex said, pouring her more wine. "No more trouble from Donna Landsman."

"Funny," Lucky said reflectively. "I never think of her as Donna Landsman. She'll always be a Bonnatti to me."

"Get over it, Lucky."

She looked at him intently. "No, Alex, you don't understand. She'll *never* go away, not unless I do something about it."

"You *did* something about it—you got your studio back."

"Donna's Sicilian, there's no way she'll quit."

"What else can she possibly do?"

"Anything she feels like," Lucky said grimly.

"You can't live the rest of your life surrounded by guards."

"I don't intend to."

"What *do* you intend to do?"

She gazed out at the sea for a moment, watching a blond boy surf the waves. "The Santangelos solve things their own way," she said at last. "We've always had to."

"Forget about taking the law into your own hands," Alex said. "You got away with it once—twice would be pushing it. And I'm telling you now, I am *not* visiting you in a jail cell. No way."

"Trust me, I know what I'm doing."

"No, *you* trust *me*," he said forcefully. "When I was in Vietnam, I had experiences that haunt me to this day. Don't even think about doing anything you'll regret."

She took a sip of red wine. "Hey, Alex—you're a writer," she said lightly. "You should be loving this."

"Lucky," he said seriously, "make me a promise that whatever you decide, you'll discuss it with me first."

"I have a policy," she said. "I refuse to make promises I'm not sure I can keep."

He looked at her for a long moment, wondering how far she was prepared to go.

No, she wouldn't do anything drastic. She was no longer the wild girl who'd shot Enzio Bonnatti. She was a woman with responsibilities who wouldn't be foolish enough to do anything that might put her family in jeopardy.

"Just remember," he said. "You have three young children. Do anything dumb, and you could go to jail for the rest of your life. I don't think you'd want to do that to your kids—not after they've lost Lennie."

She sighed. "Time to take me home, Alex, I've a lot of thinking to do."

He drove her home and dropped her off. "Are you jogging in the morning?" he asked as they stood at the door.

"Maybe," she said vaguely.

"Coffee. Same time. Same place." He kissed her lightly on the cheek, willing her to invite him in.

She didn't. She walked into her house without looking back.

Miss Cool. Only this time she'd come to him, at least that was progress.

Lucky clicked on her answering machine. There were a couple of hang-ups, a message from Venus, and another one from Boogie.

She did not feel like returning calls.

She went upstairs to the bedroom, and threw open the terrace doors so she could smell and hear the sea.

This room reminded her of Lennie so much. Lennie...Her love...Her life...

And while Donna Landsman lived, she would never be able to erase the pain.

67

Donna and George got in the Rolls and hurriedly drove to Venus's house.

"Thank God she called us instead of the police," Donna said, imagining the consequences if it had been otherwise.

George agreed. "You're going to have to do something about Santo," he said. "He needs to be sent away to a different environment—somewhere he'll get discipline."

"I know," Donna admitted reluctantly.

The guard met them at the gate. Venus was pacing around outside with Cooper, not looking pleased.

"Where is he?" Donna asked.

"In the guardhouse," Cooper replied.

Donna peered through the glass window of

the small guardhouse. Santo was huddled in a corner, his head down on his knees.

Venus was quite civilized about the incident. "I'm only glad it's not some freako," she said. "Do me a big favor—make sure there're no more letters."

"Don't worry," George said. "You have my word Santo will never bother you again."

"Get him out of here, and we'll forget it," Cooper said, anxious to be rid of the problem as quickly as possible.

Santo could hear them talking about him as if he didn't exist. It filled him with rage.

Then Venus sent for her assistant, who appeared with copies of all his letters neatly filed in a manila folder. Shit! His mother was going to see his freaking letters!

"Take a look at these," Cooper said, handing the folder to George. "My suggestion is you get the boy to a shrink fast. He needs help."

"We appreciate you not calling the police," George said.

"I couldn't take the publicity," Venus replied, rolling her eyes.

The guard shepherded Santo into the Rolls. He slouched down in the back of the car.

Donna turned around, glaring balefully at her son. She was repulsed. For the first time she saw him as he really was—a mirror image of Santino.

Face it, she told herself, *Santo is exactly like Santino. A vile, sex-crazed pig.*

"You sicken me," she said savagely. "You're

a disgusting lowlife pervert—just like your father. You even look like him."

"My father was a great man," Santo managed, hating her. "George isn't good enough to wipe his ass."

"You shut your filthy little mouth," Donna said, coldly furious. "I'll deal with you when we get home."

Venus removed a carton of orange juice from the fridge. "Some sick wacko!" she exclaimed, shaking her platinum curls. "Did you read the letters?"

"Glanced at them," Cooper replied. "Pour me some, too, hon."

"Good thing I caught him," Emilio said, reminding them of his presence.

"Yeah...really," Venus said, handing Cooper a glass of juice.

"It wasn't easy," Emilio boasted. "I coulda walked away."

"We appreciate your quick action, Emilio," Cooper said.

"He coulda had a gun."

"We know."

Emilio basked in his moment of glory. "So, y'see, little sis, I'm always lookin' out for you."

"Don't worry," she said briskly. "You'll get a check. This time you deserve it." She reached for the phone. "I'm calling Johnny Romano, he has the best security in town."

"Good idea," Emilio said, strutting around

the kitchen, wondering how generous she'd be.

"Isn't that like shutting the gate after the rabid dog has gotten out?" Cooper remarked sagely.

Venus sighed. "It'll make me feel better."

She spoke to Johnny, telling him what had taken place.

"Daniella and I are takin' a trip to Vegas," Johnny said. "I'll send a couple of my guys over. They'll put together a new security team for you. In fact, I'll have 'em bring the dogs."

"Thanks, Johnny, I appreciate it."

"You know," Cooper said thoughtfully, "in my whole career, I never had to have security."

"That's 'cause you were fast on your feet."

"I guess we live in different times now."

"It only takes one maniac," Emilio said helpfully, thrilled to be part of the family again.

"He's right," Venus agreed, shivering. "Santo happened to be Donna Landsman's son, but it could've been some crazed out-of-town freako—"

"With a gun," Emilio added quickly.

"Don't worry, Venus," Cooper said. "I'm here to protect you."

She put her arms around his neck and hugged him tightly. "Wow, Coop, I never knew you were so macho!"

Johnny put down the phone. "That was Venus," he said.

"Who?" Daniella questioned, licking her pouty lips.

Johnny looked at her quizzically. "You gotta have heard of Venus Maria."

"No."

"She's a big star. She's in *Gangsters* with me. You met her yesterday."

"Oh, yes."

"Hey—we'd better get movin'. I got a little surprise waitin' for you in Vegas. You'll love it."

"What surprise, Johnny?"

He grinned. "You'll see."

Lucky sat in her study, attempting to work. She was happy to see that in the short time Mickey had been at Panther, he'd not done too much damage. She noted he'd canceled several of her movies in development, and made deals with a group of producers she didn't approve of. Nothing that couldn't be fixed. Monday morning she'd reinstate her team, and go over everything more thoroughly. One thing she knew for sure—it was great having her studio back.

What are you going to do about Donna? an inner voice screamed in her head. *What are you going to do?*

Could she risk taking no action?

Impossible. Donna was too dangerous an enemy. She was as evil as her late husband, Santino. There had to be a resolution of some kind.

She murdered Lennie, the voice continued. *Set him up, then had him killed. She put a hit on Gino, and tried to ruin Brigette. And if that weren't enough, she took your studio. Morton Sharkey and Sara Durbon are dead because of Donna. Is your plan to sit around and let her get away with everything, or are you going to resolve the situation?*

Lucky stood up and began walking up and down the room. Her head was spinning, she didn't know what to do. She knew if she were so inclined she could put a hit out on Donna; Boogie would arrange it in a minute. But that wasn't the Santangelo way. The Santangelo way was retribution.

And yet, something was holding her back. Alex was right, she couldn't afford to do anything that might have dire consequences.

She had a desperate craving for a joint. She went to her stash in the drawer and lit up. Then she wandered restlessly around the house—unsettled and edgy.

She missed her children, but there was no way she could bring them home while Donna was still at large.

When are you going to do something about her?

I can't. I'm not the same person. Alex is right—I have responsibilities.

Oh, get a fucking life! You're a Santangelo, you can do it.

I'm not sure anymore....

Oh, yes you are. You know exactly what you have to do.

642

They sat on the terrace at the Ivy. "This is a nice surprise," Dominique said, patting her short black wig. "The two of us—dining together. Where's Tin Lee tonight?"

"Stop pushing Tin Lee on me," Alex said irritably. "She's one of the reasons I wanted to see you by myself."

"Why?"

"I felt it was time we talked."

"About what, Alex?"

"About the way you treat me."

"I treat you very nicely."

"No, you don't. I'm forty-seven, as you constantly remind me, and I have no intention of listening to your nonstop criticisms anymore. If you keep it up, I'll stop seeing you."

She looked at him with displeasure. "Alex! I'm your mother. How can you be so cruel?"

"When my father died, you turned away from me—sent me off to a military academy. You knew I was unhappy, yet you let me rot there until I was old enough to get out. It was torture."

"You needed the discipline, Alex."

"No!" he said, almost shouting. "What I needed was a loving mother who cared."

"I cared."

"Bullshit," he said harshly. "You were out with a different man every night."

"No, Alex, I—"

"I went to Vietnam," he interrupted. "You never wrote. And when I lived in New York all those years—did you ever try to find me?"

"It wasn't easy—"

"No," he continued, relieved to be saying what had been on his mind for so long. "The only time you've been halfway civil to me is since I became successful."

"Nonsense."

"If I'd turned out to be a bum, you wouldn't bother seeing me at all."

"That's untrue," Dominique objected.

"I'm not taking your shit anymore," he said angrily. "It's time you realized that it's *my* life. No more guilt trips."

He waited for her to start screaming and yelling.

She didn't. She merely looked at him and said, "This is the first time you've reminded me of your father. Gordon was a sonofabitch, but he was a strong man and in spite of all his faults—I suppose I loved him."

"So, Mom," he said carefully, sensing an opening. "Do we have an understanding?"

Dominique nodded. "I'll try my best."

Venus and Cooper entered Spago like the stars they were. A sudden silence fell over the room as everyone checked them out.

Venus squeezed her husband's hand. It felt so good being back with Cooper, they belonged together. "Gotta feeling we're making an impression," she whispered.

"You *always* make an impression," he

replied, amused by the attention they were receiving.

"*This'll* give the tabloids something to think about," she said, laughing. "Did you catch the latest headline?"

"Wasn't I supposed to be screwing an alien?" he said sardonically. "And you were busy having sex with three NBA players—simultaneously. Hmm...difficult..." He grinned. "However, knowing how talented you are..."

She giggled. "It's amazing what they can make up and get away with."

"That's 'cause nobody has the time to sue."

"Honey"—she squeezed his hand again—"I love you so much."

"You, too, baby."

They sat at a corner table for two and ordered the duck pizza, a specialty of the house.

Wolfgang Puck came running over to greet them. "You two back together?" he said, beaming.

"Where else would we be?" Venus replied, smiling sweetly.

The waiter brought over a complimentary bottle of champagne. They toasted each other, clinking glasses the old-fashioned way.

"You're so handsome," Venus said admiringly. Even though Cooper had been a movie star for many years, she knew he could never get enough compliments. It was part of his insecurity—a side of him she loved.

He pulled a face. "Used to be, I'm turning into an old man. I ran a couple of weeks ago—couldn't walk properly for a week!"

"So *that's* why you wanted to get back together," she teased. "You figure your playboy days are over."

He laughed. "Yeah, *right.*"

Venus sipped her champagne. "Don't look now," she said, "but guess who Charlie Dollar just walked in with."

"Do I get a clue?"

"One of your old girlfriends."

"Honey—they were all nothing compared to you. I was going through a midlife crisis—a dying man seeing if he could still get it up!"

"You sweet-talker you."

"Well, aren't you going to tell me who it is? Or do I have to turn around?"

"Since you're so interested, it's Leslie Kane."

"Leslie and Charlie, huh?"

"Jealous?"

"Insanely so," he joked, taking a surreptitious look. "At least she's with Charlie, not that deadbeat from the other night."

"Feeling protective?"

"I didn't treat her very nicely."

"My heart breaks."

"Where's your compassion? Leslie's not a bad girl."

"Don't push it, Coop," Venus said, losing her sense of humor. "She's an ex-hooker who was fucking my husband."

He threw up his hands. "Okay, okay—I get the message."

Venus waved at Charlie. "As long as we understand each other," she said succinctly.

"Whatever you want," Cooper said, not about to screw things up again.

Venus sipped her champagne. "Lucky never called back," she said. "I wanted to tell her about my number-one fan—dear little Santo Landsman. She'll freak!"

"Maybe it's not such a good idea to spread it around," Cooper said, thinking of the repercussions.

"Telling Lucky is hardly spreading it around."

"Think about it first."

"Whatever you say, darling." She leaned across the table with a wicked expression. "Now, tell me the truth, I've been *dying* to ask."

"What?"

"Exactly how far *did* you get with Veronica the guy?"

"Venus!"

"Yes?" she said innocently.

"I'm gonna have to spank you if you keep this up."

"Oooh...Coop, how exciting! *When?*"

He shook his head. "You really are incorrigible."

She grinned. "Tell me about it!"

68

They'd taken out his computer, but they hadn't gotten into his closet.

"What do you have in there?" Donna demanded, angrily pacing around his room. "More filth?"

He knew it was only a matter of time before his stupid mother managed to get into his closet. She'd already searched his room and discovered a couple of joints hidden in his underwear drawer, which, of course, she'd confiscated. She'd yelled some more when she couldn't open his closet, and had demanded the key.

He'd told her he'd lost it.

She didn't believe him. "Tomorrow morning I'll have a locksmith here," she threatened.

If she ever found his stash of Venus memorabilia and porno magazines, she'd go berserk. He had to smuggle his suitcase out of the house until things cooled down. Maybe if he locked it in the trunk of his car it would be safe.

He scowled. "I dunno what you're getting so mad about," he said. "I wrote to Venus Maria as a joke—somebody at school dared me."

Donna glared at him imperiously, as if he were the worst piece of shit in the world. "Who would dare you to write such vile pornography?"

He shrugged, wishing they'd both get the frig out of his room. "One of the guys. It's no big deal."

"It's a very big deal," George interrupted, puffed up with his own importance. "The trouble with you, Santo, is that you take no responsibility. You expect everything to be easy. Well, this time you've gone too far."

Who voted that the creep could have a say in his life?

If it weren't for George trying to show he had balls, everything would've been okay by now.

"You're to stay in your room until we decide what to do with you," Donna said, throwing in a contemptuous look for good measure.

We? Why was she bringing George into it? He had no say in his life.

The two of them marched out. A couple of tired old fools.

Santo went into his bathroom. He was sick of being bossed around.

Peering at himself in the mirror above the sink, he slicked back his hair with gel. Yes, with the hair off his face, he did look like his father. He was proud he bore such a strong resemblance to Santino. *He* was a true Bonnatti.

He went back into the bedroom, opened his desk drawer, and took out the wedding photograph he kept of his father and mother. Santino and Donatella. The prince and the peasant. She couldn't even speak English when his dad married her. Santo knew all about her past, in spite of the airs and graces she put on.

Santino Bonnatti was a fine man—Santo remembered him well. His dad had bought him expensive clothes, taken him out to ball games and movies, and sometimes to fancy restaurants. The two of them had always done things together.

Sometimes Donatella had tried to tag along. Santino wouldn't allow it. "Ya gotta know one thing about women," his father had taught him. "Keep 'em at home slavin' in the kitchen where they belong."

Yes, well...his mother hadn't stayed at home, had she? She'd changed her appearance with plastic surgery, lost a ton of weight, and turned into a monster. It was like she was *waiting* for Santino to die so she could undergo a transformation and marry his freaking feeble-minded accountant.

Now he fully understood why his father had always kept girlfriends.

Oh, yes, he knew about the girlfriends, too. He even remembered the last one's name—Eden Antonio, a horny blond. Santino had called Eden a business associate, but Santo knew his dad was screwing the ass off her.

It was in the house Santino had bought for Eden that he'd been shot. Boom! Just like that he'd gotten his freaking head blown off.

If Santino were alive, he wouldn't be locked in his room now.

If Santino had caught him with a girl, he wouldn't have been punished.

If Santino had found out about the letters, he wouldn't have thought it was so disgusting.

No. Santino would have laughed. "Leave the boy alone," he'd have said to Donna. "Get off his fuckin' case."

Many times he'd heard Santino say those words to her. She'd rushed off into the kitchen muttering Sicilian curses under her breath, later returning to the living room to scream insults at her husband in broken English.

Why was his father dead and not his mother? It wasn't right. It wasn't the way it should be.

He unlocked his closet, hastily removing the suitcase filled with his Venus collection. Had to smuggle it out to his car, lock it in the trunk, then maybe in a couple of days he'd get the opportunity to ask Mohammed to look after it for him.

In the meantime, he hid it under his bed, where she'd already looked.

That done, he suddenly remembered his gun. His twelve-gauge semiautomatic Magnum shotgun. Shit! If she found that, she'd really have a nervous breakdown.

The shotgun was propped in his closet, cleverly hidden behind a bunch of winter clothes. She'd have to search to find it, but knowing his mother, she'd do just that.

Maybe he'd hide the gun in his car, too. Yeah, for now, that was the safest plan.

As soon as they were asleep, he'd make a couple of trips to his car. First he'd take the suitcase, then the shotgun.

He quickly hauled it out of the closet, shoving it under the bed, next to the suitcase.

All he had to do now was wait for them to retire for the night.

Donna never drank, it did not suit her to lose control. Tonight, she was so distressed by Santo's behavior and the happenings of the last few days that she told her houseman to fix her a vodka martini.

One turned into two, then three.

By the time she sat down to dinner with George, she was swaying slightly and more than a little belligerent.

"Why are you drinking?" George asked, a disapproving note in his voice.

Ha! Like she had to explain herself to George. She'd had enough of him trying to assert himself; it was time to put him back in his place, where he belonged. "None of your business," she snapped.

"I know it's upsetting, dear," George said, attempting to soothe her.

"You have no idea how upsetting it is," Donna replied bitterly, picking up a glass of red wine and draining it just to spite him. "No idea at all."

After dinner, George announced he had work to attend to. "There're some papers you must sign before you leave," he said.

Was this her lot in life? Men placed documents in front of her and she signed them.

She had the houseman fix her another martini and carried it up to her bedroom. For the last two years she and George had maintained separate bedrooms; it suited her that way. When she wanted sex—which was less and less often—she summoned him. He had no choice in the matter.

She went into her bathroom, stripped off her clothes, and inspected herself in the mirror.

All the liposuction in the world could not bring her flesh back to the way it had been when she was a young girl in Sicily. A young girl...pursued by Furio...the belle of her village. She turned sideways. Not bad. Since she'd lost all that weight, she liked to admire her body, although it was wasted on George; he was no longer the lover he'd been when they were first married. She'd thought having control of a Hollywood studio might lead to more exciting relationships. A movie star wouldn't be bad. Lucky had a movie star, why shouldn't she?

The room was spinning, she wasn't used to drinking. She wasn't used to losing either.

She ran a hot bubble bath, sat in the tub, martini glass balanced on the side, then she stretched out and reached for the phone.

The phone rang. Lucky picked up. A woman's voice, thinly disguised, very drunk: "S' that you, *bitch*?"

"Who's this?"

"You...think...you're so goddamn...clever."

Lucky tried to stay calm. "Donna?"

"You think you're…Miss Fucking…Smart-ass."

Her voice cold, "What do you want?"

"You notta so smart, *bitch*," Donna said, weaving in and out of her former accent. "Your precious Lennie he'sa dead now. You had a chance to save him, but no…you were too busy with your studio to figure he might still be alive. Ha! You gotta Panther now, I hope you're happy. This isn't the end…this is…just the beginning."

The line went dead.

What was Donna talking about? A chance to save Lennie? There'd been no chance, he'd died in that car crash, nobody could have survived.

Unless he wasn't in the car…

But he *was* in the car. The doorman had seen him drive off.

They'd recovered the body of the driver, why hadn't they found Lennie?

Lucky's mind began racing. Was there something she'd missed?

Screw Donna Landsman. Now she was trying to mess with her brain.

She went upstairs to her bedroom, unlocked the drawer beside her bed, and took out her gun.

Back downstairs.

Another joint.

Several long drags, then she walked outside and sat down, cradling the gun on her lap.

Very soon she'd have to make a decision.

Very soon…

69

Donna snored loudly. Santo put his head against her bedroom door, listening intently. From the sound of her, she wouldn't surface until morning, which left only George to avoid.

He crept downstairs, angling himself so he could see into the library. George was busy poring over a stack of papers. If he moved quickly, he could sneak downstairs with his suitcase and gun, and hide them safely in his car before George noticed.

He hurried back upstairs, dragging the suitcase out from under his bed. It was heavy—filled not only with his Venus stuff, but his collection of porno magazines, too.

He sneaked past his mother's room—still hearing her snoring loud and clear.

Stealthily he started down the stairs, lugging the heavy suitcase behind him. It pained him that he couldn't keep his collection near him, but the cow had given him no choice.

On the other hand, what did he care about Venus anymore? She was the slut who'd exposed him—shown his letters to other people and humiliated him. Didn't she realize they were personal? That the private love messages the letters contained were supposed to be between them?

She'd taken their love and made it into

something public and dirty. What a vile bitch.

Halfway down the stairs he tripped and fell. The suitcase burst open, and videos, posters, photos, and magazines came tumbling out.

George emerged from the library and stood at the bottom of the stairs, glaring up at him. "Where do you think *you're* going?" he said.

"Where the fuck I want," Santo snarled, lumbering to his feet.

Donna appeared at the top of the stairs and switched the light on. "Whatta going on?" she screeched. "Whatta you doing?"

She sounded like the old Donatella. And she looked like a crazy woman, with her hair standing on end and her smeared makeup. She wore a diaphanous nightgown with nothing underneath. It was not a pretty sight.

"Whatta you got in the suitcase?" she demanded, swaying slightly. "You running away like your sisters? The whores, *putanas.*"

"My sisters aren't whores," Santo said, thinking that they'd made the smart choice and gotten out while they could. "They ran to get away from you. You try to control everyone. Well, you can't control me."

"Oh, yes I can," Donna said, unsteadily making her way down the stairs. "You're only sixteen. You're mine—you hear me—*mine!*"

He tried to avert his eyes because he could see right through her nightgown.

She stooped down, picking up one of his porno magazines and throwing it in his face.

"You're sick!" she yelled. "That's what you are—sick! Justa like your father."

"I'm glad I'm like him," he yelled back. "I *want* to be like him."

"You can get out," Donna shouted, holding on to the banisters. "I donta care anymore. *GET OUT!*"

"I'm going," he said, frantically picking up his stuff and attempting to jam it back in the suitcase.

"Leave," she shouted. "And donta think you're taking your car. You go in the clothes you stand up in—nothing else. I've put up with you long enough."

"Put up with *me*?" he yelled, outraged at her unfairness. "*I'm* the one who's put up with you."

"I mean it," Donna shrieked. "You're notta welcome here, Santo. You're fat and ugly. You're lazy. You're scum like your father. DIRTY FILTHY SCUM. You leave tonight."

Santo looked at George, standing silently at the bottom of the stairs. There was a twisted expression of triumph on the older man's face. "You heard your mother," George said with a great deal of satisfaction. "Pack your things and get out."

Lucky was completely calm. She went back upstairs, took a shower, pulled her hair back into a ponytail, and dressed in a simple black turtleneck, black jeans, and boots. Then she stuck her gun in the waistband of her jeans and left the house.

Donna was playing mind games, and she wasn't going to take it anymore.

She got into her Ferrari and drove fast, heading in the direction of Donna's house.

Heading for revenge.

Santo dragged the suitcase back to his room. A red film of fury swam before his eyes—little dancing devils encouraging him to do bad things.

Fat. She'd never called him fat before. Ugly. No way. She'd always told him he was handsome.

YOU'RE DIRTY FILTHY SCUM LIKE YOUR FATHER.

She wasn't fit to shine Santino's shoes.

Without really thinking about it, he took the loaded shotgun from under the bed.

Fuck them! Fuck the two of them. They deserved exactly what they were about to get.

He ran out into the hall and burst into his mother's bedroom.

She was halfway across the room. She turned when she heard him come in. "Whatta you doing..."

Before she could finish the sentence, he lifted the twelve-gauge shotgun, aiming it at her stomach. Then he pulled the trigger.

The blast almost blew her apart. Blood and

gore splattered everywhere as she fell to the ground.

A blissful feeling of peace descended over him. As if in a trance, he walked closer, put the gun to her head, and let off another shot.

Then he walked out of the room.

George stood, transfixed, at the bottom of the stairs with a horrified expression, staring up, too shocked to move.

He was easy pickings.

Easy.

70

Lennie kept moving all night, sticking close to the mountains above the sea, eventually finding himself on a coastal road that led down to isolated beaches.

After a while the land began to get very flat, surrounded by uneven clusters of rocks and a few trees. Forgetting about his aching ankle and cut foot, he concentrated on reaching a safe haven.

Several hours later, dawn began to break. He collapsed at the base of a tall tree, ravenously stuffing chunks of the bread he'd saved into his mouth. It tasted better than a gourmet meal.

He groped in his pockets. He had Claudia's flashlight and map, which he'd consulted from time to time; about six hundred dollars in crumpled American money and several thousand dollars in traveler's checks; a credit card that was probably canceled by now; and his passport. It was fortunate he'd always carried his passport and money on him when out of America—even more fortunate his captors hadn't discovered the money, which he'd kept hidden in the cave.

He'd abandoned the idea of getting to an American embassy. If he did that, he'd have to tell his story, and there'd be questions and major publicity. Plus, he didn't want Claudia getting into trouble.

His new plan was to get home as fast as possible.

Home to America and Lucky and his children, that's all he wanted.

As the light came up, he found himself heading into a picturesque valley. Goddamn it, he *had* to be safe now—he'd been walking all night.

You're free, he told himself as he trudged along. *Free, free, free.* It was a heady feeling.

A short while later he reached the outskirts of a town, and started seeing people. He didn't stop to ask for help, just kept on going.

A schoolchild pointed at him; a mangy dog ran up and growled; an ancient crone, dressed all in black, watched him pass and crossed herself. Human contact—it was strangely comforting.

Eventually he came upon a small train station. The old man behind the ticket counter looked at him oddly, and told him there'd be a train in an hour. He purchased a ticket to Palermo, then went into a small market next door and bought bread, cheese, and some kind of cooked sausage. Outside, the sun was shining. He sat on a bench and tried to eat slowly, relishing every mouthful.

By the time the train arrived, he was completely exhausted. Settling in a window seat, he slept fitfully until he arrived in the big city.

In Palermo he found a tourist shop and purchased a shirt, trousers, and shoes—which he put on in a back room the girl in the shop let him use. Staring in the mirror, he was shocked. It was the first time he'd seen his reflection since his capture. He was thin and gaunt, with a rough beard and long, wild hair. One good thing—nobody would ever recognize him. At least he could remain anonymous until he was safely home.

The shop girl spoke a little English. He asked if there was a barbershop around, and she directed him to a place five minutes away.

He went there immediately and got rid of the matted beard and long hair. It was a big improvement, although he still looked like shit.

He felt completely alone in the world, but it was a satisfying feeling. Once more he was in control of his own destiny.

Within an hour he caught a ferry service to Naples, and from there he took another train into Rome—where he went straight to the airport, using his traveler's checks to buy a bargain ticket to Los Angeles. There was a flight leaving in one hour. He bought some magazines and a cheap pair of sunglasses just in case he *was* recognized.

It wasn't until he was sitting on the plane, heading home, that he felt completely safe.

71

Santo's mind was a movie. And he was the macho action hero.

He'd killed them. Donna and George. He'd killed the bad guys, and it was a good thing. How many people got to realize their dreams?

Now that the deed was completed, he couldn't decide what to do next. There was blood everywhere, some of it had splashed on his clothes. Should he clear up the mess? Donatella wouldn't like blood all over her house—she'd be really pissed.

Someone murdered my mother. An intruder. Yes. That's what had happened. An intruder broke in and killed poor George and Donna.

Too bad.

The question was, why had they been so brutally murdered?

Simple. Venus Maria was the reason. Now she had to be punished, too.

He walked into his mother's bedroom and stood over her for a moment, staring unblinkingly at her ungainly body sprawled on the floor in a pool of dark-red blood. Her nightgown was crumpled and bloody. She didn't look neat.

He went to her dresser, took a pair of scissors, and returned to her side. Then he carefully cut the offending nightdress off her body, arranging her limbs in a more symmetrical fashion.

Satisfied, he went downstairs and inspected George's body, crumpled at the bottom of the stairs.

Santo walked around him several times, trying not to get blood on his sneakers.

George's mouth was open, so were his eyes.

Too bad they couldn't be together. Mommy and Stepdaddy, side by side.

Life wasn't perfect.

After a while, Santo took his shotgun and went outside to his car.

Carefully placing the gun on the floor, he set off toward Venus Maria's house. This time, nothing would stand in his way.

As Lucky drove toward the Landsmans's mansion, a car raced toward her, speeding in the opposite direction. She swerved to the side of the road, narrowly avoiding a head-on collision. She caught a quick glimpse of the driver and recognized the Landsmans' son.

She parked on the street outside the gates, and sat in her car for a minute.

It was one thing to rationalize, think sensibly, and imagine people would get punished properly. It never happened that way, and she knew what she had to do. Finally, she had no choice. If she didn't take care of it, Donna would never leave the Santangelos in peace.

Donna Landsman née Bonnatti had killed Lennie.

Never fuck with a Santangelo.

Lucky got out of her car and walked around the property until she found an unlocked side gate. It was a sign.

She slipped through the gate, noting that the big house was in darkness.

Moving swiftly and silently, she circled the house and was surprised to find the front door ajar. Another sign?

She entered tentatively.

Sprawled at the bottom of the stairs lay George Landsman—his head practically blown off.

Lucky's heart began pounding in her chest. He was dead. The man was dead. Oh, God, somebody had gotten here before her.

She backed away, nervously touching her gun, tucked in her jeans. Then she edged past George's body, and headed upstairs. There was an eerie silence in the house. She flashed on the memory of Santo driving past at high speed, his face a white blur. Was he running from the killer? Or was *he* responsible?

She shivered. The master bedroom door was open. She edged into the room, holding her breath.

There was Donna, lying in the middle of the floor, naked and spread-eagled, laid out for all to see.

Poetic justice.

Slowly Lucky backed out of the room, ran downstairs, and left the house.

By the time she reached her car, she was shaking.

Donna Landsman would never bother anyone again.

Santo was on a mission. Nobody could stop him now. He knew Venus Maria was responsible for everything, there was no doubt about it.

She'd killed his mother.

She'd murdered Donna.

George was dead because of her.

She was a tramp bitch who deserved everything she was about to get.

Her guards were useless, and her stupid brother must have left by now.

This time he'd get her good, no more love letters. She'd betrayed him. Let's see if she liked the shotgun better than the letters.

His gun gave him power.

His gun enabled him to shoot his way out of any situation.

He was Sylvester Stallone, Clint Eastwood, Chuck Norris. He was the quintessential American hero.

He drew up to the guard's station in his car.

"Yeah?" The man half opened the security window and peered at him suspiciously. "What can I do for you?"

Without a word, Santo lifted the gun and blasted him in the face.

Pow! The guard dropped without a sound, blood splashing on the window.

Just like in the movies, Santo thought gleefully.

Laughing to himself, he drove toward the house.

Venus sighed luxuriously—a long-drawn-out sigh of pure pleasure. Cooper made love to her like nobody else. From the tips of his fingers to his versatile tongue, hc was a master lover—transporting her to the land of ecstasy, giving her orgasms the likes of which she'd never experienced before.

He'd made her come twice—each time she'd screamed aloud with utter abandon as the climax sent her into shuddering paroxysms of rapture.

"Turn over," he said.

"No more," she said.

"Turn over."

"I can't take it."

"Do it!"

She rolled onto her stomach. He parted her legs and began licking the soft flesh of her inner thighs. Her head was buried in the sheets. She couldn't see him, only feel his burning touch. It was impossible that he could make her come again so soon.

Absolutely impossible.

And yet...the feeling began to sweep over her. The incredible mind-blowing buildup of a storm waiting to break...

Santo parked his car outside the mansion.

This mission felt good.

This mission was going to give him the clout and recognition he'd yearned for all his life.

No longer was he a sixteen-year-old fat kid. He was Santo Bonnatti. He was a big man, just like his dad. AND NOBODY COULD STOP HIM!

He got out of the car, stood in front of the tramp's house, raised his gun, and shot the fucking lock right out of the fucking door.

Venus thought she heard a gunshot, but she was too close to bliss to care.

"Honey..." she murmured. Then the thought was lost as she climaxed with an earth-shattering shudder of pure sensual lust.

She screamed her pleasure—loud, abandoned, piercing screams.

★ ★ ★

As Santo started to enter the house, he didn't notice the three dogs racing in his direction.

It was only when their vicious teeth sank into his flesh, tearing it away from the bone, that he began to scream—loud, abandoned, piercing screams.

He screamed until everything went a deadly black.

And then it was over.

72

Alex slept well for the first time in months. No sleeping pills, no Halcion—he put his head on the pillow, falling into a deep, relaxed sleep.

In the morning he awoke refreshed, rolled over in bed, and, as was his habit, reached for the TV clicker.

The TV was tuned in to HBO, where he'd left it the night before. There was a bad movie on about a drug deal gone wrong. Corny shit.

He had a positive feeling he was getting his life together at last. He'd told his mother something he should have gotten into years ago. Now, if she'd only get off his case and leave him alone.

He clicked to the next station. Another movie. Another piece of mindless violence.

The clicker was power. He moved on to a fitness show, watching for a few mindless minutes, trying to decide if he should order the piece of equipment guaranteed to give you unbelievable abs. Maybe not. Who had the time? Or the inclination.

The next channel was all news. A serious black newscaster was in the middle of a breaking story:

"Early this morning, the bodies of millionaire corporate raider Donna Landsman and her financial-advisor husband, George Landsman, were discovered shot to death in their six-million-dollar mansion in Bel Air. The grisly discovery was made by a maid, who immediately summoned the police."

Alex sat bolt upright. *Oh, God, Lucky, what did you do?*

He grabbed the phone. She answered immediately. "Lucky," he said, his voice low and distressed. "I just saw the news."

"Good morning, Alex," she said cheerfully, as if there was nothing wrong.

"*Why*, Lucky? *Why* did you do it?" he said urgently.

"I didn't," she replied calmly. "It wasn't me."

"Oh, come on."

"I promise you, Alex, I had nothing to do with it."

"So you're saying it was a convenient coincidence? That somebody else wanted her dead?"

"Get off my case, Alex," she said sharply. "If you don't believe me, that's your problem—not mine."

"I'm coming over."

Her voice was firm. "No, please don't."

"Yes," he said insistently.

She didn't want to see him, he was trying to get too close too fast. It was time to step back again. "Look," she said patiently. "I'll call you later."

"Make sure you do," he said sternly, irritating her even more. "We have to talk."

"I will."

Alex jumped out of bed and went into the bathroom. Jesus! What had she done? His mind began buzzing. She'd need help, the best lawyers....

Whatever happened, he'd be there for her.

Lucky went downstairs to the kitchen and switched on the coffee machine. Life made strange turns, sometimes too strange to follow. Were the Santangelos finally free of the Bonnattis?

Oh, God, she hoped so. The feud had taken enough lives.

Last night when she'd gotten home, she'd called Gino in Palm Springs, asking if he was in any way responsible. He'd assured her he wasn't. Gino wouldn't lie. Besides, she'd *seen* the assassin, Santo, Donna's son, fleeing from the scene of the crime in his car, almost colliding head-on with her. She wondered how long it would take the cops to figure it out.

Alex didn't believe she'd had nothing to do with the murders. She couldn't blame him; after all, she'd told him she was going to do something, and now it had happened, why would he think she was innocent?

At last she could bring her children home. It was a sweet feeling of relief knowing they were finally safe and they'd all be together again soon.

The coffee was bubbling. She took a mug from the shelf, pouring herself a cup.

"Hey—"

Her imagination was playing tricks, she thought she heard Lennie's voice.

"Hey—*you.*"

She turned around, startled. Lennie was standing behind her, smiling. "Missed me?" he said. "'Cause I sure as hell missed you."

She stared at him, speechless, utterly stunned. "Oh...my...God! Lennie..." she gasped at last.

"That's me," he said flippantly.

She was floating, dizzy, confused. This couldn't be happening. Yet it was. And Lennie was here...her Lennie...her love....

"You're alive!" she cried out. "Where did you come from? Oh...my...God! LENNIE!"

He grabbed her, hugging her fiercely to him as if he would never let her go. "Lucky...Lucky...I dreamt of this moment— it's the only thing that kept me sane."

She leaned back in his arms, softly touching his face, marveling that he was actually there. "Lennie..." she murmured, her eyes filling with tears. "Oh, God, Lennie...what *happened* to you?"

"It's a long story, sweetheart...a very long story. All you have to know for now is that I love you, I'm here, and I promise you this— we will *never* be separated again."

Los Angeles

1988

Epilogue

The extravagant premiere of Alex Woods's *Gangsters* was a major Hollywood event. Everybody who was anybody was invited, and if they weren't, they left town, or pretended to.

The venue was Mann's Chinese Theatre on Hollywood Boulevard. A red carpet stretched down to the curb, a luxurious welcoming mat for all the famous guests to parade down. Klieg lights—strategically placed—lit up the sky for miles around.

The excited crowds surrounded the theater, police barricades holding them back from mobbing the stars as they arrived.

A long line of limousines snaked around for at least ten blocks. TV camera crews were alert, ready and lined up, as were the paparazzi. Manic publicists grabbed the stars as they got out of their limos, leading them down the line of media people.

It was a major event.

Abe Panther settled comfortably in the back of his limo and winked at Inga Irving. "This is the first time I've left the house in years," he said, puffing on a fat cigar.

"You'll do anything for Lucky," Inga remarked indulgently. "She calls, you run."

"Lucky's like the granddaughter I never had," Abe mused. "She's a ballsy broad, the kind we used to have in Hollywood in the good old days. I like that in a woman."

Inga nodded; she'd finally grown to accept Abe's fondness for Lucky.

Inga had dressed for the occasion. Lucky had paid her generously for her shares, and she'd invested in a few good pieces of jewelry which she'd told Abe were fake. The man was in his nineties, and he still hung on to his money like a hooker on a bad night.

Abe leaned forward, wheezing. "Got something for you," he said gruffly, groping in the pocket of his 1945 tuxedo, which still fit him perfectly. "Since we've been married a year or two, I started thinking there's no gettin' rid of you." More wheezing as he handed her a leather ring box.

She opened it and gasped. Sparkling up at her was a magnificent eight-carat diamond ring.

"No, Abe," she said, her normally stoic face breaking into a wide smile. "There's certainly no getting rid of me."

Abe cackled. "That's exactly what I thought."

Abigaile and Mickey Stolli, along with Tabitha and her date, Risk Mace—a long-haired, heavily tattooed rocker—were sitting in the limo behind Abe's.

Tabitha had changed from an out-of-control punk to a Hollywood princess. She'd dropped out of her exclusive Swiss boarding school, informing her father she wished to become an actress. Mickey had gotten her an agent, who in turn had arranged for her to audition for a small part on a TV sitcom. To everyone's surprise, she'd gotten the role, the audience had taken to her, and within six months Tabitha was a major TV star.

Mickey was proud. Who would have thought his daughter would become a role model for teenage girls all over America?

He puffed on his cigar and thought, *Hmm...I didn't do a bad job raising my kid. At least she's making her own money.*

Abigaile sat back and thought, *Why is Tabitha wasting her time with this strange-looking rock 'n' roller? Why doesn't she find herself a decent studio executive—someone who has a chance to rise to the top and make lots of money.*

Abigaile was ignorant of the fact that Risk was a millionaire several times over. Had she known, she might have regarded him in a different light.

Tabitha was bored. She couldn't imagine why she'd agreed to come to this premiere with her parents. It was such a lame thing to do. Risk must think she was a total dweeb. Her father had insisted—he wanted the cachet of arriving at the premiere with his famous daughter on his arm. Mickey had to attend the premiere on account of the fact that Johnny Romano was due to star in his first independent movie. Yes,

677

Mickey Stolli—ex-studio head—was venturing into independent production—land of the failed studio executive.

Tabitha hoped there might be a role for her, she really wanted to break into movies.

Leslie Kane stepped out of a long white stretch limo in front of the theater, and the crowds went wild. Then her date got out behind her, and when everyone saw who it was, the screams and excitement reached fever pitch.

The paparazzi and TV crews launched into frenzied action as three publicists moved in to escort the two stars down the line.

Charlie Dollar and Leslie Kane—the good girl and the rogue—what a dynamite combination!

They both had the routine down pat. Charlie with his trademark dark glasses and maniacal grin; Leslie making sure the photographers only caught her good angles—not that she had any bad ones; early on she'd learned not to let them shoot low, or up her skirt when she got out of a car.

She hung on to Charlie's arm and smiled.

He waved to the crowds, who screamed their appreciation.

Leslie Kane and Charlie Dollar—a new front-page sensation.

Ron Machio was excited for his best friend; he'd seen a rough cut of *Gangsters*, and knew how sensational Venus was in it—certainly the performance of her career.

Anthony—in his new tuxedo—pressed down the black-tinted side window.

"Don't do that," Ron said fussily. "The fans can see in."

"I *want* everybody to notice me in a limo," Anthony said proudly. "Can you imagine—if we're on TV in London, they'll know *I'm* a star, too."

"You're not a star," Ron said. "You're still Venus's assistant."

"I'm living with *you*," Anthony said tartly. "That *makes* me a star."

A slow smile spread across Ron's face. "You say the nicest things."

Sitting across from them, Emilio scowled. Why did he have to get stuck in a car with the gay brigade?

He supposed it was better than not getting invited at all. Still...didn't he deserve his own limo?

Since he'd caught that crazed intruder on Venus's property, she'd been almost nice to him. And in return he'd quit selling stories and worked for her as a part-time assistant. Thank God he'd caught Santo that first time—if he hadn't, Venus wouldn't have called Johnny Romano and borrowed his dogs, and without the dogs on her property that night, she might not be here today....

So really, it was all thanks to him. Not that anybody appreciated it.

Occasionally, when Venus and Cooper took him to dinner at Hamburger Hamlet, they acted like they were doing him a big favor. This pissed him off—wasn't he good enough to accompany them to any of the fancy restaurants they frequented?

When Venus had invited him to her premiere, he'd said, "How'll I get there?"

"You'll go with Anthony and Ron," she'd replied. "They'll make sure you behave."

"But, little sis," he'd objected, "I thought I could take a date and get my *own* limo!"

"No, Emilio," she'd said firmly. "I don't trust you. You'll go with them."

And that had been that.

Brigette peered out of the window. "Get an eyeful of the crowds," she exclaimed. "Wow! Amazing!"

"Stay cool," Nona said. "Remember—you're a star, too."

Zandino beamed and nodded agreeably. They'd gotten married six months ago. Now Nona was five months pregnant and they were both incredibly happy.

Brigette couldn't keep still. "I'm really glad Lucky and Lennie invited us," she said. "This is *sooo* cool."

"Maybe you'll meet the hunk of your dreams," Nona said. "There's a lot of cute guys in Hollywood."

"The hunk of my dreams does not exist," Brigette said wistfully. "*Especially* in Hollywood. In fact, I'm beginning to think he doesn't exist at all."

"You're a star, Brigette—a supermodel—you never know who'll come chasing after you— hot for your gorgeous young bod. Sean Penn. Emilio Estevez. Who would you like?"

Brigette grinned. "Dunno. But if I see him, I'll be sure to let you know!"

Their limo drew to a stop outside the theater. "Out!" Nona said. "Be a star!"

"You're so bossy."

"You'd be uncontrollable if I weren't."

"Ha! Betcha no one will know who I am."

"Ten bucks. You're on."

Brigette stepped out of the car, breathed deeply, and faced the crowds.

"BRIGETTE! BRIGETTE! BRIGETTE!"

They were chanting her name. She was stunned! And a little bit thrilled.

A handsome young publicist grabbed her arm, preparing to escort her along the media walk.

"You owe me ten bucks," Nona whispered somewhere behind her.

She smiled, and faced the press.

Johnny Romano and his bride of one year, Daniella, sauntered down the red carpet with

Daniella's nine-year-old daughter clutching Johnny's hand. They made a lovely looking family. Johnny so dark and sexy, Daniella so blond and beautiful, and the little girl a mirror image of her mother.

The press considered their story to be incredibly romantic. Daniella, a French journalist, had come to L.A. to interview Johnny for a magazine. One interview and they werc in love; he'd sent for her daughter, married her in Las Vegas, and now they were the perfect Hollywood couple.

Daniella was content.

Johnny had never been so happy.

It really was a love match.

"You look gorgeous," Cooper said.

"No way," Venus replied, pulling a disgusted face. "I'm fat."

"Not fat, pregnant. There's a big difference."

"I should be looking all sleek and sexy," she worried. "My fans expect it. I should be wearing something outrageous."

"Your performance in the movie is outrageous. Everyone who's seen it says you're a dead cert for a nomination, including me."

She stared at him anxiously. "Do you *really* think so, Coop? You're not just saying that to make me happy?"

He smiled knowingly. "I have other ways of making you happy."

"Yeah, witness this," she said, ruefully patting her swollen belly.

He put his hand over hers. "I love you so much," he said. "Never thought it would happen to me."

"And to think we nearly blew it," she said, and sighed.

"Well, we didn't."

"I know. One night with Veronica and you came running back to me! I should thank him/her—whatever."

"Ha ha! Very amusing."

"Did I tell you that you look fantastically handsome tonight?"

"Thank you," he said, smiling at his adorable pregnant wife. She always knew how to make him feel like a king.

Alex was tired, but it was a good tired. He'd finished cutting the movie six weeks earlier, and since that time they'd had several test runs, which had surpassed everyone's expectations—word of mouth was phenomenal.

He knew that *Gangsters* was the movie he'd win an Oscar for. And two of his actors—Venus and Johnny—would definitely get nominated. He felt fulfilled and satisfied.

He was also thrilled for Lucky. She'd had faith in the movie *and* him—now it was payoff time for Panther.

He thought about Lucky for a moment—he'd always have a special feeling for her, but since

Lennie's return, he'd drawn back because she'd made it quite clear she loved Lennie and would always put him first.

The nice thing was that the three of them had become good friends. Lennie was a great guy; Alex not only liked him, he respected him, too.

Dominique sat opposite her son in the limo with her date—a tango-dancing stockbroker she'd met at a club on Wilshire. He was a pleasant man, older and quite dapper.

Lately Dominique was a changed woman— no more criticisms. He wondered how long it would last.

Tonight he was escorting Lili and France. They'd both worked hard on the movie, and deserved a treat.

He reflected that now *Gangsters* was finished and launched, it was time to get his personal life back on track. Who knew what was out there?

He planned on taking a vacation—traveling to Italy and finding out.

Maybe there was a wildly beautiful, unpredictable, dark-haired woman waiting for him somewhere....

Maybe...

"Well, sweetheart," Lucky said excitedly. "This is it—the premiere of *Gangsters*. I'm kinda buzzed."

"You should be," Lennie replied. "You put in plenty of time to make sure everything went smoothly."

"Thanks," she said, thinking about what an amazing year it had been, and how fortunate she was to have Lennie back.

"You look so goddamn beautiful tonight," he said, squeezing her hand. "Sometimes, I wake up in the morning and I can't believe I'm safely home in bed next to you."

"I can't believe it either," she said, marveling at how things had turned out. "It seems incredible."

"How did we both get through it?" he questioned, shaking his head.

"Somehow, we did; we're together and we're here."

"Every moment I was away, you were in my thoughts. You kept me alive."

"And you were in mine," she said softly. "Even though you didn't phone, you didn't write."

"My wife the comedian," he said wryly.

"That used to be *your* job," she pointed out.

"Oh no," he said. "I've had the acting/performing bit—no more in front of the camera for me."

She knew it was going to be a hard job persuading him to resume his career. Since his return he'd become reclusive, preferring to stay at home with the children rather than go out in public. It didn't bother her, but she knew—

for his own sake—she had to do something to get him involved in the real world again. Right now he was happy doing nothing. Eventually he'd realize it wasn't enough.

"So, your friend Alex must be happy about tonight," Lennie remarked. "Y'know, when you first introduced us, I wasn't sure about him."

"Really?" she said, her tone noncommittal.

"Yeah, but he's a nice guy. I like him."

"I'm glad, because Alex was a very good friend to me while you were gone."

He threw her a look, his green eyes probing hers. "Is that all he was?"

She didn't hesitate. "Yes, that's all."

"He's got a major crush on you."

"No way."

"Oh, yes."

They were silent for a few minutes as their limo edged its way toward the theater.

"And Claudia?" Lucky asked, breaking the silence. "You've told me what she did for you...was *she* just a friend?"

"Of course," he said quickly.

"So maybe one day we'll go visit her."

"Maybe..."

"Anyway," Lucky said, "I'm looking forward to tonight, and then—I've got a big surprise for you."

"What?"

"Guess."

"With you—I wouldn't have a chance. You give unpredictable a whole new meaning."

"I'm taking a six-month leave of absence from the studio."

He sat up straight. "You're doing *what*?"

"You heard. We're going on a trip around the world...you, me, the kids. No work, just play. I think we deserve it."

"Sweetheart—you don't have to do this for me—"

"It's for us," she interrupted, staring at him intently. "And when we get back, you can decide what you want to do."

"Y'know," he said thoughtfully. "I've been thinking...I wouldn't mind getting into directing...."

"Have I got a studio for you!"

"You're a funny lady tonight."

She grinned, her black eyes sparkling. "Whatever makes you happy."

"*You* make me happy, you always have. You're the most special woman in the world, and I love you more than I can ever put into words."

"Love you, too, Lennie," she said softly. "And I always will."

They smiled at each other and squeezed hands, and it was as if they'd never been apart.

If you have enjoyed reading this large print book and you would like more information on how to order a Wheeler Large Print Book, please write to:

 Wheeler Publishing, Inc.
P.O. Box 531
Accord, MA 02018-0531